About the Author

Paul Rudnick is a celebrated playwright, screenwriter, and novelist. His plays include *I Hate Hamlet*, *Jeffrey*, *The Most Fabulous Story Ever Told*, *Regrets Only*, *The New Century*, *The Naked Eye*, and *Valhalla*. He is the author of *I Shudder*, a collection of humorous personal essays, and the novels *Social Disease* and *I'll Take It*. He wrote the screenplays for the movies *In & Out* and *Addams Family Values* and is a frequent contributor to *The New Yorker*. He is rumored to be quite close to *Premiere* magazine film critic Libby Gelman-Waxner, whose collected columns have been published under the title *If You Ask Me*. Born in Piscataway, New Jersey, he now lives in New York City.

"Paul Rudnick, ever the stylish and witty playwright, pressed foot to the pedal on his imaginative overdrive to see how far it would take him into his new comedy, and it seems to have taken him into an elegant terrain."

—Playbill.com

ON *THE NEW CENTURY*

"The one-liners fly like rockets in *The New Century*, the rollicking bill of short plays by Paul Rudnick . . . Frivolity for his characters is a solid existential choice in a threatening universe."

—Ben Brantley, *New York Times*

"The evening contains so many gut-busting one-liners that those with heart conditions are advised to steer clear."

—*New York Post*

"It's not every day that a comedy writer gets a laugh on every line he intends to be thigh-slappingly funny, but Paul Rudnick does so with *The New Century*."

—Theatermania.com

"Paul Rudnick may be the funniest playwright around."

—*The Journal News*

"Deliriously funny and instructional at the same time."

—Associated Press

Also by Paul Rudnick

Novels

Social Disease
I'll Take It

Essays

I Shudder
If You Ask Me (as Libby Gelman-Waxner)

The Collected Plays of Paul Rudnick

AKED EYE REGRETS ONLY THE NEW CENTURY JEFFREY I HATE HAML
LLA THE MOST FABULOUS STORY EVER TOLD THE NAKED EYE REGRE
THE NEW CENTURY JEFFREY I HATE HAMLET VALHALLA THE MOST FAB
STORY EVER TOLD THE NAKED EYE REGRETS ONLY THE NEW CENTU
EY I HATE HAMLET VALHALLA THE MOST FABULOUS STORY EVER TO
AKED EYE REGRETS ONLY THE NEW CENTURY JEFFREY I HATE HAML
LLA THE MOST FABULOUS STORY EVER TOLD THE NAKED EYE REGRE
THE NEW CENTURY JEFFREY I HATE HAMLET VALHALLA THE MOST FABU
STORY EVER TOLD THE NAKED EYE REGRETS ONLY THE NEW CENTUR
EY I HATE HAMLET VALHALLA THE MOST FABULOUS STORY EVER TOL
AKED EYE REGRETS ONLY THE NEW CENTURY JEFFREY I HATE HAMLE
LLA THE MOST FABULOUS STORY EVER TOLD THE NAKED EYE REGRET
THE NEW CENTURY JEFFREY I HATE HAMLET VALHALLA THE MOST FABU
STORY EVER TOLD THE NAKED EYE REGRETS ONLY THE NEW CENTUR
EY I HATE HAMLET VALHALLA THE MOST FABULOUS STORY EVER TOL
AKED EYE REGRETS ONLY THE NEW CENTURY JEFFREY I HATE HAMLE
LLA THE MOST FABULOUS STORY EVER TOLD THE NAKED EYE REGRET
THE NEW CENTURY JEFFREY I HATE HAMLET VALHALLA THE MOST FABU
STORY EVER TOLD THE NAKED EYE REGRETS ONLY THE NEW CENTUR
EY I HATE HAMLET VALHALLA THE MOST FABULOUS STORY EVER TOL
AKED EYE REGRETS ONLY THE NEW CENTURY JEFFREY I HATE HAMLE
LLA THE MOST FABULOUS STORY EVER TOLD THE NAKED EYE REGRET
THE NEW CENTURY JEFFREY I HATE HAMLET VALHALLA THE MOST FABU
STORY EVER TOLD THE NAKED EYE REGRETS ONLY THE NEW CENTUR
EY I HATE HAMLET VALHALLA THE MOST FABULOUS STORY EVER TOL
AKED EYE REGRETS ONLY THE NEW CENTURY JEFFREY I HATE HAMLE

THE COLLECTED PLAYS OF
Paul Rudnick

Paul Rudnick

itbooks

AN IMPRINT OF HARPERCOLLINS*PUBLISHERS*

!t
itbooks
AN IMPRINT OF HARPERCOLLINS PUBLISHERS

Contents

Introduction

I am an infant. I've been trying to come up with some thoughtful, suitably scholarly opening remarks for this collection, and all I keep secretly thinking is—yay! A whole book of my plays!

I'll try to be more adult. Yay!!! Look at all my plays!!! I'm sorry, that won't happen again. The plays appear in roughly chronological order, so here are some comments and memories—first of all, *I Hate Hamlet* was inspired by Manhattan real estate. I actually did live in an apartment which had once been the home of John Barrymore. So sometimes that's how plays get written: The apartment insists. *I Hate Hamlet* had a somewhat rambunctious Broadway debut, owing to the deranged behavior of its star, but the play has since been produced all over the world, without, as far as I know, similar drunken violence.

About a year after the *I Hate Hamlet* fracas, I wrote *Jeffrey*. This play was initially rejected by every theater in New York, and many other theaters around the country; it was a comedy about AIDS, featuring unabashedly gay leading characters, and the nicest rejection letter I received was from an artistic director who wrote, "Well, I thought the play was funny, but our subscribers would never stand for it!" My agent, Helen Merrill, finally marched the play over to the office of Kyle Renick, who ran the tiny WPA Theater on Twenty-third Street, and she refused to leave until Kyle had read the script. Kyle, who quickly became my hero, may have in fact agreed to produce the play because he was afraid of Helen.

Jeffrey was intended for a three-week run, and many of the actors in

New York were warned by their agents and managers not to audition for it. One particularly repellent agent informed her clients that appearing in my play would end their careers. The original cast was both brave and spectacular, and I am forever in their debt. I remember sitting on a wooden bench at the back of the theater, taking notes during previews, and I started to cry. I'm not big on tears, but here's why I was so upset: The play was working. The audience, a mix of all ages, genders, and sexual orientations, was laughing, and all I kept thinking was: If this play is a bomb, I'm going to be really depressed.

Jeffrey opened to shockingly wondrous reviews, and after an extended, sold-out run, the play moved to a larger theater for a commercial life. I was especially grateful on behalf of the actors, several of whom won awards, almost all of whom can't stop working, and at least one of whom fired his agent. As the play's run continued, more than one person told me, "Oh, this'll do great in New York and L.A., but nowhere else." *Jeffrey* has since been performed all across the country and around the world, including in France where, for some reason, and without my consent, the title was changed to *Sex, Drugs, and Sequins*.

Jeffrey changed my life for many reasons, but mostly because it was the first time I'd ever written something of which I was really proud. I'm not claiming that this makes *Jeffrey* a good play; that's for audiences to decide. But personally, I felt like I'd dealt with a subject which I cared passionately about, in my own style.

While *Jeffrey* was running, the play's director, Christopher Ashley, and I were sitting in a diner near the theater, talking about how religious fundamentalists like to justify their bigotry by insisting, "God made Adam and Eve, not Adam and Steve." I looked at Chris and asked, "Well, what if God did make Adam and Steve?" And that's how I came to write *The Most Fabulous Story Ever Told*, which covers not just the first gay men, but the first lesbians, Jane and Mabel, as well. During the run of the play, I received hundreds of identical postcards from a single religious group, which was deliriously named something like the Society of Mary. The cards said that God was all-loving and all-forgiving, and that I was going to burn in Hell. I like to think that the most current editions of the Bible now include the phrase, "God is all-loving and all-forgiving, except for Paul Rudnick."

I'm sometimes asked if I mind being dubbed a gay writer, and I usually reply that I'm fine with it, as long as everyone calls, say, David Mamet a straight writer and asks him why he likes to write about straight people. I love being gay, and I'm deeply grateful to be living in an era when gay subject matter is no longer forbidden. But I've never written anything that's only about homosexuality; *Jeffrey* concerns life and death, and *The Most Fabulous Story* covers God and faith. Because, oddly, gay people care about such things, too.

Valhalla is a sort of historical fever dream. It's a tribute, in part, to the life of Ludwig, who was called both the Dream King and the Mad King, of Bavaria. Ludwig spent most of his reign building wildly theatrical castles, one of which, Neuschwanstein, is the template for Cinderella's castle in all of the Disney theme parks. I intertwined Ludwig's story with that of an entirely fictional character, a Texas teenager named James Avery. I was sparked, however, by the true story of a gay soldier stationed in Europe during World War II, who'd surreptitiously shipped stolen, gem-encrusted artworks back to his Texas home. What intrigued me was that this guy never tried to sell his loot; he just wanted to enjoy his treasures, and to introduce their beauty into his otherwise parched Lone Star days. Somehow, across time and space, Ludwig and James were a match.

The Naked Eye was first produced, under a different title, at the WPA, but I wasn't satisfied with my work, so I kept rewriting, and Chris Ashley and I presented the revised version printed here at the American Repertory Theater in Cambridge, Massachusetts. Both productions included two sublime actresses, Marybeth Peil and J. Smith Cameron, as the well-bred mother-and-daughter team of Nan and Sissy. *The Naked Eye* was inspired by the life of and the controversy surrounding the photographer Robert Mapplethorpe. My photographer, Alex DelFlavio, isn't specifically based on Mapplethorpe, but I'm a big fan of Mapplethorpe's work and his ability to charm and outrage. I wrote *The Naked Eye* because I've always loved the notion of polite museumgoers admiring Mapplethorpe's photos of huge erect penises, and maybe purchasing a souvenir postcard. Maybe I should rename the play yet again, and call it *The Polite Penis*.

As of this writing, legalizing gay marriage is still the subject of heated international debate. As a citizen, I think of marriage as a basic civil right which should be available to everyone, but as a playwright, I'm drawn to the furor. As a comic playwright, I'm intoxicated by the social uproar surrounding such topics as religion, sex, and marriage; when people get offended or militant or embarrassed, they're usually pretty funny. The premiere of *Regrets Only*, at the Manhattan Theater Club, gave me the opportunity to work with another blissful cast, including the incomparable Christine Baranski and, in one of his last roles, George Grizzard, a theater legend who managed to be devilish, warmhearted, and entirely delightful, onstage and off.

Some critics didn't go for *Regrets Only*, finding it trivial. I was also accused of writing gay stereotypes. The leading man in *Regrets Only* is a gay fashion designer, and he's also the most deeply moral and imaginative character in the play. Political correctness can often be the death of comedy—that's why I'm smitten with characters who just can't behave. And this can make some critics, gay or straight, very nervous and sometimes shrill. It's always a lovely moment when a bitchy queen approaches me and commands, "You shouldn't write gay characters as bitchy queens!"

My response to all of this political lunacy can be found in *The New Century*. The first three short pieces in *The New Century* were written and revised over a ten-year period. I wrote "Pride and Joy" after meeting a gay man who had four gay siblings, and I instantly wondered about his parents. It's easy to be liberal and accepting towards one gay child, but after the fourth kid comes out, Mom or Dad might start to wonder—was it the breakfast cereal? "Mr. Charles, Currently of Palm Beach" was written for and is dedicated to the glorious actor Peter Bartlett. To this day, many ear-

Praise for the Plays of Paul Rudnick

ON *JEFFREY*

"Wildly funny . . . just the sort of play Oscar Wilde might have written had he lived in 1990s Manhattan and taken aim at an epidemic that was decimating his circle of friends . . . for all its fun, *Jeffrey* captures the strained social tenor of Manhattan life as it is lived right now perhaps more acutely than any play."

—Stephen Holden, *New York Times*

"Rudnick is a born showbiz wit with perfect pitch for priceless one-liners. Far from being escapist, the laughter along the way is a battle cry, a defiant expression of who these idiosyncratic characters were before AIDS arrived, and who they will still be after it has gone."

—Frank Rich

"Explicit, provocative and hilarious . . ."

—*New York*

"A dazzling, bittersweet travelogue about gay New York. I don't expect to see a funnier play this year."

—*New York Daily News*

"In daring to laugh, then to cry, it reveals itself as a cunning twist on the old-fashioned Broadway comedy. All with unfettered wit and a lot of heart. Who could ask for anything more?"

—*Time*

ON *THE MOST FABULOUS STORY EVER TOLD*

"Line by line, Mr. Rudnick may be the funniest writer for the stage in the United States today. . . . One-liners, epigrams, withering put-downs, and flashing repartee: these are the candles that Mr. Rudnick lights instead of cursing the darkness, although he does a lot of cursing, too . . . a testament to the virtues of laughing . . . and in laughter, there is something like the memory of Eden."

—Ben Brantley, *New York Times*

"You will find yourself laughing uncontrollably throughout the evening . . ."

—*New York Daily News*

ON *VALHALLA*

"You can be sure that a winsomely wicked bon mot will fly by every minute or so . . ."

—Ben Brantley, *New York Times*

"Paul Rudnick's most ambitious and . . . his strongest work yet."

—*The New Republic*

"If, as Paul Rudnick contends, 'opera is music gone mad,' what's it called when a giddy profusion of one-liners achieves the lunatic rhythm of music?"

—*New York Newsday*

ON *REGRETS ONLY*

"One of the funniest quip-meisters on the planet . . . the temptation is to quote as many of those one-liners as space allows . . ."

—Ben Brantley, *New York Times*

"Hilariously witty . . ."

—*Show Business Weekly*

"A devastatingly accurate political and social satire."

—*Backstage*

nest gay politicos decree that in the future, when equality is assured, gay people and straight people will become indistinguishable. For me, true equality never means sameness, but limitless options for everyone. I've also found that sometimes, out of necessity, the most flamboyant creatures can become impressively tough and courageous. For anyone who tries to tell gay people, or straight people for that matter, to calm down, I say: Meet Mr. Charles.

The third section of *The New Century* belongs to Barbara Ellen Diggs, an ardent craftsperson from Decatur, Illinois. Responding to the play's initial production at Lincoln Center, some New Yorkers began to fret over Barbara Ellen, concerned that I was patronizing her. I beg to differ. I agree with Barbara Ellen on just about everything, and I think she's a true artist. Only those vibrating Manhattan types can't imagine that art can include sock monkeys and scrapbooks, created without irony.

So there they are, my plays. Yes, there are common themes, and idle graduate students everywhere are welcome to chart them, kicking off with art and life, barreling through sex comedy and arriving, with amazing frequency, at death. The highest possible stakes can often foster the funniest comedies. And, as a playwright, my lust for comedy is either my greatest strength or my most crippling flaw. I don't regard comedy as an evasion or an escape, but as a triumph over, and an entirely suitable revenge against, a world that can be cruel, dull, and exasperating. Comedy can mock reality, upend it, ravish it, and leave it gasping. For me, comedy is often the only feasible antidote to a completely justifiable, but not very entertaining hopelessness; sometimes, a wisecrack is a weapon.

I'm suspicious, however, of comic pretension, of longwinded plays which are acclaimed as "brilliantly witty" or "soul-searingly comic"; this can mean that the audience is checking its collective watch, and not laughing very much. I prefer the go-for-broke challenge of making an audience really lose it, especially when the audience members are surprised and even shocked by their own giddy response. There's a moment in *Jeffrey* when a character reveals that he's HIV-positive, and at every performance,

I could hear the crowd grow very quiet, as everyone became convinced that the play was no longer a comedy, until a few seconds later, when folks were roaring again. The jokes hadn't cured a terrible disease, but they'd earned Steve, the man who was HIV-positive, a certain power and, by the end of the evening, a kiss.

I'd also like to take this occasion to boundlessly thank Christopher Ashley, who directed the original productions of most of these plays. Chris is both ferociously talented and deeply kind, as I've always been able to phone him at 3 AM and batter him with eight possible new punchlines, none of which are even remotely funny. Chris will then, with his trademark tact and supportiveness, say something along the lines of "But I like where you're going," rather than "Why are you bothering me, you talentless hack?" Christopher is a dear friend, and invaluable ally, and a constant inspiration. I'd also like to thank Rakesh Satyal, my wonderful editor at HarperCollins, who is also a surpassingly talented writer and singer, for making this collection possible.

And to sum up, to reveal the far too deeply buried meaning and authority of my plays, all I can say is—yay!!! Here they are!!!

—Paul Rudnick

The Collected Plays of Paul Rudnick

ONE

I Hate Hamlet

For Helen Merrill

I HATE HAMLET was originally produced at the Walter Kerr Theatre (Jujamcyn Theaters, James B. Freydberg, Robert G. Perkins and Margo Lion, Producers), in New York City, on April 8, 1991. It was directed by Michael Engler; the set design was by Tony Straiges; the costume design was by Jane Greenwood; the lighting design was by Paul Gallo; the sound design was by Scott Lehrer; fight direction was by B. H. Barry and the original music was by Kim Sherman. The cast was as follows:

FELICIA DANTINE	Caroline Aaron
ANDREW RALLY	Evan Handler
DEIRDRE MCDAVEY	Jane Adams
LILLIAN TROY	Celeste Holm
JOHN BARRYMORE	Nicol Williamson
GARY PETER LEFKOWITZ	Adam Arkin

I Hate Hamlet

ACT ONE

Scene 1

Time: The present.

Place: The top floor apartment of a brownstone just off Washington Square in New York City. The apartment's architecture is highly theatrical, a Gothic melange of oak beams, plank floors and plaster work designed to resemble roughhewn stone. There is a deep window seat stage left, with treetops visible through a leaded bay window. Upstage right is the front door to the apartment, and an open archway reveals a hall, presumably leading to a kitchen and bedrooms. Center stage is a grand marble fireplace, as regal and gargoyled as possible. Beside the fireplace stands an elaborately carved wooden stairway, which curves first to a landing and then up a short flight to an impressive, rounded gothic door, which leads to the roof. The design of the apartment must be, above all, exceedingly romantic and old world, a Manhattan interpretation of a King Arthur domicile; think Hollywood/Jacobean.

At present almost all of the apartment is shrouded in dropcloths and sheets, providing an ambience of ghost-provoking mystery. The apartment's current occupant has only just moved in; cardboard cartons are stacked about, amid mounds of partially unpacked goods. The sparse furnishings are stark and modern, functional at best. There is a square-ish couch off to one side, upholstered in white canvas. Folding chairs and the stacks of cartons provide additional seating.

As the curtain rises, the stage is in darkness. Mystic music, and a supernatural lighting effect might precede the action.

The doornob on the front door rattles, and the door is flung open. Felicia Dantine bursts into the room, and immediately bustles around the apartment, switching on lights. Felicia is a tall, imposing woman with a mane of boldly streaked hair. She wears high suede boots, and a long vest of ragged purple leather and fur. Felicia is a real estate agent, with an almost carnal passion for Manhattan apartments. She speaks in a hoarse, buoyant voice, with a hint of Queens nasality, a jubilant New York honk.

Andrew Rally, the apartment's new tenant, follows Felicia into the apartment. Andrew is an actor, in his late twenties or early thirties; he is handsome and charming, possessing the polished ease of a television star. Andrew could easily glide through life, wafting on a cloud of good looks and affability. He is not without ego, however; he is more than accustomed to being the center of attention.

This is Andrew's first Moment in the apartment; he carries a box of personal belongings. He stares at his new surroundings, with a mixture of awe and uneasiness.

ANDREW. (*Looking around.*) Oh my God.

FELICIA. Isn't it fabulous? I'm so glad you took it sight unseen. I just knew it was perfect.

ANDREW. It's amazing, but . . . gee, I'm sorry. This isn't what we talked about. I was thinking of, you know, something . . . less.

FELICIA. But it's a landmark! John Barrymore, the legendary star! And now you, Andrew Rally, from *LA Medical!* I loved that show! You were adorable! Why did they cancel it?

ANDREW. Bad time slot, shaky network—I don't think I can live here, this isn't what we discussed.

FELICIA. I know, I know—but honey, I'm not just a broker. I want you to be happy! You belong here.

ANDREW. Don't worry, it's my mistake, I'll move back to my hotel, it's fine.

FELICIA. (*Gesturing to the cartons.*) But your things are here! It's a match! You and Barrymore!

ANDREW. (*Flattered.*) Please, I'm no Barrymore.

FELICIA. Of course you are, Dr. Jim Corman, rookie surgeon! I even love those commercials you do! What is it—Tomboy Chocolate?

ANDREW. Trailburst Nuggets. It's a breakfast cereal.

FELICIA. (*Delighted.*) And . . . ?

ANDREW and FELICIA. (*Singing the jingle.*) "An anytime snack!" (*The doorbell buzzes.*)

FELICIA. An anytime snack! I love it! I love that ad! (*Felicia goes to the intercom, which is located in a niche beside the front door. Into the intercom.*) Hello? He sure is! (*Passing the receiver to Andrew.*) For you! Your first guest!

ANDREW. (*Into the receiver.*) Hello? Sure . . . come on up. Please! (*To Felicia.*) It's my girlfriend. She can't wait to see the place.

FELICIA. (*Excited.*) Do I know her? Was she on your show?

ANDREW. No, I met Deirdre in New York. But I'm from LA. I like modern things. High tech. Look at this place—I mean, is there a moat? (*There is a knock on the front door. Andrew opens it. Deirdre McDavey is standing outside, clutching a bouquet of roses. Deirdre wears a green wool cape, a long challis skirt, a lacy antique blouse and pointy, lace-up Victorian boots. Her hair streams down her back, Alice-in-Wonderland style. Deirdre is Andrew's girlfriend; she is twenty-nine years old, but appears much younger. Deirdre is the breathless soul of romantic enthusiasm. She is always on the verge of a swoon; to Deirdre, life is a miracle a minute. Deirdre is irresistibly appealing, a Valley girl imagining herself a Brontë heroine. Deirdre stands in the doorway, trembling and on the verge of tears. Her eyes are clenched shut. She is practically hyperventilating; she speaks in a passionate, strangled whisper.*)

DEIRDRE. Andrew . . . ?

ANDREW. (*With amused patience.*) Yes, Deirdre?

DEIRDRE. Andrew . . . am I . . . here?

ANDREW. This is it. (*Deirdre steps into the apartment and opens her eyes. She gasps. As she tours the premises she removes her cape and hands Andrew the roses and her velvet shoulderbag.*)

DEIRDRE. Oh, *Andrew* . . . his walls . . . his floor . . . the staircase to his roof . . . the air he breathed . . . oh Andrew, just being here makes you a part of history!

FELICIA. And I'm the broker!

DEIRDRE. (*To Felicia.*) I worship you! (*The doorbell buzzes again.*)

ANDREW. I'll get it.

FELICIA. (*Handing Deirdre her business card.*) Hi. Felicia Dantine.

ANDREW. (*Into the intercom receiver.*) Hello? Come on up.

FELICIA. Isn't this place amazing? The Barrymore thing? The morning it comes on the market, I get Andrew's call.

DEIRDRE. (*Impressed.*) No.

FELICIA. Two famous actors! It's freaky. Are you in the business? (*There is a knock on the door. Andrew opens the door; Lillian Troy is outside. Lillian is a striking, silver-haired woman in her seventies; she wears an elegant mink coat over a simple navy dress, and carries a bottle of champagne. She is smoking an unfiltered Camel cigarette. Lillian speaks with a regal German accent, and has a no-nonsense manner, combined with a delight at any sort of highjinks. Lillian is Andrew's agent. As the door opens, Lillian is coughing, a real smoker's hack.*)

ANDREW. Lillian, Lillian, are you okay?

LILLIAN. (*Finishing her coughing.*) I am fine. (*Passing Andrew the champagne.*) Take it. (*Surveying the premises.*) This is it. As I remember.

ANDREW. What?

LILLIAN. I have been here before. But I had to be certain. (*As Deirdre curtsies.*) Deirdre, you I know. (*To Felicia.*) Hello. I am Lillian Troy. I am Andrew's agent. The scum of the earth.

FELICIA. Hi. Felicia Dantine. Real estate. I win.

ANDREW. (*To Lillian.*) What do you mean, you've been here before?

LILLIAN. It was in, oh, the forties I imagine. I had just come to America. (*Looking around.*) It was magical. This great window. The cottage on the roof. Fresh flowers everywhere. I had a little fling. Andrew, perhaps you have found my hairpins.

ANDREW. Lillian—you had a fling here?

FELICIA. In this apartment?

DEIRDRE. With who?

LILLIAN. Whom do you think?

ANDREW. Barrymore?

DEIRDRE. (*Awestruck.*) Lillian—you and . . . Barrymore?

FELICIA. Here?

LILLIAN. I am an old lady. The elderly should not discuss romance, it is distasteful. And creates jealousy. And Andrew has such marvelous news—does everyone know?

DEIRDRE. What? What news?

ANDREW. I haven't told because . . . I'm not sure how I feel about it.

DEIRDRE. What? Andrew, what haven't you told me?

ANDREW. Well . . . you know Shakespeare in the Park, right? The open-air theater, by the lake?

FELICIA. I went once. It poured. Right on Coriolanus. Didn't help. They kept going.

DEIRDRE. (*To Andrew.*) What? Tell us!

ANDREW. Well, this summer they're doing *All's Well,* and . . . another one.

DEIRDRE. Which one?

ANDREW. (*Taking a deep breath.*) *Hamlet.*

DEIRDRE. Oh my God. Wait. Laertes?

ANDREW. Hamlet.

DEIRDRE. The *lead?*

ANDREW. Yeah, Hamlet.

LILLIAN. Ya! Isn't that extraordinary? (*Deirdre is starting to hyperventilate again. She holds up her hands, and backs away from Andrew.*)

DEIRDRE. You . . . are . . . playing . . . Hamlet? My boyfriend is playing Hamlet?

ANDREW. I don't know why they cast me.

LILLIAN. Because you are talented. You auditioned five times. They saw something.

FELICIA. Dr. Jim Corman! You'll pack the place! I'll even come. Is it the real *Hamlet?* Or like, a musical?

ANDREW. The real one. And she's right, of course, I'm sure they only asked me because of the TV show. I'm a gimmick. I don't know why I said yes.

LILLIAN. Schnookie—we are talking about *Hamlet.*

DEIRDRE. Wouldn't it be great if we could like, go back in time and tell Barrymore?

FELICIA. Why?

DEIRDRE. I mean, he was the greatest Hamlet of all time—isn't that what people say?

LILLIAN. That is true. And Andrew, you know—he lived here for many years. Perhaps when he played Hamlet.

DEIRDRE. And now you're here—I bet this is all happening for a reason.

FELICIA. 'Cause you were cancelled! (*Looking around, sniffing the air.*) I get this feeling sometimes, in special apartments. About the people who lived there. (*Felicia climbs the staircase to the first landing. She raises her arms. Intoning.*) Barrymore. Barrymore! (*In the distance, a bell tolls, from a belltower. Everyone looks up.*)

LILLIAN. What was that?

FELICIA. The church, down the street. The clock in the belltower.

ANDREW. But . . . it's six o'clock. It only struck once.

DEIRDRE. Oh my God. Just like in *Hamlet.* Right before the ghost of Hamlet's father appears. He comes when the clock strikes one.

FELICIA. Which means . . . ?

ANDREW. That we live in New York. Where everything's broken.

DEIRDRE. But what if it's an omen?

FELICIA. Right. Barrymore. Hamlet. The connection. Maybe he's trying to contact us.

ANDREW. (*Pointing to the messy batch of menus which have been slipped under the front door.*) Yeah. Maybe he's the one who's been slipping all these take-out menus under the door.

DEIRDRE. Andrew!

FELICIA. (*Still on the landing.*) Don't joke. Maybe he's . . . around. It's possible. Totally.

DEIRDRE. Oh my God. What if we could reach out to him, across time and space? Wouldn't that be a great idea?

LILLIAN. Don't ask me about great ideas. I am German.

FELICIA. (*Coming down the stairs.*) Wait. Guys. You know—I'm psychic.

DEIRDRE. Oh my God!

LILLIAN. What do you mean?

FELICIA. I've made contact. With the other side. I go into this pre-conscious state, like a trance. And I speak to a spirit guide.

ANDREW. A spirit guide?

FELICIA. Yeah—my Mom. We were real close. After she died, I went into such a slump. I tried everything, therapy, encounter groups, you name it. Finally I saw this ad, for a course—"Spiritual Transcommu-nication: Beyond The Physical Sphere."

LILLIAN. So you talk to your mother?

FELICIA. Right. Is your Mom gone too? Would you like to contact her?

LILLIAN. No. Why break a habit?

DEIRDRE. The clock. This apartment. Hamlet. This is pre-ordained. I think we should do it.

ANDREW. Do what?

DEIRDRE. Contact Barrymore. A seance. Right now. (*There is a pause, as everyone looks at each other; the women are all extremely excited at the prospect of a seance, while Andrew has his doubts.*)

FELICIA. I've never tried anyone but Ma. But I'm game!

ANDREW. I don't think so.

LILLIAN. But who can tell? Barrymore might return. As he promised me.

DEIRDRE. Lillian—were you really here? With Barrymore?

LILLIAN. Ask him yourself.

ANDREW. No, come on—this is just an apartment. It's not magical, and there aren't any ghosts or supernatural phenomena. And we're not having a seance. (*The door to the roof creaks open, and then slams shut, all by itself.*) Do we need candles?

FELICIA. Candles are great. (*Andrew rummages through a box to find a candle.*)

DEIRDRE. Felicia, what about a table?

FELICIA. Perfect. (*During the next few speeches, Deirdre and Felicia move a card table to C., and set chairs or crates around it. Lillian supervises.*)

DEIRDRE. (*As she moves the table.*) This is just like at the beginning of *Hamlet,* when the guards call out to the ghost. (*With gusto.*)
"Stay, illusion!
If thou hast any sound or use of voice,
Speak to me!"

LILLIAN. (*Holding out her arms.*)
"If there be any good thing to be done
That may to thee do ease and grace to me
Speak to me!"

DEIRDRE. "O, speak!"

LILLIAN. "Stay and speak!"

ANDREW. Oh my God. Felicia, is this how you usually operate? Seances? Shakespeare?

FELICIA. Honey, I've been a broker for almost fifteen years. In Greenwich Village. Try human sacrifice. And cheese. (*Surveying the table.*) Okay, everybody sit. How should we do this? I know—first I'll try and contact Ma, and then see if she can get ahold of Barrymore. (*By this point, Deirdre, Lillian and Felicia are all seated around the table.*)

LILLIAN. May I smoke? Does anyone mind?

DEIRDRE. Oh Lillian, it's such a terrible thing to do, and we all love you so much, do you have to?

LILLIAN. (*Sighing.*) Very well. (*She puts down her cigarette.*) You know, I really must stop.

DEIRDRE. Smoking?

LILLIAN. No—asking. (*Andrew has located a candle and stuck it in a bottle. He sets the bottle on the table.*)

FELICIA. (*To Andrew.*) Now hit the lights, okay, hon? I'm gonna enter this trance state, so Andy, think about what you want to ask Barrymore.

DEIRDRE. Has he met Shakespeare?

LILLIAN. Is it hot?

DEIRDRE. Lillian, Barrymore is not in Hell. I'm sure Felicia never even deals with people . . . down there.

FELICIA. Well, if I have a legal problem . . . okay everybody, put your hands on the table, palms down, it helps the flow. Now close your eyes. (*By now Andrew has dimmed the lights; the room is lit only by the candle. Andrew has joined the others seated around the table. Everyone joins hands and closes their eyes.*) Now just clear your minds, totally blank, clean slate. Deep, even breathing. (*Everyone is now breathing in unison, very deeply. Lillian coughs. Everyone continues breathing. Felicia lifts her head. A convulsion shakes Felicia's body; her head drops. As her head rises, she utters a long, guttural, effectively bizarre moan. Finally, as contact is made, Felicia's head pops up, and she assumes a cheery brightness, as if talking on the phone. Her eyes remain shut during her conversation with her mother.*) Yeah Ma, it's me . . . fine, fine, you? (*Confidentially, to the group.*) I got her! . . . Ma, listen to me, I need your help, I'm here with Andrew Rally . . . yeah, "LA Medical" . . . Ma, listen, he wants to talk to someone, over there . . . no Ma, he's seeing someone . . . Ma, I think he's having a career crisis, he's gonna do Shakespeare, and he needs to talk to Barrymore, right, John Barrymore . . . from the movies . . . okay, okay—hang on . . .

(*To Andrew.*) She needs to know, what do you want to ask Barrymore? What's your question?

DEIRDRE. (*Thrilled.*) Andrew, ask!

ANDREW. Ask him what?

DEIRDRE. Ask him about *Hamlet!*

LILLIAN. Ask him for advice!

ANDREW. But I don't want advice, and I don't want to play Hamlet, I mean I don't think I do, I mean, I hate *Hamlet!* (*As Andrew says "I hate Hamlet," there is a deafening crack of thunder. A gust of wind fills the apartment, extinguishing the candle. There is a second thunderclap, and a bolt of lightning streaks across the sky. An enormous shadow is thrown across the wall, of a handsome profile. Only Andrew sees the shadow.*)

LILLIAN. Andrew!

DEIRDRE. Don't say that! (*Felicia is again overtaken by a convulsion, as the astral contact is broken. She makes a wild hacking noise, as if coughing up a furball. She rocks, and leaves the table, her body spasming.*) Felicia! (*Andrew rises and runs to the lights. He flips on the switch.*)

FELICIA. What? Is he . . . hold on. Yeah? What happened? Did I get her? Ma?

DEIRDRE. You talked to her, and she tried to contact Barrymore, but something happened! There was lightning!

LILLIAN. It was marvelous!

FELICIA. Did you see anything? A sign? A woman with rhinestone glasses?

DEIRDRE. I don't think so . . .

ANDREW. (*Firmly.*) No. We didn't see anything. No Barrymore.

LILLIAN. As far as we know.

FELICIA. I'm sorry, you know . . . Ma's really the only one I get. It's emotional, there's gotta be a real need. Andy, I'm sorry.

ANDREW. No, please, you were fine. And I'm glad about your Mom and I can't believe I even considered playing Hamlet. This is all . . . not possible.

LILLIAN. Rally—do me a favor. Do not be like all the others. Everywhere I look, I am disappointed. You must have faith. Barrymore would insist.

DEIRDRE. He could still appear.

FELICIA. Sometimes you gotta bribe 'em—the spirits. You need something they really liked, when they were alive. Especially the first contact.

DEIRDRE. Really? What did your mother like? What did you use?

FELICIA. It was tough, I tried everything. Jewelry, sponge cake, finally I just said Ma, it's after ten, the rates are down. Bingo! Should we try again?

DEIRDRE. Of course!

ANDREW. No. Absolutely not. No more.

LILLIAN. Oh Rally, where is your sense of adventure? Television has ruined you. (*The sound of thunder and rainfall is heard, increasingly heavy.*) I must go. I only wanted a look at the place.

FELICIA. I'd better split too. Before it starts pouring.

LILLIAN. (*Gazing around.*) It is . . . as I recall. Perhaps smaller. But still a jewel. The elevator is new. (*She starts coughing.*)

ANDREW. Lillian, are you okay? Have you been to the doctor?

LILLIAN. (*Cutting him off.*) Doctors. I have seen too many doctors. Mostly played by you. Enough. Rally, when do rehearsals begin?

ANDREW. I'm not discussing it.

LILLIAN. But I need to negotiate, on your behalf. It is Shakespeare in the Park. It is non-profit. I will make them bleed. (*Felicia and Lillian now have their coats on.*)

FELICIA. (*Taking a last look at the apartment.*) It's a great space. Don't listen to me, I say that in cabs. Someday they're gonna say, Andrew Rally lived here!

DEIRDRE. A great Hamlet!

LILLIAN. And an anytime snack.

ANDREW. Out!

FELICIA. Bye, kids!

LILLIAN. Wait. (*Lillian pauses, feeling an emanation. She goes to the mantel, and finds an object. She gleefully holds the object aloft.*) My hairpin! (*A chord of ghostly music is heard. Felicia and Lillian exit. Andrew and Deirdre face each other, both excited at being alone together.*)

DEIRDRE. Andrew . . . (*Deirdre runs into Andrew's arms, and they embrace.*) Hamlet! Why didn't you tell me?

ANDREW. Because I knew you would be the most excited. And I knew you would tell me I have to do it.

DEIRDRE. Of course you have to!

ANDREW. But why? Just because it's supposed to be this ultimate challenge? Because everyone's supposed to dream of playing Hamlet?

DEIRDRE. No—because it's the most beautiful play ever written. It's about how awful life is, and how everything gets betrayed. But then Hamlet tries to make things better. And he dies!

ANDREW. Which tells us . . .

DEIRDRE. At least he tried!

ANDREW. But why do I have to be Hamlet? I can get another show, maybe even movies. I don't need Hamlet.

DEIRDRE. But Andrew—you went to drama school.

ANDREW. Only for two years.

DEIRDRE. But wasn't it wonderful? The great plays—Ibsen, O'Neill—nothing under four hours. And Shakespeare—didn't you love it?

ANDREW. Sometimes. But I left.

DEIRDRE. Why?

ANDREW. (*Thrilled by the memory.*) LA Medical! The bucks! TV Guide. My face at every supermarket check-out in America, right next to the gum. I felt like—every day was my Bar Mitzvah. Everyone I saw was smiling, with an envelope with a check. That's what California is, it's one big hug—it's Aunt Sophie without the pinch.

DEIRDRE. Andrew, Jim Corman was terrific, but now you're back.

ANDREW. On a whim. The show was dead, I thought, okay, try New York, why not? Take some classes, maybe do a new play, ease back in. But now—this place. (*He gestures to the apartment.*) *Hamlet.* That's not the plan.

DEIRDRE. Of course it is! It's your old plan, your real one! You know the only thing that would be better? Better than *Hamlet?*

ANDREW. The Cliff notes?

DEIRDRE. *Romeo and Juliet.* Remember, when we did that scene in class? (*Deirdre runs up the stairs to the roof, stopping at the landing, which she will use as Juliet's balcony. Her acting should be long on eagerness, if somewhat lacking in technique. She is very big on expressive hand gestures. As Juliet.*)

O, swear not by the moon,
(*She points to the moon.*)
the inconstant moon
(*She points to the moon again.*)
That monthly changes in her circled orb
Lest that thy love
(*She points to Andrew.*)
prove likewise variable.
(*Andrew leaps up to the landing, with the bannister still separating him from Deirdre.*)

ANDREW. (*As Romeo.*) What shall I swear by?

DEIRDRE. Do not swear at all,
Or if thou wilt, swear by thy gracious self
Which is the god of my idolatry,
And I'll believe thee.

ANDREW. My heart's dear love . . . (*Andrew climbs over the railing, and they kiss. Passionately.*) Oh, Deirdre . . .

DEIRDRE. Andrew . . . (*Another kiss.*)

ANDREW. Will you . . . stay?

DEIRDRE. Yes. Upstairs. Isn't there an extra room? On the roof?

ANDREW. Deirdre.

DEIRDRE. Andrew—you said you understood. I can only give myself to the man I'll love forever. The man I'll marry.

ANDREW. So marry me!

DEIRDRE. Andrew, that's so sweet.

ANDREW. Why won't you take me seriously? I'm not just talking about sex. You believe in things. And you almost make me believe. You *are* Juliet.

DEIRDRE. Exactly! And you'll be Hamlet! I can see it! (*Descending the stairs.*) Andrew, I do want to get married, and I do want to have sex, it's just . . . I've waited so long. I have so much invested in this. I mean, if it wasn't absolutely perfect, it would all just be wasted. I'd feel so silly.

ANDREW. (*Following her down the stairs.*) Deirdre, you're a twenty-nine-year-old virgin. And you tell everyone. I think fear of silliness is not the issue.

DEIRDRE. Oh, but won't it be wonderful, once I know for sure? Won't you be glad that we waited?

ANDREW. (*Kneeling beside her.*) Deirdre, sex *is* wonderful. Take my word. It's right up there with unicorns and potpourri, and antique lace and bayberry-scented candles. Deirdre, even Laura Ashley had sex.

DEIRDRE. That's true . . .

ANDREW. When will you know? When will you be sure?

DEIRDRE. Soon . . . maybe. I know I'm being impossible, but it's not that I'm a prude. I just want—everything! And it's happening!

ANDREW. It is?

DEIRDRE. Of course! You're going to be Hamlet, and I'm going to be . . . *Ophelia.* Oh Andrew, could I audition? Would they let me?

ANDREW. I guess I could ask them . . .

DEIRDRE. Would you? And it wouldn't be sleazy, because I'm not sleeping with you! Isn't that perfect?

ANDREW. Deirdre, that's nuts. It's like . . . show business for Mormons. (*Deirdre grabs her shoulderbag and runs up the stairs to the roof.*)

DEIRDRE. It's going to be the best! Good night, sweet . . .

ANDREW. Don't say it! If I can't have sex, I don't know why I should play Hamlet.

DEIRDRE. Sweet prince! (*Deirdre exits out the door to the roof.*)

ANDREW. (*To the heavens.*) What is this—a test? No sex? Shakespeare? It's like high school! (*He goes to the phone and dials; he holds Lillian's bottle of champagne in his free hand. Into the phone.*) Lillian? It's Andrew. When you get back, please call the people at the theater. Tell them I'm cancelling. And I'll be back at the hotel tomorrow. So goodbye, Hamlet, and good night, Barrymore! (*Andrew opens the bottle of champagne. As the cork pops, thunder and lightning explode. The lights all go out, and the wind moans. The clock from the belltower tolls again. As much melodrama as possible. A spotlight hits the door to the roof, at the top of the stairs. The door swings open, and smoke pours out. A triumphant trumpet flourish is heard, followed by a grand musical processional, which should continue under Barrymore's entrance. A figure is silhouetted in the doorway to the roof. The spotlight illuminates the figure: it is John Barrymore, striking a dramatic, melancholy pose. He is dressed as Hamlet; he wears black tights, a black velvet tunic with a wide, slashed neck, and a jewelled belt from which a golden dagger hangs. A full-length cape swirls about him. He is phenomenally sexual and dashing; he is the very image of a sly, romantic hero. Barrymore lifts his head, still appearing quite severe. He smiles rakishly. He surveys the apartment; he's been gone a long time. He slowly descends the staircase, studying what has become of his former residence. Finally, Barrymore sees Andrew. Andrew is frozen, holding the champagne bottle. Barrymore smiles at him.*)

BARRYMORE. Dear fellow. (*Barrymore spots the bottle. He grabs a glass and heads for Andrew; he hasn't had champagne in ages. He holds out the glass, gesturing to the bottle.*) May I? (*Andrew remains frozen. He tries to speak; only choking sounds emerge from his throat.*) Pardon? (*Andrew tries to speak again, but cannot. He holds out the bottle; Barrymore takes it, fills his glass and drinks, with vast enjoyment.*)

ANDREW. You're . . . him.

BARRYMORE. Am I?

ANDREW. You're . . . dead.

BARRYMORE. You know, occasionally I'm not truly certain. Am I dead? Or just incredibly drunk?

ANDREW. You're . . . Barrymore.

BARRYMORE. Yes. Although my father's given name was Blythe; he changed it when he became an actor, to avoid embarrassing his family. Your name?

ANDREW. (*Still completely unnerved.*) Andrew. Rally. It's really Rallenberg. I changed it, to avoid embarrassing . . . the Jews.

BARRYMORE. (*Surveying the premises.*) Behold. My nest. My roost. (*Indicating where things had been, perhaps with musical cues.*) A grand piano. A renaissance globe. A throne.

ANDREW. You're dead! You're dead! *What are you doing here?*

BARRYMORE. Lad—I'm here to help.

ANDREW. Wait—how do I know you're a ghost? Maybe you're just . . . an intruder.

BARRYMORE. (*Toying with him.*) Perhaps. Cleverly disguised as Hamlet. (*Andrew slowly sneaks up on Barrymore. He touches Barrymore's forearm. Barrymore is very nonchalant.*) Boo.

ANDREW. But—I can touch you. My hand doesn't go through.

BARRYMORE. I'm a ghost, Andrew. Not a special effect.

ANDREW. But . . . ghosts are supposed to have powers! Special powers!

BARRYMORE. I just rose from the dead, Andrew. And how was *your* morning? Now shall I truly frighten you?

ANDREW. (*Not impressed.*) I'm not afraid of you.

BARRYMORE. Shall I cause your flesh to quake?

ANDREW. (*Very cocky.*) You couldn't possibly.

BARRYMORE. Shall I scare you beyond all human imagination?

ANDREW. Go ahead and try.

BARRYMORE. In just six weeks time, you will play Hamlet. (*Andrew screams.*)

ANDREW. (*Genuinely terrified.*) Oh my God, you really are him, aren't you?

BARRYMORE. John Barrymore. Actor. Legend. Seducer. Corpse.

ANDREW. So—it worked. The seance. Felicia, her mother—she brought you back, from over there.

BARRYMORE. Not at all. You summoned me.

ANDREW. I did?

BARRYMORE. As a link in a proud theatrical tradition. Every soul embarking upon Hamlet is permitted to summon an earlier player. From Burbage to Kean to Irving—the call has been answered.

ANDREW. Wait—you mean you're here to help me play Hamlet? Because you did it?

BARRYMORE. Indeed.

ANDREW. Okay. Fine. Then the problem's solved. Because I'm not going to play Hamlet. No way. So you can just . . . go back. To . . . wherever.

BARRYMORE. I'm afraid that's not possible.

ANDREW. Why not?

BARRYMORE. I cannot return, I will not be accepted, until my task is accomplished. Until you have . . .

ANDREW and BARRYMORE. Played Hamlet.

BARRYMORE. Precisely.

ANDREW. (*Completely floored.*) Oh no. Oh my God. You mean, if I don't go through with it . . .

BARRYMORE. Then I'm here to stay. Within these walls. Trapped for all time, with a television actor.

ANDREW. Well, excuse me—I happen to be a very good television actor! And I don't need any dead ham bone to teach me about anything! Even if I were going to play Hamlet, which I'm not, I could do just fine! All by myself! (*Barrymore glares at Andrew. He removes a small leatherbound copy of* Hamlet *from a pouch on his belt, and tosses it to Andrew.*)

BARRYMORE. Very well then. Hamlet. "To be or not to be."

ANDREW. That happens to be the speech I did at my auditions. And I got the part. (*Andrew tosses the copy of* Hamlet *back to Barrymore.*)

BARRYMORE. Proceed. (*Barrymore reclines full length on the couch. Andrew, very full of himself, decides to show Barrymore a thing or two. He strides U., and turns his back. He hunches over.*) Yes?

ANDREW. I'm doing my preparation.

BARRYMORE. Your . . . preparation.

ANDREW. Yes. My acting teacher taught me this. Harold Gaffney.

BARRYMORE. Harold Gaffney?

ANDREW. The creator of the Gaffney technique. Act To Win. I can't just do the speech cold, I have to get into character. I have to become Hamlet. I'm doing a substitution.

BARRYMORE. A substitution?

ANDREW. I'm thinking about something that really happened to me, so I can remember the emotion, and recreate it.

BARRYMORE. And what are you remembering?

ANDREW. It's a secret. Otherwise it won't work. Be quiet, I'm going to act.

BARRYMORE. Why do I feel we should spread newspapers about? I'm sorry, I shall be silent. Out of deep respect. Road closed—man acting. (*Andrew turns, and moves D., facing out. He makes a small snuffling noise. He loosens up his shoulders, like a prizefighter shadow-boxing. He makes a few faces; he is being ultra-naturalistic, very Method. He makes an ungodly howling noise, then slaps his own face. He repeats this. Barrymore watches all this, appalled.*) You know, Andrew, I am dead, and I shall be for all eternity. But I still don't have all day. (*Andrew begins again. After a few lunges, he begins to speak. His forehead is furrowed with intensity; his speech patterns are reminiscent of a Brooklyn tough guy, in the Brando/ DeNiro mode.*)

ANDREW. To be . . . nah. (*He paces. A thought occurs.*) Or . . . not . . . to . . . be. That, *that* is the question. Whoa. Whether . . . (*He holds up a hand.*) Whether 'tis nobler . . . huh . . . in the mind, right . . .

BARRYMORE. Wrong.

ANDREW. What?

BARRYMORE. No.

ANDREW. What "No?"

BARRYMORE. No.

ANDREW. No, what? No you disagree with my interpretation, no my interpretation wasn't clear, no you think I'm totally horrible?

BARRYMORE. Yes.

ANDREW. I'm horrible?

BARRYMORE. At the moment. What were you doing?

ANDREW. I was internalizing the role. I was finding an emotional through-line.

BARRYMORE. Why?

ANDREW. Why? So the character will come alive! So I'll achieve some sort of truth! *(Barrymore rises, aghast.)*

BARRYMORE. Truth! Your performance—the pauses, the moans, all that you clearly consider invaluable—it's utterly appalling. We must never confuse truth with asthma.

ANDREW. What?

BARRYMORE. I understand the impulse, God help me, I lived just long enough for the introduction of truth into the modern theater. As I recall, it accompanied synthetic fibers and the GE Kitchen of Tomorrow.

ANDREW. Oh—so you just want me to ham it up.

BARRYMORE. I beg your pardon?

ANDREW. Hamming. Mugging. Over the top. Too big. Too . . .

BARRYMORE. *(With a grand gesture.)* Barrymore?

ANDREW. Well, you did have that reputation. As someone . . . larger than life.

BARRYMORE. What size would you prefer? Gesture, passion—these are an actor's tools. Abandon them, and the result? Mere reality. Employ them, with gusto, and an artist's finesse, and the theater resounds! I do not overact. I simply possess the emotional resources of ten men. I am not a ham; I'm a crowd! Andrew, who is Hamlet?

ANDREW. A prince?

BARRYMORE. A star.

ANDREW. What?

BARRYMORE. A star. The role is a challenge, but far more—an opportunity. To shine. To rule. To seduce. To wit—what makes a star?

ANDREW. Talent? *(They exchange a look.)* Sorry, I wasn't thinking.

BARRYMORE. A thrilling vocal range? Decades of training? The proper vehicle? *(He shakes his head, no.)* Tights.

ANDREW. Tights?

BARRYMORE. Tights. Where are you looking? Right now?

ANDREW. I am not!

BARRYMORE. Of course you are! The potato, the cucumber, the rolled sock—this is the history of Prince Hamlet.

ANDREW. You mean—you padded yourself?

BARRYMORE. Unnecessary. Even for the balcony. *(Pause, as he gazes upward.)* The second balcony.

ANDREW. So Hamlet should be . . . horny?

BARRYMORE. Hamlet is a young man, a college boy, at his sexual peak. Hamlet is pure hormone. Ophelia enters, that most beguiling of maidens. Chastity is discussed.

ANDREW. Please, don't joke. Not about chastity.

BARRYMORE. Why? What?

ANDREW. I can't talk about it.

BARRYMORE. Oh dear. Your beloved? A problem?

ANDREW. A nightmare. Five months.

BARRYMORE. What?

ANDREW. Nothing.

BARRYMORE. Truly?

ANDREW. Necking at the Cloisters. Picnics on Amish quilts. Sonnets.

BARRYMORE. Not . . . sonnets.

ANDREW. Yes. And I've been faithful. Totally. It's unnatural. Do you know what happens when you don't have sex?

BARRYMORE. No.

ANDREW. Thanks.

BARRYMORE. But why?

ANDREW. Why her, or why me? Deirdre won't have sex because . . . she's not sure. Because she's the victim of a relentlessly happy childhood, which she fully expects to continue.

BARRYMORE. And you?

ANDREW. Me? Why do I put up with all this? Why have I begged Deirdre to marry me, practically since the day we met? Because, in the strangest way, she's the most passionate woman I've ever met. Because when she sees a homeless person, she gives them a fabric-covered datebook. Deirdre's just . . . she makes me think that love is as amazing as it's supposed to be. She's romantic, which means she's insane. I know I love her, because I want to strangle her. Does that make sense?

BARRYMORE. Of course. A virgin goddess.

ANDREW. Please—don't encourage her.

BARRYMORE. She is to be treasured, and honored. I have known few such women in my sensual history. Perhaps only five hundred. They are the most adorable saints. But . . . there are ways.

ANDREW. (*Eagerly.*) What?

BARRYMORE. No. It would be unthinkable.

ANDREW. *What?*

BARRYMORE. I could never condone such Casanova-like tactics. Such Valentino mesmerism.

ANDREW. Such Barrymore deceit.

BARRYMORE. (*Mortally offended.*) Cad.

ANDREW. Yes?

BARRYMORE. Knave.

ANDREW. Please?

BARRYMORE. Hamlet!

ANDREW. No! Stop with that.

BARRYMORE. Hamlet, to cunningly expose his father's murder, feigns madness. To perfect the pose, he must spurn his beloved, the fair Ophelia. She is undone.

ANDREW. But doesn't she kill herself? I don't want to hurt Deirdre.

BARRYMORE. You'll be merciful.

ANDREW. No, that would be dishonest.

BARRYMORE. You would prefer, perhaps, some form of therapy? Continued discussion? What is the present-day epithet— "communication?" That absolute assassin of romance? (*The door to the roof swings open. Deirdre enters, in a long, Victorian, white cotton nightgown, carrying a book. Deirdre will not be able to see Barrymore. Spotting Deirdre; aglow.*) Ahh!

DEIRDRE. Andrew?

ANDREW. (*Surprised.*) Deirdre.

BARRYMORE. (*Gazing at Deirdre, appreciatively.*) Darling.

DEIRDRE. Who were you talking to? (*Andrew turns to Barrymore.*)

BARRYMORE. No. She has no need to see me.

ANDREW. (*To Deirdre.*) No one. I was just . . . running my lines. The soliloquies.

DEIRDRE. I've been reading your Barrymore book. He was incredible.

BARRYMORE. Nymph.

DEIRDRE. But his life—it was so tragic. Did you know, he was a major alcoholic. Toward the end, when he couldn't find liquor, he would drink cleaning fluid.

BARRYMORE. A black lie!

DEIRDRE. And perfume.

BARRYMORE. As a chaser.

DEIRDRE. I mean, he was magnificent, but he was married four times.

BARRYMORE. I was?

DEIRDRE. He would fall madly in love with these women, and then he'd become insanely jealous. And then he'd cheat on them. Andrew—I want you to promise me something. I know that Barrymore is your hero, and that we should all worship him, but please—promise me you'll never be anything like him. (*Andrew stands at C., midway between Deirdre and Barrymore. Deirdre takes Andrew's hand.*) Do you promise? (*Barrymore takes Andrew's other hand.*)

BARRYMORE. (*Beseechingly.*) Swear it.

ANDREW. Deirdre—maybe Barrymore wasn't so bad.

BARRYMORE. Maybe?

ANDREW. I mean, he was very talented, and I'm sure he had a few . . .

BARRYMORE. Sterling attributes?

ANDREW. Good days. (*Deirdre is now seated, paging through the Barrymore book.*)

DEIRDRE. Oh, no. He was . . . well, do you know, the first time he had sex, he was only fourteen?

BARRYMORE. Which book is this?

DEIRDRE. With his own stepmother. Can you imagine?

BARRYMORE. I'm a Freudian bonus coupon.

DEIRDRE. And after that, there was no stopping him, he must have been with every woman in New York. He was a matinee idol, before he did *Hamlet*. He starred in these trashy plays, and women would swoon, right in the aisles. There are these pictures of him . . . (*She holds open the book.*) from when he was young. He was so . . . cool.

ANDREW. Deirdre?

DEIRDRE. Look at this picture—it's him rejecting Ophelia. See, he wore all black, sort of open at the neck. And tights. (*Barrymore is delighted.*)

ANDREW. (*To Barrymore.*) Shut up!

DEIRDRE. (*Thinking Andrew was speaking to her.*) What? What do you mean? Oh, I get it. You're treating me the way Hamlet treats Ophelia. Andrew, do you think Hamlet slept with Ophelia?

BARRYMORE. Only in the Chicago company.

ANDREW. (*To Barrymore.*) Shut up!

DEIRDRE. (*Almost swooning.*) Oh, Andrew. Hamlet's so mean to Ophelia.

He says, "Get thee to a nunnery." A nunnery! Oh, if you said that to me . . . I'd die.

ANDREW. (*To Barrymore.*) I'm not kidding.

DEIRDRE. Oh Andrew, say it. Like in the play.

ANDREW. What? Get thee to a nunnery?

DEIRDRE. No—like Barrymore!

BARRYMORE. (*With tremendous authority.*) Barrymore. Begin! (*Barrymore begins another lesson. He gazes at Deirdre, and lightly strokes her face. Ghostly music. He turns away. He motions for Andrew to do the same. Andrew gazes at Deirdre, and strokes her face. No music. Andrew's actions are perfunctory; he tries not to participate. He gestures—"See? It didn't work."*)

DEIRDRE. (*Very disappointed.*) Andrew . . . (*Barrymore is outraged at Andrew's lack of cooperation.*)

BARRYMORE. (*Howling.*) GET THEE . . . (*Andrew is shocked by Barrymore's roar; he moves into action, also at fever pitch.*)

ANDREW. TO A NUNNERY! (*Deirdre is shocked and thrilled at this new Andrew.*)

DEIRDRE. Yes!

BARRYMORE. (*Still very passionate.*) Why wouldst thou be a breeder of sinners? (*Andrew has grabbed the copy of Hamlet; he hurries after Barrymore. Together they stalk Deirdre, with great sensual intensity.*)

ANDREW. I am myself indifferent honest, but yet I could accuse me of such things . . .

BARRYMORE. Pause. Consider. Destroy!

ANDREW. (*With enormous authority.*) . . . that it were better my mother had not *born me!*

DEIRDRE. *No!*

ANDREW. I am very proud . . .

BARRYMORE. Revengeful . . .

ANDREW. With more offenses at my beck than I have thoughts to put them in . . .

DEIRDRE. (*Backing around the couch.*) Andrew, this is making me very nervous . . .

ANDREW. Imagination to give them shape, or time to act them in! (*Andrew takes Deirdre in his arms; they embrace and kiss with wild abandon. Barrymore stands nearby, urging them on and enjoying the spectacle.*)

BARRYMORE. What should such fellows as I do crawling between earth and heaven? We are arrant knaves all, believe none of us! (*Andrew literally sweeps Deirdre off her feet. He carries her to the couch.*)

ANDREW. Go thy ways to a nunnery! (*Andrew tosses Deirdre onto the couch; she reaches out to him. He regards her with majestic disdain, thoroughly rejecting her.*) Call my machine!

DEIRDRE. No! (*Deirdre moans, and continues reaching out to Andrew, imploringly. Andrew turns to Barrymore; they shake hands, both very full of themselves and their success. Andrew turns back to Deirdre. She pleads.*) My lord Hamlet!

ANDREW. Fair maiden. (*Andrew lowers himself onto the couch, into Deirdre's arms. They kiss passionately; just as things are about to progress, the doorbell buzzes. Unbearably frustrated.*) NO! (*The doorbell buzzes repeatedly.*) GO AWAY! (*Deirdre leaps up and goes to the intercom.*)

DEIRDRE. (*Into phone, composing herself.*) Hello?

BARRYMORE. Poor boy! Within one couplet! Shakespeare—the most potent aphrodisiac.

ANDREW. (*In frantic despair.*) I was almost there! I was going to have sex!

DEIRDRE. (*Still on the intercom.*) It's Gary!

BARRYMORE. Gary?

ANDREW. A friend. A director. From LA. He did my show. Why is he here? Why?

BARRYMORE. You are Hamlet. A study in frustration. Thwarted action. (*Deirdre has opened the front door, and is peering out into the hall. Gary Peter Lefkowitz appears. Gary is in his thirties; he personifies LA shaggy-chic. He wears extremely expensive casual clothing; an Armani suit or a $5,000 suede*) *jacket with a baseball cap. Gary should be played as an extremely happy, over-grown child, an oddly appealing creature of pure appetite. Reality is of very little consequence to Gary; the deal is all.)*

GARY. Dee Dee!

DEIRDRE. Gary! *(Gary and Deirdre hug.)* What are you doing here? Why aren't you in LA?

GARY. I'm here for my man. My man Andrew Rally. Andy boy! *(Gary opens his arms to Andrew.)* Talk-time, Andy man. Fusion has occurred. Yes! *(Gary goes into a brief physical spasm, a celebratory combination of war dance and gospel fervor.)*

DEIRDRE. I'll let you guys talk. I'm going to finish my reading. *(Deirdre begins ascending the stairs to the roof. She turns to Andrew, longingly.)* My liege?

ANDREW. *(Disgruntled.)* Yeah, to a nunnery. *(Deirdre trembles visibly, and utters a passionate moan.)*

DEIRDRE. Oooh! *(She runs upstairs and out the door to the roof.)*

GARY. Reading? She's reading?

ANDREW. I don't understand it.

GARY. Still no . . . ? *(He makes an obscene hand gesture denoting sexual intercourse.)*

ANDREW. No, Gary. Still no hand gestures.

GARY. Whoa. Man, if I was with a lady for that long, and there was still no return, I don't know, I might start thinking trade-in. Turn-around. And who's this? *(Gary gestures to Barrymore. Andrew looks at Barrymore, shocked that Gary can see him.)*

BARRYMORE. Of course he can see me. Because it won't make any difference. *(Introducing himself to Gary.)* John Barrymore.

GARY. Barrymore. Right. Disney? VP?

BARRYMORE. No. I'm an actor.

GARY. An actor! Whoa! Not another one. Good luck, big guy. I mean it. See, that's what's great about you guys. You're both actors, you're like in direct competition, but you can still give the appearance of friendship. See, I'm fucked up, I can't be friends with anyone like me.

BARRYMORE. We understand.

GARY. I mean, the way I monitor, there's only bungalow space for so many hyphenates, right?

BARRYMORE. Hyphenates?

GARY. Writer-producer-director. Gary Peter Lefkowitz.

BARRYMORE. Ah. I see. So, if you also designed the scenery, would you require an additional name?

GARY. Cute. That's cute. (*Admiring Barrymore's outfit.*) Great look. What is that? Japanese? Washed silk?

BARRYMORE. Hamlet. Shakespeare.

GARY. Right. Nice. Retro.

BARRYMORE. Sixteenth century.

GARY. Whoa. God, other centuries. Like, people who weren't me. Okay, tell me, total truth, am I like the most self-obsessed person you've ever met? My answer? Yes. Okay, enough about me. Figure of speech. Andy, Andy boy, Andy my love—we got it. Green light. The go-ahead. Network approval! A pilot and five episodes!

ANDREW. A pilot and five episodes—of what?

GARY. Of the show! Of *our* show!

ANDREW. What are you talking about?

GARY. Okay, I didn't tell you. Because I didn't want you to be disappointed, and blame me, if it didn't go. But it went! I used your name to tip it through the hoop. I told the network it was your all-time favorite project, that you were ready to roll. And after Jim Corman, you're network candy, they're crawling.

ANDREW. Really?

GARY. America cries out! Your commitment was just the push!

BARRYMORE. But he's not committed. He's playing Hamlet.

ANDREW. Well . . .

GARY. Wait a second—which network?

BARRYMORE. In the park. This summer.

GARY. What, it's like for some special? Hallmark Hall of Fame?

BARRYMORE. It's not for anything. It's . . . theater.

GARY. Wait, let me get this. It's Shakespeare, right, it's like algebra on stage. And it's in Central Park, which probably seats, what, 500 tops. And the only merchandising involves, say, Gielgud cassettes and Mostly Mozart tote-bags. And on top of this, it's free. So Andy, tell me, who the hell is representing you nowadays?

ANDREW. Lillian is all for it.

GARY. Lillian! Jesus, of course. Andy, I love her, but she's a war criminal. I'm not kidding. She's a ten hour documentary waiting to happen. Okay Andy, fine, do your little show in the park. Is it a deduction? I mean, it's not even dinner theater. What, they sell whole wheat brownies and little bags of nuts and raisins. It's snack theater. It's Shakespeare for squirrels. Wait, just answer me one question, one simple thing: why? Why are you doing this? Are you broke?

ANDREW. No. I have savings.

GARY. Is there a bet involved?

ANDREW. No!

GARY. Andy—are you in some sort of trouble?

ANDREW. Yes Gary, that's it, you finally hit it. The producers have my parents.

GARY. *Hamlet.* Andy, I have to say this, 'cause we're buds, and I cherish that budship—but think reputation. Word on the street. When folks—let's call 'em Hollywood—when they hear that you're doing the greatest play in the English-speaking world, they're gonna know you're washed up!

ANDREW. Gary . . .

GARY. I'm serious. You haven't had offers? Nothing? What about the commercials? That Trailburst crap?

ANDREW. Gary, have you ever seen those ads? Have you seen what I have to work with?

BARRYMORE. What?

GARY. A puppet. A furry little chipmunk. It's cute.

ANDREW. It's a *hand puppet.* (*To Barrymore.*) Have you ever worked with a puppet? There's some guy, kneeling down near your crotch, working the puppet. And he's doing a chipmunk voice, into a microphone. And the guy, the chipmunk operator, he says, (*In a high-pitched, cutesy chipmunk voice.*) "Oh Andy, can I have a Trailburst Nugget?" And I say no, they're for people, not chipmunks. And he starts . . . to cry. And I . . . (*Andrew can't quite continue.*)

BARRYMORE. You what?

ANDREW. (*Mortified.*) I . . . kiss him. On the top of his little chipmunk head.

GARY. It's great!

ANDREW. It's disgusting! It's humiliating! I didn't spend four years in college and two in drama school to end up comforting someone's fist! It's not even a decent product. Trailburst Nuggets are like sawdust dipped in chocolate, and they have more calories than lard.

GARY. And that's why you're doing *Hamlet?*

ANDREW. Gary, you don't understand, about the theater. About why people do Shakespeare.

BARRYMORE. They do it because—it's art.

GARY. (*After a beat.*) Andy. Andy my honey, Andy my multi-talented prime-time delight. You don't do art. You buy it. You do TV, or a flick, you make a bundle and you nail a Monet. I was at this producer's place in Brentwood on the weekend. Incredible. Picassos. Van Gogh. A Rembrandt. And all from his TV shows.

ANDREW. But Gary, I don't want to just buy art. I mean, which would you rather do, paint a Picasso or own one?

GARY. Are you kidding? I'd like to sell one. At auction. Cash-flow. See, that's what I like—balls in the air. Activity. You're my Rembrandt.

ANDREW. I am?

GARY. How much are you gonna clear from this Shakespeare deal? Zip, right? Actually, you're paying them, because your time is valuable. A pilot and five episodes, high six figures. And if it hits, you get participation.

ANDREW. (*Impressed.*) Participation? In syndication?

GARY. Yup. You'll get paid every time it airs, first run, rerun, four AM in Singapore in the year 3000. Basically, you'll be able to afford to buy England, dig up Shakespeare, and get him to write the Christmas show!

BARRYMORE. This television program you're promoting, this goldmine—what is it exactly?

GARY. Okay—the pitch. Gather ye round. It's not cops, it's not young doctors, none of that TV crap.

ANDREW. Great.

GARY. You're a teacher. Mike Sullivan. You're young, idealistic, new to the system. Inner city high school. Rough. Dope. M-1's. Teen sex.

ANDREW. Wow . . .

GARY. No one cares. All the other teachers are burn-outs. Not you.

BARRYMORE. Why not?

GARY. Because . . . you care. You grew up in the neighborhood. You want to give something back.

ANDREW. (*Sincerely.*) You know, that sounds sort of . . . okay. It's almost realistic. I mean, you could deal with real problems. I could be vulnerable. I could mess up sometimes.

GARY. And at night, after the sun goes down, you have superpowers.

BARRYMORE. Superpowers?

GARY. Sure. I mean, who wants to watch that caring-feeling-unwed mothers bullshit? It's over. But, after sundown, you're invincible. Modified X-ray vision. You can fly, but only about ten feet up. See, we're keeping it real. Gritty. And so, after dark, you help the community, you help the kids, with your powers.

ANDREW. Do they know it's me? When I have superpowers?

GARY. No. You're in leather, denim, they just think it's some great dude.

Great title, killer title—*Night School.* Dolls. Posters. The clothes. You could get an album, easy.

ANDREW. But . . . I can't sing.

GARY. Someone can. You can keep the Trailburst gig, there's no conflict—they'll probably extend, 'cause now you're a teacher! So think about it. What's to think, you've got a network commitment. Just forget this *Hamlet* crap—I mean, who are you kidding?

ANDREW. What do you mean?

GARY. Andy, I know you. I gave you your break. You're no actor.

ANDREW. What?

GARY. You're better than that. An actor, what, that's just some English guy who can't get a series. Look, I'm in town, I'm at the Ritz. I'll talk to Lillian, get things rolling. (*Gary hugs Andrew. He shakes Barrymore's hand.*) Great to meet you. You act, right?

BARRYMORE. John Sidney Barrymore.

GARY. We'll keep you in mind. Barrymore—any relation to the dead guy?

BARRYMORE. Distant.

GARY. (*At the door.*) Death. Man. Think about it—the third coast. (*Gary exits, out the front door.*)

ANDREW. (*Defensively.*) Don't say it! He's right, he's totally right!

BARRYMORE. *Night School?*

ANDREW. I don't know what to do! Think about the money—you had that kind of money!

BARRYMORE. Yes, as I grew older. Wealth is obscene in the young, it stunts ambition.

ANDREW. But . . . but . . . what about security?

BARRYMORE. What is this mania for security? What's the worst that can happen?

ANDREW. That I play Hamlet and Gary's right. And no one will hire me, and soon I'm face down in the gutter, wearing rags, without a job or anywhere to go.

BARRYMORE. Shouldn't every evening end like that?

ANDREW. Why am I talking to you? And it's not just the money, I'm not that superficial. It's the *fame*. Do you know how many people will watch *Night School*, even if it's a bomb?

BARRYMORE. Of course. There is fame in that sort of work. You may be admired, lusted after. You may acquire all the attributes of a well-marketed detergent. But there is fame—mere celebrity—and there is glory. Do you appreciate the difference?

ANDREW. Of course. Fame pays better. Fame has beachfront property. Fame needs bodyguards.

BARRYMORE. Glory, only an audience.

ANDREW. Oh, come on! That audience has changed! Don't you think that if Shakespeare were around now, he'd be writing normally?

BARRYMORE. I beg your pardon? (*Andrew grabs the* Hamlet *script.*)

ANDREW. You know, wouldn't the characters say, how are you, instead of how dost thou, my liege? What is a liege, anyway? And what's a fardel? In "To be or not to be," there's this line; Hamlet is thinking about suicide, right? And he tells about how awful life is, the whips and scorns of time.

BARRYMORE. Correct.

ANDREW. And he says, why should anyone put up with all this "when he himself might his quietus make with a bare bodkin." Quietus? Bodkin?

BARRYMORE. Quietus means death; a bodkin is a dagger.

ANDREW. And this next sentence, "Who would fardels bear . . ."

BARRYMORE. A fardel is a burden. Any burden.

ANDREW. So why can't we change it? Why can't I just say, so with all this garbage in the world, why not just stab yourself? Instead of dragging your fardels around? Then it would be clear, then people would get it!

BARRYMORE. Angels and ministers of grace, defend us! Tell me—if you loathe Shakespeare, if Los Angeles is so alluring—why did you audition?

ANDREW. Because my agent made me! And because Deirdre loves *Hamlet!* And because—because they asked me!

BARRYMORE. Because they asked you?

ANDREW. Because somewhere, someone thought that maybe, just maybe—I could do it. That I wouldn't have to be just Jim Corman, rookie surgeon, for the rest of my life. On TV, no one cared if I was talented, I had the right twinkle, the demographic appeal. And after a while, I started to think maybe that's all I had. That if I didn't show up, they could just use the poster. But I came to New York and somebody said, wait. Maybe Andy Rally could do Shakespeare. Onstage. Say those lines.

BARRYMORE. Act!

ANDREW. Yes. But they were wrong! I belong on TV, I know that. And it's not a crime. And I'm sorry I got you down here, and I'm sure that if you go back and talk to whomever, you can get this whole *Hamlet* deal cancelled. Because I'm really tired, and my girlfriend won't sleep with me, and I think my agent is very ill but she refuses to discuss it. And my life is an embarrassing joke, so if you'd please just leave, I'd appreciate it!

BARRYMORE. Can you imagine you're the first performer to experience such misgivings? Can you possibly believe that every prospective Hamlet did not tremble, and pale, and bolt? *Hamlet* will change you, Andrew, make no mistake. And the deal, as you term it, cannot be cancelled. And I cannot depart these premises until you have fulfilled your destiny. You approach a crossroads, and a decision must be made. What are you to be—artist, or lunchbox?

ANDREW. Stop it!

BARRYMORE. You are no longer Jim Corman.

ANDREW. Get out.

BARRYMORE. And you are not yet sensitive Mike Sullivan.

ANDREW. You don't know that.

BARRYMORE. You are Hamlet!

ANDREW. No! (*Andrew and Barrymore are facing off; neither will give an inch. Barrymore finally makes a decision.*)

BARRYMORE. Right! (*Barrymore strides to a tall, bulky object standing in a corner; the object is completely shrouded in a sheet. With a flourish, Barrymore tugs the sheet away, revealing a carved mahogany cabinet.*)

ANDREW. (*Astonished.*) That's not mine! How did that get there? (*Barrymore opens the cabinet, and removes a sword, a duelling rapier. He tosses the sword to Andrew, who catches it.*) A sword? Oh my God. (*Barrymore strides to the opposite side of the room. He tugs a sheet from another shrouded object, revealing a suit of armor.*) I should call the movers. (*Barrymore removes a second sword from the suit of armor. He tests the sword, bending it, and then raises it above his head. He points it at Andrew.*)

BARRYMORE. En garde!

ANDREW. *What?*

BARRYMORE. The drama's conclusion. Hamlet's duel and death. (*Barrymore begins to advance on Andrew, brandishing his sword.*)

ANDREW. Excuse me? I can't fence.

BARRYMORE. Hamlet can. I can. (*Barrymore takes a swipe at Andrew, who jumps back.*)

ANDREW. Stop that! I hate swords! I hate violence! (*Barrymore takes another swipe. Andrew breaks away, rapidly.*) I have a gym excuse!

BARRYMORE. As does Hamlet, until the closing moments of the drama. At last, he takes action. He assumes a tragic stature. (*Barrymore feints at Andrew, who jumps again.*)

ANDREW. He dies!

BARRYMORE. A hero! (*He slashes the air with his sword, bounding about in his best swashbuckling manner.*) This is why one acts! This is why actors are envied! We are allowed to *do* this sort of thing!

ANDREW. Not anymore. We have stunt people. Doubles.

BARRYMORE. Of course—for the soliloquies! (*Barrymore advances on Andrew, who runs and hides in the passage beneath the staircase. Andrew then backs out, on the other side of the staircase. Barrymore has anticipated this, and*) *has circled around to meet him. The exact fight choreography is, of course, left to the discretion of any individual production. Barrymore feints at Andrew who, for the first time, raises his sword to defend himself.)* Well done!

ANDREW. No! Stop it! I can't do this. (*Andrew lays down his sword. During Andrew's next speech, Barrymore might stand on the couch, bouncing and slashing the air with his sword, in a playful if dangerous mood.*) I'm stopping, okay? You're very cute, but I'm not going to play. You think you can force me to be like you, to be Hamlet. To be bold, and dashing, and vengeful. Well, no. I don't do that. I'm a liberal. So no duels. No macho behavior. Not in my house.

BARRYMORE. (*Outraged.*) Your house! (*Barrymore leaps from the couch. He and Andrew face off. Barrymore raises his sword. Decisively, he slashes the couch, ruining the upholstery.*)

ANDREW. (*In disbelief.*) My couch. You slashed my couch.

BARRYMORE. It offended me. So modern. (*Barrymore looks around. He raises his sword, and sweeps a lamp off a table. It crashes to the floor.*)

ANDREW. Stop it! That's my lamp! You're making a mess!

BARRYMORE. Buy a new lamp! Residuals! (*Barrymore sweeps a vase off a shelf with his sword; the vase shatters. Alternately, and to save money, Barrymore might pick up a vase and hurl it offstage, through the archway, from which appropriate crashing noises might issue. Andrew, livid at the destruction of his property, picks up his sword and brandishes it. He becomes a decisive man of action.*)

ANDREW. That's enough! The girl doesn't come until Friday! *Someone is going to vacuum!*

BARRYMORE. (*Delighted.*) Not I! (*Barrymore gestures, and exciting, galloping swordfight music begins, very Errol Flynn. He and Andrew begin some serious fencing. Andrew lunges at Barrymore; they cross swords, above their heads.*)

ANDREW. Again! (*Andrew and Barrymore fence, moving across the stage. Barrymore fences with one hand, and swigs from the bottle of champagne with the other. At one point, Barrymore uses the bottle to fence with.*)

BARRYMORE. Nicely done! (*Barrymore shakes the bottle of champagne, and *sprays Andrew with the fizz. They continue to fence, with great brio, all over the stage. Andrew backs Barrymore up the staircase. He disarms Barrymore, whose sword falls. Andrew's sword is now at Barrymore's throat.)*

ANDREW. Say it! Say I don't have to do it! No Hamlet!

BARRYMORE. But Andrew—you're already doing it. Look! *(Andrew is distracted, and Barrymore kicks the sword out of Andrew's hand, grabbing it for himself. He backs Andrew down the stairs, at swordpoint. Gleefully.)* Hamlet—rookie prince! *(Andrew retrieves Barrymore's previous sword, and they continue to fence.)* Hamlet?

ANDREW. I can't!

BARRYMORE. Then shall I kill you? *(Barrymore knocks the sword from Andrew's hand; Andrew is now defenseless, as Barrymore advances on him.)* Right now? Curtail your precious mediocrity? Imagine your epitaph— "Andrew Rally, Beloved Coward. Beloved Hack. Here Lies No One!" *(Barrymore feints at Andrew, and seemingly wounds him. Andrew clutches himself and moans; he slumps to the floor. His injury is highly believable. Barrymore is aghast; he had not intended to actually hurt Andrew.)* Lad?

ANDREW. *(Trying to speak, clearly in great pain.)* No . . . you're right . . .

BARRYMORE. *(Kneeling.)* What? Are you . . . shall I call someone? A physician?

ANDREW. No.

BARRYMORE. I'm sorry, I didn't intend to . . . wound you.

ANDREW. *(Barely able to speak.)* Call . . .

BARRYMORE. Call whom? Deirdre? *(Andrew leaps to his feet, fully recovered and triumphant. He grabs his sword and points it at Barrymore.)*

ANDREW. Shakespeare!

BARRYMORE. Ha! *(Barrymore grins, and makes an arm gesture; a jubilant trumpet flourish is heard.)*

CURTAIN

ACT TWO

Scene 1

Place: The same.

Time: Opening night, six weeks later.

The apartment has been transformed, into a true medieval lair. All of Andrew's furniture has been replaced by elaborately carved, heavy dark oak pieces. There is a richly upholstered chaise, and an ottoman center stage. An ornate throne sits off to one side, and the glorious fireplace is now fully revealed. A tapestry hangs on one wall, with a chandelier above. A renaissance globe stands near the staircase. The floor is covered with oriental carpets, stacks of antique leather-bound books, and atmospheric mounds of brocade cushions. Various candelabra and sconces are located around the room, as yet unlit. The suit of armor and other appropriately Gothic pieces complete the lavishly theatrical mood.

Several vases of flowers have been placed about; other boxes of flowers are stacked by the front door.

As the curtain rises, Barrymore descends from the roof, singing to himself. He crosses to the globe, which opens to reveal a fully-stocked bar. Barrymore pours himself a drink. He is still dressed as Hamlet.

Felicia enters, very dressed up, from the archway. She cannot see Barry-
more. She stares at the apartment's new furnishings, shaking her head.

FELICIA. Oh my God. What got into him? (*Deirdre enters, also from the*
archway, carrying a vase of flowers. Deirdre is dressed in a flowing velvet, medi-
eval-style gown, complete with a lengthy train and trailing sleeves. She is playing
one of Ophelia's ladies-in-waiting, and a wreath of flowers has been braided
into her hair.)

DEIRDRE. Isn't it incredible? It's Barrymore! Andrew says this is exactly
what it used to look like! He says it's been helping him, to get in the
mood.

FELICIA. Well I hope he's there—in the mood. It's opening night! (*Deir-*
dre and Felicia shriek with excitement. They are wildly excited; this entire scene
should be played with an air of giddy anticipation and suspense.)

DEIRDRE. Opening night! *Hamlet!*

FELICIA. So where is he? Doesn't he have to get to the theater?

DEIRDRE. He's upstairs, getting ready, on the roof. He's in costume,
too, he wears it everywhere. And he talks to Barrymore.

FELICIA. Really? He got through?

DEIRDRE. No, he just imagines. I catch him at it all the time. Do you
think he's here? Watching over us?

FELICIA. Barrymore?

DEIRDRE. Yes! Oh John Barrymore, wherever you are! Bless this evening! Bless Andrew! (*As Deirdre invokes Barrymore, she runs through*
the room, seeking the ghost. Barrymore follows her, skipping along behind her,
highly amused. Finally he stretches out on the chaise.)

FELICIA. Honey, you better calm down. (*Barrymore beckons to Deirdre from*
the chaise. He opens his arms.)

DEIRDRE. I know, I've been like this all day, all week, I can't sit still . . .
(*Deirdre, pulled by unseen forces, sits on the chaise beside Barrymore. She lies*
down, as he gently strokes her hair. She is unaware of his presence, but he has his

effect.) Felicia, what's it like? Sex? (*Felicia is busily putting finishing touches on her makeup, inspecting herself in the mirror of her compact.*)

FELICIA. Sex? Oh, that's right—you're still on the bench. No wonder you're nervous. Sex is great. With the right guy.

DEIRDRE. Really? But what about with the wrong guy?

FELICIA. (*After a beat.*) Better.

DEIRDRE. Felicia, you're terrible! (*Barrymore kisses Deirdre's neck.*) Stop it!

FELICIA. What? (*Deirdre leaps up, flustered. Barrymore rises as well, and heads for the staircase.*)

DEIRDRE. (*Unnerved.*) Nothing. Felicia—how do you know? If you're really in ultimate love? If it's . . . Shakespeare?

FELICIA. What's to know? Andy's the best. I mean, he's a star, he must have girls coming outta the woodwork. And he's waiting for you.

DEIRDRE. That's true. It's just—sometimes I think I'll never marry anyone. I mean, anyone alive. (*Barrymore, on the staircase, turns and salutes Deirdre's last phrase—"anyone alive." He raises his glass in a toast. Then he heads up the stairs and exits to the roof.*)

FELICIA. Hon?

DEIRDRE. I've always wanted to be Joan of Arc, or Juliet, or Guinevere. And I want to love someone like Hamlet, or King Arthur, or Socrates.

FELICIA. You're rich, right?

DEIRDRE. No—why?

FELICIA. Well, the way you think, I mean I love it, but, you don't have to make a living, right?

DEIRDRE. No, I'm not rich, really. Just my parents. They're so great, they've been married for almost forty years. And that's what I want— eternal love! For the ages! And tonight, Andrew's playing Hamlet. And I'll know. (*Gary enters, from the archway, carrying a glass and a bottle of champagne. He wears a tuxedo, a model both luxurious and trendy.*) Gary, that's bad luck! The champagne is for afterwards, to celebrate!

GARY. Oh, sorry. (*Deirdre grabs the champagne from Gary and exits*

through the archway, leaving Gary alone with Felicia.) Hey—big night!
Hot stuff!

FELICIA. I can't wait!

GARY. You know, I love Andy, he's a great actor, but—what if he really
sucks? (*Deirdre re-enters.*)

DEIRDRE. He won't! He's going to be glorious! Don't even think that!

FELICIA. I hope he's good. Although, you know, with Shakespeare—
how can you tell?

GARY. Exactly. I mean, maybe it's foolproof—maybe, with Shakespeare,
there's no difference between bad and good. And everybody's afraid
to say it. I mean, at the movies, on the tube—either you're funny, or
you're cancelled. You're good-looking, or you're best-supporting. I
mean, you can tell. But Shakespeare—it's just real hard to tell who's
good, without nudity.

DEIRDRE. Gary—have you ever been to the theater?

GARY. Yeah. Not lately. Can I be frank? I don't get it. The theater. It
doesn't make sense. It's like, progress, right? Take it step by step.
Back in Neanderthal times, entertainment was like, two rocks. Boom
boom. Then, in the Middle Ages, they had theater. Then came radio.
Then silent movies. Then sound. Then TV. That's like, art perfected.
When you watch TV, you can eat. You can talk. You don't really have
to pay attention, not if you've seen TV before. Nice half-hour chunks.
Or even better, commercials. Thirty seconds. Hot girl, hot guy, the
beer, it's all there. It's distilled. I mean, when I go to the theater, I
sit there, and most of the time I'm thinking—which one is my arm-
rest? (*The door to the roof swings open. Andrew appears, dressed as Hamlet,
in a black costume similar to, although not identical, to Barrymore's. Andrew's
Hamlet might have modern touches, but it must include tights and a codpiece,
as well as a sword and a dagger. Andrew has been drinking, although he is by
no means drunk. His vocal and physical style now resemble Barrymore's; he has
acquired a grandeur, and is somewhat larger than life. He carriers a bottle of
champagne.*)

ANDREW. OUT!

DEIRDRE. Andrew!

GARY. Big guy!

ANDREW. Out! Tonight I shall play Hamlet. I must be alone.

DEIRDRE. Andrew, honey, can't we take you to the theater?

ANDREW. Nay! I have dressed, I have drunk, I seek only solitude. (*Andrew stands on the landing halfway up the stairs. Gary climbs the stairs to meet him.*)

GARY. I hear you. And Andy, it's working like a charm. I told the network, Andy's not sure. He's thinking, he's doing *Hamlet*—they love it. They know it's a trick. So I'm going for half-ownership of the show— or you'll do Lear.

ANDREW. AWAY!

GARY. (*Imitating Andrew, delighted.*) AWAY! I love this guy! Hey, what does opening night mean? A party?

DEIRDRE. Of course.

GARY. Photographers?

FELICIA. Really?

GARY. Critics?

DEIRDRE. Andrew, don't listen! They'll love you, and it's not important!

GARY. Not in movies or TV. That's the great thing—you can really blow, and no one can stop you. But tonight—watch out, right? They're out there! (*Gary starts moving back down the stairs. As he turns his back on Andrew, Andrew pulls out his dagger and points it at Gary's back; Gary does not see this, and Andrew returns his dagger to its sheath. Reaching C.*) You know, when I heard you were goin' through with this, I went, hey, maybe Andy's right. Maybe I should just chuck everything, leave LA, just produce, direct and write Shakespeare. But I woke up. Your turn, Andy boy. I gotta car downstairs—anybody?

FELICIA. A car? A limo?

GARY. You do real estate, right? You gotta come to Beverly Hills.

FELICIA. I know, I dream about it. Beverly Hills—that's my *Hamlet*.

ANDREW. NOW!

GARY. We're going, we're going!

FELICIA. We'll see you after. (*She takes a last look at Andrew; she is enraptured.*) Look at you! You are so adorable! Just like Peter Pan, but for evening!

ANDREW. Farewell! (*Gary and Felicia exit, out the front door.*)

DEIRDRE. Are you sure you don't want me to stay? I'll go with you, to the theater.

ANDREW. Be gone, wench. (*Andrew comes down the stairs. As he does so, Deirdre gets her first good look at his codpiece. She blushes, and looks away, then steals a second glance. Andrew unsheathes his sword, and practices a few feints. Deirdre picks up a pair of oversized, extremely modern high-topped sneakers, Reeboks, which she has hidden behind the staircase. She carries the sneakers to the throne, and sits. During her next speech, she will remove her period slippers, and put on the enormous sneakers.*)

DEIRDRE. I know you're going to be—the best. And I'm so proud of you. And I'm so glad we're in the play together, even if I am just one of Ophelia's ladies-in-waiting. And even if I don't have any lines. The director took me aside yesterday, at the dress rehearsal. He said I was very good, but that when they announce that Ophelia is dead, I shouldn't scream. Or stagger. Or grab your sword and try to stab myself. He said the play wasn't called "The Tragedy of Ophelia's Best Friend." But I understand. (*Deirdre now has her sneakers on. Daintily holding her skirt, she walks toward the front door, past Andrew.*)

ANDREW. My lady.

DEIRDRE. My Lord. (*Andrew takes Deirdre's hand, and twirls her into a passionate embrace, with Deirdre bent backward. He then twirls her out of the embrace, and her sleeves whirl around her. Deirdre steadies herself, almost swooning. She glances at Andrew, and moans voluptuously. Deirdre goes to the front door. With her back to Andrew, she gathers her long, unwieldy skirts into a huge ball in her lap. She turns, carrying her bundle. She gives Andrew one last torrid look, and exits. Barrymore appears at the door to the roof. He carries a bottle of champagne, and salutes Andrew. They are now grand, lusty, Elizabethan comrades, bold and dashing.*)

ANDREW. Blythe!

BARRYMORE. Rallenberg!

ANDREW. Tonight—*Hamlet!*

BARRYMORE. The Dane!

ANDREW. The Bard!

BARRYMORE. The bottle!

ANDREW. The best! (*Barrymore has now descended the stairs, and the men toast each other ceremoniously.*)

BARRYMORE. And Deirdre!

ANDREW. Deirdre?

BARRYMORE. For certain. She shall witness your portrayal. She imagines herself Ophelia. She shall wed you, or drown.

ANDREW. We have accomplished much!

BARRYMORE. Vocal assurance.

ANDREW. (*Gesturing with his sword.*) Physical technique.

BARRYMORE. Even, dare I say it, an appreciation of the text.

ANDREW. Indeed. Our achievement is twofold—not only do I revere the play, but for the first time, I have finished it.

BARRYMORE. Welcome Rallenberg—to the royal order of Hamlets. (*The two men stride forward, their arms around each other's shoulders.*)

ANDREW. The elite!

BARRYMORE. The august!

ANDREW. Princes and players.

BARRYMORE. We do not step . . .

ANDREW. We stride.

BARRYMORE. We do not speak . . .

ANDREW. We beseech . . .

BARRYMORE. We whisper . . .

ANDREW. We roar!

BARRYMORE. Brother Hamlet!

ANDREW. (*With a deep bow.*) Player King.

BARRYMORE. The moment is nigh. I name my rightful heir. Kneel, Rally! (*During Andrew's investiture, and perhaps during the preceding scene, glorious, Pomp-and-Circumstance style music might be used as underscoring, emphasizing the evening's ritual aspects. Andrew kneels before Barrymore. Barrymore uses his champagne bottle as a sword, tapping Andrew on each shoulder.*) I hereby dub thee Prince Hamlet, of all lower Manhattan. You join an illustrious line. You shall henceforth be known as the greatest American Hamlet.

ANDREW. Of all time?

BARRYMORE. Of your generation. (*Andrew stands, a bit unsteadily. The reality of his situation is beginning to catch up with him.*)

ANDREW. Of my generation?

BARRYMORE. And why not?

ANDREW. It's just, I keep thinking . . . tonight.

BARRYMORE. Of course—the performance. Minutes from now.

ANDREW. No, no, I'm fine, I'm fine. Hamlet. Whoa. Hamlet.

BARRYMORE. Glory!

ANDREW. Glory . . .

BARRYMORE. Shakespeare!

ANDREW. Shakespeare . . .

BARRYMORE. Blind, unspeakable terror!

ANDREW. That's it!

BARRYMORE. Of course you're shaking. And for the noblest of reasons. The role. The moment. The test.

ANDREW. Come with me. Be there.

BARRYMORE. I cannot. You know that.

ANDREW. Then help me. There must be some . . . ancient secret of the Hamlets. A trick, something you've been saving.

BARRYMORE. Of course. (*Barrymore looks around, checking to see that no one is listening. He seats Andrew, perhaps on a pile of cushions on the floor. Barrymore sits beside him, on the throne, as if about to impart confidential in-*

formation.) Speak the speech, I pray you, as I pronounced it to you, trippingly on the tongue. But if you mouth it, as many of our players do, I had as lief the town crier spoke my lines. Nor do not saw the air too much with your hand, thus, but use all gently; for in the very torrent, tempest, and, as I may say, whirlwind of your passion, you must acquire and beget a temperance that may give it smoothness. Be not too tame neither, but let your own discretion be your tutor. Suit the action to the word, the word to the action, with this special observance, that you o'erstep not the modesty of nature. For anything so o'erdone is from the purpose of playing, whose end, both at the first and now, was and is to hold as 'twere the mirror up to nature, to show virtue her own feature, scorn her own image, and the very age and body of the time his form and pressure. Now this overdone or come tardy off, though it makes the unskillful laugh, cannot but make the judicious grieve. Go make you ready. (*Barrymore has delivered the speech magnificently. Andrew rises, quite shaken.*)

ANDREW. I don't think so.

BARRYMORE. Go make you ready. It's all there. In the text. At your service.

ANDREW. I can't do that. What you just did. I'm . . . who do I think I am?

BARRYMORE. Andrew—your fear has a history. My opening night— good Lord.

ANDREW. But—you were Barrymore.

BARRYMORE. Barrymore? I was a light comedian, attempting Olympus. There was a family reputation knotted about my neck. Before the curtain rose I sat on the stage in darkness, paralyzed with fear.

ANDREW. But you weren't . . . some TV clown. You were still doing theater.

BARRYMORE. Don't overestimate the form. Would you like the titles of my boulevard triumphs? *The Fortune Hunter. Claire de Lune. Princess Zim Zim.*

ANDREW. But—what if Gary's right? What if the critics hate me?

BARRYMORE. (*Scornfully.*) Oh, newspapers.

ANDREW. What if *I* hate me?

BARRYMORE. You have prepared for this evening.

ANDREW. But, when you played Hamlet, you prepared for six months. In the country. Just learning the role.

BARRYMORE. You have been diligent.

ANDREW. Sure, but—six weeks? And tonight—people are gonna be there. Not just critics—my friends. My family. People who saw me in my second grade school play. And who might expect an improvement. And Deirdre.

BARRYMORE. She'll adore you.

ANDREW. It's not automatic. Deirdre wants me to be . . . a hero. An immortal. What if that doesn't happen, what if I disappoint her?

BARRYMORE. Impossible!

ANDREW. Up till now I've been plugging away, trying to be Hamlet, trying to be like you, but now . . .

BARRYMORE. Andrew—this is not your first opening night. Your panic, your doubt—this is all to be expected.

ANDREW. This isn't just stage fright. This is . . . something else.

BARRYMORE. What?

ANDREW. Common sense! I had this idea, that I could come back to New York, that I could prove some ridiculous point, to myself, to everybody. Instant actor! Just add Shakespeare! But I don't think it works that way!

BARRYMORE. And why not?

ANDREW. Because I'm going to be on that stage with real actors, with people who know what they're doing! Jesus, why did I listen to you? I could be in LA right now! Making a fortune! In pants!

BARRYMORE. Is that what you'd like? Is that what I've taught you?

ANDREW. That's what I know!

BARRYMORE. Enough! You unbearable brat! Your snivelling is a disgrace! The words of Shakespeare—be worthy! The role of Hamlet— be grateful!

ANDREW. Oh, come off it!

BARRYMORE. What?

ANDREW. Listen to yourself!

BARRYMORE. Excuse me?

ANDREW. After you played Hamlet, you left the theater! And you never came back!

BARRYMORE. Unimportant! (*Andrew begins to stalk Barrymore, as their fight grows increasingly brutal.*)

ANDREW. I read about it—after 101 performances, you went right to Hollywood!

BARRYMORE. For a time!

ANDREW. For the rest of your life!

BARRYMORE. That is my affair!

ANDREW. You lived in a mansion, in Beverly Hills. With a yacht, and a screening room, and—how many wives?

BARRYMORE. Quite a few!

ANDREW. You made movie after movie . . .

BARRYMORE. Some of them classics!

ANDREW. Most of them garbage!

BARRYMORE. Yes! And after awhile I even had trouble with those! (A beat.) There was a day, on a set, when the cameras rolled, and . . . I couldn't remember a line. Nothing. Take after take. Not a word, not a speech, just haze and then—terror. And I wasn't drunk, no, stone sober. And everyone was more than kind, and the words were scribbled on shirt-sleeves, and cardboards held just out of camera range. But I knew—I knew instantly—I could never go back on the stage.

ANDREW. (*Maliciously.*) John Barrymore, the great classical actor! The example to us all!

BARRYMORE. The hopeless, unemployable lush! The public embarrassment! The off-color joke! (*With vicious intensity.*) Yes, I ran to Hollywood, you're quite right—and you can't imagine the life I led! I was a movie star, do you know what that means? My face five stories high, and six zeroes wide! (*A pause.*) But before all that, in my prime—I faced the dragon. I accepted a role so insanely complex, so fantastic and impossible, that any attempt is only that—an attempt! And I stood in the light, before a crowd fully prepared to dismiss, to deride, and to depart. And I shook them, I wooed them, and I said, yes, you will stay, and yes, you will remember! And for one moment in my life, I used all that I knew, every shred of talent, every ounce of gall! I was John Barrymore! And for those sacred evenings, there was no shame. I played Hamlet! Have you? (*By the end of this speech Barrymore is utterly drained; he staggers to a chair. His battle with Andrew has stunned both of them, and neither can speak. After a pause, the doorbell buzzes. Andrew goes to the intercom.*)

ANDREW. (*Into the receiver.*) Yes? Okay, okay, I'm coming. (*A Moment passes between Andrew and Barrymore. Then Andrew opens the front door. Lillian steps into the room. She looks quite beautiful, in a silvery evening gown. She is very angry.*)

LILLIAN. Rally! The car is waiting! Go! (*Andrew looks to Barrymore for some final word. None is forthcoming.*) Go! (*Andrew runs out the door. Lillian turns, and sees Barrymore. To Barrymore.*) You. You look terrible.

BARRYMORE. (*Surprised that Lillian can see him.*) What? (*Andrew sticks his head back in.*)

ANDREW. Lillian—are you coming?

LILLIAN. I will catch up—in a cab.

ANDREW. Lillian—I have to do this, don't I?

LILLIAN. No. You can stay here, and cancel the production. I'd be so proud. Go! (*Andrew leaves. Lillian faces Barrymore.*) Yes, I can see you, you swine.

BARRYMORE. How?

LILLIAN. I am very old. I see everything. And it so happens I know you.

BARRYMORE. You do?

LILLIAN. Ha! I knew you would not remember.

BARRYMORE. (*As he stares at her.*) Could it be?

LILLIAN. (*Challenging.*) What?

BARRYMORE. No. Yes. Is it . . . you?

LILLIAN. I was very young.

BARRYMORE. A young wife. Of . . . a conductor.

LILLIAN. A violinist.

BARRYMORE. A violinist. Yes. With a mistress.

LILLIAN. Bravo.

BARRYMORE. (*Circling her.*) I was in town promoting a film. There was a cocktail party. Your husband was to meet you. He did not.

LILLIAN. Do not be smug. You were married as well. To an actress.

BARRYMORE. To an actress? Is that legal? I found you sobbing, in a coatroom.

LILLIAN. I did not sob!

BARRYMORE. Out of anger. We came here.

LILLIAN. Out of madness. Temporary insanity.

BARRYMORE. We had a fire. (*Barrymore makes a sweeping gesture, and a fire springs up in the fireplace.*)

LILLIAN. And candlelight. (*Barrymore makes another gesture, and all the candles, located throughout the room, suddenly glow. The stage lights dim, creating an impossibly romantic mood. A moon might appear at the window.*)

BARRYMORE. We stole champagne, from the party.

LILLIAN. And bought chocolate bars, from the five and dime.

BARRYMORE. We broke every commandment. We made love.

LILLIAN. And gained weight.

BARRYMORE. (*Delighted.*) You were impossible.

LILLIAN. You were . . . Barrymore. (*The mood has become very intimate; Barrymore and Lillian are almost in an embrace. Barrymore breaks away.*) What?

BARRYMORE. No!

LILLIAN. What is the matter?

BARRYMORE. You are far too kind. I am undeserving. I have failed utterly. I return for a single purpose, and now . . .

LILLIAN. What? What is your purpose?

BARRYMORE. That Andrew should play Hamlet.

LILLIAN. So? It is done.

BARRYMORE. But there's more, so much more. I wanted Andrew . . . to learn.

LILLIAN. To learn what?

BARRYMORE. From all that he accuses me of! From my sorry excuse for a life! I was offered—the planet. Every conceivable opportunity. Andrew is my last vain hope. My cosmic lunge at redemption.

LILLIAN. Tell me, Barrymore—when did it happen?

BARRYMORE. What?

LILLIAN. When did you turn—scoutmaster?

BARRYMORE. Excuse me?

LILLIAN. Rally is a big boy. You have pushed him, as have I. He needed that. But—tonight must be his. And his alone.

BARRYMORE. So why do you stay? What do you want?

LILLIAN. I am like anyone else. I have come to see Barrymore.

BARRYMORE. A sideshow.

LILLIAN. A three-ring circus. A true oddity. A movie star, and a Danish prince. A womanizer, but never a beast. A drunkard, but—at least until recently—never a bore. Tonight I had hoped for—one last encounter. An encore. But it was long ago. Perhaps I remember incorrectly. I will go. (*She starts to leave.*)

BARRYMORE. Lillian?

LILLIAN. (*Pausing.*) Yes?

BARRYMORE. Will he be all right? Andrew?

LILLIAN. Who can say?

BARRYMORE. Have I helped him? In any way?

LILLIAN. Ask him. When he returns. Any more questions?

BARRYMORE. Just one. Your husband—is he well?

LILLIAN. I hope not. We are divorced. You were named in the lawsuit.

BARRYMORE. (*Pleased.*) Divorced . . . (*After a beat.*) One last encounter? (*Barrymore gestures. Music—a lush, sweepingly romantic melody begins. Barrymore holds out his arms. Lillian resists.*)

LILLIAN. I am old.

BARRYMORE. I am dead.

LILLIAN. I no longer dance.

BARRYMORE. Make an exception.

LILLIAN. Fool.

BARRYMORE. Fraulein.

LILLIAN. My Hamlet. (*Lillian goes to Barrymore. They dance. They pause.*) Tell me—where one goes, where you have come from—I am assuming it is heaven?

BARRYMORE. Sad to say.

LILLIAN. Is there . . . smoking?

BARRYMORE. Of course. It's heaven.

LILLIAN. Should I . . . be afraid?

BARRYMORE. Of death? Never. Only of life.

LILLIAN. Actors.

BARRYMORE. (*Offended.*) What?

LILLIAN. I love them. (*They continue to dance. They pause.*)

BARRYMORE. You know, Lillian, there is another question that many ask. A question regarding certain activities, and their practice in the next world.

LILLIAN. You mean, activities of a physical nature.

BARRYMORE. Aren't you curious?

LILLIAN. Surprise me. (*Barrymore laughs. They begin to dance again, as the lights dim, and the curtain falls.*)

Scene 2

Place: The same.

Time: 7 AM, the next morning.

Barrymore is slumped on the chaise, his shirt open and askew. He is surrounded by junk food wrappers and open bags of chips. A small portable TV is balanced on the ottoman. The romantic song from Barrymore's dance with Lillian now comes from the TV.

The music is interrupted by the Trailburst Nuggets TV commercial. Barrymore watches the commercial, transfixed and appalled.

CHIPMUNK. (*On TV.*) Please Andy—can I have a Trailburst Nugget?

ANDREW'S VOICE. (*On TV.*) I'm sorry—Nuggets are for people, not chipmunks. (*The chipmunk cries, loudly.*) Oh, all right, but remember— Trailburst Nuggets are a delicious breakfast treat. And an anytime snack. (*The Trailburst Nuggets jingle plays. Andrew has entered the apartment, quietly. He sings along with himself on the commercial. Andrew is still dressed as Hamlet, but he also wears sunglasses, a denim Levi's jacket and sneakers. Once Barrymore realizes Andrew is in the room, he shuts off the TV and leaps to his feet.*)

BARRYMORE. (*Eagerly.*) Yes?

ANDREW. (*After a pause.*) Yeah?

BARRYMORE. The morning after! So?

ANDREW. So?

BARRYMORE. Your performance! Tell me! (*Andrew exits through the archway, further frustrating Barrymore.*) What, am I to remain despised? An ogre beyond question? Denied the result of my labor, forbade so much as a word, some meager report? (*Andrew re-enters from the archway, swigging from a carton of orange juice. He has removed his sunglasses.*)

ANDREW. So . . . you want to know? What happened? Last night?

BARRYMORE. If you wish to impart the information. If you have not grown too grand, too swollen with triumph.

ANDREW. Who writes you?

BARRYMORE. Tell me! I've earned it!

ANDREW. (*After a pause.*) First—you tell me. Your deal, up there. Once I've played Hamlet, you can go back, right?

BARRYMORE. Correct.

ANDREW. And we'll never have to see each other again, right?

BARRYMORE. Agreed.

ANDREW. So nothing depends on . . . the quality of the performance.

BARRYMORE. I don't believe so. Why?

ANDREW. Because . . . it did not go very well. In fact—I was awful.

BARRYMORE. (*Refusing to believe him.*) No.

ANDREW. Sorry. I mean, I got through it, I remembered my lines. But— that's about all.

BARRYMORE. Impossible. This is all modesty. I'm sure you were marvelous.

ANDREW. I wasn't. Take my word. Or ask around. It wasn't a fiasco, but maybe that would have been better. Or at least more memorable. Like the *Hindenburg.* Or a power blackout. Yeah, years from now, people could ask, where were you on the night Andy Rally played Hamlet? Nine months later, hundreds of unexpected babies would be born. Laughing hysterically.

BARRYMORE. Cheap vengeance, this is cheap vengeance against me. I'm sure you were . . . more than acceptable. Far more.

ANDREW. No. (*A beat.*) I've been walking all night.

BARRYMORE. Where?

ANDREW. Every place. The park. Fifth Avenue. All the way down to the Battery.

BARRYMORE. All night? Were you accosted?

ANDREW. Once. Two guys, with a knife. I just said, guys, look at me. What do you want? A farthing? A doubloon? Then they recognized me—from TV. The wrong show. I kept walking. (*The doorbell buzzes. Andrew goes to answer it.*) It's 7 AM. What is going on around here? (*Into the receiver.*) Hello? Sure. Come on up. (*To Barrymore.*) It's Gary.

BARRYMORE. Gary? That cloud of Malibu ozone, that cultural cavity? *Night School?* Is that what you're doing?

ANDREW. I guess we'll find out.

BARRYMORE. Well done, Andrew! (*He toasts Andrew, with a bottle of champagne from the mantle.*) Here's to all the money you can make, and all the pride you can swallow! Here's to challenge, and risk, and (*He gestures to himself.*) the worst possible role models! Why don't you join me, Andrew, this is very good champagne! After all, you can afford it! Lucky dog! (*Andrew goes to the door. Gary enters, dressed in his usual top-of-the-line casual wear. He carriers a sheaf of newspapers.*)

GARY. (*To Andrew.*) Hey! Hamlet! (*To Barrymore.*) Big guy! Where were you last night? You missed it! (*A beat.*) Look what I got! The papers! Or did you already see 'em?

ANDREW. No.

GARY. Well, let's have a look. (*Unfolding a newspaper.*) Aren't you curious?

BARRYMORE. There is something about a person who brings the papers, with glee. Shouldn't you be hooded? (*Barrymore exits, through the archway.*)

GARY. (Scanning the review.) Uh-oh . . .

ANDREW. Don't. Let me. (*Improvising.*) "A not uninteresting attempt. Far to go. If Mister Rally is to seriously consider a career on the boards, blah, blah, blah, fine supporting cast, dee dee dee, remember, it's free."

GARY. (*Impressed.*) Not bad. You left out "TV lightweight," but that's not so terrible, huh? Coulda been worse. Personally, I thought you were terrific. Like I could tell.

ANDREW. Gary . . .

GARY. I warned you, I said Andy, it's not for you, but hey—you learned, right? In front of all those people. Shuffling all those feet.

ANDREW. I was there.

GARY. I know. I know. Anyway, it's all over—back to reality. I wanted to see you, before I took off, so I can call the network. Are we on? All systems go? Start pre-production? (*Before Andrew can speak.*) Wait. I know you're gonna say yes, it's all set, but let me . . . polish the party. Tickle the treat.

ANDREW. Gary, cut it. What's the offer?

GARY. The money. It was a feeding frenzy. The first season, twenty-four episodes, guaranteed—three million. That's right.

ANDREW. Three million dollars? For one season?

GARY. Even if it's a dud, one year and out—it's enough, to breathe, to lay back. A house. Houses. Cars. No—for your folks. For all they've done. Or, if you hate 'em, rub 'em out—the money's there. And if the show hits, okay, you're tied up for a few years, but—triple it. Quadruple. Keep going. Picture it. One day, you wake up, and whatever happens—you're rich. Something goes wrong, something breaks, it's not so bad, it's never gonna be so bad. Why? You're rich!! It's like they say, the rich are different from you and me—(*Searching for a superlative.*) they're RICH!!! (*Barrymore re-enters, and sits on the chaise, with a drink.*) On the other hand, and I'm just blowin' smoke here, pretend like you're outta your mind, pretend you say no. Pretend . . . you stick around here. The theater. El footlights. And in a few years . . . (*He gestures to Barrymore.*) Here you are. No offense, but—another out-of-work actor. Not so young, not so network. Maybe you wait tables. (*To*

Barrymore.) Sorry—maitre'd. Pretty soon you move, 'cause you can't afford this place. But hey, once in a while—you get work. Off-off-*no-where.* It's Chekov. It's a basement. It's July. And there's folding chairs. I'm not trying to scare you, I'm just doing my job, as a bud.

ANDREW. Three *million* dollars?

GARY. Plus all expenses and personal staff. Folding chairs, Andy! And you fold 'em up, after every show. AA needs the hall. Andy-boy? Are we on?

ANDREW. Am I in? A network commitment . . .

GARY. Full season . . .

ANDREW. Three million dollars . . .

GARY. No tights.

ANDREW. (*After a pause.*) No.

GARY. No?

BARRYMORE. (*Shocked.*) No?

ANDREW. No.

GARY. No? What, no, you still don't like the figures, no, you're not happy with the time slot?

ANDREW. No. Just no.

GARY. Wait. You don't get it. In LA, there is no "no." You know, like "yes" means sure, unless I get a better offer. And "no" means "yes," with more money.

ANDREW. No. This is a New York "no." A real no. A surgical no. A final, terminal no.

GARY. Oh. A maybe.

ANDREW. No. Gary, it's a no like in, Gary, would you be interested in doing a documentary on acid rain for PBS?

GARY. (*To Barrymore.*) Talk to him. Talk sense.

BARRYMORE. (*Increasingly gleeful.*) No.

ANDREW. No!

GARY. Andy, you're sayin' this now, but what about tomorrow? The next day? When the bills start comin' in. When you're flyin' coach!

ANDREW. I'm sorry.

GARY. (*Falling to his knees.*) Andy—think about me. Think about the money *I* could make on this. Don't be selfish!

BARRYMORE. (*Delighted.*) Have pity, Andrew—he's begging.

GARY. (*To Barrymore.*) You! This is all your fault! You made him do that *Hamlet* crap!

BARRYMORE. (*Innocently.*) Me? I didn't even see the play. I was home, watching television. I'm an American.

GARY. (*Utterly bewildered.*) Jesus, what happened here? Andy, what am I going to tell the network?

ANDREW. Tell 'em—who needs Andy Rally? Dime a dozen.

GARY. (*Delighted.*) Yeah! That's good. That's great! Who can I get?

ANDREW. Gary!

BARRYMORE. (*To Gary.*) Three million dollars? (*Considering it.*) When would you need me? (*Felicia, dressed for travel in her usual gaudy fashion, pokes her head in from the front door.*)

FELICIA. Gar?

GARY. Babe—in the car.

FELICIA. We're gonna miss the plane.

ANDREW. Felicia?

FELICIA. Hi, hon.

GARY. Andy, I gotta make some calls. Damage control.

ANDREW. In the kitchen. (*Gary exits, through the archway. Felicia gives Andrew a big hug.*)

FELICIA. Hon, what can I say? Last night—were you terrific or what? I mean, the part I saw.

ANDREW. The part you saw?

FELICIA. Well, I caught the first act, where you were so confused. But at intermission I got thirsty, and Gary has a bar in the limo, and—Andy, I'm sorry. One thing led to another!

ANDREW. Wait—the two of you?

BARRYMORE. (*Tickled.*) Perfection!

FELICIA. (*Thrilled.*) Yeah! And all thanks to you—and Shakespeare!

ANDREW. So you only saw one act—both of you?

FELICIA. Honey, I'm sorry. So how did it end? You're king now, right?

ANDREW. No—Felicia, are you going away with Gary?

FELICIA. Yeah, to LA. Long weekend. (*Admiring the apartment.*) This is a great place. I told you. I just wish we could've contacted Barrymore. But I've been thinking—you know, maybe ghosts don't really exist. Even Ma, maybe it's all in my mind. No afterlife, no other side—nothing. (*During this speech, Barrymore has crept up behind Felicia. His arms encircle her waist, from behind. He now kisses her neck passionately. She is completely oblivious.*) Who knows? (*Gary re-enters, from the archway.*)

GARY. We gotta split. But Andy—this isn't over. I'm comin' back for you. And if I have to tie you up, drug you, and slam you into a cage—you're makin' money.

ANDREW. Aren't you flying somewhere?

FELICIA. We'll call you!

GARY. (*Making a phone gesture.*) From the plane, buddy. (*At the door.*) Andy, this theater thing—we'll beat it, together. (*Gary and Felicia exit. The door to the roof swings open. Deirdre appears, in a nightgown. Her hair is wild, and tangled with flowers. Her eyes are half-shut, and she rubs her upper arms. She moans; she is in a pleasure stupor. She leans against the door frame, rubbing up against it, like an extremely satisfied cat.*)

ANDREW. Deirdre?

DEIRDRE. Mmmm . . .

ANDREW. Deirdre?

DEIRDRE. MMMMM . . .

ANDREW. Deirdre, are you okay?

DEIRDRE. Mmmmmhuh . . .

ANDREW. Deirdre, I'm sorry I took off last night, after the show. I hope you went to the party. Did you . . . have a good time?

DEIRDRE. *MMM* . . .

ANDREW. Deirdre, what is going on? (*Deirdre, who has been slinking her way down the stairs, stroking the bannister, now leaps into Andrew's arms. She looks deep into his eyes and gives him a volcanic, passionate kiss.)*

DEIRDRE. Hi.

ANDREW. Hi.

DEIRDRE. Mmmm . . .

ANDREW. Stop that.

DEIRDRE. Stop what?

ANDREW. Stop . . . moaning. Deirdre, did you go to the party?

DEIRDRE. Party?

ANDREW. The party. After the play. We were in *Hamlet* last night, re-member?

BARRYMORE. *(Starting up the stairs.)* Perhaps I should leave you two alone.

ANDREW. No! Stay.

DEIRDRE. Of course I'll stay. Oh, Andrew. Last night, you were so won-derful.

ANDREW. No, I wasn't. Deirdre, I'm not . . . what you want. You're waiting for someone legendary, for a total hero, for Lancelot, or Mark Antony. And you should. I wish I'd been good, I wish I'd been—everything. For you. And I'm sorry.

DEIRDRE. *(With real wonder.)* Andrew—I watched you on stage last night, and I thought—he has worked so hard. He's put his heart and soul into this, and at least partly for me. And he's . . . so *bad*. And I thought I'd be demolished, but—something happened. I mean, people were coughing, and a plane, it just *flew* overhead, and there were all those mosquitoes.

ANDREW. Right in my mouth.

DEIRDRE. And you just kept on going! And I thought—what makes a hero? It's just someone who tries to do what's right, despite impos-sible odds. Like you playing Hamlet! You're the bravest, noblest man I've ever met!

ANDREW. *(Eagerly.)* Really?

DEIRDRE. Yes! But then I thought about how I'd put you off, and how I was just a lady-in-waiting, and I thought . . . I'm not worthy.

ANDREW. Deirdre . . .

DEIRDRE. So you know what I decided to do?

ANDREW. Something sensible?

DEIRDRE. (*Really re-living it.*) Exactly! I decided to drown myself! Like Ophelia, in Central Park Lake! Isn't that perfect? (*She runs to the chaise and stands on it.*) So I went behind the theater, and I stood on a rock and braided wildflowers into my hair! And I sang Ophelia's bawdy song . . . (*Singing.*)

>Hey nonny nonny
>
>Hey nonny no . . . no . . .

(*Desolate.*) But I couldn't jump in. I lost my nerve!

ANDREW. I'm glad.

DEIRDRE. And I was so upset that I came back here and ran up to the roof! (*She tears across the stage and runs up the stairs to the landing. Barrymore is waiting; he stands right behind her. She speaks with great yearning.*) And I stood at the edge, and I gazed up at the moon! And I said, oh Mister Moon, you're so *big*, and *round*, and *yellow* . . .

ANDREW. Deirdre . . .

DEIRDRE. (*Very frustrated.*) I know. Please. I thought Deirdre, everyone's right. Get some help. And that's when I felt it.

ANDREW. Felt what?

DEIRDRE. This breeze, on the back of my neck. (*Barrymore blows gently on Deirdre's neck.*) Except it wasn't just a breeze, it was more like . . . a hand. (*Barrymore lightly strokes Deirdre's neck.*)

ANDREW. A hand?

DEIRDRE. A caress.

ANDREW. No. No. (*Barrymore makes a rather grand cross, moving from the staircase to the chaise, on which he stretches full out. He passes directly in front of Andrew. He is smiling, like a cross between the Mona Lisa and the Cheshire Cat.*)

DEIRDRE. Yes! And that's all I can remember, except I woke up this morning in the room up there, and there was a rose on my pillow.

BARRYMORE. A red rose.

ANDREW. (To Deirdre.) A red rose?

DEIRDRE. For passion. And my copy of Romeo and Juliet was lying open, right to one of Juliet's speeches:

> My bounty is as boundless as the sea,
> My love as deep; the more I give to thee
> The more I have, for both are infinite.

And all I could think about was you. Andrew—I'm *worthy*. (*Deirdre glides up the door to the roof. She turns to Andrew. As a sensual command.*) Get thee . . . right now! (*Deirdre might also toss Andrew a rose at this point. She exits to the roof, beckoning for Andrew to follow. Andrew turns to Barrymore, absolutely furious.*)

ANDREW. (To Barrymore.) I wish I could kill you! You . . . you . . .

BARRYMORE. Me? She was suicidal! She felt unworthy of you!

ANDREW. What *did you do*?

BARRYMORE. Andrew—I'm a ghost! A spirit!

ANDREW. A Barrymore!

BARRYMORE. How dare you!

ANDREW. Swear it! Nothing happened, between you and Deirdre!

BARRYMORE. Please! You wouldn't understand! It was . . . a moment of Shakespeare. A purely poetic communion, between two lyric souls, as assisted by moonlight. (*A beat.*) A midsummer night's dream.

ANDREW. (*After a beat, warily.*) Much ado about nothing?

BARRYMORE. (*Grandly, comforting him.*) As you like it.

ANDREW. So—all's well that ends well.

BARRYMORE. Indeed. Yet—I am utterly perplexed. Three million dollars. And your precious LA. Why not go?

ANDREW. Why not? Do you know what stopped me? Of all things? *Hamlet*.

BARRYMORE. But . . . you were ghastly. You said so. Deirdre agreed.
The papers—everyone in New York.

ANDREW. I heard. And that's part of it. Last night, right from the
start, I knew I was bombing. I sounded big and phony, real thee and
thou, and then I started rushing it, hi, what's new in Denmark? I
just could not connect. I couldn't get ahold of it. And while I'm . . .
babbling, I look out, and there's this guy in the second row, a kid,
like sixteen, obviously dragged there. And he's yawning and he's
jiggling his legs and reading his program, and I just wanted to say,
hey kid, I'm with you, I can't stand this either! But I couldn't do
that, so I just keep feeling worse and worse, just drowning. And I
thought, okay, all my questions are answered—I'm not Hamlet, I'm
no actor, what am I doing here? And then I get to the soliloquy, the
big job, I'm right in the headlights, and I just thought, oh Christ,
the hell with it, just do it!

To be or not to be, that is the question;
Whether 'tis nobler in the mind to suffer
The slings and arrows of outrageous fortune,
Or to take arms against a sea of troubles and by opposing, end
them.

And I kept going, I finished the speech, and I look out, and there's
the kid—and he's listening. The whole audience—complete silence,
total focus. And I was Hamlet. And it lasted about ten more seconds,
and then I was back in Hell. And I stayed there. But for that one little
bit, for that one speech—I got it. I had it. *Hamlet.* And only eight thousand lines left to go. (*The preceding monologue must grow extremely passionate; Andrew must be transported back to the previous evening onstage in the
park. A lighting change and musical cues are possibilities. All of Andrew's frus-
trations, with his career and his life, must impact on the speech; when he reaches
"To be or not to be" he should be D.C., using the audience in the theater as the
audience in the park. Andrew's delivery of the soliloquy fragment should show
real talent, and great emotional force. The play arcs to this Moment, during*

which Andrew reveals the result of Barrymore's teachings; the speech should be as moving and as theatrically effective as possible.)

BARRYMORE. There it is! The glory of Shakespeare. *Hamlet* has changed you. Altered your course.

ANDREW. *(Sincerely.)* Yes. And I love this apartment! Because—it's like a stage set. It's the theater. And because, once upon a time—you lived here.

BARRYMORE. Brother Hamlet.

ANDREW. Player King. *(They embrace.)* Stay. Teach me.

BARRYMORE. You have already learned all that is important. You've tasted glory—now, reach skyward. Surprise everyone. *(Very solemn.)* And someday, and Andrew, this I promise you—someday you will perform . . . indoors. I must go. You have a performance this evening. And . . . *(He gestures to the roof.)* a matinee.

ANDREW. Get out of here.

BARRYMORE. I'm on my way. But I have a parting request. I was unable to witness your debut, but I must see your bow.

ANDREW. My bow? *(Barrymore nods. Andrew, puzzled, demonstrates his bow, which is quite ordinary, a simple bend from the waist.)*

BARRYMORE. As I suspected.

ANDREW. What?

BARRYMORE. It was . . . perfunctory. A bow should be theater incarnate. *(Andrew gestures—"So show me." Barrymore pretends to resist, then gives in.)* Oh . . . very well. Begin in a daze, still lost in the drama. *(Barrymore turns away from the audience; he might move U., and lean against the bannister of the staircase, as if utterly exhausted. He then turns toward the audience, looking dazed and spent, not sure where he is, destroyed by his own genius. Peering out.)* Good Lord—is that . . . an audience? *(Barrymore hears an ovation; he spots the audience, and looks shocked and confused. Pointing a trembling finger at himself.)* Me? *(He moves haltingly toward the footlights, as if the audience were pulling him helplessly forward.)* Into the light . . . *(Barrymore stands at C., still stunned by the applause. He stretches out his* *arms to the orchestra section, acknowledging the love.*) All my children . . . (*Barrymore crisply raises his arms to the balcony.*) And the poor! (*He gestures to either side, acknowledging the rest of the cast.*) The company . . . (*He flips his hands up, dismissing the cast, and returns to self-acknowledgement.*) Don't spoil them. The finale. Your humble servant. (*A deep bow from the waist, as florid as possible. Still bent over, he lifts his head, as the ovation continues.*) Oh, stop. (*He stands erect, and crosses his hands over his heart.*) I love you all . . . (*He taps his heart with his right fist, then raises the fist in a salute, with the pinky and thumb extended—this is sign language for "I love you." As he salutes.*) Especially the deaf! (*He blows a kiss, using both hands.*) And off. (*He walks backward, his arms at his sides, his head bowed. He turns and faces Andrew.*)

ANDREW. Virginia Smokehouse!

BARRYMORE. On rye! Now you. (*Barrymore positions Andrew at C.; Andrew is still not quite sure what is going on.*) For the full effect . . . (*Gesturing to the proscernium.*) Ring down the curtain! (*The curtain falls, then rises* immediately. *Andrew is alone onstage; Barrymore has vanished. Andrew is looking around for Barrymore, frantically. As he searches, he spots the audience. He points a trembling finger at himself—"Me?" He begins an abbreviated version of the grand Barrymore bow, acknowledging the orchestra, then the balcony, then performing the "humble servant" bend and the salute to the deaf. As Andrew salutes the deaf, a spotlight hits the chaise, illuminating the leather-bound copy of* Hamlet. *Andrew picks up the copy, and looks to heaven, as the lights on the stage dim, except for the spotlight now on Andrew. Andrew smiles.*)

CURTAIN

TWO

Jeffrey

For My Father

Jeffrey received its premeire at the WPA Theatre (Kyle Renick, Artistic Director; Donna Lieberman, Managing Director), in New York City, on December 31, 1992. It was directed by Christopher Ashley; the set design was by James Youmans; the lighting design was by Donald Holder; the costume design was by David C. Woolard; the sound design was by Donna Riley and the production stage manager was John Frederick Sullivan. The cast was as follows:

JEFFREY	John Michael Higgins
MAN #1 IN BED, GYM RAT, SKIP WINKLY, CASTING DIRECTOR, WAITER IN HEADDRESS, MAN #2 WITH DEBRA, MAN IN JOCKSTAP, THUG #2, DAVE, ANGELIQUE	Patrick Kerr
MAN #2 IN BED, GYM RAT, SALESMAN, THE BOSS, MAN #1 WITH DEBRA, MAN IN CHAPS, THUG #1, FATHER JULIAN, SEAN	Daryl Theirse
MAN #3 IN BED, GYM RAT, DON, TIM, DAD, FATHER DAN, CHUCK FARLING	Richard Poe
MAN #4 IN BED, DARIUS	Bryan Batt
MAN #5 IN BED, STERLING	Edward Hibbert
MAN #6 IN BED, STEVE	Tom Hewitt
WOMAN IN BED, SHOWGIRL, ANN MARWOOD BARTLE, DEBRA MOORHOUSE, MOTHER TERESA, SHARON, MOM, MRS. MARCANGELO	Harriet Harris

The WPA production of *Jeffrey* was moved to the Minetta Lane Theatre (Thomas Viertel, Richard Frankel, Steven Baruch, Jack Viertel, Mitchell Maxwell and Alan Schuster, Producers), in New York City in May, 1993. In this production, the part of MAN #2 IN BED was played by Scott Whitehurst.

Jeffrey

ACT ONE

The play takes place in a wide variety of locations, all of which should be suggested as simply as possible. The staging should be fast-paced and fluid, always a few steps ahead of the audience.

As the play begins, we see a series of slides projected on the front curtain or scrim, accompanied by lush, moody music such as a Gershwin* score. The slides include various ultraromantic views of the Manhattan skyline, the streets of Greenwich Village, and, finally, the windows of an appealing brownstone. It is late at night.

Jeffrey is in his thirties, attractive and well put-together. He is an innocent; he is outgoing and optimistic, cheerful despite all odds. Jeffrey believes that life should be wonderful.

In half-light, we see two men making love, and then:

JEFFREY. Ooh! Oh, oh, I'm sorry!
MAN #1. What?
JEFFREY. It broke. *(The lights come up fully on Jeffrey and Man #1 in bed, C.)*
MAN #1. *(Panicking.)* It broke?
JEFFREY. *(Reassuring.)* Don't worry.

---

* See Special Note on Songs and Recordings on copyright page.

MAN #1. It broke?

JEFFREY. It's okay.

MAN #1. It broke?

JEFFREY. Do you have another?

MAN #1. On the table—the wicker basket.

JEFFREY. (*Looking in the wicker basket.*) It's empty.

MAN #1. Don't you . . . ?

JEFFREY. That was my last one. What should we do? (*Man #1 turns away but remains in bed. Man #2 pops up in bed. The full cast will gradually emerge from the bed, in the manner of clowns piling out of a tiny circus car. Their route of entry will be disguised by the bed's sheets and blankets. As each actor appears, he or she will remain in the bed, which will become quite crowded. Man #2 has a too-sincere, gooey personality.*)

MAN #2. Let's just cuddle.

JEFFREY. Cuddle?

MAN #2. Like little bunnies.

JEFFREY. Bunnies?

MAN #2. Or like little babies.

JEFFREY. Babies?

MAN #2. Can we?

JEFFREY. (*Agreeably.*) Well, okay. (*They begin to cuddle.*)

MAN #2. Isn't this better?

JEFFREY. Than what?

MAN #2. Than sex.

JEFFREY. Sure.

MAN #2. I wuv you, Mommy. (*Jeffrey pulls away. Man #3, a hustler, very slick, pops up in bed. He has a smooth, sexy style.*)

MAN #3. Just relax.

JEFFREY. Gee, I've never paid for sex before.

MAN #3. Just tell me what you want. I'll do anything. (*He strokes Jeffrey's face.*) Hey, you're hot. (*Very bored and professional.*) Okay, I am so turned on now. Let's do it all. Let's get wild. Let's burn down the fuckin' house. Just tell me what you want.

JEFFREY. (*Excited.*) I want to have sex!

MAN #3. (*After a beat.*) You're nuts. (*Man #4 pops up in bed. Jeffrey embraces him.*)

MAN #4. Don't you just adore sex?

JEFFREY. I do!

MAN #4. Even nowadays, isn't it just the best thing ever?

JEFFREY. Oh, yeah!

MAN #4. I always have a great time, even with being careful!

JEFFREY. That's incredible!

MAN #4. I just don't like you. (*Man #5 pops up in bed. He is rather imperious.*)

MAN #5. Yes?

JEFFREY. (*Handing him some papers.*) Here's my latest medical report.

MAN #5. (*Inspecting the papers.*) Um-hmm.

JEFFREY. (*Handing over a form.*) And here's the results of my blood test from a month ago.

MAN #5. (*Wary.*) A month ago?

JEFFREY. (*Handing him another form.*) Last week.

MAN #5. Last week?

JEFFREY. (*Handing him still another form.*) This afternoon.

MAN #5. (*As he checks Jeffrey's throat, eyes, and the glands under his jawline.*) Um-hmm. I'll also need the name of your internist, your most recent X-rays, your passport, and a list of all of your previous sexual contacts.

JEFFREY. Well, okay, but isn't that a little extreme?

MAN #5. Do you *want* the apartment? (*Man #6 pops up in bed. His body is heavily draped in Saran Wrap, head to toe. He also wears rubber surgical gloves and a surgical mask.*)

JEFFREY. Are you ready? (*Man #6 nods yes.*) Do you feel safe? (*Man #6 nods yes.*) I'm just going to stand way over here—*way* over here—and maybe I'll . . . jerk off. (*Man #6 looks suspicious and makes a warning noise through his surgical mask. Trying to be cooperative.*) Okay! I won't touch myself! Or you! I'm just going to look at you and—have erotic thoughts. I'm wearing eight condoms, and I won't come! I swear! I promise! (*Man #6 nods okay, a bit doubtfully. Very carefully, very soothingly.*) Okay . . . here we go . . . this is totally safe. I'm just going to look at you, that's right . . . one, two, three . . . (*Jeffrey turns and looks at Man #6. Man #6 panics and screams through his surgical mask. Jeffrey refuses to give up and speaks eagerly to the group on the bed.*) Can we—?

MAN #1. No!

JEFFREY. Oh, but maybe just—

MAN #2. No!

JEFFREY. Oh, oh, but how about just under the—

MAN #3. No!

JEFFREY. And we'll be really, really careful—

MAN #1 and MAN #6. No!

JEFFREY. And we'll stay totally aware at all times—

MAN #4, #5, and #6. No!

JEFFREY. But *please*—

ALL THE MEN EXCEPT JEFFREY. No!

JEFFREY. But I swear, I promise—

ALL THE MEN EXCEPT JEFFREY. NO!

JEFFREY. But just for one tiny little second—

ALL THE MEN EXCEPT JEFFREY. NO! NO! NO! (*A woman pops up in bed; she is lovely and soft-spoken, in a silk negligée.*)

WOMAN. Hi.

ALL THE MEN, INCLUDING JEFFREY. (*After a beat, a bit shocked.*) NO! (*Everyone except Jeffrey collapses onto the bed, as if asleep or unconscious.*)

JEFFREY. Oh my God, oh no, I wonder if maybe it's really happening! You can feel it coming—oh my God, maybe from now on . . . (*All the people on the bed rise up.*)

ALL. NO MORE SEX! (*Jeffrey climbs out of bed. Lights down on the bed and everyone in it. Jeffrey steps forward and begins to get dressed. He speaks to the audience.)*

JEFFREY. Okay. Confession time. You know those articles, the ones all those right wingers use? The ones that talk about gay men who've had over five thousand sexual partners? Well, compared to me, they're shut-ins. Wallflowers. But I'm not promiscuous. That is such an ugly word. I'm cheap. I *love* sex. I don't know how else to say it. I always have—I always thought that sex was the reason to grow up. I couldn't wait! I didn't! I mean—sex! It's just one of the truly great ideas. I mean, the fact that our bodies have this built-in capacity for joy—it just makes me love God. Yes!

But I want to be politically correct about this. I know it's wrong to say that all gay men are obsessed with sex. Because that's not true. All *human beings* are obsessed with sex. All gay men are obsessed with opera. And it's not the same thing. Because you can have good sex.

Except—what's going on? I mean, you saw. Things are just—not what they should be. Sex is too sacred to be treated this way. Sex wasn't meant to be safe, or negotiated, or fatal. But you know what really did it? This guy. I'm in bed with him, and he starts crying. And he says, "I'm sorry, it's just—this used to be so much fun."

So. Enough. Facts of life. No more sex. Not for me. Done!

And you know what? It's going to be fine. Because I am a naturally cheerful person. And I will find a substitute for sex. Sex Lite. Sex Helper. I Can't Believe It's Not Sex. I will find a great new way to live, and a way to be happy. So—no more. The sexual revolution is over! England won. No sex! No sex. I'm ready! I'm willing! Let's go! *(Lights up on Gym Rat #1. He is working out, wearing a Walkman. We hear the music on his Walkman—hip-hop. Lights up on Gym Rat #2. He is working out, wearing a Walkman. We hear the music on his Walkman—throbbing disco. Lights up on Gym Rat #3. He is working out, wearing a Walkman. We hear the music on his Walkman—soaring grand opera. The Gym Rats will continue their workouts during the following scene. Jeffrey bounds into the gym, wearing workout clothes.*) It's the answer! I'll pour all my physical needs into working out! Endorphins, not hormones! No sex! Just sweat! (*Jeffrey is now standing beside a barbell resting on supports over a workout bench.*) Can I get a spot? (*Steve, a good-looking, extremely sexual man in his thirties, turns around. Steve is a master at outrageous, successful flirtation; he knows what he wants.*)

STEVE. You got it.

JEFFREY. Oh my.

STEVE. (*Referring to the weights.*) How much do you want on?

JEFFREY. Oh, forty-fives are fine.

STEVE. I just joined. Do you like it here?

JEFFREY. Oh yeah, a lot. (*He lowers his voice to a more masculine pitch.*) Yeah.

STEVE. (*Offering his hand.*) Steve.

JEFFREY. Jeffrey. (*Lowering his voice.*) Jeff.

STEVE. Are you okay?

JEFFREY. Sure. (*He giggles from nervousness.*) I'm sorry, I'm butching it up. I don't know why I'm doing that. I guess it's to seem sexier—you know, more masculine. (*In an exaggeratedly nelly voice.*) This is the way I really sound. (*In his normal voice.*) I'm sorry.

STEVE. No, don't be. We all do that. Change our personalities, to seem . . . hotter. I'm doing it right now.

JEFFREY. Are you?

STEVE. Technically, we haven't even met yet. (*Putting out his hand.*) Steve.

JEFFREY. (*Shaking Steve's hand; romance is now clearly in the air.*) Jeffrey.

STEVE. So, do you want to . . . do your set?

JEFFREY. Oh. Yes. Sure. (*Jeffrey lies down on the weight bench. Steve spots Jeffrey on the bench press, monitoring the weight. Steve's crotch is now directly over Jeffrey's face.*)

STEVE. Ready?

JEFFREY. Oh yeah. (*Jeffrey starts bench-pressing, as Steve urges him on, rather erotically.*)

STEVE. One . . . two . . . that's right . . . three . . . four . . . you love it . . . five . . . six . . . one more—come on, you're ready—I'm with you—it's so good—don't stop—get it up—pump it—keep it coming, baby, baby, you're there, you're doing it—go, go, go, *owww!!! (The workouts of all the other Gym Rats are now in sync with Jeffrey and Steve; all of the men have reached a truly orgasmic crescendo. As Jeffrey's set ends, everyone drops his weights onto the floor with a thud. Steve helps Jeffrey lower the barbell back onto the supports. All of the men in the gym, including Jeffrey and Steve, are now panting, exhausted, as if postorgasm. Jeffrey remains lying on the bench.)* Cigarette?

JEFFREY. What?

STEVE. Great set.

JEFFREY. *(Gazing up at Steve's crotch.)* You too.

STEVE. What?

JEFFREY. *(Sitting up.)* I mean, thanks. For the spot.

STEVE. Anytime. You look great.

JEFFREY. Thanks. You look . . . terrific.

STEVE. Jeffrey? Jeff?

JEFFREY. Yeah?

STEVE. What would happen . . . if I kissed you? Right now?

JEFFREY. What?

STEVE. Do you want to?

JEFFREY. *Steve* . . .

STEVE. We could drive this place crazy. Everyone's being so butch. We could probably kill people.

JEFFREY. Steve . . .

STEVE. Chickenshit.

JEFFREY. I am not!

STEVE. Then get over here.

JEFFREY. I can't. I have to—*(Steve grabs Jeffrey and kisses him passionately; Jeffrey responds. As the kiss continues, all of the Gym Rats look at Steve and Jeffrey and, in unison, give a sincere schoolgirl sigh of romantic appreciation.)*

GYM RATS. Awww . . . *(Jeffrey pulls away.)*

JEFFREY. No! I won't let this happen! No more! I grabbed my stuff and I ran out of there! (*As he runs across the stage and begins to pull on his street clothes.*) I said no sex and I meant it! No backsliding, no loopholes! And I didn't linger in the locker room and tie my shoe five times while he took off his shorts, I didn't admire my knapsack until he got out of the shower, I didn't accidentally have sex with him—oops!—in the steam room! I erased him, from my mind, from every part of my body! Because I am the new Jeffrey, no longer a slave to my libido, to my urges, or to my reputation as the pushover of lower Manhattan. I just left, with a new inner peace, a serenity. I didn't even glance back to see if he was still watching me. (*Jeffrey glances back; Steve is watching him.*) No! I won't! I ran right up the stairs and into the street! (*Mother Teresa enters. She wears her distinctive full-length white sari with striped blue trim. We do not see her face, which will remain completely hidden in the veil of her sari.*) And I see her. Mother Teresa. Near Blockbuster Video. Was it a hallucination? Or was that really her? I read, later on, that she was actually in the neighborhood, having her cataracts removed at St. Vincent's. But was it her? Or just a truly perverse drag queen? A comfortable one? Well, whoever, or whatever, she was, I know an omen when I see one. (*Mother Teresa crosses the stage and exits.*) But what does it mean? What's her message? I guess it's—be good. Behave. But— what's good? Okay. First step. Goodbye. (*Steve exits. Sterling Farrell enters. Sterling is in his thirties or forties; he is superbly regal and beautifully dressed. Sterling is never bitchy or cruel; he adores his life and his friends, and exults in stylishness. Sterling is an ideal host, generous and amusing. He is Jeffrey's best friend.*)

STERLING. You saw Mother Teresa?

JEFFREY. I swear. She was standing right there. On Eighth Avenue.

STERLING. Well, how did she look?

JEFFREY. I don't know, she was walking. She looked great.

STERLING. Oh, please. She's had work done. I saw her on CNN, she looked sixty. (*We are now in an elegant men's shop. A Salesman—pure at-*

titude—is waiting on Sterling. He holds up two expensive sweaters; Sterling is trying to decide between them.) Teal? Or slate?

JEFFREY. *(As the Salesman indicates the correct choice.)* Teal. *(Sterling tosses one of the sweaters over his shoulders dramatically, like a cape; the sleeves dangle. He turns his body in profile.)*

STERLING. Can I do this? Or do I look like some sort of gay superhero? *(Sterling continues to drape the sweater, ever more outlandishly.)*

JEFFREY. Sterling, I think I'm . . . giving up sex.

STERLING. You are? Why?

SALESMAN. Did I miss an issue of *New York* magazine?

JEFFREY. I just think it's time. I love sex so much, but everything's gotten too scary. It's too . . . overwhelming.

STERLING. My dear, what you need is a relationship.

JEFFREY. A relationship?

SALESMAN. *(Examining Jeffrey's shoes; he snorts.)* Humph. And shoes.

STERLING. If you had a boyfriend, you could relax. You'd set the rules once and then you'd be fine. That's what Darius and I did, and we've been together for almost two years. *(The Salesman helps him into a jacket.)* Do you like this? I mean, on me?

JEFFREY. But aren't you incredibly frustrated?

STERLING. Of course. I'm hard to fit.

JEFFREY. About sex!

STERLING. *(As the Salesman fusses with him, straightening the jacket, removing lint, etc.)* Darling, love is more than just sex. I mean, even trolls can have sex. What you need is a boyfriend. Someone to nest with, wake up with, just lie around the beach house with. *(Delicately pushing the Salesman away.)* Sweetheart. Like Darius.

JEFFREY. But Darius is a dancer.

STERLING. Exactly. I said you needed a boyfriend, not a person. I love having a boyfriend. Not having to worry about going out and finding one. Just having someone there, and I mean this in the best possible way, like a wonderful pet that can feed and walk itself. *(Sincerely.)* I mean, I really do love Darius. I love his body, I love his smile, and he has great hands and feet. On some dancers the toes are all smushed, and I mean I would just say "Sorry, Misha, uh-uh, not without socks." And Darius loves me, Lord knows why. (*Handing the jacket to the Salesman.*) Charge.

JEFFREY. How is Darius? Is he back in *Cats*?

STERLING. Of course. He's fine. It was just a reaction to the AZT. They adjusted the dosage. He's great.

JEFFREY. Of course.

STERLING. You think I don't know what I sound like. Of course I know. But I have made a decision. I have always been lucky, all my life. Obviously. And I have simply decided to stay lucky. *N'est-ce pas?*

JEFFREY. And you still have sex?

STERLING. Of course. Safe sex. The best. (*The Salesman hands Sterling a shopping bag with his purchases.*) Thank you. I mean, Jeffrey—it's just sex. (*A blast of raucous music is heard. A slide of a handsome, fairly unclothed man might fill the stage.*)

JEFFREY. Just sex? Just sex? (*Another blast of music, and perhaps more erotic slides. Skip Winkly, a smarmy, upbeat game-show host, appears, in a flashy tuxedo. He is accompanied by a vapid Showgirl.*)

SKIP. Hi! I'm Skip Winkly, and welcome to "It's Just Sex!"—the show where we explore human sexuality and win big prizes! (*The Showgirl cues canned applause; slides of garish big prizes might appear. The Salesman, Sterling, and Jeffrey now stand behind glittery podiums with buzzers. A sign or slide reads, in Vegas-caliber letters, "It's Just Sex!"*)

SALESMAN. Hi, Skip.

STERLING. Hey, Skip.

JEFFREY. Hi!

SKIP. What a great set of contestants—three gay men! And now let's play "It's Just Sex!" And remember—each question may have more than one correct answer. The most stylish reply wins! (*The Showgirl hands him a card.*) Here we go—question number one! What seemingly harmless events can now be fatal if they occur during sex? (*The Sales-man, Jeffrey, and Sterling all hit their buzzers, one after the other.*)

SALESMAN. A paper cut.

JEFFREY. Recent dental work.

STERLING. Fluorescent lighting.

SKIP. (*Pointing to Sterling, as the Showgirl cues more applause.*) Yes, for seventy points!

JEFFREY. I knew that.

SALESMAN. Is my buzzer working?

SKIP. We'll find out! Question number two: Who is your favorite sexual fantasy? (*The Salesman, Jeffrey, and Sterling all hit their buzzers again, one after the other.*)

SALESMAN. Denzel Washington!

JEFFREY. That guy at the gym.

STERLING. Yoko Ono. (*Everyone stares at Sterling questioningly. He rolls his eyes at their obtuseness.*) To see the apartment.

SKIP. (*Pointing to Sterling.*) Yes again, for seventy points!

JEFFREY. (*Regarding Sterling.*) He was coached before the show.

SALESMAN. I have a slow buzzer!

SKIP. Now, now! It's time for our bonus round, when everything could change, for five *hundred* points! Yes! Here we go: Let's say there's a fella who just loves having sex more than anything. What will happen to him if he suddenly just flat-out dagnabbit *stops*? (*There is a pause. No one buzzes.*)

SALESMAN. (*At a loss.*) Gee . . .

STERLING. (*At a loss.*) Skip . . . (*Jeffrey is suddenly afire with inspiration, and he hits his buzzer.*)

SKIP. Yes! Gay Man #2, with that hopeful, deluded look!

JEFFREY. Skip, my answer is this: If the fella stops having sex, he will pour himself into his career. And all that rechanneled energy will create incredible career karma, and he'll be a huge success and fantastically happy!

SKIP. (*Looking off-stage.*) Judges? What do you say? Will his career compensate? (*He listens to the off-stage judges.*) That's absolutely right! (*The music goes crazy, confetti rains down, and frenzied applause is heard. The Showgirl hands Jeffrey a dozen roses and places a rhinestone tiara on his head. Jeffrey is ecstatic.*) Wait! Hold it! Just a minute! Judges? (*He listens.*) They have a question—it's nothing really, just a minor technicality. A soaring career can compensate for no sex, but—just what is your career?

JEFFREY. Well, I'm an actor . . . waiter. (*A pause.*)

SKIP. Which means . . .

STERLING. (*Stepping out from behind his podium.*) I win! (*The wild music and confetti resume. The Showgirl grabs Jeffrey's roses and tiara and gives them to Sterling. Skip, the Salesman, and the Showgirl all exit. Sterling begins to exit, and then notices the audience. He beams, and gives a gracious royal wave as he walks offstage. Jeffrey is alone.*)

JEFFREY. Okay, so I'm an unemployed actor. I mean, I'm talented—I think I am. I mean, last week I read for a part, on a TV show! (*A Casting Director appears, very smug and patronizing, seated, holding a clipboard. Jeffrey is now at an audition. He tries to be ingratiating.*) Hi. Jeffrey Calloway.

CASTING DIRECTOR. (*Handing Jeffrey some pages.*) Page thirty-three. Police Officer #2. Remember, there are no small parts. Well, actually, there are. All right. You've just burst in on the evil ghetto drug lord. Action.

JEFFREY. (*Reading from the pages.*) "Hold it right there, Diego! Freeze!"

CASTING DIRECTOR. (*Not happy.*) You're a hero. You mean business. Again. Action.

JEFFREY. (*A bit more intense.*) "Hold it right there, Diego! Freeze!"

CASTING DIRECTOR. You've been hunting him for months. You've finally got him with the goods. But he might have a gun! Action!

JEFFREY. (*More intense.*) "Hold it right there, Diego! Freeze!"

CASTING DIRECTOR. You hate him! More! Action!

JEFFREY. (*Pouring it on.*) "Hold it right there, Diego! Freeze!"

CASTING DIRECTOR. You loathe him! You scorn him! Make me feel it! More! Prime time!

JEFFREY. (*With ultimate fury, his voice squeaking girlishly as he uses both hands to aim an imaginary gun.*) "Hold it right there, Diego! Freeze! Oh, I just hate you!" (*There is a pause.*)

CASTING DIRECTOR. Perhaps you'd like to read for our gay role. It's not a caricature, it's a very full human being.

JEFFREY. Sure. The gay role?

CASTING DIRECTOR. Page sixty-eight. The neighbor. (*Lights down on the Casting Director. Jeffrey steps forward and addresses the audience.*)

JEFFREY. I got the part. The gay role. Two lines. It was the first time I'd worked in almost a year. Which is why I am a waiter. (*Another Waiter appears, hands Jeffrey a starched white service jacket, and exits. Jeffrey puts the jacket on.*) A cater waiter, to be exact. I work for various party outfits—you've heard of them. Glorious Food. Sublime Service. Arugula with Attitude. It's actually kind of fun, because I get to go everywhere, with my shiny black shoes and my garment bag. I've been to private homes, museums, tents in Central Park. It's like gay National Guard. (*The other Waiter reappears. He now wears a bandanna at his throat, cowboy-style. He hands Jeffrey a beaded headband with a feather. Jeffrey puts the headband on as the Waiter exits.*) If you're anyone at all, you've ignored me. But I don't mind, because I've tried on your fur. (*Music begins. Lights up on the ballroom of the Waldorf, decorated with hay, pinto-patterned tablecloths, cacti, and gingham for a country-western theme. Chandeliers descend, also draped in gingham. Steve enters; like Jeffrey and the other waiter, he wears the standard cater-waiter uniform of service jacket, black pants, white shirt, and black bow tie. Steve also wears a red cowboy hat, and perhaps a bandanna. Everyone's country-western accessories should appear fairly ridiculous. Jeffrey and Steve spot one another.*)

STEVE. Kemo sabe?

JEFFREY. Pardner?

STEVE. Howdy!

JEFFREY. Howdy! (*As Jeffrey and Steve greet each other, the Boss enters. He wears a waiter's uniform and an absurdly oversized cowboy hat. He is a barking bully, perhaps with a Jamaican accent.*)

BOSS. Gentlemen? What do you think you're doing?

JEFFREY. (*To Steve, as Jeffrey and the Boss exit.*) Roundup! (*Steve takes his place behind a bar, which is draped with a pinto-patterned tablecloth and set with bottles and glassware. During Ann Marwood Bartle's speeches, he freezes in half-light. Lights up on Ann Marwood Bartle. She is a giddy socialite in an elaborate ball gown accessorized with a sequined cowboy hat, fringed gauntlet gloves, and a holster with pistols. Ann is thrilled beyond measure to be the evening's hostess. She should not be played as southern; think Connecticut lockjaw.*)

ANN. Good evening, everyone. I'm Ann Marwood Bartle. And I'd like to welcome you to Country-Western Nite here at the Waldorf! A Hoedown for AIDS. Now more than ever we need to combat this terrible disease with funding, education, and gingham. (*She indicates the ribbons on her bodice.*) The red ribbon I wear stands for AIDS awareness. The lavender ribbon is in memory of those who have died. And the diamond spray is a gift of my first husband. And now I'd like to introduce our honorary board of directors at table number one. Hold your applause, please, for Lauren Bacall! Donna Karan! Mr. and Mrs. Henry Kravis! And our very own, the Honorable Mayor Rudolph Guiliani. In the chaps. (*Ann freezes in half-light. Jeffrey enters with a tray.*)

JEFFREY. I need a vodka rocks with a twist, and two spritzers.

STEVE. (*As he makes the drinks.*) I was hoping I'd run into you. I wanted to apologize about the other day, at the gym. I came on a little strong.

JEFFREY. No, you were great. I'm sorry I took off. I was just acting weird. I'm . . . an actor.

STEVE. I thought so. Have I seen you in something?

JEFFREY. Well, did you see *Manhattan Precinct* two weeks ago? Near the end of the show? The gay neighbor? (*Doing sincere, TV-style acting.*) "You know, Karen, I have the same problem . . . with Bob."

STEVE. You were great! (*The other Waiter enters, disgruntled, in a full-tilt feathered Indian headdress and a beaded breastplate.*)

JEFFREY. (*Indian-style, to the Waiter.*) How.

WAITER. (*Morose.*) Why? (*The Waiter exits.*)

STEVE. (*Handing Jeffrey a drink in a glass shaped like a cowboy boot.*) Here you go.

JEFFREY. So—what do you really do?

STEVE. I'm actually, really—a bartender. I sort of acted and I sort of wrote, but mostly . . .

JEFFREY. What?

STEVE. I watch you.

JEFFREY. (*Pleased.*) You do? (*The Waiter reappears.*)

WAITER. He does. (*The Boss appears.*)

BOSS. Spritzers! Table fifteen! (*Jeffrey and the other Waiter begin to exit to opposite sides of the stage. The waiter pauses and speaks to Jeffrey, regarding Steve.*)

WAITER. Nice work, Little Feather.

JEFFREY. Bitch.

WAITER. Squaw. (*The Waiter, Jeffrey, and the Boss exit. Lights up on Ann.*)

ANN. Is everyone ready to kick up their heels and rustle their petticoats for a new outpatient lounge? Cowhands, cowgals, I give you a very special treat! They've been practicing for—weeks! Let's have a big whoop-ti-aye-ay for Dr. Sidney Greenblatt and his Mount Sinai Ramblers! (*A raucous country-western square dance tune begins. Jeffrey enters with an empty tray. He stares at the dance floor.*)

JEFFREY. Oh my God . . . (*Ann begins clapping her hands and calling the square dance.*)

ANN. Come on, everyone! Get out on the floor! Here we go! It's a square dance! Yee-haw!

JEFFREY. (*To Steve.*) Isn't this bizarre? But I think they're raising a fortune.

STEVE. You're making small talk.

JEFFREY. I need a Bloody Mary and two more spritzers.

STEVE. Am I making you nervous?

JEFFREY. Yes!

STEVE. I like you nervous.

JEFFREY. Why?

STEVE. I have to tell you something. At the gym—that wasn't the first time I saw you.

JEFFREY. It wasn't?

STEVE. No. I've seen you at parties—at the Met, the Armory. You are always chattering away.

JEFFREY. Oh no.

STEVE. What?

JEFFREY. I have this image of myself as . . . a normal person—you know, a guy. But I've always known that I'm secretly really . . . a teenage girl.

STEVE. No! You're great! You're a great teenage girl! The other waiters, they're moody, they're Brando. But you—you have a ball. You belong at the party.

JEFFREY. So do you. (*The Waiter appears in his headdress with a tray.*)

WAITER. (*À la* Poltergeist.) He's baaack . . . (*The Boss enters, very angry.*)

BOSS. What is this, a social club? Do you want to be fired?

WAITER. I want my land.

BOSS. Move! (*The Waiter and Jeffrey exit, followed by the Boss.*)

ANN. C'mon, y'all! (*Calling the square dance.*) Swing your partners, round you go, allemande left, then do-si-do! (*Speaking normally.*) Isn't this fun? You little dogies! (*Jeffrey enters with an empty tray.*)

STEVE. So have we talked enough? Can I see you? After the party?

JEFFREY. I need two glasses of champagne.

STEVE. California?

JEFFREY. No—the good stuff. (*Steve starts to pour two glasses of champagne.*)

STEVE. Do you have a lover?

JEFFREY. No.

STEVE. Are you seeing someone?

JEFFREY. No.

STEVE. Do I care?

JEFFREY. You are unbelievable!

STEVE. Find out. (*He laughs.*) I'm sorry, I keep hitting on you. Don't you love this part?

JEFFREY. What part?

STEVE. The part where you can't find out enough, about the other person. Where it's all interesting, where it all seems . . . sexy. First steps.

JEFFREY. To where?

STEVE. To my place. Or your place. Or happiness. Or . . . more.

JEFFREY. You move fast.

STEVE. Catch up. Because if I don't touch you very soon, I may explode.

JEFFREY. You know, until about a minute ago, I had a very strong reason not to go out with you.

STEVE. Which was? No, wait—is it because . . . I'm a cowboy, and you're . . . a waiter?

JEFFREY. We're a proud people.

STEVE. What a shame.

JEFFREY. (*Toasting Steve with the champagne.*) You know, in a better world, I could ask you to square dance.

STEVE. Really? You want to square dance? (*Steve holds up his hand. He looks at Ann Marwood Bartle.*)

ANN. Bow to your partner, then once more . . . (*Steve snaps his fingers.*) Cater waiters, take the floor! (*The lights grow brighter. Steve steps out from behind the bar. He bows to Jeffrey and holds out his hand. Jeffrey takes Steve's hand and they begin to dance a rousing, sexy two-step, the Cotton-Eyed Joe. As Steve and Jeffrey dance, the Waiter and the Boss appear and begin to dance as well, as a couple. Ann Marwood Bartle joins the number, she might hold a hobbyhorse or fire her pistols. The number becomes a spirited, miniature version of a real Busby Berkeley hoe-down complete with square dancing and "Yee-haw!"s. As the number grows in wildness, Steve begins to remove Jeffrey's clothing; he tosses the discarded items to the other people on stage. Jeffrey's headband comes off, and then his jacket; everyone surrounds Jeffrey and begins to caress him. Jeffrey pulls away from Steve and the group.*)

JEFFREY. No! (*The music stops abruptly, and Ann, the Waiter, and the Boss exit.*)

STEVE. You can't do that. This is my fantasy.

JEFFREY. (*Very torn.*) I have to circulate. Table 22.

STEVE. Come on—one more do-si-do.

JEFFREY. I'm working!

STEVE. What is going on with you?

JEFFREY. (*Very distraught.*) We're not allowed to have fantasies! Not anymore!

STEVE. Come on. Let's go.

JEFFREY. I can't!

STEVE. Why not?

JEFFREY. It's . . . I can't explain! It's not you! Yes, it *is* you!

STEVE. What?

JEFFREY. I have to go! (*Steve and the hoe-down vanish. As they do, Sterling
enters, wearing something outrageous, perhaps Chinese-inspired lounging pajamas.*)

STERLING. So—he was really cute, this bartender? (*We are now in Sterling's elegant, if somewhat overdone, Upper East Side apartment. Sterling holds
a cigarette and a cocktail.*)

JEFFREY. He was fantastic. But I just got so—I don't know! I went nuts!

STERLING. Jeffrey—you are beginning to have a problem. (*Darius, Sterling's boyfriend, enters, wearing an overcoat. Darius is a true innocent, a handsome, completely sweet dancer in his twenties.*)

DARIUS. Hi, guys.

STERLING. Hello, sweetheart.

DARIUS. What a day. I am exhausted. (*Darius takes off his coat. He is wearing his costume from* Cats, *which consists of a heavily painted body suit, accen-
tuated with yarn and fur, elaborate leg warmers, knitted gauntlets, and a tail.
He has already removed his makeup.*)

JEFFREY. Darius—aren't you supposed to leave your costume at the theater?

DARIUS. We were filming a commercial, the new one, and it went late, I
got stuck. So you're not having sex anymore. (*Darius sits beside Sterling;*

they are very easy and affectionate with one another. Their love affair is real and lasting. The friendship between Jeffrey, Sterling, and Darius should also be one of great pleasure and devotion.)

STERLING. What he needs is to fall in love and have a relationship. And then this sex thing will fall into place.

DARIUS. Exactly. Look at us. Look at how happy we are. Don't we make you want to fall in love?

STERLING. You know, sometimes I think we should be on a brochure for Middle America. So that everyone can say, "Oh, look, a wholesome gay couple!"

JEFFREY. Excuse me? You're not wholesome. You're a decorator—excuse me, an interior designer—there, I said it without giggling. And you—you're a dancer. You two are like Martha Stewart and Ann Miller. Which, believe me, I prefer. I hate that gay role models are supposed to be just like straight people. As if straight people were even like that.

STERLING. That's true. I was watching these two guys on *Nightline*, on Gay Pride Day? And one of them said, "I'm Bob Wheeler and I'm a surgeon. And my lover is an attorney. And we'd like to show America that all gays aren't limp-wristed, screaming queens. There are gay truck drivers and gay cops and gay lumberjacks." And I just thought, "Ooh—get *her*."

DARIUS. Who's Martha Stewart?

STERLING. She writes picture books about gracious living. Martha says that nothing else matters, if you can do a nice dried floral arrangement. I worship her.

DARIUS. And who's Ann Miller?

STERLING. Leave this house. (*Jeffrey and Sterling freeze. Darius addresses the audience.*)

DARIUS. Some people think I'm dumb, just because I'm a chorus boy with an eighth-grade education. Well—I live in a penthouse and I don't pay rent. I go to screenings and I take cabs. Dumb, huh? And yes, I'm in *Cats*. Now and forever. And I love it! I do! I figure I was too young for *A Chorus Line*, and too happy for *Les Miz*. I never got that show—*Les Miz*. It's about this French guy, right, who steals a loaf of bread, and then he suffers for the rest of his life. For *toast*. Get over it! (*Back to the scene.*)

JEFFREY. That's why I came over. To be convinced about this love-and-relationship bit. Because I do believe that you two are truly in love. You have that special . . . smugness. You're like an advertisement for connubial bliss.

DARIUS. What's "connubial"?

STERLING. It's when one of us can afford a cleaning woman. (*The doorbell rings. Steve enters, carrying a bouquet of flowers.*) Steven! Hi!

DARIUS. What a surprise!

JEFFREY. Oh my God . . .

STERLING. Jeffrey, this is Steven. I met him at the showhouse opening, and we talked.

DARIUS. We love him.

STEVE. (*Handing Jeffrey the flowers.*) Hi there.

JEFFREY. How are you?

STERLING. I think they're perfect for each other.

DARIUS. Me too.

STERLING. Steve's a bartender, so they'll have something in common. They can fall in love and cater together—it'll be like *Roots*.

JEFFREY. (*To Steve, with great, accelerating passion.*) Steve—since the first second I saw you, at the gym, I have thought of nothing and no one else. I have fantasized about you—naked—about you kissing me and talking to me and walking down the street with me, and letting you do things to me that I have only permitted with five thousand other men. I think you could change my life and change the world and I would love more than anything to do exactly the same for you and I think it's completely and totally possible that we could be the happiest people alive except—I'm not having sex anymore so—sorry! (*Jeffrey, in agony, hands the flowers back to Steve and collapses into a chair.*)

STERLING. Wait—you two already know each other.

STEVE. We do.

DARIUS. Oh my God. Oh my God. (*To Sterling.*) It's like I told you. I'm psychic—I can predict boyfriends!

JEFFREY. We're not boyfriends! (*Steve, Sterling, and Darius surround Jeffrey, standing or kneeling around his chair.*)

STEVE. Jeffrey, calm down. Stop hyperventilating.

JEFFREY. I can't!

STEVE. Take a deep breath. (*As conducted by Sterling, all four men take a deep breath.*) Better?

JEFFREY. Sort of.

STEVE. Okay. Now, I want to see you. We can take this as slow as you like. First step. How about—tomorrow night?

JEFFREY. I'm working! Till ten!

STEVE. Afterwards. We'll have dinner.

STERLING. (*To Jeffrey.*) You must.

DARIUS. You can't ignore the karma. It's too dangerous.

STERLING. You have to get over this bizarre sex thing.

DARIUS. You'll have fun! You'll have appetizers!

STERLING. We're your friends.

DARIUS. We love you.

STERLING. You must obey us.

STEVE. You have no choice, Jeffrey. Dinner?

STERLING. (*To Jeffrey.*) Dinner?

DARIUS. (*To Jeffrey.*) Dinner?

JEFFREY. Well . . .

DARIUS. Oh, come on. You're gay. You're single.

STERLING. It isn't pretty.

JEFFREY. Yes! (*Sterling, Darius, and Steve cheer.*)

STERLING. (*Hugging Jeffrey.*) I'm so proud of you! You're dating again!

STEVE. How about the Paris Commune? On Bleecker? I know the maître d'.

JEFFREY. Yes!

STEVE. And Jeffrey?

JEFFREY. Yes?

STEVE. I just . . . okay, just so there are no surprises . . .

JEFFREY. Uh-huh.

STEVE. I'm HIV-positive.

JEFFREY. (*After a beat.*) Um, okay, right.

STEVE. Does that make a difference?

JEFFREY. No. No. Of course not.

STERLING. (*Dismissing any doubt.*) Please.

DARIUS. HIV-positive men are the hottest.

STEVE. I mean—I'd understand. I'd be hurt and disappointed, but—I
just wanted to be clear.

JEFFREY. No, really, it's fine—I mean, come on, it's the nineties, right?
The Paris Commune, at ten. I can't wait.

DEBRA. (*Entering from the rear of the theater.*) Do you feel lost? (*Lights down
on Steve, Sterling, Darius, and the apartment. Jeffrey steps forward.*)

JEFFREY. I do! (*Debra is an attractive, vibrant, magnetic woman in a stylish
Armani suit. She is in turn ferocious, deeply compassionate, abusive, and a red-
hot mama. She is the evangelist as pop star, capable of seducing and threatening
her audience—she is the most confident person on earth.*)

DEBRA. (*Approaching the stage.*) So you come to me, and you say, "Debra,
what can I do to feel better about myself and the world?," and you
know what I say?

JEFFREY. What?

DEBRA. Love. It's real. It works. Go for it!

JEFFREY. (*To the audience.*) Debra Moorhouse—the nation's hottest post-
modern evangelist. (*Jeffrey leaves the stage to watch from the audience.
Debra picks up a microphone and begins to work the crowd—she will use the
actual theatergoers as her flock.*)

DEBRA. I'm not here as a priest, or a guru, or as any sort of religious
leader. I'm just someone who—likes to talk. And people come to me,

and they say, "Debra, I'm in love with an alcoholic, what should I do?" And I tell them, "Don't look to me for answers—look to yourself. And then turn it all over to some higher power, whether that power is simply the collective strength of all the love in the world, or some dude named—Jesus Christ. (*She offers a nod and a salute to heaven.*) Find that source of unconditional love, find that all-encompassing, ultimate love, surrender to that unending, infinite love that will let you say, 'Hey (*Her voice shifts from cajoling to a harsh bellow*)—FUCK YOU! Get out of my house until you stop drinking!' " (*She smiles radiantly.*) Let's have some questions. Yes? (*Various trembling, sincere followers raise their hands, yearning for Debra's attention. Debra points to a lucky male Acolyte.*)

ACOLYTE #1. Um, Debra, first of all, I just want to thank you for speaking to us tonight . . .

DEBRA. You bet. What's up?

ACOLYTE #1. Well, um, I just broke up with my lover.

DEBRA. Well, we've all been there, haven't we?

ACOLYTE #1. (*Puzzled.*) With my lover?

DEBRA. Spill, baby.

ACOLYTE #1. (*As Debra holds out the microphone.*) Well, Brad and I have lived together for almost five years, but then he lost his job and started doing cocaine. And he wouldn't look for work and I was paying for everything and we would have these terrible fights and . . . he even tried to hit me with the car. *My* car.

DEBRA. Whoa. Man.

ACOLYTE #1. But I still love him!

DEBRA. (*Almost laughing, looking at Acolyte #1 as if he's crazy.*) Okay. Okay. Let me cook on this! Okay. Okay. (*Serious again.*) It sounds like you've got a problem with everybody's favorite—low self-esteem. Of course, I don't know you. Maybe you *should* have low self-esteem.

ACOLYTE #1. I just want a relationship.

DEBRA. You want a relationship because you're afraid! It all goes back to mother, doesn't it? Did you love your mother?

ACOLYTE #1. Well, I guess so . . .

DEBRA. Don't lie to me. I'll call her. Did she withhold? Was there . . . abuse?

ACOLYTE #1. (*Choked up.*) Sometimes . . .

DEBRA. Go see her. Tell her, "Mom, you were chilly." (*Acolyte #1 bursts into sobs; Debra takes him in her arms.*) "You forgot my birthday. You beat me with a baseball bat. But I understand. I forgive. I *love* you. And Mom, now you're old. You've got a plastic hip. (*Triumphantly.*) And I've got the bat!" (*She pushes Acolyte #1 away.*) Next?

ACOLYTE #2. Debra, Debra, Debra!!! (*Acolyte #2, another man, is wildly overemotional; he leaps onto the stage.*) First of all, I want to say that I listen to your audiocassettes at least eight times a day, even in the car on my way to and from work.

DEBRA. Good.

ACOLYTE #2. I've memorized most of them, and sometimes I recite right along with you. (*Debra makes a gesture "And?"*) I used to be afraid all the time, but you've really helped me to have a life!

DEBRA. *You've* helped you to have a life. (*Acolyte #2 smacks his forehead in recognition of this great truth. He pulls a pair of hand-crocheted baby booties out of his pocket.*)

ACOLYTE #2. And I just wanted to give you this pair of booties that I hand-crocheted for your baby. I know you discourage gifts, except donations, but—I just had to! (*Acolyte #2 hands Debra the booties. Overcome, he gives her a big wet kiss on the cheek and bounces off the stage. Debra surreptitiously wipes her cheek with the booties.*)

DEBRA. Well, thank you! These are adorable. But remember, I'm not your idol, your Elvis. Don't worship me—*love* me! Do you see the difference?

ACOLYTE #2. Yeah, okay!

DEBRA. One more!

JEFFREY. Hi, Debra. Debra, I think that sex is the best thing ever, but I've met someone, and he's HIV-positive, and I'm beginning to self-destruct. Now, I'm a waiter, so I can't afford your cassettes, or the mug, or the calendar. Do they mention this problem?

DEBRA. They sure do. It's in my book, chapter ten—cheap waiters! (*She laughs at her joke, then grows serious.*) No, no, no. What you're talking about is evil, am I right? Why is there disease? Why was there a Hitler? (*She holds up the booties.*) Why are these acrylic? Ha! Isn't laughter the best medicine? (*Acolyte #2 gives a half-hearted laugh; Debra dismisses him.*) Anyway. Here's the lowdown on evil: it's the absence of love. Ta-da. That's it. Case closed. Where you don't have love, illness makes a home.

JEFFREY. Wait, Debra—are you saying that people get sick because they don't love enough, or because no one loves them?

DEBRA. It may sound simplistic, it may sound cruel, it may sound like I am blaming people for their own illness, and maybe I am. (*Perky again.*) That's Debra!

JEFFREY. Debra, that's crazy.

DEBRA. Think about it! That's it! I'd like to end tonight's session with five minutes of guided meditation. First, I'd like everyone to take the hands of the people on either side of you. (*Jeffrey holds hands in between Acolyte #1 and Acolyte #2.*) Close your eyes. Close 'em up. I'd like you to picture yourself as a very young child. You're four or five, you're innocent, open to love. For maybe the last time in your life, you're very appealing. Can you see that child?

ACOLYTE #1. I see him!

ACOLYTE #2. I see him!

DEBRA. (*To Jeffrey.*) What about you, Mr. I'm-on-a-Budget?

JEFFREY. I . . . I think I see him.

DEBRA. Give him a kiss! Take that child in your arms! Hug him! Squeeze him! Tickle him till he can't breathe and the eyes roll back in his head! Now tell him—"I love you!"

ACOLYTE #1, ACOLYTE #2, and JEFFREY. I love you!

DEBRA. I can't hear you!

ACOLYTE #1, ACOLYTE #2, and JEFFREY. (*Louder.*) I LOVE YOU!

DEBRA. Make him believe it!

ACOLYTE #1, ACOLYTE #2, and JEFFREY. (*As passionately as possible,*
howling.) I LOVE YOU!!!

DEBRA. (*She can't resist.*) Debra!

ACOLYTE #1, ACOLYTE #2, and JEFFREY. DEBRA!!!

DEBRA. (*Suspensefully.*) Next week's topic: Dead-end job? Dead-end marriage? Dead-end life? (*Ferociously.*) Stop whining, you big baby! (*With a*
wave and a smile.) 'Night! (*Lights down on Debra and her acolytes. We hear*
a phone ring.)

STEVE'S VOICE. (*On his answering machine.*) Hi, this is Steve. I'm not in
right now. Please leave a message after the beep. Have a great day.

JEFFREY. (*To the audience.*) I'm sorry.

JEFFREY'S VOICE. (*On Steve's answering machine.*) Steve, hi, it's Jeffrey.
And . . . I'm working later than I thought. Private party, you know.
So can we reschedule? Next week? Maybe? I . . . I can't wait, and I'll
call you, and . . . I . . . take care.

JEFFREY. (*To the audience.*) I know what you're thinking. What a sleazoid,
what a major-league, hall-of-fame rat. And maybe you're right. It's just
. . . okay, what am I so afraid of? Him getting sick? Me getting sick?
Why is the idea of a simple dinner now like an evening of Russian
roulette? And I felt like a complete creep, and I couldn't go home and
be alone with myself, and I was so horny. Why is that my response to
everything? (*Lights up on a shirtless, well-built Man in a leather biker's jacket*
and a jockstrap.)

MAN IN JOCKSTRAP. Hey.

JEFFREY. Why can't I drink? (*Lights up on another man, in leather chaps and a*
harness. He speaks in a deep, practiced, ridiculously sexual basso.)

MAN IN CHAPS. Uh-huh.

JEFFREY. And if I can't touch anyone else, who can I touch? (*Lights up on*
Don, a tough guy wearing a leather vest over his bare chest, a leather top man's
cap, and Levi's.)

DON. Welcome—to the Lower Manhattan Gentlemen's Masturbation Society. Or, as we call it in our brochure, Beats All. I'm Don, tonight's sergeant-at-arms. Anyone not following our basic guidelines will be asked to leave and, if necessary, ejected. There will be no bodily contact, and no exchange of fluids. Please feel free to remove as much clothing as you like. We are into hot men, mutual getting off, and masculine appreciation. (*We hear the sounds of a heavy iron door slamming shut and locks turning.*) The doors have been locked, and we think it's going to be a very hot night. (*The Men are now standing in separate down lights; the atmosphere is very rough and shadowy. As they speak, in their lowest, huskiest, most seductive voices, the Men pinch, rub, and slap various parts of their bodies. Jeffrey stands in the center of the group a bit D. The other Men eye him.*)

MAN IN JOCKSTRAP. Hey.

DON. Hey.

MAN IN CHAPS. Hey.

JEFFREY. (*Pleasantly.*) Hey.

MAN IN JOCKSTRAP. Hot bod, man.

DON. Real hot.

MAN IN CHAPS. Uh-huh.

JEFFREY. Okay . . .

MAN IN JOCKSTRAP. Nice tits, man.

DON. Hot tits.

MAN IN CHAPS. Uh-huh.

JEFFREY. (*Starting to rub his chest, tentatively.*) Hot.

DON. Nice butt, man.

MAN IN JOCKSTRAP. Hot fuckin' *butt.*

MAN IN CHAPS. Uh-huh.

JEFFREY. Thank you.

MAN IN JOCKSTRAP. Hot *bubble* butt.

JEFFREY. Thank you very much.

DON. I want to see you touch that butt.

MAN IN JOCKSTRAP. Touch that hot butt.

MAN IN CHAPS. Uh-huh.

JEFFREY. Okay . . . (*The Man In Chaps has started to slap his own butt with both hands. Jeffrey starts to rub his own butt.*)

DON. That's right.

MAN IN JOCKSTRAP. Hot fuckin' butt!

MAN IN CHAPS. Uh-huh.

JEFFREY. (*Growling.*) Yeah . . . (*Everyone but Jeffrey begins to rub his own crotch.*)

MAN IN JOCKSTRAP. Do it, man.

DON. Touch that dick.

MAN IN CHAPS. Uh-huh.

JEFFREY. Touch it? (*Jeffrey begins to rub his own crotch. He continues to rub his butt with his other hand.*)

DON. That's right.

MAN IN JOCKSTRAP. Go for it, man!

MAN IN CHAPS. Uh-huh.

JEFFREY. (*As he rubs his crotch and his butt.*) Why do I feel like—I'm on the subway? This isn't working, not for me. I wonder if I can just kind of . . . slip out . . . (*Jeffrey stops rubbing himself. He tries to leave. The other Men do not approve.*)

DON, MAN IN JOCKSTRAP, MAN IN CHAPS. (*Very threatening.*) UH-UH! (*The other Men begin to encircle Jeffrey, coming closer and closer.*

JEFFREY. Oh my God . . .

DON. Take 'em down!

JEFFREY. What?

MAN IN JOCKSTRAP. Let's see that butt!

JEFFREY. Guys . . .

DON. Come on, man!

MAN IN JOCKSTRAP. Here we go! Take 'em down! Rip 'em down!

DON. Gettin' hot!

MAN IN CHAPS. Uh-huh! (*As the Men begin to unbutton their jeans, we hear a shrill blast on a whistle. Everyone freezes.*)

STERLING. Stop that!

DARIUS. Leave him alone! (*Sterling and Darius have entered, wearing black T-shirts with huge pink paw prints on them. They also wear pink berets and silver whistles on thongs around their necks. They confront the Men from the masturbation club, who scamper away. The lights grow bright again.*)

STERLING. We are the Pink Panthers! (*Sterling and Darius strike a dramatic pose as conquering heroes.*)

JEFFREY. (*Very entertained.*) You are?

STERLING. We just got off our shift. We're part of a citizens' patrol to prevent gay bashing. We patrolled with five other guys, from Christopher to Bank Street.

DARIUS. From Seventh Avenue to the river. And we have whistles, and walkie-talkies. (*Sterling displays his walkie-talkie as if it were in a showroom.*)

JEFFREY. I'm so impressed!

STERLING. We're keeping the streets safe. It was Darius's idea.

DARIUS. I wanted to do something.

STERLING. Something with a T-shirt. Don't you love it? (*Sterling and Darius twirl and pose, modeling their T-shirts with great flair.*) I'm sorry, those students in Tiananmen Square were very misguided. Where were the graphics? All it would've taken was one silk-screen. Mao with a *Ghostbusters* circle. (*He demonstrates the circle with a line through it, on his chest.*)

DARIUS. Or that *Miss Saigon* doodle.

STERLING. We heart cultural freedom.

DARIUS. (*Admiring his T-shirt.*) These are going to be very rare. We have to change our name.

JEFFREY. Why?

STERLING. MGM has started a lawsuit. They own the rights to all the *Pink Panther* movies and they claim it's a copyright infringement.

DARIUS. Even though we are a non . . .

STERLING and DARIUS. (*Sterling helps Darius with the phrase.*) Profit . . .

DARIUS. . . . organization to prevent violence.

STERLING. They claim it's not homophobia, but you know it is. So we're testing all the other studios. We've come up with a great new name for our patrol.

JEFFREY. What?

STERLING. Fantasia.

DARIUS. So how was your date? Where's Steve?

JEFFREY. He . . . I had to cancel. I just got off work.

DARIUS. Did you call him?

JEFFREY. Of course. I left a message on his machine.

DARIUS. Left a message? Call him again! He's a doll! (*The beeper on Sterling's walkie-talkie goes off.*)

STERLING. (*Into his walkie-talkie, in a very butch voice.*) Hello. Pink Panthers. (*More social.*) Oh, hello, darling.

DARIUS. Is someone in trouble?

STERLING. (*Listening to the walkie-talkie, very upset.*) Really . . . No . . . Oh no.

JEFFREY. What?

STERLING. We have to get over to Washington Square right away. It's Todd, that huge bodybuilder from the gym!

DARIUS. Oh, no. Not Todd!

STERLING. In shorts! (*Sterling and Darius blow their whistles and exit at a gallop. Jeffrey watches them go. Steve enters from the opposite side of the stage.*)

STEVE. Jeffrey.

JEFFREY. Steve! Did you—?

STEVE. I got your message. That party. You poor guy. But I was all revved up, so I went out anyway. Dancing.

JEFFREY. Great. I . . . I . . .

STEVE. I know.

JEFFREY. No, I really . . .

STEVE. Jeffrey, it's not the first time this has happened to me. You freaked. Cold feet.

JEFFREY. That's not true . . .

STEVE. Stop it. I can understand, about the HIV thing. It's not easy. But I don't like lying about it. I don't like . . . politeness. Not anymore.

JEFFREY. I'm sorry. I just—couldn't deal with it. Not right now.

STEVE. Okay. Fine. (*A beat.*) There's lots of things we could do. Safe things. Hot things.

JEFFREY. I know . . .

STEVE. But you just . . . don't want to.

JEFFREY. I'm sorry.

STEVE. You're sorry. I'm sorry. It's the new national anthem. You said that you . . . thought about me. That you . . . fantasized.

JEFFREY. I know.

STEVE. Do you? Still?

JEFFREY. (*After a beat.*) Yes.

STEVE. But . . . Jesus Christ. Jesus *Christ*. I can take being sick, I can fucking take dying, but I can't take this.

JEFFREY. You should have told me.

STEVE. I did.

JEFFREY. Sooner! Before . . . things happened!

STEVE. Before I kissed you!

JEFFREY. Yes!

STEVE. Okay! You didn't have all the . . . information. Okay. I've been positive for almost five years. I was sick once, my T-cells are decent, and every once in a while, like fifty times a day—an hour—I get very tired of being a person with AIDS. A red ribbon. So sometimes . . . I forget. Sometimes I choose to forget. Sometimes I choose to be a gay man with a dick. Can you understand? At all?

JEFFREY. Yes.

STEVE. Can I . . . forget again?

JEFFREY. No.

STEVE. Can I do something, say something, that will let this happen? I want you, Jeffrey. I may very well even love you. And that means nothing? That should beat anything. That should win!

JEFFREY. I know.

STEVE. Then why are you the one with the problem? Why do I get to be both sick and begging? (*A beat.*) Why won't you kiss me? (*Jeffrey moves toward Steve. They are about to kiss. Jeffrey pulls away.*)

JEFFREY. I'm sorry—no, I'm sorry I said I'm sorry! I'm sorry you're sick! And I'm sorry I lied! I'm sorry it's not ten years ago, and I'm sorry that life is suddenly . . . radioactive!

STEVE. (*After a beat, staring at Jeffrey.*) Apology accepted. (*Steve exits.*)

JEFFREY. (*Exploding.*) I hate sex! I hate love! I hate the world for giving me everything, and then taking it all back! (*Two Thugs appear from the shadows on either side of Jeffrey.*)

THUG #1. What's up?

JEFFREY. (*Unsure.*) Hey.

THUG #2. Are you . . . gay?

JEFFREY. (*After a beat.*) Mom?

THUG #1. You a faggot?

JEFFREY. Yes.

THUG #2. You queer?

JEFFREY. Please—don't do this.

THUG #1. Suck my dick.

JEFFREY. Do you really want me to do that?

THUG #1. Yeah. No!

THUG #2. Fuck you, man.

JEFFREY. Look, why are you doing this? On Christopher Street?

THUG #1. What is this, like, sacred ground?

JEFFREY. Maybe.

THUG #1. You think you're so special? What are you, one of them fancy faggots? You go to the gym, you got nice friends, you think you're so hot?

JEFFREY. No.

THUG #2. You think you're better than us?

JEFFREY. I'm a waiter.

THUG #1. A waiter? Like at a restaurant?

JEFFREY. Sort of.

THUG #1. They let you touch food? Put your faggoty fingers on it?

JEFFREY. Yes they do. I touch it all the time. I spit in it.

THUG #2. Jesus. What restaurant?

JEFFREY. (*Sizing up the Thugs.*) Pizza Hut.

THUGS #1 and #2. (*Very grossed out.*) Uck! Damn! Shit!

THUG #1. Let's dust his ass.

JEFFREY. Fine. Kill me. You're the ones who'll suffer. The rest of your lives. Buffet style.

THUG #2. Shut the fuck up.

JEFFREY. You have weapons. So do I.

THUG #1. I got a knife. What do you got?

JEFFREY. Irony. Adjectives. Eyebrows.

THUG #2. Fuck you. Hold him! (*Thug #1 holds Jeffrey while Thug #2 punches him in the stomach. Jeffrey doubles over in pain. The Thugs throw Jeffrey onto the ground and kick him. One Thug holds Jeffrey's arms while the other goes through Jeffrey's pockets.*) Shit.

THUG #1. (*Digging in Jeffrey's pocket.*) He's got cash! (*They hear a distant siren. As the Thugs panic, Jeffrey bites the leg of Thug #2.*)

THUG #2. Shit, he's bitin' my leg! I'm gonna get AIDS! (*The siren grows louder.*)

THUG #1. Come on! (*Thug #2 gives Jeffrey one more, particularly vicious kick. The two Thugs run off. Jeffrey moans. He struggles to sit up.*)

JEFFREY. Shit. Owww. (*Mother Teresa enters. She kneels beside Jeffrey, cradling him.*) Terry. (*Mother Teresa strokes him.*) Oww. (*To Mother Teresa.*) You know, when that asshole started kicking me, I had this horrible stupid thought, this flash, that at least it was . . . physical contact. Well, I think I've found my substitute for sex. A substitute for everything. Bruises. Phone machines. Fear. (*Mother Teresa takes Jeffrey's hand. Jeffrey looks up at the night sky. He looks at Mother Teresa. He begins to sing, a bit of the Gershwins' "Nice Work If You Can Get It."*)*

Holding hands at midnight
'Neath a starry sky
Nice work if you can get it
And you can get it if you try
Loving one who loves you
And then taking that vow
Nice work if you can get it
And if you get it
Won't you tell me . . . how . . .

(*The lights fade.*)

---

* See Special Note on Songs and Recordings on copyright page.

ACT TWO

A slide sign appears, reading "Sexual Compulsives Anonymous."

There is a microphone on a stand at center stage. A Man enters and moves to the microphone.

TIM. Hi. My name is Tim, and I am a sexual compulsive.

CHORUS OF OFFSTAGE VOICES. HI, TIM!

TIM. Today I have already performed oral sex on three different people. I can't help myself. I'm an agent. *(Tim leaves the stage. Sharon enters, a clearly depressed woman. She stands at the microphone.)*

SHARON. *(With great difficulty.)* Hi. My name is Sharon, and I . . . I'm a sexual compulsive.

CHORUS OF OFFSTAGE VOICES. HI, SHARON!

SHARON. Oh, that felt good. *(She takes a deep breath.)* I feel like . . . I'm on my way. Admitting I have a problem is the first step to healing. *(Unconsciously, she begins to stroke the microphone stand, up and down, with her hand.)* Now, for the first time in my life, I feel like I don't need a man to define myself. *(She notices a guy in the front row.)* Hi there. *(Sharon, very frustrated, leaves the stage. Dave enters and stands at the microphone.)*

DAVE. Hi. My name is Dave, and I'm sexually compulsive.

CHORUS OF OFFSTAGE VOICES. HI, DAVE!

DAVE. I just love sex. Maybe it's because I have a constant erection, twenty-four hours a day. Or because my penis is fourteen inches long.

CHORUS OF OFFSTAGE VOICES. (*Very interested.*) Oooh. Hi, Dave. (*Sharon reappears, staring at Dave, completely smitten. He nods his head, and she follows him off-stage. As they exit, Jeffrey enters and stands at the microphone.*)

JEFFREY. Hi. My name is Jeffrey, and I'm . . . just like you.

CHORUS OF OFFSTAGE VOICES. Jeffrey . . .

JEFFREY. I'm a sexual compulsive. But I haven't had sex in almost six months! (*Applause from off-stage.*) I never even think about sex, not anymore. And I used to . . . be compulsive. (*More applause and cheers.*) All because of Billy Kearny. I blame him! That's where it started. He kept daring me. "I dare you to take off your clothes—even your underpants." "I dare you to kiss me—on the mouth." Oh God. Two naked fourteen-year-old boys, in front of the big mirror in my parents' bedroom. I'm having sex. And I'm watching myself have sex. Please don't do that. Please don't stop. (*Jeffrey's memory has become very alive and emotional.*) Stop. (*Lights up on the full stage. Jeffrey is wearing his waiter's uniform. He takes his place behind a long rectangular table covered with a floral chintz tablecloth. There is a silver chafing dish on the table, along with china and linen napkins. To the audience.*) I'm working. A memorial. Another one. At a townhouse. It's for a curator, at the Met. The speakers are great. His straight brother. His doctor. His gorgeous Italian boyfriend. (*Jeffrey smiles at the boyfriend, across the room.*) Oh, my God, I am so disgusting. Do you know what I'm doing? I'm cruising a memorial. (*Sterling enters, in a stylish black suit, with a cocktail.*)

STERLING. Oh, please—everybody is. That boyfriend. Carlo. I'm telling you, while Jessye Norman was singing that hymn, everyone was watching *that* him. It's not that we're not sad, it's just . . . there are all these guys here.

JEFFREY. And we've been through so many of them—memorials. Each one more moving and creative than the last.

STERLING. The Gay Men's Chorus doing Charles Ives.

JEFFREY. Vanessa Redgrave reading Auden.

STERLING. Siegfried and Roy.

JEFFREY. (*Looking across the room.*) Who is that? Talking to Darius?

STERLING. It's Todd Malcolm.

JEFFREY. What?

STERLING. You know, from the gym.

JEFFREY. Oh my God.

STERLING. Jeffrey . . .

JEFFREY. He must weigh eighty pounds.

STERLING. He just got out of the hospital.

JEFFREY. He's blind, isn't he?

STERLING. It's a side effect—they think that ninety percent of the vision will return.

JEFFREY. Oh my God.

STERLING. Don't stare.

JEFFREY. Don't stare? When I first came to this city, he was . . . a god. I'd never seen anything like that. I used to watch him, dancing with his lover. People would gasp. (*He begins taking off his service jacket.*) I'm sorry.

STERLING. What are you doing?

JEFFREY. I can't work here. I can't go to one more of these. I can't see one more twenty-eight-year-old man with a cane.

STERLING. Don't be ridiculous.

JEFFREY. What are we doing? Cruising? Giggling? Pretending it's all some sort of hoot? I can't keep passing hors d'oeuvres in a graveyard! I went out with Todd! I just saw him in the hospital, and I don't even recognize him!

STERLING. Stop it! (*Darius enters, in a dark suit, with a cocktail.*)

DARIUS. Hi, guys. Did you see Todd?

STERLING. Of course.

DARIUS. He looks better.

JEFFREY. Darius, Todd is dying! (*Darius faces him; Jeffrey realizes his mistake.*) He's . . . doing okay, I guess.

DARIUS. At least he's out of St. Vincent's. I mean, three months! Remember that collage he made on the wall? With all those Armani ads, and anything with Ann-Margret? (*He realizes something is wrong.*) What's going on here?

STERLING. Jeffrey is just having some sort of anxiety moment.

DARIUS. About Todd, right? It's okay. Do you know what we were talking about? This memorial. The cannoli are frozen. The drinks are watered. And I hated that singer. At my memorial, I want Liza!

STERLING. You are not having a memorial.

DARIUS. I mean, like, in a million years.

STERLING. You are not going to get sick. I thought I'd made that clear.

DARIUS. But I *was* sick. I had pneumonia, and it went away. But I want—the Winter Garden. I do! And I want all the other cats to come out . . . and sing "Darius" to the tune of "Memory." (*He sings, to the tune of "Memory," while making paw-like gestures.*) "Darius, we all thought you were fabulous . . ."

STERLING. Fine. And the service will run for years.

JEFFREY. Sterling!

STERLING. What?

JEFFREY. I mean . . . aren't we all being just a bit much? About all this?

DARIUS. What do you mean?

JEFFREY. I mean—it's a memorial.

DARIUS. So?

JEFFREY. We're making remarks. We're dishing it.

STERLING. Really, darling. Picture mine. And Jeffrey, do remember—open coffin. They can say it to my face.

JEFFREY. (*Viciously.*) Good idea.

DARIUS. Well, I like it. I mean, cute guys, and Liza, and dish—it's not a cure for AIDS, Jeffrey. But it's the opposite of AIDS. Right?

STERLING. Shh, bow your heads. We're supposed to be praying. (*They all bow their heads.*)

JEFFREY. (*To Sterling.*) What are you praying for?

STERLING. What do you think? No more disease, no more prejudice.

DARIUS. And?

STERLING. (*Glancing around.*) No more chintz.

NURSE'S VOICE. (*On PA system.*) Scott Elliman to the front desk—Scott Elliman. Visiting hours are over in fifteen minutes. Fifteen minutes. Regular visiting hours are ten AM to four thirty. And six to eight PM. (*Lights fade on the memorial. Lights up on a row of fiberglass waiting-room chairs. There is an exit sign, a sign reading "St. Vincent's," and a metal cart holding an array of medical paraphernalia. Jeffrey sits in one of the chairs. Steve enters; he and Jeffrey see each other.*)

JEFFREY. Are you following me?

STEVE. Of course, I always follow men into clinics.

JEFFREY. How are you?

STEVE. Still positive. Darn.

JEFFREY. Okay . . .

STEVE. And you? What brings you to St. Vincent's high-profile outpatient facility? White sale?

JEFFREY. Blood test. (*Steve grins and crosses his fingers on both hands.*)

STEVE. I'm sorry. There was one thing I never told you. I'm HIV-positive—and obnoxious.

JEFFREY. I knew.

STEVE. Still no acting work?

JEFFREY. No.

STEVE. Still no day job?

JEFFREY. No.

STEVE. Still no sex?

JEFFREY. Steve.

STEVE. You know, Jeffrey, St. Vincent's is not just another Blue Cross pavilion and biopsy barn. Oh no.

JEFFREY. What is it with you?

STEVE. Oh, I don't know. Being here, in my living room, and seeing you—it's a killer combo. It's just got me all a-tingle. What shall I wear?

(*Steve goes to the medical cart and begins holding up various items. His tone is that of a haughty, scintillating host at a fashion show.*) What will today's sassy and sophisticated HIV-positive male be wearing this spring, to tempt the elusive, possibly negative waitperson? Let's begin with the basics—a gown! (*With a flourish, he unfurls a green hospital gown and puts it on over his clothes.*) It's crisp, it's cotton, it's been sterilized over five thousand times—it always works. (*He begins to model the gown, as if on a runway.*) It's a go-nowhere, do-nothing look, with a peekaboo rear and (*Indicating a blood-stain.*) a perky plasma accent. Add pearls and pentamidine, and you're ready for remission!

JEFFREY. Only in green?

STEVE. Please! Green is the navy blue of health care. But it's the accessories that really make the man. Earrings . . . (*He holds two syringes up to his ears and aims them at Jeffrey.*) Careful! Hat . . . (*He places a bed pan on his head as a chapeau; he removes the bed pan and reads the label.*) "Sanicare"! And of course . . . (*He holds up two surgical gloves.*) Gloves!

JEFFREY. (*Very entertained, applauding.*) I'll take it!

STEVE. Cash or charge? (*He pretends to take a charge card from Jeffrey.*) Oh no—but according to this, madam is HIV-negative. This is not for you. This is only for a select few, the truly chic, the fashion plates who may not live to see the fall collections.

JEFFREY. Steve . . .

STEVE. Can I show you something in—a healthy person? Someone without complications? Someone you could bear to touch?

JEFFREY. Look . . .

STEVE. Okay. Okay. Show's over. (*He curtsies.*) Merci.

JEFFREY. Are you all right?

STEVE. (*Tugging off the gown.*) What do you care? Stop being so compassionate. No one's watching.

JEFFREY. Jesus Christ!

STEVE. I'm sorry, I'm a little manic today. And I didn't expect to see you here. I'm being a jerk.

JEFFREY. No, you're fine. I admire your spirit. And your humor.

STEVE. Don't admire me! Fuck me! Admiration gets me an empty dance card, except for the chest X-rays and the occasional march on Washington. Admiration gets me a lovely memorial and a square on the quilt!

NURSE'S VOICE. (*On PA system.*) Jeffrey Calloway to examining room one—Jeffrey Calloway.

STEVE. Your table is ready.

JEFFREY. Do you want to go first?

STEVE. What?

JEFFREY. I don't mind.

STEVE. Jeffrey, I am not here to see the doctor. Surprise!

JEFFREY. You're not?

STEVE. No, I'm on my way to the tenth floor, to see the AIDS babies.

JEFFREY. Why?

STEVE. As a volunteer. The last time I was up there, there were eight. They were all abandoned, or their parents had died. And no one would touch them—the nurses were all scared, or busy. The first baby I saw was just lying there, staring, not even crying. But when I held her, she finally smiled and gurgled and acted like a baby. We're all AIDS babies, Jeffrey. And I don't want to die without being held. (*Steve exits, lights fade on the clinic. Jeffrey's Dad enters; he is a straightforward midwestern man, in a cardigan and Sansabelt slacks. He is on the phone.*)

DAD. Well, howdy, stranger. (*To off-stage.*) It's Jeff!

MOM. (*From off-stage.*) Oh!

JEFFREY. Can you tell if you're having a nervous breakdown? Or do you just wake up in a strait jacket, and notice the bars on the windows? I called my parents. (*Jeffrey picks up a phone receiver and continues to address the audience.*)

DAD. Well, isn't this a special occasion!

JEFFREY. I love them. I mean, I wasn't kicked out or abused or anything. But they still live in Wisconsin, and we just sort of agree not to get too personal.

DAD. Your mother's right here. (*Jeffrey's Mom enters, in a cardigan, a wrap skirt, and sneakers. She is wholesome and sensible.*)

JEFFREY. But what if I could really talk to them? What if they really had some answers? Or would that just be too weird?

DAD. So how are things in the Big Apple?

JEFFREY. (*Into the phone.*) Dad—I've stopped having sex.

DAD. (*To Mom.*) Eileen, Jeff's stopped having sex.

MOM. (*Concerned.*) Let me get on the other line. (*She picks up an extension.*) No sex? You mean just safe sex, don't you, dear?

JEFFREY. No, Mom, I hate safe sex.

DAD. Wrestling with those condoms.

MOM. Water-based lubricants.

DAD. Dry kissing.

MOM. Sweetheart—are you a top or a bottom?

JEFFREY. Mother!

DAD. Have you tried any of those workshops?

MOM. What about a jerk-off club?

DAD. How about—phone sex?

JEFFREY. What?

MOM. Fred, let's help him out. (*To Jeffrey.*) Darling, what are you wearing?

JEFFREY. Jeans and a shirt.

DAD. (*Very matter-of-fact.*) Oh, that's hot.

MOM. That's very hot.

DAD. Are you alone?

JEFFREY. Dad! I am not going to have phone sex with you and Mom!

MOM. Oh, don't be such a stick-in-the-mud. This is your mother. I've bathed you. I've changed your diapers.

DAD. Is that what you like?

JEFFREY. (*Panicking.*) Operator?

MOM. Darling, you can't just resign from the human race. Have you looked at any videos?

JEFFREY. Videos?

DAD. Hard-core. Have you explored masturbation?

MOM. As if we have to ask. Sometimes I never did get into that bathroom.

DAD. We like that new Jeff Stryker film. *Powertool II.*

MOM. Jeff isn't in that one, dear. It's got Lex Baldwin. He's a little short, but he's got beautiful skin. And oh, that scene in the prison laundry!

DAD. I like Jeff. I say stick with the best. *Powertool. The Young and the Hung.* I'm from Wisconsin.

MOM. Dear, do you like it when they shave their assholes?

JEFFREY. Shave their *what?*

DAD. And what about this fellow Steve? Seems very nice.

JEFFREY. Dad—Steve is HIV-positive.

MOM. And a dreamboat. Check the basket. (*Jeffrey hangs up.*)

JEFFREY. Oh my God. I'm sorry, I'm sorry. That is not really the way it went. (*Mom and Dad switch their phone receivers to opposite ears.*)

DAD. So, you keeping busy?

JEFFREY. Oh yes, I worked five nights last week.

MOM. That big city. It sounds very exciting.

JEFFREY. Sometimes. So how are you? Doing okay?

DAD. A touch of arthritis. Can't complain.

MOM. Have you tried Motrin? We love it!

JEFFREY. No, not yet.

DAD. So—when will we see you again?

JEFFREY. Soon. As soon as I can take some time off. Christmas for sure.

MOM. I love you.

DAD. Take care.

JEFFREY. Dad . . . (*Lights down on Mom and Dad. A stained-glass window begins to glow. An altar railing appears. Sacred music is heard. We are in St. Patrick's Cathedral. Jeffrey puts on a jacket and kneels at the railing, his back to the audience. He crosses himself, bows his head, and begins to pray. A priest, Father Dan, enters, wearing the traditional collar and full-length cassock. He kneels beside Jeffrey, crosses himself, bows his head, and begins to pray. After* *a Moment, Father Dan's hand reaches out and grabs Jeffrey's behind. Jeffrey stares at the priest, who withdraws his hand. Both men bow their heads and resume praying. Once again Father Dan's hand reaches out and grabs Jeffrey's behind, with a great deal of conviction. Jeffrey squirms and stares at Father Dan.)* Excuse me? *(Father Dan rises with great dignity. He stands, and motions with his head.)*

FATHER DAN. Come on. *(Father Dan exits. Jeffrey, quite perplexed, follows him. Lights down on the altar. Lights up on a storeroom somewhere in the cathedral, with piles of hymnals and a Gothic bench. Father Dan enters, followed by Jeffrey. Father Dan is very working-class, a tough, two-fisted guy. He is passionate in his beliefs; he is a dedicated, thoughtful, lusty man, clinging to sanity while surrounded by absurdity and horror. This scene must be played with great ferocity and need; it is not just a chat or debate.)* In here.

JEFFREY. Where are we?

FATHER DAN. A storeroom. Some old hymnals. They need to be rebound. *(Father Dan grabs Jeffrey and kisses him. Jeffrey pulls away.)*

JEFFREY. Hey!

FATHER DAN. What? What's wrong?

JEFFREY. *(Stunned.)* Excuse me?

FATHER DAN. Is it the collar? Is that a turn-off? Aren't you Catholic? *(Father Dan makes another lunge at Jeffrey, chasing him around the room. Jeffrey fends him off.)*

JEFFREY. Wait! Are you really a priest?

FATHER DAN. Of course.

JEFFREY. But what's going on? Why did you bring me here?

FATHER DAN. I'm attracted to you. The door's locked.

JEFFREY. Wait—you're a priest? And you cruise guys at St. Patrick's?

FATHER DAN. Yeah! And what were you doing in the pews?

JEFFREY. I was not! Aren't you supposed to be straight? And celibate?

FATHER DAN. Wait—maybe you didn't hear me. I'm a Catholic priest. Historically, that's somewhere in between chorus boy and florist.

C'mere. (*Father Dan chases Jeffrey again. Jeffrey pushes him away with great fury.*)

JEFFREY. No! Get away from me! Don't touch me!

FATHER DAN. (*Holding up his hands, backing off.*) All right! All right! I won't! What's wrong? (*Jeffrey tries to pull himself together. During the following speech, his despair, rage, and yearning will overwhelm him.*)

JEFFREY. Two nights ago I was at the ballet, with my friends. It's *Nutcracker.* And it's intermission, and we're walking down this wide marble staircase, and suddenly—Darius falls. He just crumples up, and pitches forward, and keeps tumbling, and his legs are all bent, and there's blood everywhere, and Jesus—he's a dancer! He's just a kid! And he's so dehydrated from some fucking AIDS drug that he can't even stand up! And all the parents are screaming about their kids, and the blood, and we get him into an ambulance, and he's home now, but I've been walking for forty-eight hours! And I finally come here, to church, where I haven't been since I was twelve, and all I keep thinking is—what if it was Steve? How could I love someone, and watch that happen?

FATHER DAN. Wait—who's Darius? Who's Steve?

JEFFREY. (*Exploding.*) Why did He do this? Why did God make the world this way, and why do I have to live in it? You're a priest—you have to tell me! Don't you?

FATHER DAN. All right. If I tell you—if I show you the true face of God—will you listen?

JEFFREY. Of course! That's why I'm here!

FATHER DAN. Will you really listen?

JEFFREY. Yes! (*Father Dan sits Jeffrey down.*)

FATHER DAN. First, here's how you see God. He's a Columbia recording artist.

JEFFREY. What?

FATHER DAN. You got your idea of God from where most gay kids get it—the album cover of *My Fair Lady*. Original cast. It's got this Hirschfeld caricature of George Bernard Shaw up in the clouds, manipulating Rex Harrison and Julie Andrews on strings, like marionettes. It was your parents' album, you were little, you thought it was a picture of God. As, I believe, did Shaw. Right?

JEFFREY. (*Surprised.*) Yeah.

FATHER DAN. Well, you were almost there. Because God is on that record. Lerner and Loewe! "Why Can't the English." "Wouldn't It Be Loverly." I'm telling you, the only times I really feel the presence of God are when I'm having sex, and during a great Broadway musical!

JEFFREY. You're nuts.

FATHER DAN. Excuse me? All you people, you're worshipping resurrections, virgin births, Ben-Hur, and I'm nuts?

JEFFREY. I'm talking about a plague! About, I don't know—evil!

FATHER DAN. Yes! Satan! Well, that's another story. I've seen him. He's among us. He's real.

JEFFREY. What? Disease? Hospitals? Fear?

FATHER DAN. *Phantom. Miss Saigon. Sunset Boulevard!* Know ye the signs of the devil: overmiking, smoke machines, trouble with Equity.

JEFFREY. (*Rising to leave.*) Gotta go . . .

FATHER DAN. Why? Because I haven't told you the secret of life, in five words or less? You're getting antsy?

JEFFREY. I need to know!

FATHER DAN. Okay, okay. I am so horny! Do you know what it's like in that confessional? "Father, I abused myself eight times last week." "Father, I'm attracted to my brother-in-law." "Father, I'm having impure thoughts about my soccer coach." Where are the Polaroids? What am I, a mind reader? Say six Hail Marys and bring me his shorts! (*Jeffrey starts to leave again.*) Okay, okay—secret of life. All of those people out there, in the pews, they're not so bad, most of them. They're just like you—you just want a few mindless answers, some autocomfort, and you're a little too uptight for Madame Zora in her storefront. But you've only got one problem—you're completely wrong!

JEFFREY. I am?

FATHER DAN. Of course! Who's your God? Some prissy classroom monitor, nodding at the brown-nosers, and smacking anyone who gets out of line? A God who does what—sends us Mussolimi and brain cancer to test us, for our own good? That's not God—that's Aunt Betty with an enema!

JEFFREY. So what—there's no God? It's all just random, luck of the draw, *bad* luck of the draw!

FATHER DAN. Darling, my darling—have you ever been to a picnic? And someone blows up a balloon, and everyone starts tossing it around? And the balloon drifts and it catches the light, and it's always just about to touch the ground, but someone always gets there just in time, to tap it back up. That balloon—that's God. The very best in all of us. The kindness. The heavy petting. The eleven o'clock numbers.

JEFFREY. But what about the bad stuff? When the balloon does hit the ground, when it bursts?

FATHER DAN. Who cares? Evil bores me. It's one-note. It doesn't sing. Of course life sucks; it always will—so why not make the most of it? How dare you not lunge for any shred of happiness?

JEFFREY. With Steve, who's sick? Who I'm afraid to touch?

FATHER DAN. So maybe you need a rubber or a surgical mask or a roll of Saran Wrap! But how dare you give up sex, when there are children in Europe who can't get a date! There is only one real blasphemy—the refusal of joy! Of a corsage and a kiss!

JEFFREY. So what're you telling me? Perk up? Look on the sunny side? Get out more?

FATHER DAN. What's your alternative? When did despair become enjoyable? Grief, yes; tears, of course; but terminal gloom? Who does that help? Even Brecht wrote musicals.

JEFFREY. If you believe all this, all this smile-button gospel, if those people out there have it all wrong—then why did you become a priest?

FATHER DAN. I'm working from within. That's why I have to stick around, kiss a few rings, get to be a cardinal. 'Cause the next time we choose a pope, I've got the guy.

JEFFREY. What? Who?

FATHER DAN. Tommy Tune! Perfect, huh? Someone upbeat? I know it's nuts, of course it's ridiculous—who could afford him? But that's my church—high kicks to heaven.

JEFFREY. *(Backing away.)* You're no priest! I don't know what you are! You're just some sort of lunatic, dressed up in a priest suit!

FATHER DAN. Isn't that redundant? *(Pursuing Jeffrey again.)* Here we go!

JEFFREY. Get away from me!

FATHER DAN. I told you the meaning of life! Now put out! *(Father Julian, an earnest young priest, knocks on the door.)*

FATHER JULIAN. Father Maginnis, please! I don't know what to do! You have to help me!

FATHER DAN. All I wanted was a quickie. *(He opens the door.)* Yes, my son?

FATHER JULIAN. Father, Mass is about to begin. The congregation is starting to worry.

FATHER DAN. Oh, all right! Those people! What would happen if I didn't show up? Animal sacrifice?

FATHER JULIAN. *(Shocked.)* Father!

FATHER DAN. *(To Father Julian.)* You're new. You'll learn. *(To Jeffrey.)* Think about what I said. Will you do that? And call me?

JEFFREY. I can't.

FATHER JULIAN. Father, the altar boys are in place!

FATHER DAN. *(To Father Julian.)* Don't tease. *(Father Dan and Father Julian exit, followed by Jeffrey. The scenery for the storeroom begins to vanish. Joyous, irresistible disco music is heard. Steve appears, wearing an official Gay Pride T-shirt. He carries a bullhorn and a clipboard. We hear parade noise.)*

STEVE. (*Into bullhorn.*) The parade is about to begin! The first unit will be as follows: Dykes on Bikes! (*The roar of motorcycles is heard.*) Concerned Pan-Asian Bisexuals! (*A cheer is heard.*) Black Gay Republicans! (*There is no response.*) Hello? (*A middle-aged woman runs on. She wears a New Jersey Mafia princess look: stretch pants, high heels, bouffant hair, outsize sunglasses, lots of gold jewelry, a quilted lamé bag, and a glitzy sequined sweatshirt with shoulder pads. Animal prints might also be a favorite. She speaks with a nasal Jersey accent; she is rowdy and forthright, clearly a social leader and a take-charge person. She is Mrs. Marcangelo.*)

MRS. MARCANGELO. (*To Steve.*) Excuse me! Are you with the parade? I'm lost!

STEVE. No problem. Which group are you with? (*Angelique Marcangelo enters. Angelique is the woman's son, in drag, and they are dressed somewhat alike, overdone and cheery.*)

ANGELIQUE. Ma! Did you find out? (*To Steve.*) We're marching together.

MRS. MARCANGELO. (*Sincerely.*) I am so proud of my preoperative transsexual lesbian son! (*Jeffrey enters, carrying a full laundry bag.*)

JEFFREY. Steve.

STEVE. Jeffrey! We're about to start! Who are you marching with?

MRS. MARCANGELO. (*To Jeffrey.*) Excuse me—could you take our picture? With this nice man? (*She hands Jeffrey her camera and poses with Steve and Angelique.*) It's for my album. It's our first parade!

ANGELIQUE. We're going to be on a truck!

STEVE. (*To Jeffrey.*) Parents of Transsexuals.

ANGELIQUE. Preoperative Transsexual Lesbians.

JEFFREY. Okay . . .

MRS. MARCANGELO. Believe me—

JEFFREY. (*Snapping the photo.*) Smile!

MRS. MARCANGELO. —at first I was as confused as anyone. (*She takes back the camera.*) More confused. When Anthony first came to me—

ANGELIQUE. Angelique, Ma.

MRS. MARCANGELO. You were still Tony, at the time. He said, "Ma, I want to be a woman—I've always felt like one." I said, "What, are you gay?" He said, "No, I'm not gay—I'm a lesbian!"

ANGELIQUE. Exactly!

MRS. MARCANGELO. And my first thought is, when I was pregnant with you, what did I do? Did I Tilt-a-Whirl? Did I bungee jump?

ANGELIQUE. But you didn't judge.

MRS. MARCANGELO. Listen, alone, late at night, I judged plenty. I judged you, I judged me, I said, I don't understand, why does he need this? And you know what made me feel better?

STEVE. What?

MRS. MARCANGELO. Those Summer Olympics. I was watching them on TV, feeling sorry for myself. And they kept showing the parents, of all those girls in the pool, those . . .

ANGELIQUE. Synchronized swimmers.

MRS. MARCANGELO. Exactly. And the parents were all crying, and waving little flags, and I just thought, Hey—if they can be proud of their kids, just because they can stand on their heads in the deep end, then I can be proud of mine! (*Sterling enters, wearing sunglasses and carrying a large, rolled-up banner.*)

STERLING. Jeffrey! Steven! (*Sterling and Steve kiss.*)

MRS. MARCANGELO. Look at that—two men kissing! (*She snaps a photo and says to Angelique.*) Why can't you be like that?

ANGELIQUE. *Ma* . . . do we need sunscreen?

MRS. MARCANGELO. (*Rummaging through her shoulder bag.*) Right here.

STERLING. Has anyone seen Darius? I lost him somewhere near the S&M people. I swear, I saw this terrifying man, wearing a dog collar, a harness, and jackboots, snarling at me. And I look closer, and it's my upholsterer. (*Darius runs in, wearing a T-shirt, shorts, and boots, very excited.*)

DARIUS. Should I get my nipples pierced?

STERLING. What?

DARIUS. I just saw this big guy, totally naked, except for a jockstrap and two big gold rings, right here and here. (*He gestures on his chest.*)

STERLING. For guest towels.

MRS. MARCANGELO. Which group are you with?

STERLING. Gay Men Who Need a Cigarette. (*Sterling and Darius unfurl their banner, which stretches between them on a pole. The banner is beautifully lettered and decorated with expensive fringe and tassels. Sterling and Darius read aloud the words on the banner.*)

DARIUS. "Interior Designers Fight AIDS."

STERLING. "Care with Flair." (*Loud parade noise is heard—bands, motorcycles, disco, etc.*)

STEVE. We're starting! (*Into bullhorn.*) Parents of Pre-Ops! Prepare to move!

ANGELIQUE. (*To her mother.*) How do I look?

MRS. MARCANGELO. (*Tenderly.*) Gorgeous!

ANGELIQUE and MRS. MARCANGELO. (*Protecting their coiffures as they attempt to hug.*) Hair! (*The Marcangelos exit, very excited.*)

STERLING. Come along, Jeffrey—help with this thing.

JEFFREY. (*Holding up his laundry bag.*) Delicate hand washables—I'll catch up.

DARIUS. All right! (*To Sterling.*) Move it! (*Sterling and Darius exit, carrying their banner.*)

STEVE. Dump that stuff. I'll put you on the best float—with the porn stars.

JEFFREY. No, it's okay. I'm not marching.

STEVE. You're not marching?

JEFFREY. Not this year. I can't. I am not an asset to this parade.

STEVE. Jeffrey, I hope this doesn't have anything to do with me. I know I gave you a pretty tough time.

JEFFREY. You didn't.

STEVE. I tried. But it really is good to see you. You look great. And I'm not hitting on you.

JEFFREY. Why not?

STEVE. Oh, Jeffrey. (*They stare at each other, in an awkward Moment of renewed longing.*)

JEFFREY. I should go. I'm meeting someone.

STEVE. (*With a leer.*) Pardon me?

JEFFREY. My sublet. I hope.

STEVE. Your sublet? Are you moving? Where?

JEFFREY. It doesn't matter.

STEVE. *Where?*

JEFFREY. I shouldn't have said anything!

STEVE. Come on!

JEFFREY. Back to Wisconsin.

STEVE. Wisconsin?

JEFFREY. Not for a month! I have to go . . .

STEVE. Wait a minute!

JEFFREY. It's a very good idea! There are no car alarms, no potholes . . .

STEVE. No parades. What about Sterling? And Darius?

JEFFREY. Don't tell them!

STEVE. *What?*

JEFFREY. I'm going to—I just have to find a spare moment, we've all been so busy . . .

STEVE. You are leaving town? Now?

JEFFREY. Darius is doing much better! He looks great! He's off the Intraconozal, he's gained his weight back . . .

STEVE. You are really a piece of work.

JEFFREY. (*After a beat.*) Yes I am! I'm a shit, and I'm a coward, and I'm a traitor. And I'm running away, just as fast as my frequent flier miles can carry me! Because if I stay here, I will lose it! And how does that help anyone?

STEVE. And what are you going to do? In Wisconsin?

JEFFREY. Live! Breathe! Hide! Until it's all over!

STEVE. Until what's all over? AIDS? Or your life?

JEFFREY. (*Very distraught.*) Either.

STEVE. Good to have known you. A growth experience.

JEFFREY. Okay, look, maybe I'll come back. Who knows? Someday.

STEVE. There is the difference between you and me. In that one word. "Someday." A real luxury item. (*Sean, another marcher, enters. He is attractive and appealing.*)

SEAN. There you are! (*Sean and Steve kiss. Steve gets rather passionate.*)

STEVE. Sean, this is Jeffrey.

SEAN. (*Very friendly.*) Really? At last! I've heard way too much about you!

JEFFREY. Oh, those tabloids. Are you guys . . . ?

STEVE. (*To Sean.*) For what? Two months now?

SEAN. (*To Jeffrey.*) We met on the parade committee. (*To Steve.*) They need you. (*To Jeffrey.*) Great to meet you. (*Chuck Farling, a TV reporter, enters, in a blazer and a startlingly blond blown-dry hair style. He carries a microphone and speaks to the camera. He is vain and fatuous, very full of himself and his own importance.*)

CHUCK. (*Adjusting the hidden headset in his ear.*) Yeah, I know we've got to cover this thing, but why me? (*Smiling for the camera.*) Good afternoon, this is Chuck Farling, here at Manhattan's some would say notorious Gay Pride March. Homosexuals have made great strides in recent years, and—I'm surrounded by them. Your names?

STEVE. Steve Howard.

SEAN. Sean Bailey.

CHUCK. And are you . . . homosexuals?

STEVE. Yes, Chuck, we are.

SEAN. We are righteous members of the Queer Nation!

STEVE. And you?

CHUCK. No! Oh no, I'm . . . with Channel 9 Action News. (*Sterling and Darius enter and spot Chuck.*)

DARIUS. (*Crazed.*) Chuck!

CHUCK. Yes, young man? (*To the camera.*) Another gay marcher.

DARIUS. I love your show! You are so cute! (*Trying to compose himself, for the camera.*) Hi. We're here, we're queer . . . (*Unable to control himself.*) . . . and we're on TV!

STERLING. Chuck, I'm truly sorry. He gets overexcited. (*Sterling has been staring at Chuck's hairpiece. Sterling reaches over and touches Chuck's hair, lightly. Chuck pulls back. Sterling reassures him.)* No, it's working, really.

CHUCK. Spirits are running very high here in Washington Square! *(He spots Jeffrey.)* And here's a regular fellow—why, he could be anyone, your son, your brother, the guy next door. Your name? *(Chuck strides over to interview Jeffrey. Darius, Sterling, Steve, and Sean all move right along with Chuck; they are all eager to stay on camera. They group themselves behind Sterling and Darius's banner.)*

JEFFREY. Jeffrey.

CHUCK. And how are you celebrating Gay Pride Day?

JEFFREY. I'm . . . doing my laundry.

STEVE. His laundry! Just like a regular person! You see, all gays are not flamboyant and overtly . . . extreme. *(Darius flamboyantly kicks one leg out from behind the banner.)* So you're doing your laundry, here on Gay Pride Day.

JEFFREY. Yes, Chuck, I am.

CHUCK. *(To the camera.)* Provocative. *(The Marcangelos enter. They see Chuck and scream. Jeffrey exits.)*

MRS. MARCANGELO. Chuck!

ANGELIQUE. Chuck Farling!

MRS. MARCANGELO. We love you! *(The Marcangelos run over to Chuck and look into the camera.)* Hi, Theresa—hi, Mrs. Russamano—it's us! We're on TV! With Chuck Farling!

CHUCK. Well, it seems we have a mother-and-daughter team here with us—is that right?

ANGELIQUE. That's right!

MRS. MARCANGELO. Don't ask.

CHUCK. And what are you ladies doing to celebrate this Gay Pride occasion? Something very special?

ANGELIQUE. You bet, Chuck! We're going to ride on a flatbed truck, for all the world to see!

MRS. MARCANGELO. Because we are proud of who and what we are!

CHUCK. And after the parade?

STERLING. (*Taking Chuck's microphone.*) Angelique is going to remove her penis. (*Everyone cheers "YAY!!!", as Chuck looks distinctly uncomfortable and motions with a finger across his throat to his film crew—"Cut!"*)

NURSE'S VOICE. (*On PA system.*) Dr. Matthews to ICU—Dr. Matthews. Joel Garber to the front desk—Joel Garber. (*Lights dim on the parade. Lights up on St. Vincent's waiting room. Sterling enters and sits in one of the fiberglass chairs. He is alone. After a beat, Jeffrey enters.*)

JEFFREY. How is he?

STERLING. No change.

JEFFREY. Can I see him?

STERLING. No. He won't know who you are. Or talk. It's a coma.

JEFFREY. Do you need anything?

STERLING. No, I'm okay. Where were you?

JEFFREY. Working. My last job. The Hilton. A whimper. Is his mom in there?

STERLING. No. She's back at our place, getting some rest. He doesn't recognize anyone.

JEFFREY. You never know, for sure—

STERLING. (*Cutting him off.*) No he doesn't. He's dead.

JEFFREY. What?

STERLING. Half an hour ago. I . . . that's the first time I've said it. Out loud. A brain hemorrhage. That's why it was so fast. Brain things. That's why three weeks ago, he was marching on Fifth Avenue. With me.

JEFFREY. Sterling, I am so sorry.

STERLING. You're what? (*Jeffrey tries to embrace Sterling. Sterling pulls away.*) You're sorry? Thank you, Jeffrey. Thank you. Darius is dead. I'm sorry too. (*He takes a breath, and then, sincerely.*) I'm sorry.

JEFFREY. Is there anything I can do?

STERLING. (*Very straightforward, not emotional.*) I wasn't . . . enough. I wasn't important enough. I couldn't snub it. I couldn't scare it off, with a look. I couldn't shield him, with raw silk, and tassels, and tie-backs. The limits of style.

JEFFREY. You loved Darius. He loved you.

STERLING. Jesus, Jeffrey, how can you?

JEFFREY. What?

STERLING. Jeffrey, I don't know why, I'm obviously out of my mind, but right now—no, I don't. I don't hate you.

JEFFREY. You hate me?

STERLING. (*Standing, moving away.*) Jeffrey, perhaps you should just not be here. Just right now.

JEFFREY. Sterling, please—let me help you. What can I do?

STERLING. What can you do? Nothing! You're leaving. You're going away, to . . . someplace insane.

JEFFREY. I can stay. For a few more days.

STERLING. No. Please go. You are not part of this. This has nothing to do with you. (*Jeffrey, very upset, starts to leave.*) You know, Darius said he thought you were the saddest person he ever knew.

JEFFREY. (*Stunned.*) Why did he say that?

STERLING. Because he was sick. He had a fatal disease. And he was one million times happier than you.

JEFFREY. (*After a beat.*) You loved Darius. And look what happens. Do you want me to go through this? With Steve?

STERLING. Yes. (*Mother Teresa appears. She gestures at Sterling; he freezes. She gestures again, and Darius enters, in a dazzling, all white version of his* Cats *costume.*)

DARIUS. Jeffrey—guess what?

JEFFREY. Sterling!

DARIUS. (*Sitting on one of the fiberglass chairs.*) You know that tunnel of light you're supposed to see, right before you die? It really happens! The first person I saw was my Aunt Berniece. She had emphysema. She hugged me and she said (*As Aunt Berniece, crossing his legs, taking a drag on a cigarette and speaking in a gravelly voice*), "Darling, can you get me a pair for the matinee?"

JEFFREY. (*Staggered.*) What are you? Some sort of grief-induced hallucination? Are you a symptom? Why did you come back?

DARIUS. To see you. I figured you got here too late, after I was already in the coma. Did you bring me anything?

JEFFREY. Um . . . flowers!

DARIUS. (*Looking around.*) Where?

JEFFREY. I was in a hurry!

DARIUS. Jeffrey, I'm dead. You're not.

JEFFREY. I know that.

DARIUS. You do? Prove it.

JEFFREY. What do you mean?

DARIUS. Go dancing. Go to a show. Make trouble. Make out. Hate AIDS, Jeffrey. Not life.

JEFFREY. How?

DARIUS. Just think of AIDS as . . . the guest that won't leave. The one we all hate. But you have to remember.

JEFFREY. What?

DARIUS. Hey—it's still our party. (*We hear an orchestra tuning up. Darius stands.*) That's the orchestra. I have to go.

JEFFREY. But . . . but is that it? Is that all you can tell me?

DARIUS. Be nice to Sterling. (*Mother Teresa gestures. Gorgeous romantic music begins, perhaps the Gershwins' "Embraceable You."* Sterling unfreezes. He and Darius gaze at each other and smile. The music swells.*) See you! I'm on. (*Darius exits. Sterling exits in the opposite direction. The lights change. The skyline of Manhattan appears, beneath a glorious full moon. A railing and perhaps a telescopic viewer appear. The clinic vanishes; we are now on the observa-*

---

* See Special Note on Songs and Recordings on copyright page.

tion deck of the Empire State Building. There is a sports jacket hanging over the railing. A red balloon is also attached to the railing. Mother Teresa helps Jeffrey into the jacket; she checks his appearance. She hands him the balloon. She exits. Steve enters, looking around.)

STEVE. Jeffrey?

JEFFREY. Steve! You showed up!

STEVE. What is this? A scavenger hunt? Am I on a list? "Meet Steve on the top of the Empire State Building"?

JEFFREY. I wasn't sure you'd come, when I left the message. I didn't know if . . . John would let you.

STEVE. Sean. Have you seen Sterling?

JEFFREY. Yeah. He's doing okay. He liked the memorial.

STEVE. So did I.

STEVE and JEFFREY. *(After a beat, they sing softly to the tune of "Memory.")* "DARIUS, WE ALL THOUGHT YOU WERE FABULOUS . . ."

STEVE. Nice balloon.

JEFFREY. It was a gift.

STEVE. And what are you still doing here? I thought you were headed west, or north.

JEFFREY. I need a favor.

STEVE. This is very Hitchcock.

JEFFREY. I have to ask you something.

STEVE. And your phone was shut off. Gay castration.

JEFFREY. Be serious. Can I ask you my favor?

STEVE. I'm here.

JEFFREY. Dump Sean.

STEVE. What?

JEFFREY. Leave him. Tell him it's over. Be really mean.

STEVE. It's a little late for that!

JEFFREY. Why?

STEVE. He's gone. He . . . dumped me.

JEFFREY. He did? *Really?*

STEVE. Oh, calm down. He couldn't take it. The sex. He was exhausted. He's twenty-two.

JEFFREY. Were you upset?

STEVE. Of course!

JEFFREY. A whole bunch?

STEVE. Jeffrey!

JEFFREY. Steve, if I asked you to, could we have sex? Safe sex? Some kind of sex? Tonight?

STEVE. On the top of the Empire State Building?

JEFFREY. Wherever. I needed . . . a moon. You haven't answered my question.

STEVE. Wait a minute! What is this? You think it's so easy? You leave a message, snap your fingers? Jeffrey, I'm still HIV-positive.

JEFFREY. So?

STEVE. So—it doesn't go away! It only gets worse!

JEFFREY. I know.

STEVE. Don't do this. Don't pretend. I will not be your good deed!

JEFFREY. Oh, you're not. I'm too selfish. I don't want a red ribbon. I want you.

STEVE. Say we have sex. Say we like it. And say tomorrow morning you decide to take off, for Wisconsin!

JEFFREY. I won't!

STEVE. How do I know that?

JEFFREY. Because I'm a gay man. And I live in the city. And I'm not an innocent bystander. Not anymore. (*Steve is now somewhat convinced. He studies Jeffrey for a Moment.*)

STEVE. So . . . how bad do you want it?

JEFFREY. Find out.

STEVE. I like this. This is nice. You want it. Suddenly it's my decision. I get to be Jeffrey.

JEFFREY. Fuck you.

STEVE. Maybe.

JEFFREY. *Maybe?*

STEVE. You know, I think you should woo me. Maybe dinner. Maybe dancing.

JEFFREY. Yes!

STEVE. And then . . .

JEFFREY. Unbelievably hot sex!

STEVE. Not yet.

JEFFREY. (*Very frustrated.*) What do you want?

STEVE. Jewelry.

JEFFREY. Yes!

STEVE. No, wait. What did my horoscope say this morning? "You will meet an incredibly fucked-up guy. Happiness is impossible. Go for it."

JEFFREY. Yes! (*After a beat.*) Yes?

STEVE. (*After a Moment.*) Yes.

JEFFREY. But Steve—first you have to promise me something.

STEVE. (*Exasperated.*) What?

JEFFREY. Promise me . . . you won't get sick.

STEVE. (*After a beat.*) Done.

JEFFREY. And you won't die.

STEVE. Never.

JEFFREY. (*Staring at Steve, very emotional.*) Liar. (*Jeffrey and Steve move toward each other. Steve pulls back.*)

STEVE. Jesus. We shouldn't do this. We are really asking for it. Give me one good reason. Give me one reason why we even have a prayer.

JEFFREY. You want one good reason?

STEVE. I do.

JEFFREY. (*After a beat.*) I dare you. (*They stare at each other. Jeffrey tosses the balloon to Steve. The balloon almost hits the ground, but Steve leans forward and catches it. He holds the balloon for a Moment and then tosses it back to Jeffrey. They move U, and toward each other, tapping the balloon back and forth. The balloon is caught in the light of the moon and glows translucently. Finally, Jeffrey catches the balloon. He and Steve embrace and kiss as the lights dim.)*

CURTAIN

THREE

The Most Fabulous Story Ever Told

For John Raftis

THE MOST FABULOUS STORY EVER TOLD was originally produced by the Williamstown Theatre Festival (Michael Ritchie, Producer), in Williamstown, Massachusetts, on July 1, 1998. It was directed by Christopher Ashley; the set design was by Michael Brown; the costume design was by Marion Williams; the lighting design was by Rui Rita; the sound design was by Kurt B. Kellenberger; and the stage manager was Judith Tucker. The cast was as follows:

STAGE MANAGER	Dara Fisher
ADAM	Alan Tudyk
STEVE	Bobby Cannavale
MATINEE LADY, WHISKERS, MOM #1, FTATATEETA, RABBI SHARON KLOPER	Maggie Moore
PRIEST, BUGS, RHINO, DAD #2, BRAD, KEVIN MARKHAM	Michael Wiggins
LATECOMER, PETER, ZIZI, DAD #1, PHARAOH, TREY POMFRET	Peter Bartlett
CHERYL MINDLE, MITTENS, FIFI, MOM #2, PEGGY	Michi Barall
JANE	Becky Ann Baker
MABEL	Jessica Hecht

THE MOST FABULOUS STORY EVER TOLD was originally produced by New York Theatre Workshop, in New York City, on December 14,

1998, and subsequently produced off-Broadway by Scott Rudin, Viertel/ Frankel/Baruch/Routh, Paramount Pictures, Maxwell/Balsam/Harris, and the New York Theatre Workshop, at the Minetta Lane Theatre, on February 2, 1999. It was directed by Christopher Ashley; the set design was by Michael Brown; the costume design was by Susan Hilferty; the lighting design was by Donald Holder; the sound design was by Darron L. West; and the production stage manager was Charles Means. The cast was as follows:

STAGE MANAGER	Amy Sedaris
ADAM	Alan Tudyk
STEVE	Juan Carlos Hernandez
FATHER JOSEPH, RABBIT #1, RHINO, DAD #2, BRAD, KEVIN MARKHAM	Orlando Pabotoy
MIRIAM MILLER, BABE, MOM #1, FTATATEETA, RABBI SHARON	Lisa Kron
LATECOMER, RABBIT #2, DAD #1, PHARAOH, TREY POMFRET	Peter Bartlett
CHERYL MINDLE, FLUFFY, MOM #2, PEGGY	Joanna P. Adler
JANE	Becky Ann Baker
MABEL	Kathryn Meisle

At the Minetta Lane Theatre the role of STAGE MANAGER was performed by Peg Healey, and the role of STEVE was performed by Jay Goede.

The Most Fabulous Story Ever Told

ACT ONE

Throughout the play, the audience will hear the Stage Manager's voice, amplified through a microphone, calling various cues for sound, lights, and scenery. The play begins with the curtain down.

STAGE MANAGER'S VOICE. House to half, go, house out and pre-set, go. Creation of the world, go.

The curtain rises on a bare stage, in darkness. The Stage Manager sits at a small table or desk, at the side of the stage. She is a sleek, incredibly capable woman, dressed in a black turtleneck and close-fitting pants. She wears her microphone on a headset, leaving her hands free. She speaks in a low, authoritative, sexy voice, like a very smart flight attendant with an agenda. She is the ultimate professional: confident, aloof, and slightly swaggering. She knows what she's doing.

Music begins, something grand and propulsive, like Wagnerian pop or a rolling, percolating dance mix of "Thus Sprach Zarathustra."

STAGE MANAGER. Monday, go. Light, go. I love this.

A shaft of light hits the stage. More light appears, illuminating the bare stage from every possible direction. Finally, the entire stage is ablaze with blinding white light.

STAGE MANAGER. First sunset, go.

The stage returns to darkness.

STAGE MANAGER. Tuesday, go. Oceans, go.

The stage is again filled with light. Yards of blue silk are released from high above the stage, cascading to the stage floor, shimmering and undulating. Sounds of the ocean are heard. The silk is then either mechanically removed, or the Stage Manager leaves her desk, gathers up the fabric, and stashes it in a corner. All of this happens very quickly, as the music builds.

STAGE MANAGER. Sunset at the beach, go.

The light is again extinguished.

STAGE MANAGER. Wednesday, go. Land, go.

The lights come up. A large rock, suitable for sitting on, is now tugged center stage, either mechanically or by the Stage Manager, using a rope. A horizon line appears in the distance.

STAGE MANAGER. Sunset over the mountains, go.

Blackness.

STAGE MANAGER. Thursday, go. Garden of Eden, go.

The lights come up, as the Garden of Eden begins to fill the stage.

STAGE MANAGER. Sunset in paradise, go.

Blackness.

STAGE MANAGER. Friday, go. Creatures of the earth, go.

Lights up on the full garden. We now hear sounds of animal life, everything from barking dogs to laughing monkeys to roaring lions. The sounds should be vigorous but happy. The Stage Manager slaps a mosquito which has landed on her neck. She squashes a bug with her foot.

STAGE MANAGER. Sunset at the zoo, go.

Blackness.

STAGE MANAGER. Saturday, noon-ish, go.

The lights come up on the Garden, gorgeously sunlit, as we hear something like the "I had a dream" notes from "Everything's Coming Up Roses" in the musical Gypsy.

Adam enters, perhaps through a door upstage center. He is an attractive, innocent, wide-eyed fellow in his twenties. He wears only a jockstrap. He looks around, filled with a combination of wonder, awe, and shock. Throughout the play, Adam will remain overwhelmingly, passionately curious, in love with the world's possibilities. His ebullient, aggressive need to know everything will always hurtle him joyously forward.

ADAM. (*after a beat*) Hello? (*a beat*) Yes? (*looking around*) Well. *My.* (*He looks around, really taking in the garden, more and more impressed*) Whoa. Nice! Very nice! And there are trees and flowers, and a clear blue sky . . . (*Adam has now leapt atop the rock, and he studies the landscape*) I mean, I would put the lake over *there*, but—I am so jazzed about this! All right, I'll just say it, right out loud—this garden is fabulous! Stop it! Wait. Who am I talking to? Where am I? Who am I? What am I? Am I—gay? (*He thinks for a second, and then, with exuberant, grateful relief*) Yes! (*He carefully checks his hair, smoothing the sides into place*) And I'm alone.

 The Stage Manager strikes a crisp, bell-like note on a small chime. Steve enters, from the wings, or any different entrance than Adam's. Steve is a handsome guy, a bit more solid than Adam. He is good-natured but firm in his opinions, and more grounded than Adam. He also wears only a jockstrap. He and Adam spot each other with huge enthusiasm.

STEVE. Hey!

ADAM. Hey!

STEVE. Hey!

ADAM. Hey! (*awkwardly extending his hand, inventing the handshake*) Adam.

STEVE. Steve. (*they shake hands vigorously*)

ADAM. Nice to meet you!

STEVE. Yeah!

ADAM. Really nice!

STEVE. (*perhaps taking an appreciative glance at Adam's body*) Yeah.

ADAM. Can I ask you something?

STEVE. Sure!

ADAM. (*with great urgency, the words tumbling out, all in one breath*) Where did we come from? How did we get here? Who made us, who made this garden, and why? Are we the only ones here, are we meant to be together, are there things we're supposed to do, how will we know, will our relationship be good for the both of us, will we be together forever, what's forever, and is all of this part of some plan, or did it just happen?

STEVE. (*a bit overwhelmed*) I should go.

ADAM. Oh, oh, me too.

STEVE. Good to meet you.

ADAM. Can I . . . can I see you again?

STEVE. I'd like that.

ADAM. But how will I find you?

STEVE. Call me.

ADAM. (*After a beat, yelling*) Steve!

STEVE. Yeah?

STAGE MANAGER. First date, go.

Adam and Steve begin walking together, through the garden, appreciating their surroundings. They share the giddy nervousness of a first date.

ADAM. (*pointing*) Grass!

STEVE. (*pointing*) Vine!

ADAM. (*pointing*) Rock!

Steve sits on the rock, gesturing for Adam to join him. Adam sits beside him, and Steve rapidly puts his arm around Adam's shoulders.

STEVE. First base.

ADAM. (*pointing to Steve's feet*) Feet!

STEVE. (*pointing to Adam's knees*) Knees!

ADAM. (*pointing to Steve's stomach*) Abs!

STEVE. (*pointing to Adam's arms*) Arms!

ADAM. (*pointing to Steve's hands*) Fingernails!

STEVE. (*looking into Adam's eyes*) Eyes.

ADAM. (*pointing to Steve's lips*) Soft face-hole things.

Steve leans over to kiss Adam. Adam pulls away, confused.

ADAM. What . . . what are you doing?

STEVE. I . . . I don't know. I just—I wanted to put my soft face-hole things on yours.

ADAM. Really? Why?

STEVE. I don't know. I just, I was looking at your soft face-hole things, and I just—if you don't want to, it's okay . . .

ADAM. No, no, I mean, it's just . . .

Adam turns his head away for a second, and cups his hand over his mouth, exhaling sharply and checking his breath. Satisfied, he turns back to Steve.

ADAM. Sure!

Adam and Steve kiss. The kiss begins extremely awkwardly, as they aim their open mouths at each other, but end up landing on chins or cheeks. Gradually, slurping and contorting, they achieve a real kiss. Adam then pulls away, and runs a few yards away.

STEVE. I'm sorry!

ADAM. No, no, don't be . . .

STEVE. What's wrong?

ADAM. It's just, when I first got here, I thought that everything was perfect. And now it just got—more perfect!

Adam runs back to Steve, and they kiss again, even more passionately. Things begin getting a bit physical.

STAGE MANAGER. Boners, go.

Adam runs away again, even more hyper and upset.

ADAM. Oh my!

STEVE. What?

ADAM. I just, I started to feel . . . (*He is getting an erection, to an almost painful degree. He begins to rub his crotch, to relieve the pressure.*) I'm sorry!

STEVE. No, don't be.

ADAM. But . . .

STEVE. (*also rubbing his crotch*) I feel like that too!

ADAM. (*panicking wildly*) What is happening to us?

STEVE. I have an idea.

ADAM. Yeah?

STEVE. What if I took my mouth, and my lips, and my tongue, but not my teeth, and I put them on your . . . (*indicating Adam's crotch*)

ADAM. (*thrilled*) You!

STEVE. (*also delighted*) And later, you could do the same thing for me!

ADAM. (*even more giddy*) Yes! If I wasn't too tired!

STEVE. Deal!

As Steve begins to kneel before Adam, we hear:

STAGE MANAGER. Privacy, go.

The stage is plunged into blackness.

STAGE MANAGER'S VOICE. Sorry, folks. Oh, get over it!

From the darkness, we hear:

ADAM. Great idea! Thank you!

STEVE. (*His mouth full, a bit garbled*) You're welcome! (*a beat, and then, not garbled*) I have another idea!

ADAM. (*from the darkness*) OUCH!

STAGE MANAGER. Lights twenty-nine, go.

The lights come up. Adam is bent over the rock, facing the audience. Steve stands close behind him; they're having anal sex. They both still wear

*their jockstraps. They will continue to have vigorous sex during the fol-
lowing conversation.*

STEVE. What, what's wrong?

ADAM. That hurts!

STEVE. I'm sorry—should I stop?

ADAM. No. It's just that I've never done this before, you know, using a
person.

STEVE. What did you use?

ADAM. Well, those shiny green things, you know, that grow on the
ground . . .

STEVE. Sure . . .

ADAM. Oh, and sometimes those pointy orange things, that grow under
the ground . . .

STEVE. (*interrupting*) Adam?

ADAM. Yes?

STEVE. Do you wish that I was, you know, more like those other things?

ADAM. No, oh no! You are wonderful, you are so special! (*continuing
to have sex, Adam reaches around to slap Steve on the thigh, encouragingly.*)
They were just . . .

STEVE. What?

ADAM. Salad!

*Steve is relieved; the sex grows even more vigorous, as both guys begin
moaning ecstatically with pleasure.*

STAGE MANAGER. Lights thirty, go.

The lights go out, as the sex continues.

STAGE MANAGER. First simultaneous orgasm ever, go.

From the darkness, we hear both men enjoy an exuberantly loud, enormously lusty and joyful orgasm.

STAGE MANAGER. Thank you, thank you. Lights thirty-one, go.

When the lights come up, the two men are seated back-to-back on the rock, their heads thrown back in post-orgasm afterglow. We hear sultry, sexy, film noir-ish saxophone music play. Adam is eating a banana, while Steve munches a carrot, as if they were both smoking post-coital cigarettes.

STEVE. Adam?

ADAM. Right here.

STEVE. I love you.

ADAM. What?

STEVE. I love you.

ADAM. What's that?

STEVE. Love is—well, it's hard to explain it, exactly.

ADAM. Is it that thing that makes you bring me presents?

STEVE. (*handing ADAM a small rock*) Here's another rock.

ADAM. (*thrilled*) Thank you! (*Adam extends his arm and places the rock on his ring finger, considering the rock as if it were a diamond engagement ring; he's very pleased*)

STEVE. Love is—something I know. I don't know how we got here, I don't know why touching you makes me so happy, but I know—that seeing you, or even thinking about seeing you, makes me feel like—I don't need to know anything else.

ADAM. Really?

STEVE. You're my answer.

Adam stands and strides away from Steve, across the stage.

STEVE. What? What is it?

ADAM. I just . . . you didn't kiss me, and I didn't fall down, but—I can't catch my breath. It's that thing, that you said.

STEVE. I love you?

ADAM. Stop! Don't! I can't—I can't look at you.

STEVE. Why not?

ADAM. Because I will break, I will burst, into one million tiny pieces of joy! I will be so happy that I won't be able to be a creature anymore, I'll become—pure happiness!

Steve has begun to pursue Adam all over the stage. Adam might end up standing on the rock, across the stage from Steve.

STEVE. You will?

ADAM. So I have to stay just like this, perfectly still, frozen, so I can always be someone who just heard you say, "I love you."

STEVE. Adam?

ADAM. (*not looking at him*) I can't.

STEVE. (*enjoying the chase*) This is really fun. I can torture you.

ADAM. Stay away!

STEVE. Here I come . . .

ADAM. Stop! I'm not looking!

STEVE. I love you! I love you!

ADAM. No! No more!

STEVE. Okay. Good-bye.

Steve begins to stride offstage, away from Adam.

ADAM. What? Steve?

STEVE. (*pausing*) Yeah?

ADAM. (*after a beat*) I love you.

They run to each other, and begin to make love. The sultry saxophone music is heard again. Adam and Steve are now on the ground, kissing and embracing.

FATHER JOSEPH. Stop!
ADAM. What?
FATHER JOSEPH. Stop it this minute!
ADAM. Excuse me?

Father Joseph Markham, a priest in traditional clerical garb, has stood up from a seat in the audience. He holds a small, leather-bound Bible. He is extremely angry; he just couldn't put up with Adam and Steve's story for one more second.

Only Adam will interact with the audience members. Once Adam is standing, Steve will remain on the ground, asleep.

FATHER JOSEPH. I'm Father Joseph Markham, and I'm sorry, but this is all wrong! It wasn't Adam and Steve, that's nonsense! This isn't the Bible!
ADAM. The Bible? What's the Bible?
MIRIAM. Don't ask!

Miriam Miller, a matinee lady, has stood up from her seat in the front row. She wears a nice dress from Loehmann's, accessorized with gold jewelry, an important purse and maybe a coordinated shawl. She is not shy. She introduces herself, in a friendly manner, to Adam and the audience.

MIRIAM. I'm Miriam Miller, and I'm with the theater party from Temple Beth El. And I like this story! I think it's very sweet!
STAGE MANAGER. Houselights!
LATECOMER. Oh, I'm sorry!

*As the houselights come up, illuminating the entire audience, a Latecomer
has entered the theater, coming down an aisle from the back of the house.
He is nattily dressed and carries several shopping bags from upscale stores.
He is a sophisticated, highly strung Manhattanite.*

ADAM. Who are you? All of you?

LATECOMER. I'm late, I'm sorry, but I had my mother and my shrink
and my AA meeting, so I needed to shop.

MIRIAM. *(sympathetically)* Of course.

ADAM. Shop?

LATECOMER. What have I missed?

MIRIAM. Well, the world got created.

FATHER JOSEPH. The wrong world!

MIRIAM. But it's gorgeous, like Aruba, or Cancun.

ADAM. Cancun? What's Cancun?

LATECOMER. It's over.

MIRIAM. And then these two guys showed up.

LATECOMER. Two guys?

ADAM. Steve and me!

FATHER JOSEPH. Which is not historically accurate! I have pamphlets!
(He offers pamphlets to real audience members) Do you want some pamphlets?

ADAM. *(excited and curious)* Wait! Everybody! Where are you all from? Is
there a world—outside the garden?

FATHER JOSEPH. Of course!

MIRIAM. No, no! Oh no!

LATECOMER. Take a look!

ADAM. How?

LATECOMER. Climb a tree!

*Adam runs to a tree, or the proscenium, and begins climbing, as high as he
can get.*

MIRIAM. Stop! It's a wonderful garden! You have fruit, you have foliage, don't push it!

ADAM. (*eagerly*) But why not? So far it's all been fabulous! Why can't I see everything?

LATECOMER. Why can't he see more?

MIRIAM. Because it's a terrible world! It's unpleasant! He'll find out things he doesn't want to know!

ADAM. Like what?

FATHER JOSEPH. (*holding up his Bible*) It's all right in here!

LATECOMER. According to whom?

FATHER JOSEPH. According to the truth!

MIRIAM. According to you!

ADAM. But I want to know who made me! And why! I want to thank them, for everything! For Steve! I want . . .

FATHER JOSEPH. Revelation!

ADAM. Yes!

MIRIAM. (*now standing near the front of the stage*) But shouldn't you ask your . . . (*She gestures at Steve, trying to find the correct term*) friend, about leaving the garden?

ADAM. He loves me. I love him.

LATECOMER. (*regarding Steve*) He's heaven. (*to Adam*) I hate you!

MIRIAM. But if you leave, things can happen. People can get hurt.

ADAM. (*who's never heard the word before, and doesn't know what it means*) Hurt?

FATHER JOSEPH. They can betray the people they care about.

ADAM. Betray?

LATECOMER. You could lose—everything.

ADAM. But I don't understand! And I want to!

MIRIAM. You could be alone—again.

ADAM. No—Steve will come with me. We'll go together!

STAGE MANAGER. Adam, we need a decision.

ADAM. But what's out there? All I can see is more garden!

Adam, trying to see more, swings out from the tree and Momentarily loses his footing. Everyone screams, as Adam regains his footing.

STAGE MANAGER. (*during the hubbub*) Heads up!
CHERYL. Adam?

Cheryl Mindle, a young woman from Utah, stands up in the audience. She is primly dressed and clutches her Playbill.

ADAM. Yes?
CHERYL. I just got here, to the big city, from Utah. And I still don't have a place to live, or a steady job. And I'm really scared, and really excited. And Utah was great, but—I had to leave.
MIRIAM. But why?
LATECOMER. It was Utah.
CHERYL. To find out. What would happen. What comes next. If you don't take a chance, you'll never know anything!
STAGE MANAGER. Stand by, fifty-seven L and garden, out.
ADAM. Fifty-seven L?
STAGE MANAGER. (*to Adam*) Strike the garden? You have to call it.
MIRIAM. Don't!
FATHER JOSEPH. Learn!
LATECOMER. Why not?
CHERYL. Ask!

Adam, from his perch in the tree, looks at everyone. He takes a deep breath.

ADAM. Show me . . . (*He looks at Steve*) Show us—everything!
STAGE MANAGER. And the cue?
ADAM. Fifty-seven L!
FATHER JOSEPH. Wait!

STAGE MANAGER. What?

FATHER JOSEPH. (*going to the stage*) If you're going to leave the garden—take this. (*He places his Bible on the stage*)

ADAM. Why?

FATHER JOSEPH. It is all you will ever really need.

MIRIAM. And take this too.

ADAM. What is it?

MIRIAM. (*placing a small item from her purse atop the Bible*) A moist towelette.

STAGE MANAGER. Adam?

ADAM. Go!

There is a huge crash of sound and light, as the stage is plunged into darkness. A few seconds later, the lights come up on the stage. The garden has vanished. Miriam, Father Joseph, the Latecomer, and Cheryl are all gone. The stage is empty and harshly lit. The space is cavernous, dark, and frightening.

Adam is now lying on the ground, having fallen from the tree. Steve is gone.

ADAM. (*realizing he's been hurt in the fall*) Owww! (*looking around*) Steve? Steve? (*standing and searching for Steve, very frightened*) Oh no! *Steve!*

Steve runs on. He and Adam are now both truly naked.

STEVE. What happened?

ADAM. (*looking around*) Where . . . where did . . .

STEVE. (*staring at Adam*) Adam . . .

ADAM. Yeah?

STEVE. (*stunned*) Adam—you're naked.

Adam looks down at his body; he is shocked and yelps, leaping about as if his body is suddenly a foreign object. He looks up at Steve.

ADAM. Steve . . .

STEVE. What?

ADAM. So are you! (*Steve looks down at his own body, shocked*) You know what this means . . .

STEVE. I have to get to a gym!

ADAM. I need some khakis!

Jane stalks onstage. She is a hefty, proudly and impressively butch woman, wearing a pair of primitive overalls made from leaves and bark. Jane is boisterous and tough-minded, with a short fuse. She is also very warm-hearted and generous, earthy and wonderfully sane. At the Moment she is violently pissed off.

JANE. What the hell are you doing?

Adam and Steve both scream and try to cover their naked flesh.

ADAM and STEVE. AHHH!

JANE. Oh, please! Like I could care!

ADAM. Who are you?

JANE. Jane.

MABEL. (*from offstage*) Jane?

Mabel runs onstage. She is a thin, quivering, sprite-like waif with a cloud of long, frizzy, pre-Raphaelite hair. She wears a long dress, also made from leaves and bark. She always responds emotionally to any situation; she is tremulous, hopeful, and sympathetic to everyone. As soon as Mabel sees Adam and Steve, she screams.

MABEL. *AHHH!*

ADAM and STEVE. (*screaming right back*) *AHHH!*

MABEL. (*regarding Adam and Steve*) Jane—who are those poor, ugly women?

JANE. They're not women. But I have a feeling they did something to the garden, and I'm gonna find out what!

MABEL. No, no—let me.

Mabel approaches Adam and Steve, gingerly. She speaks in her best, hostess-y manner, using a loud, distinct voice, as if talking to children.

MABEL. Hel-lo.

ADAM. Hi.

STEVE. Hello.   (*at the same time*)

MABEL. (*pointing to Jane*) Jane. (*pointing to herself, perhaps with a curtsey*) And Mabel.

ADAM. What are you?

JANE. We're the first people!

ADAM. Excuse me?

MABEL. (*graciously*) We're the first human beings ever. We were living in the garden, enjoying eternal peace and happiness.

ADAM. (*condescending*) I'm sorry.

JANE. Yeah, what?

ADAM. I was actually the first person.

STEVE. (*to Adam*) You were not.

ADAM. Yes I was. I got there first.

STEVE. And what was I?

ADAM. The first boyfriend.

JANE. Excuse me, buddy!

STEVE. What?

JANE. We were here first. We were sitting in that garden, minding our own business . . .

MABEL. (*sweetly*) Enjoying all the wonder of nature . . .

JANE. When somebody came along after us, and fucked things up!

STEVE. How do you know? Maybe you're the ones who fucked things up! Maybe the garden was getting a little crowded!

JANE. It was a women's garden!

MABEL. Although we had special nights for other creatures, with discussion groups . . .

STEVE. It was *our garden!*

JANE. You wanna make something of it?

STEVE. Try me!

Steve and Jane face off, circling each other, balling up their fists, preparing for a fight.

ADAM. Steve, don't!

MABEL. Violence is never the answer—look at what happened to your breasts!

JANE. (*taunting Steve*) Come on, nature boy . . .

STEVE. (*to Jane*) Hey, who cut your hair? Lightning?

As Steve turns toward Adam to laugh at his wisecrack, Jane shoves Steve from behind. He stumbles and turns on her.

JANE. Hit me! Come on, pal! You want a piece of this?

STEVE. You're not a man! I bet you don't even have a dick!

MABEL. We have vaginas! They're our friends!

JANE. Faggot!

STEVE. Dyke!

Just as Steve and Jane lunge forward and are about to hit each other, Adam, in agony, stops the bout.

ADAM. Stop it! It's all my fault! I ruined the garden!

STEVE. You did?

JANE. I knew it!

ADAM. I climbed a tree, and I was asking questions, and then the garden disappeared!

JANE. (*incredulous, pissed off*) You were asking questions?

STEVE. *Why?*

ADAM. And now Steve and I are naked!

MABEL. We were naked too!

ADAM. And what happened?

JANE. The minute the garden disappeared . . . (*referring to Mabel*) she got crazy. She started jogging.

MABEL. Do I look fat?

JANE. No!

STEVE. (*to Jane*) And what did you do?

JANE. Nothing! I like my body.

ADAM. So why are you wearing clothes?

JANE. I need pockets.

STAGE MANAGER. North wind, go.

We hear sounds of gusting wind, and the rumble of approaching thunder.

ADAM. (*shivering*) It's windy.

STAGE MANAGER. Goosebumps, go.

For the first time in their lives, Adam, Steve, Jane, and Mabel feel the effects of bad weather; they are starting to feel very lost and exposed.

JANE. It's gonna rain.

MABEL. We have to get inside!

STEVE. Inside *what?*

MABEL. Where are we?

ADAM. The world.

STAGE MANAGER. Lightning, go. Thunder, go. Barren wilderness, go.
There is a huge clap of thunder and a bolt of lightning; the stage is plunged into darkness.

Campfire, go.

The lights come up on a small area of the stage. Jane and Mabel are asleep together, on the ground. Steve sits up, wrapped in a blanket, unable to sleep. Adam, also in a blanket, sits nearby. The light from the campfire casts eerie shadows.

ADAM. Steve? (*Steve refuses to speak to Adam*) Is everyone really mad at me? You know, just because the garden disappeared and we're in a barren wilderness and there's no food and we're starting to smell?
STEVE. Why didn't you ask me? About leaving the garden?
ADAM. Because I thought that you might—say no.
STEVE. Bingo!
ADAM. But—I've never heard you talk like this. You sound like I've—hurt you.

(*For the first time, Adam realizes the meaning of the word "hurt"*)

STEVE. You did!
ADAM. Hey. Hey, Mister Cranky-Face. Mister-I-got-kicked-out-of-Para-dise-so-I'm-not-gonna-smile.
STEVE. That's right!
ADAM. (*spotting an object a few yards away*) Oh come on—look! Everything didn't vanish! We still have—this!

Adam has run over to pick up the Bible, which Father Joseph had left on the stage. He brings the Bible back to Steve.

STEVE. What's that?

ADAM. (*investigating the Bible; neither he nor Steve has any concept of books or reading*) I'm not sure. It's filled with these little markings.

Steve rips a page out of the Bible and begins eating it.

ADAM. (*grabbing the Bible*) No!

STEVE. I'm starving!

ADAM. So—does everybody hate me?

STEVE. (*after a beat, opening his arms, so that Adam can lie beside him*) No. Never.

JANE. (*still lying down, without moving*) I hate you.

ADAM. (*noticing something in the sky*) Look! I feel like—singing. So the moon will know we're here.

MABEL. (*singing, in a high, screechy voice, with more yearning and emotion than melody or pitch*) Hello, moon! We're down here! We love you! Especially Mabel!

EVERYONE. (*joining in, using high screechy voices to imitate Mabel's song*) HELLO, MOON! WE'RE DOWN HERE! WE LOVE YOU!

JANE. (*singing, with gusto*) AND ADAM IS AN IDIOT WHO RUINED EVERYTHING!

EVERYONE. AND ADAM IS AN IDIOT WHO RUINED EVERYTHING!

ADAM. (*Sung in a tentative, apologetic, high-pitched voice*) By accident!

EVERYONE. (*continuing to sing, even louder and more atrociously*) HELLO, MOON . . .

STAGE MANAGER. (*Interrupting, as they sing*) Lights sixty-four, go. Fast! *The lights go to black.*

MABEL. (*from the darkness, indignant*) Hey!

Adam, Steve, Jane, and Mabel exit in the darkness. The lights come up on the Stage Manager, crossing the stage, carrying a piece of crude, Western-

style wooden fence. She speaks as she walks, eventually depositing the fence somewhere across the stage.

STAGE MANAGER. Crude implements, go. Division of labor, go. Fence posts, go. Harvest, go. Ethnic jewelry, go. (*She has deposited the fence. As she crosses back to her desk, she spots an offensive garment on someone in the audience; she points to that audience member*) That shirt, no. Hoe-down, go. Yee-ha, go.

Some extremely sprightly music begins, perhaps the high-stepping Aaron Copland score for Rodeo. *Lights up on the full stage, which has become a bit more sunny and welcoming. The landscape, while remaining Biblical and barren, has a hint of Midwestern, pioneer spirit.*

Adam leaps onstage, wearing roughhewn clothing, crudely hand-stitched. He carries a crude ax. He holds out his ax to the audience; he loves his ax. He begins to dance with his ax, in a high-spirited, klutzy version of a number from Seven Brides for Seven Brothers *or* Oklahoma. *Jane enters; she looks disgusted with Adam's dance. Adam dances over to her, pauses, and then hands her the ax. She takes it, puts it over her shoulder and exits. Adam is thrilled, because Jane will be the one to actually chop the wood; he dances offstage in the opposite direction, leaping and clicking his heels.*

As Adam has been dancing, Steve has entered far upstage, with a bow and arrow, stalking some unseen, small animal. He also wears a new, rough-hewn outfit. Mabel follows close behind him, watching his every move. She wears a new dress, perhaps with long, fluid, macramé accents.

As Adam dances and deals with Jane, Steve and Mabel execute a fullstage cross. The dance, Jane's entrance, and Steve and Mabel's hunting cross should be choreographed to happen together, for a feeling of simultaneous action.

As Adam exits, Steve heads downstage, stalking something.

STEVE. (*to Mabel*) Shh . . .

MABEL. Shh . . .

STEVE. (*whispering intensely*) We must move very slowly, and we make no
sudden moves, and then . . .

As Steve draws back his bow, Mabel leaps out from behind him, to warn
his prey.

MABEL. (*to the animal*) Run, little one. Fear the white man!

If Steve is being played by a non-white actor, Mabel's line should read
"Run, little one! Warn the others!"

STEVE. (*furious*) Mabel!

MABEL. How would you like it if someone did that to you?

Mabel grabs Steve's arrow and pricks his arm.

STEVE. Oww! That hurt!

MABEL. You see? That felt—strangely arousing . . .

STEVE. Exactly! When I see these creatures, I feel this urge. To chase! To
pounce! To kill!

MABEL. Let's talk about that.

STEVE. It's the natural order!

MABEL. It's evil!

STEVE. What?

MABEL. It's the opposite of goodness. Goodness is bunnies and caring
and respect for all living things.

STEVE. And evil?

MABEL. (*brightly, as she and Steve exit together*) Evil is anything I don't like!

As Mabel and Steve exit, Jane enters, carrying a crude shovel. She stands near the fence posts. She calls out:

JANE. Adam!
STAGE MANAGER. Laundry, go.

A clothesline appears, with some primitive burlap clothes and a muslin sheet pinned up. Adam enters, with a basket, and starts taking down the laundry.

ADAM. Jane?
JANE. I need a hand, with these fence posts.
ADAM. Fence posts? Well, if you'll help me, with the laundry.
JANE. Shit.

Jane drops her shovel, and might belch. She pulls a sheet off the clothesline and starts bunching it up; laundry is not her area of expertise.

ADAM. (*horrified*) Jane!
JANE. What? What'd I do?
ADAM. We do not grab and bunch!
JANE. We don't?
ADAM. We fluff and fold!

Adam begins demonstrating correct laundry behavior, as he and Jane fold the sheet.

JANE. Okay . . .
ADAM. Jane, can I ask you a personal question?
JANE. Like what?
ADAM. When you and Mabel are alone together, and you take off all of your clothes, just what exactly do the two of you sort of—do?

JANE. Do? Well, first I might take my tongue . . .

ADAM. (*interrupting, running to the other side of the clothesline, terrified*) No! Stop!

JANE. Why?

ADAM. No, I can do this, keep going, tell me the whole thing . . .

JANE. (*very matter-of-fact*) So I take my tongue, and I lick her eyeball. I suck it out of her head, chew on it, roll it in the dirt, then I rub the eyeball on my butt, oh, and then we both come.

ADAM. (*proud of himself, for taking it well*) Okay. We should try that.

JANE. Adam! For cryin' out loud!

ADAM. What?

JANE. That isn't what we do. We kiss and suck and lick and finger and have a great time, just like you and Steve! And we're not grossed out by what you do with your fleshy little things.

ADAM. They are not little! Mine isn't.

JANE. There are only two of you in the whole world, and you're comparing?

ADAM. We're both huge, and you're just jealous because you wish you had a fleshy humongous thing!

JANE. What would I do with it? Mix drinks?

ADAM. You'd be proud of it!

JANE. Adam, if we're going to create the world, we have to respect our differences.

ADAM. But why? Why are we all so different? What do you do, when it all starts to overwhelm you, and you can't sleep and you stand outside, asking and needing and crying out to the stars?

Mabel enters, from the opposite side of the stage, looking into the cosmos.

MABEL. Stars!

STAGE MANAGER. Stars, go. Midnight, go. Crickets, go.

The lights change dramatically, for a feeling of enchanted midnight, beneath a full moon. Jane exits, with the laundry. Mabel glides into a circle of moonlight, enraptured, conducting a private ritual.

STAGE MANAGER. Dance of the pagan earth goddess, go.

Music begins, mostly primitive but alluring rhythmic sounds, which will grow in intensity as the scene progresses. Mabel begins to dance, her arms flung wide, as Adam watches her, from behind a tree. The Stage Manager circles Mabel, cueing her dance.

STAGE MANAGER. Spirit of the forest, go. Full moon, go. Isadora Duncan, go. (*Mabel dances with fluid, trailing, Duncan-style moves.*) Martha Graham, go. (*Mabel's dance becomes abrupt and angular, in Martha Graham style.*) Stevie Nicks, go. (*Mabel starts to spin in a witchy, airy-fairy manner, pointing at the audience, à la Stevie Nicks in concert.*) Interloper, go.

Mabel pauses, realizing that Adam is watching her. Adam approaches Mabel, holding out his Bible.

STAGE MANAGER. That thing, go.

Adam and Mabel both touch the Bible, and raise their free hands, mirroring each other.

STAGE MANAGER. Kindred spirits, go.

Adam and Mabel take each other's crossed hands, and begin to dance, spinning together. The music grows wilder and more pounding, and the dance becomes increasingly passionate and out of control, in pagan ecstasy.

STAGE MANAGER. (*as the dance builds*) Giddy high spirits, go. Dizzi-
ness, go. Loss of self, go. Lack of oxygen, go. Sparks of blinding white
light, go.

*Mabel and Adam have been spinning wildly and independently. Mabel
falls to her knees, overcome.*

STAGE MANAGER. Possible existence of God . . .

*The Stage Manager leans down and kisses Mabel. Then she stands back,
with a certain satisfied swagger.*

STAGE MANAGER. Go.

*Mabel has felt the kiss, but she has not seen the Stage Manager. She has
experienced a form of wondrous revelation. Adam watches her.*

MABEL. (*reaching upward*) Oh my—God.
ADAM. God?
STAGE MANAGER. Dance of the divine, go.

*The music grows even more frenzied, and Adam and Mabel resume danc-
ing, leaping into the air with cries of joy. They dance offstage, to opposite
sides. The Stage Manager remains at center stage.*

STAGE MANAGER. Lights sixty-five, go.

*The lights change, from midnight in the clearing to something brighter and
domestic. The Stage Crew brings out a pair of benches, a fur rug, a floor
lamp, and a tray holding four primitive goblets. They create Adam and
Steve's house, as the Stage Manager supervises their placement of each item.*

STAGE MANAGER. Stage crew, go. Adam and Steve's house, go. Seating, go. Floor lamp, go. Area rug, go. Stemware, go.

The Stage Crew exits, as the Stage Manager surveys the premises, satisfied.

STAGE MANAGER. Early Ikea, go.

Steve enters, wearing fresh white linen clothing, very loose and flowing, but more tailored than his earlier outfits. He carries a tray of hors d'oeuvres.

STEVE. They're gonna be here any minute!
Adam enters, also in fresh linen clothing, very excited.

ADAM. You look so handsome.
STEVE. (*proudly*) I know.
ADAM. I just want everything to be perfect!
STEVE. But why? What's going on?
ADAM. It told you, it's a surprise. The best one ever!
MABEL. (*entering*) Knock, knock!
JANE. (*following Mabel onstage*) We're here!

Jane and Mabel enter, carrying a bottle of wine; they also wear white linen outfits. Jane's look will always be a variation on overalls, for practicality. Mabel's outfits will always be more flowing and romantic. The foursome greet each other very socially, with hugs and air-kisses. They have all clearly become experts at brunch behavior.

ADAM. Jane!
STEVE. Mabel!
MABEL. We brought you something!
Jane or Mabel hand Steve the bottle of wine.

STEVE. Wine!

JANE. We made it, from our own grapes.

STEVE. (*reading the label on the bottle, impressed*) "Jane and Mabel. Monday."

ADAM. Come in, sit down.

STEVE. (*holding the tray of hors d'oeuvres*) Can I offer anyone some of these things that Adam made?

JANE. What are they?

ADAM. Well, I had this idea. What if, before the actual meal, we all got to taste some smaller, more complicated food.

MABEL. But—we already do that.

ADAM. (*his trump card*) On a cracker?

Everyone goes "Oooh!", tasting the hors d'oeuvres, impressed at Adam's innovation.

ADAM. (*as he pours wine into the goblets and distributes them*) Now, after the garden, I know that we all thought that maybe—we weren't going to make it. That because of what I did . . . (*everyone protests vigorously— "No, no!" "Leave it alone!" "It was ages ago!" etc.*) No no no no no, that because of my wanting a revelation, we were doomed. But as of today, we have all been together for 400 years. And I think we look great! *Everyone raises their goblets and agrees, in a wholehearted group toast:*

JANE: Yes to that!

STEVE: Here, here!

ADAM: Way to go!

MABEL: Rock on!   (*all at the same time*)

ADAM. And I would just like to mention some of the wonderful things we have invented, including the lever, the pulley system, and the wheel.

STEVE. (*toasting Jane and Mabel, with great respect*) Thank you, ladies.

MABEL. And let's not forget about shampoo and conditioner in one!

JANE. (*with respect*) Adam.

Everyone toasts Adam, who holds up his hands—"What can I say?"

ADAM. And yet—our happiness hasn't been complete. We have each other, we have so much, but still—we know nothing. We have no answers. Until—right now!

STEVE. Is this your surprise?

JANE. What? What is this?

ADAM. Mabel?

MABEL. (*standing, with a real sense of the Momentous occasion*) All right. Well, last night, I—made contact.

STEVE. Contact?

MABEL. We were out dancing, and the sky was so clear, and the stars were so bold, and I just wanted to reach out and say, I love everything!

STEVE. (*amused*) Mabel.

JANE. Mushrooms?

MABEL. No! And as I raised my arms, to embrace the universe, I felt—a kiss.

JANE. A kiss?

MABEL. And I opened my eyes, and I said, "Oh my *God*."

ADAM. She did. I heard it!

STEVE. God?

JANE. God?

MABEL. God is—this is so cool—the creator of the cosmos, and the source of all spiritual and moral nourishment.

Adam looks at Steve and Jane; he is very impressed with Mabel's story. Jane and Steve exchange a glance.

JANE. Too much free time.

STEVE. Let's eat.

Jane and Steve stand and begin to leave.

ADAM. You guys! It really happened!

MABEL. And we think that all of God's teachings may be in this.

Adam holds up his Bible.

JANE. An object which makes no sense.

ADAM. Not yet.

STEVE. Mabel, I love you, and Adam, I know you ask questions, but guys—this is the most dangerous idea I have ever heard.

ADAM. Why?

STEVE. Because we have all worked very hard. To grow food, to build our homes. To create a casual yet elegant lifestyle. And now you want to take that away, to say, oh no, something called God did it?

MABEL. That's not what we're saying.

STEVE. (*to Mabel*) If any of this nonsense is true, then how come you're the only one who really made contact?

MABEL. That's fair. And I've thought about it. Okay. Now if you had to choose someone from among, say, the four of us, someone to receive a vision of spiritual wonder, now whom would you pick? (*looking around the room*) Hmmm. Well, it wouldn't be Adam, because he's so sweet, but he isn't exactly stable.

ADAM. I'm not?

MABEL. (*sitting on the bench beside Adam and taking his hand; she speaks to him in a totally sweet and sympathetic manner*) One word, sweetie: "garden"? (*She chortles adorably, tweaks Adam's nose or shakes a you-naughty-boy finger at him. Then she glides over to Steve*) And Steve, you're so hard-working and clear-eyed, only you lack any imagination or a larger sense of life. (*She says this without a trace of rancor, as if it's the best compliment*) Not that that's a bad thing. Necessarily. (*After patting Steve's chest, she goes to Jane, and puts her arms around her, speaking in the warmest, most loving tone imaginable*) And of course I adore Jane, but she's still in recovery.

STEVE. In recovery? From what?

JANE. These conversations.

MABEL. And I'm, well, I'm open and sensitive and more highly evolved. And I have the best hair.

ADAM, JANE, and STEVE. (*vehemently*) You do not!

MABEL. People? So, God chose me. It's no big deal.

STEVE. Wait. Mabel?

MABEL. Yes?

STEVE. I'm not judging, but—is this some sort of women's thing?

JANE. Excuse me?

STEVE. You know, like making tea from bark and keeping a journal and inventing those big, ugly brown sandals?

JANE. (*who's wearing those sandals*) They're very comfortable!

STEVE. For evening?

ADAM. Steve!

MABEL. Let's all join hands and offer ourselves to God!

ADAM. We could try! This is so exciting!

JANE. Maybe after dinner.

STEVE. Not in my house.

ADAM. Your house?

STEVE. I will not believe in something I can't see or smell or touch.

ADAM. You believe in love.

STEVE. Not at the moment.

MABEL. You love Adam. God made Adam. So you should thank God. You should show God you're grateful.

STEVE. Grateful? I'm sorry, but I will not suck up to some invisible, non-existent being!

ADAM. Wait! Be careful! What if God, okay, what if something as powerful as God, heard what you just said and got angry?

STEVE. I don't care!

MABEL. Don't say that!

JANE. I know—let's invent Charades!

STEVE. We are not going to be punished for having a conversation! What are you so afraid of?

MABEL. The wrath of God!

STEVE. There is no God!

STAGE MANAGER. Flood, go.

There is a huge clap of thunder, and suddenly the stage goes black. A torrential rain is heard.

ADAM. Just for the record—that was Steve!

STAGE MANAGER. El Niño, go.

More thunder is heard, and the rain gets even heavier. Adam, Steve, Jane, and Mabel exit, as the Stage Crew, led by the Stage Manager, pulls billowing yards of blue silk across the entire stage, as the flood. The Stage Manager and her crew all wear bright yellow rain slickers and matching hats. Booming, urgent, movie-style hurricane music is heard.

STAGE MANAGER. Ark, go, surviving creatures, go. Two by two, go.

During these cues our foursome make a full-stage cross, fighting the gale-force winds and rain, making their way onto the ark, as we hear the sounds of a ship's whistle amid the music and hurricane din. The group might wear rainwear; Jane carries a duffel bag, Mabel carries a guitar case with floral decals, Steve carries the floor lamp over his head, and Adam carries his Bible and a garment bag. As our foursome make their cross and exit, they are followed by two actors dressed as Rabbits. The Rabbits have big floppy ears and cottontails, and also wear brightly colored, touristy sportswear, including Bermuda shorts, Hawaiian shirts, Day-Glo fanny packs, etc. Before exiting, the Rabbits pause briefly. They are thrilled to be going on a cruise: Rabbit #1 poses, while Rabbit #2 snaps his picture with a Kodak Instamatic, including a flash. Then the Rabbits hurry offstage, making a brief hop in unison. Various scenic pieces can also be brought onstage during all of this hubbub. They include a ship's bar and a section of railing. The benches from Adam and Steve's house can be rearranged to form a straight line upstage center.

STAGE MANAGER. Promenade deck, go. Contents of Adam's stomach, go.

Lights up on a section of railing, with a life preserver. Adam runs on and leans over the railing. He almost vomits, but doesn't. Steve runs on after Adam, concerned.

STEVE. Are you okay?
ADAM. Make it stop! The rain. The flood.
STEVE. How?
ADAM. (*holding out his Bible*) Ask God! Tell God you're sorry!
STEVE. Why?
STAGE MANAGER. Thunderbolt, go.

A bolt of lightening pierces the sky; it is very frightening.

STEVE. Okay, fine, I'll try!

Adam hands Steve the Bible; Steve stands at the railing and addresses God, looking upward.

STEVE. God, even though you're just one of Mabel's spinning-induced hallucinations, and this is totally stupid, I'm really sorry, so stop the flood. Thank you.
ADAM. Steve.

STEVE. What?

ADAM. Nice try! Do you think God is gonna hear that? And pay attention? Say you're sorry!

Adam gestures to God, regarding Steve—"I don't know what he's thinking." Steve leans at the railing and tries again, with more fervent intensity. Adam stands behind him, acting as a coach.

STEVE. God . . .

ADAM. Be charming.

STEVE. (*in a deep, almost English voice, to God*) My darling . . .

ADAM. Be respectful!

STEVE. My Lord . . .

ADAM. Get chummy!

STEVE. Lookin' good!

ADAM. Pour it on!

STEVE. I love your work!

ADAM. You are *hot.*

STEVE. You are *hot.*

ADAM. You are *it!*

STEVE. You are *it!*

ADAM. Oh, you big damn juicy God baby . . .

STEVE. Oh, you big damn juicy—(*still to God*) Can I ask you something?

ADAM. What?

STEVE. (*to God*) If you made everything, then who made you?

We hear a thunderclap.

ADAM. (*to God*) Not an issue!

STEVE. (*to God*) And if you're so wonderful, then why are we afraid of you?

Another thunderclap, even louder.

ADAM. (*to God, regarding Steve*) Don't listen!

STEVE. (*turning to Adam*) Adam, do you love God?

ADAM. Of course!

STEVE. More than you love me?

> *A thunder crash, as Adam and Steve stare at each other. Lights down on the*
> *railing, as Adam and Steve exit, perhaps taking the railing with them.*

STAGE MANAGER. Mid-Atlantic, go.

> *Lights up on the ark dining room. This may be suggested simply by having*
> *Jane and Mabel sitting beside each other on a bench. Their body language*
> *tells us that all is not well between them; Jane is sipping from a flask. They*
> *have just finished a meal, in silence. Mabel waves to someone across the*
> *room.*

MABEL. Hi!

> *Mabel barks like a dog, loud and sharp. Then, acknowledging another*
> *friend, she snorts noisily, like a pig. Spotting a third friend, she quacks like a*
> *duck or squawks like a chicken.*

JANE. (*barely controlling herself*) Could you please not do that?

MABEL. Do what?

JANE. Make animal noises, at dinner.

MABEL. Well, I have to talk to someone.

JANE. Meaning?

MABEL. We haven't spoken for the last two weeks.

JANE. So what's there to talk about? "Hey, you think it's gonna *rain?*"

MABEL. We're a couple, we're not supposed to run out of things to say!

JANE. It's been *four hundred years.* (*she sips from the flask*) And thirty-nine
days . . .

MABEL. It's just that sometimes . . .

JANE. Sometimes what?

MABEL. (*getting increasingly shrill*) Nothing! I love you! It's just that sometimes I can't stand you!

JANE. Well, I love you too, but if I hear that whiny little baby-talk voice
one more time, I'm gonna scream!

*Sexy, mambo music is heard. Fluffy, an extremely sexual cat, enters, clearly
on the prowl. Fluffy walks upright, and her costume might include elements
of human attire, but she is immediately recognizable as a cat—she has
whiskers, pointy ears, paws, and a tail. She purrs her way over toward Jane
and Mabel, heating up the atmosphere considerably.*

FLUFFY. Hi, Jane.

MABEL. Jane?

JANE. (*aroused*) Hey there, Fluffy.

MABEL. Fluffy?

FLUFFY. (*joining them on the bench, getting physical*) And this must be
Mabel. I've heard so much about you.

MABEL. How?

JANE. We met last night, after you fell asleep.

MABEL. (*to Jane*) You went out?

FLUFFY. Heavy petting.

JANE. (*to Fluffy*) So where's your better half?

*Babe, a pig, enters. Babe is a lusty, life-of-the-party pig, a sexually vora-
cious, good-time sow. Her personality combines elements of a frat guy and a
Shriner out for a wild night on the town. She also walks upright, but is pure
pig; she has pig ears, a sizable snout, and a curly tail.*

BABE. Jane!

FLUFFY. (*to Babe*) Sweetheart!

MABEL. Jane?

BABE. (*offering her hoof, introducing herself to Mabel*) Babe.

FLUFFY. All the animals are mixing.

BABE. (*who has joined the others on the bench, nuzzling with Fluffy*) Last night, we had sex with a goldfish.

MABEL. A goldfish?

BABE. She died happy!

FLUFFY. But this is so much better.

MABEL. But I don't think that females really enjoy open relationships. Women are naturally monogamous.

BABE. You really think so?

MABEL. Of course!

JANE. (*standing, eyeballing Babe lasciviously*) Oink.

Fluffy grabs Mabel and kisses her passionately.

BABE. (*swaggering, to Jane*) I should warn you—I'm Canadian.

FLUFFY. (*breaking the kiss*) What's wrong—cat got your tongue?

MABEL. No!

FLUFFY. I know that you're scared, so was I, my first time . . .

BABE. (*to Mabel*) What's wrong? You kosher?

MABEL. No . . .

JANE. (*to Mabel*) You always say we should be open to new experiences . . .

MABEL. (*increasingly panicked*) But—with animals?

BABE. (*very offended*) Hey! What's wrong with animals?

MABEL. Nothing! I love animals!

FLUFFY. *Prove it!*

Fluffy lets loose with a shrieking, passionate meow, whips the bench with her tail, and chases Mabel offstage.

MABEL. (*on her way out, desperately*) Jane!

JANE. (*totally up for sex, as a lusty love call, to Babe*) Soo-eee!

BABE. (*as Jane exits, following Fluffy and Mabel*) That's right, baby! Try the other white meat! *Babe exits, in heat.*

STAGE MANAGER. Admiral's Club, go.

Loud, thumping disco music begins. Steve enters, in a rage, and heads for the bar. The Bartender turns around—he is a Rhino. He is very sexy, perhaps shirtless or wearing a leather vest over his bare skin. He has an enormous, rough horn in the middle of his face, at least 15".

STEVE. Gimme a beer!

RHINO. (*handing him a beer*) Here you go.

STEVE. (*explosive*) Have you ever been in love?

RHINO. Sure!

STEVE. I hate it! Everything's all my fault! There's just mildew and sulking and animals!

RHINO. You know who I was in love with?

STEVE. Who? What?

RHINO. (*gesturing*) Over there, by the door. Simba.

STEVE. Simba?

RHINO. They call him the Lion King. I don't think so.

STEVE. Really?

RHINO. I found out, he was fucking everything on this boat. Dumbo. Daffy. Goofy came to me in tears. He said, all Simba wants is a big career in show business. And now I guess he's gonna get it. See who he's with?

STEVE. (*looking across the room*) You're kidding . . .

RHINO. That's right. Mickey! With the gloves and the buttons! Can you imagine? (*in a high-pitched Mickey Mouse voice*) "Oh Simba, do me!"

STEVE. You poor guy.

RHINO. We both need it bad.

STEVE. It's been weeks . . .

RHINO. You are making me so hot . . .

Steve and the Rhino have begun fondling each other.

STEVE. (*trying to break away*) But we can't . . .
RHINO. Your boyfriend doesn't know what he's got . . .
STEVE. But he's a great guy, I mean, on land . . .
RHINO. But we're not on land, we may never get back on land . . .
STEVE. We could be out here for eternity, with the water rising, and the walls closing in . . .
RHINO. With Adam telling you all about God . . .
STEVE. How can I love Adam so much, and still not push you away . . .

The *Rhino has pursued Steve, stepping out from behind the bar. Steve reaches out and begins to stroke the Rhino's horn, closing his hand around it, his strokes becoming more vigorous, as the Rhino moans with passion. Then Steve licks his middle fingers and slaps the Rhino's horn, which makes the Rhino yelp with lust. The Rhino and Steve, overcome by the Moment, grab each other and begin kissing passionately. Adam enters from the opposite side of the stage, wrapped in a blanket. When he sees Steve and the Rhino, he is stunned, and genuinely hurt.*

ADAM. Steve?

Steve and the Rhino break apart.

STEVE. Adam!
ADAM. No . . .
RHINO. (*to Adam*) Can I get you something?
STEVE. I can explain . . .
ADAM. Steve . . . (*as Steve approaches him*) Get away from me!
STEVE. I was upset, I was angry . . .

RHINO. Hey, he said you were having problems . . .

ADAM. (*to Steve, regarding the Rhino*) You told him? About our personal lives?

STEVE. We *are* having problems!

ADAM. Which you won't talk about!

STEVE. We don't do anything but talk! When was the last time we had sex? ·

ADAM. Excuse me, I've been vomiting!

STEVE. Oh, so now who won't talk about it?

ADAM. How come this is suddenly about me? I'm the one who just walked in on you, fondling some—some butch can opener!

RHINO. A rhino! You got a problem with that?

ADAM. (*to Steve*) I have a problem with the fact that I loved you so much, up until thirty seconds ago. And now, for the first time, I feel so—betrayed.

MABEL. (*from offstage*) No! Stop it! Leave me alone!

Mabel runs onstage, sobbing, very upset, wrapped in a blanket.

ADAM. Mabel?

MABEL. I'm sorry, I'm sorry, but I just can't!

Mabel huddles on the bench, as Jane runs on, buttoning her clothes.

JANE. That was incredibly rude!

Mabel starts to hack and cough, making a series of horrible rasping noises, trying to get something out of her throat.

STEVE. (*regarding Mabel's spasm*) What's wrong with her?

MABEL. (*finally coughing something up, and looking at it, in her hand, totally grossed out*) Oh my God! It's a furball!

JANE. We were having fun!

MABEL. I wasn't! Why do you need that? Why aren't I enough?

JANE. You were there! You were part of it!

MABEL. (*with volcanic fury*) She was a *PIG!*

STEVE. Mabel!

RHINO. Whoa!

JANE. In a blanket!

MABEL. It was against God's law!

JANE. It's your law!

STEVE. Why do we need laws?

MABEL. So people won't hurt each other!

ADAM. And cheat on each other!

MABEL. With sows!

ADAM. (*referring to the* RHINO) With luggage!

FLUFFY. (*from offstage*) Don't touch me!

BABE. (*from offstage*) Get back here!

Fluffy runs on, disheveled and very upset.

FLUFFY. It's over!

JANE. What's wrong?

FLUFFY. I can't live like this! Not anymore!

Babe runs on and pursues Fluffy, who might jump atop the bar.

BABE. Get back to the sty!

FLUFFY. I won't. You're too exhausting! (*to the group*) She's got six nipples!

MABEL. Why can't everyone just stay together?

ADAM. The way God intended!

JANE. Because the world is more interesting than that!

STEVE. Because God is what's fucking us up!

BABE. Stop it! You're upsetting the lower primates!

We hear all the animals on the ark begin to yelp and roar.

RHINO. They're gonna stampede!
FLUFFY. (*to Babe*) I hate you!
ADAM. (*to Steve*) I hate you more!
MABEL. (*to Jane*) You've ruined everything!
JANE. (*to Mabel*) You're insane!
STEVE. (*to Adam*) You're hysterical!
RHINO. Hey—it's stopped raining.
STAGE MANAGER. Sunshine, go. Blue sky, go. Rainbow, go.

Everyone stops fighting as the ark vanishes, and Fluffy, Babe, and the Rhino exit. The sky clears, and a vibrant, glowing sun appears. The ark might disappear simply by having the Stagehands and the Stage Manager remove the various set pieces. The action should remain continuous.

ADAM. (*pointing into the distance, toward the audience*) Look—land!
STAGE MANAGER. Dove, go.

Adam, Steve, Jane, and Mabel all follow the path of a dove, flying high above their heads. Dad #1 enters. He is a wholesome, good-natured, suburban-style fellow.

DAD #1. Hey there!
ADAM. Who . . . who are you?
MABEL. Oh my God . . .
JANE. There—there are more of us!
STAGE MANAGER. Rest of the world, go.

Through slides or a painted drop or some other scenic device, the image of thousands of other people appears, filling the stage.

ADAM. This is incredible!

STEVE. There are all these people!

MABEL. All these friends!

JANE. But where did they—where did all of you come from?

MABEL. From God!

STEVE. Let them answer!

DAD #1. We came from—across the ocean. There was a flood, which destroyed everything, but we got onboard this other ark.

JANE. Spooky . . .

Dad #1 is joined by his wife, Mom #1, and another happy, heterosexual couple, Dad #2 and Mom #2. The couples should be in no way cartoony or vicious; they are welcoming, sociable, and curious. They are dressed in a not-quite-modern-yet-suburban style, possibly all in white; their outfits might include Bermuda shorts, shirt-waist dresses and windbreakers. The two Moms might wear sleek blonde pageboy hairdos, although they shouldn't match. The Moms and Dads stay together as a group, although the couples should be very affectionate with their spouses.

STEVE. But—there are so many of you.

MOM #1. More every day!

ADAM. But how? How did that happen? How do you . . . make more of you?

DAD #1. (*very jovial*) Well, I just take my penis . . .

MOM #1. (*brightly*) And he puts it in my vagina!

Adam, Steve, Jane, and Mabel stare at the newcomers in horror and disbelief. After a beat

ADAM, STEVE, JANE and MABEL. *GROSS!*

DAD #2. (*very affable*) No, really, it's great fun. I ejaculate, and then, oh, about nine months later . . .

MOM #2. A baby! Happens all the time!

Adam, Steve, Jane, and Mabel look at each other; they are all deeply skeptical. Adam steps forward, taking command.

ADAM. Excuse me.
DAD #1. Yes?
ADAM. Now—all right. Okay. Joke over. What you're saying, what you're claiming, is that the men—have sex—with the women?

Adam, Steve, Jane, and Mabel burst out laughing. The heterosexuals aren't offended by this response, just politely puzzled.

MOM #2. But we do!
DAD #1. Every chance we get!
DAD #2. Like fallin' off a log!
MOM #1. Works for us!
ADAM. Well, that is just *wrong!*
JANE. That is unnatural!
MABEL. How could there be any possible pleasure in it?
STEVE. That is just not what God intended!

Everyone stares at Steve; he looks around.

STEVE. Who said that?
DAD #1. God?
MABEL. Well, with the way you behave, I'm sure you've probably never heard of God.
MOM #1. But of course we have!
DAD #1. We love God!
MOM #2. We worship God!
DAD #2. We're God's chosen people!

MOM #2. (*politely, for information*) And you are . . . ?

ADAM. We're—we're God's chosen people!

DAD #2. But there are so few of you. Only four.

JANE. Because we're gay!

STEVE. We don't have children!

ADAM. We have taste!

MABEL. But how can there be two different gods?

STEVE. How can there be any?

ADAM. (*holding up his Bible*) But we have this! Our Bible!

DAD #1. Just like ours!

The Moms and Dads all take out their own Bibles, which are more deluxe than Adam's.

MOM #1. (*stroking her Bible's binding*) Only in leather.

ADAM. But—can you read them?

MOM #1. Of course! Every day!

ADAM. But—what do they say?

DAD #2. (*opening his Bible*) Well . . .

MOM #2. (*opening her Bible*) Let's take a look . . .

DAD #1. (*pointing to a passage*) Oh, I love this . . .

MOM #1. (*pointing to another passage*) No, honey, here . . .

From offstage, we hear a baby cry.

DAD #1. Uh-oh!

JANE. What was that?

MOM #2. That's the new baby! He's hungry!

We hear more babies begin to cry.

DAD #1. We better get busy!

Even more babies begin to cry, and we hear older children calling out "Mommy!" and "Daddy!"

MOM #1. We've got to run! You understand. Nice to meet you.

DAD #1. We'll get together! When we can find a sitter!

MOM #2. Call us!

DAD #1. We mean it!

DAD #2. I bet you'll all make great aunts and uncles!

MOM #1. And—entertainers!

MOMS and DADS. Bye!

The four straight people run off. Adam, Steve, Jane, and Mabel stare at each other, trying to process what they've just seen and heard.

ADAM. What was *that?*

JANE. The world is getting very strange . . .

STEVE. So, do you still believe in God? After all that?

MABEL. Yes.

STEVE. Mabel!

MABEL. And I think that God—is trying to teach us something.

ADAM. Teach us what?

MABEL. I don't know. Maybe something about—babies. (*gazing offstage*) Look at them—they're like teeny, tiny little people. Like lawn ornaments.

JANE. They're so noisy, and smelly.

STEVE. What if those people move near us, with all those children?

MABEL. (*turning to Jane, with great, yearning determination*) I want one!

JANE. You do not!

MABEL. I want another one of us! Of you and me!

JANE. Well, I don't think that's gonna happen! Didn't you hear what you have to do to get one of those? (*Mabel turns to Steve*)

MABEL. Steve?

STEVE. What?

MABEL. (*seductively*) Steve?

Mabel flips her hair flirtatiously and walks over to Steve, with her version of a sexy walk. Somewhat awkwardly, Mabel and Steve kiss. Adam and Jane watch them, as the kiss grows more intense. Finally, Mabel and Steve break the kiss.

MABEL. Why . . . why did I just feel this huge drop in my self-esteem?

JANE. You see what happens?

ADAM. But those babies are really adorable . . .

STEVE. Adam?

MABEL. Adam?

ADAM. I'm not saying it's a good idea, but—what if it is? Wouldn't that be amazing? A little Adam running around? We could do things with him, guy things!

JANE. Guy things?

ADAM. Like cooking, and skincare, and the theater!

STEVE. But what if the baby's a girl?

ADAM. We could try again.

MABEL. Adam!

ADAM. (*to the women*) Or we could give her to you.

JANE. Hold it! If God wants any of us to have a baby, well, we can just do it the right way!

MABEL. How?

JANE. (*gesturing to the offstage people*) We can steal one!

STEVE. How can you all talk about having babies together, and what God wants? Weren't you on that ark? When we were all ready to kill each other?

JANE. When we learned a little too much?

ADAM. That's right. What about—us?

MABEL. Us?

ADAM. Does God want us to stay together?

STEVE. Do *we* want to?

The foursome are not just referring to the relationships of the two couples, but to the group as a whole. The foursome is at a crisis point, on every level.

MABEL. We need to talk, before we go any further. We need some rules.

JANE. No more rules!

ADAM. What if we have a baby, and the baby asks—where did I come from? Who made me?

PHARAOH'S VOICE. (*boomingly amplified, so it resounds throughout the theater*) I AM THE ONE TRUE GOD!

JANE. (*looking around*) *What the fuck was that?*

PHARAOH'S VOICE. I AM IMMORTAL!

STEVE. Don't listen!

PHARAOH'S VOICE. COME UNTO ME!

Ftatateeta, a female Egyptian guard, appears wearing a headdress, armor, a pleated white skirt, lace-up sandals, and Cleopatra eyeliner. She carries a spear. She marches downstage center and assumes an Egyptian pose. She has the attitude of a gum-chewing waitress in a spotlight.

FTATATEETA. Welcome—to the grand imperial court of Raman-hotep, beloved Pharaoh of all Egypt.

STAGE MANAGER. All Egypt, go.

Grand, booming, Ten-Commandments-style imperial music is heard, and ancient Egypt appears. The atmosphere should suggest Egypt by way of the MGM Luxor Hotel in Las Vegas, with an emphasis on gold draperies, boldly colored hieroglyphs, palm fronds, and perhaps some pyramids and a sphinx. Peggy, a second female guard in an identical outfit, also with a spear, joins Ftatateeta. Finally, the Pharaoh is brought forth, as the music peaks; he might be wheeled on inside a pyramid or arrayed on a garish, ornamental throne. He rises, and strides forward, displaying his magnificence. His striped headdress and flowing, glittering robes are reminiscent of the blindingly golden attire of Tutankhamen, by way of Ziegfeld. His eyes are made up Cleopatra-style. He holds out his arms, his pleated cape billowing majestically. He is truly regal, convinced of his own godhead.

PHARAOH. *(referring to his outfit)* Too busy?
FTATATEETA. All hail Egypt's immortal Boy-King!
PEGGY. Bow down!

The guards threaten Adam, Steve, Jane, and Mabel with their spears, and the foursome kneel on the ground.

PHARAOH. You are surrounded by my ferocious Amazon guards. They are lesbians, trained in the deadly arts of torture, gouging, and intramural field hockey.

Peggy and Ftatateeta, stationed on either side of the Pharaoh's throne, execute identical, crisp field hockey moves with their spears, thwacking imaginary pucks.

PHARAOH. May I present—Ftatateeta.

Ftatateeta and Peggy have resumed their military positions beside the throne.

FTATATEETA. Yo!
PHARAOH. And—Peggy.
PEGGY. Hi, everybody!

PHARAOH. I have enslaved hundreds of thousands of homosexuals, to build my pyramids. (*He steps forward, looking into the audience*) Oh, look at them all, just sitting there. (*a beat*) Criticizing. (*in a whiny voice*) "Why can't we build a beach house?" (*in imperial tones*) Get to work!

ADAM. Your Highness?

PHARAOH. Who speaks?

ADAM. Are you really—God?

PHARAOH. (*referring to himself*) Behold!

ADAM. Did you create the world?

PHARAOH. Ask anyone!

ADAM. Did you create—me?

PHARAOH. You, you, you, it's all about you!

ADAM. Did you?

PHARAOH. I suppose. Why are you questioning me?

ADAM. Because, if you're the ultimate supreme being, then this is the most important day of our lives, and our quest is ended. But it's just, if you're really God . . .

PHARAOH. Yes?

ADAM. Then why are you wearing so much eye makeup?

FTATATEETA. (*threatening Adam with her spear*) Silence!

PHARAOH. (*striding over to Adam, after a beat*) Bitch!

ADAM. And why have you brought us here before you?

PHARAOH. Because—I grieve.

ADAM. Your Highness?

PHARAOH. I am—in love.

JANE. Watch out.

STEVE. (*to the Pharaoh*) Whom are you in love with?

PHARAOH. I found him many years ago, in the bulrushes.

ADAM. After work?

PHARAOH. (*after swivelling to glare at Adam*) He was floating, in a crude wooden cradle. I had never glimpsed such a beautiful child. I decreed, let him be raised in my palace, as a prince!

MABEL. What did you call him?

PHARAOH. (*proudly*) Brad.

JANE. Brad?

PHARAOH. It means, "He who never wishes to work."

ADAM. And what happened?

PHARAOH. We laughed together, played together, we shared every Egyptian interest—slavery, sand, sketching each other in profile. And soon, he grew to boyhood, and then, all too quickly, he became a young man. I questioned our relationship—were we friends, brothers, immortal Boy-King and grateful swamp Jew? And lo, one evening he came unto me. I pushed him away, I said I shall not have this, you must not feel this is demanded of you.

ADAM. And he said . . . ?

PHARAOH. He protested, he wept, he said, yes, you are immortal, yes, you command all Egypt, and yes, I am but Brad of the bulrushes . . .

During the Pharaoh's last speech, Brad has entered, staring passionately at the Pharaoh. Brad is a handsome, well-built young fellow, wearing a white pleated skirt, a yarmulke with a bobby pin, and a tallis, the traditional Jewish prayer shawl, over his bare chest. He is earnest and ardent.

BRAD. (*to the Pharaoh*) But I love thee!

PHARAOH. Brad!

BRAD. (*to the group*) I love him! I call him by a special title!

ADAM. Which is?

PHARAOH. "The Mouth of the Nile." (*The Pharaoh is thrilled and overcome by this phrase. He almost swoons, then pulls himself together, and turns to Jane and Mabel.*) Could you die?

BRAD. But he's afraid! He hesitates! He will not commit!

ADAM. But why not?

PHARAOH. Because I am immortal—but is our love?

JANE. What?

PHARAOH. I have had all of you captured for this very reason. I am told that you have loved, in a time before time. That yours were the first loves on Earth. So I must know, you must answer the legendary riddle of the Sphinx: Can love endure?

BRAD. Answer, I beseech thee!

Brad is now posed becomingly at the Pharaoh's feet.

PHARAOH. (*with a grand gesture*) Approach, lesbians!

Jane and Mabel stand.

PHARAOH. Guards—slay the younger!

Mabel is hurled to the ground, and Ftatateeta holds her spear at Mabel's throat. Peggy keeps Jane at bay with her spear. Adam, Steve, Jane, and Mabel all cry out; there should be a real sense of life-and-death danger.

JANE. No!

MABEL. (*to the Pharaoh*) You are not God, mister! I will call upon the true God to smite you!

PHARAOH. The true God?

MABEL. Dear Lord in heaven—smite him!

Everyone onstage looks to heaven—nothing happens. Everyone looks back to Mabel.

PHARAOH. Yes, dear?

MABEL. (*to heaven*) Smite him eventually!

JANE. Leave her alone!

MABEL. Jane?

PHARAOH. Answer the riddle—would you die for this woman?

ADAM. Jane?

STEVE. Jane?

Everyone onstage turns to Jane. Jane has her hands raised, the spear at her throat. She speaks with passion and fury.

JANE. Yes, I would die for her!

MABEL. You would?

JANE. She's insane, and she tries to find higher meaning in just about everything, and she's nowhere near as open and free as she thinks she is, and I'm totally split on the God thing, let alone the baby thing, but if anyone gets to kill her—it should be me!

MABEL. (*overwhelmed*) Jane!

PHARAOH. (*to the guards, regarding Mabel*) Release her! Threaten the males!

The guards release Jane and Mabel, who embrace. Ftatateeta puts her spear to Adam's throat, while Peggy keeps Steve at bay with her spear. Everyone screams.

PHARAOH. (*to Adam*) Would you die for this man?

ADAM. Yes!

PHARAOH. So you love him forever?

ADAM. I . . . I did.

STEVE. You—did?

ADAM. In the garden. When there were only the two of us. When we had no choice.

STEVE. We always had a choice.

PHARAOH. And now?

ADAM. The world has become enormous. There are so many people.

STEVE. They don't matter! We don't have to listen to them!

ADAM. But I want to listen, I need to. That's what you don't understand. You won't ask questions. You won't even ask directions.

STEVE. Why should I?

ADAM. (*genuinely being torn apart*) You see? That's what drives me crazy! You are so sure of yourself, of everything, which is what I love about you, that strength, but it's also what I hate! Half the time I want you so bad I ache from it, and half the time I want to throw you off a cliff!

STEVE. That's what love is!

ADAM. Which part?

STEVE. (*with equal fervor*) All of it! I love you because you're passionate and eager and optimistic, and because you're a total mess!

ADAM. But—you have been with other men!

STEVE. I have not!

ADAM. On the ark!

STEVE. That was a rhinoceros!

PHARAOH. (*After a beat, he raises his arms, and all but swoons again, trying to picture this Rhino Moment*) A—rhinoceros?

STEVE. (*to Adam*) And what about you and your little Bible? You haven't exactly been a picnic!

ADAM. Oh yes I have!

STEVE. Who got us thrown out of the garden?

ADAM. Into the world!

STEVE. Which has caused all of our problems!

ADAM. Yeah, well, who started the flood that drowned just about everything?

STEVE. That wasn't my fault! I just said that I didn't believe in God!

JANE. Here we go!

PHARAOH. You don't believe in me?

MABEL. (*to the Pharaoh*) You're not God!

STEVE. There is no God!

BRAD. Wait! (*to the Pharaoh*) You lied to me! You said that you were God!

PHARAOH. I am God!

BRAD. Not according to these people! (*to the foursome*) He never lets me meet anyone!

Brad, in a major snit, strides over to the Pharaoh's throne and sits, crossing his legs.

PHARAOH. Excuse me! I give you gold ornaments, I dress you in precious silks!

BRAD. Last year's!

JANE. (*to BRAD, regarding the Pharaoh*) He's a rotten boyfriend!

STEVE. (*to BRAD*) You can do better!

BRAD. You know it! You've been there! You've been taken for granted!

PHARAOH. (*to BRAD*) You are listening to someone who fucked a rhinoceros!

ADAM. That's right. All right, let's get it all out in the open. Steve, you just have problems because I'm the butch one.

STEVE. (*incredulous*) *You're* the butch one?

MABEL. Why does anyone have to be the butch one?

JANE. *I'm* the butch one!

ADAM. (*to Steve*) You don't respect me, or my Bible!

PHARAOH. Your Bible?

ADAM. (*examining his Bible*) It could tell me what to do! I think it holds the answers to everything!

PHARAOH. (*sincerely, with great yearning*) Even—*stains?*

STEVE. Adam! I am right here, in front of you! Where I have been since the beginning! Why do you need a book, or a god, to tell you to love me? Are you that pathetic? Are you that weak? (*a beat*)

ADAM. No. I am that strong. Strong enough to believe.

MABEL. Yes!

ADAM. I am leaving! I am going to lead my people into the desert!

PHARAOH. Your *people?*

ADAM. (*facing the audience, addressing the hundreds of thousands of slaves*) Who wants to find a righteous way to live, in a world filled with deception?

A recorded crowd roars its approval.

ADAM. Who wants to discover the true nature of God, and the purpose of the universe?

The crowd roars even louder.

ADAM. Who wants to prove that love does not endure? Not once you leave the garden. In the world, you will be hurt. And betrayed. And you will be better off—alone.

STEVE. Is that what you believe?

ADAM. (*to the crowd*) Follow me.

STEVE. Adam!

Adam exits, with his Bible. After a beat, Peggy drops her spear and follows him. As she exits, she pauses to make a strangled cry of romantic distress.

FTATATEETA. Peggy!

Brad, furious, also exits with great petulance, following Adam and Peggy.

PHARAOH. Brad!

MABEL. Steve, don't worry! We'll find Adam, we'll bring him back!

JANE. He's headed for the Red Sea!

Jane and Mabel run off, after Adam.

STEVE. I don't want him back! I want a new boyfriend! No, I want lots of new boyfriends! A new one every night, every minute! I'm sick of being in love! Where can I go? To meet every man who isn't Adam?

FTATATEETA. You want to go some place sensual, godless, and depraved?

STEVE. Tell me!

FTATATEETA. I'd say—Sodom.

STEVE. Sodom?

PHARAOH. (*appalled*) Off-season? No . . .

STEVE. I don't care!

Steve stalks off, in the opposite direction from Adam.

PHARAOH. Let them go! Let them all go! I am the Boy-King of all Egypt! I am immortal! (*facing the audience, calling out to the hundreds of thousands of slaves*) Sing, gay slaves! Sing as you toil! Sing a gay slave song!

FTATATEETA. Sing to your Pharaoh!

GAY SLAVES. (*recorded, a thousand voices strong, a song like "One" from* A Chorus Line, *very bright and snappy*)

As the song continues, the Pharaoh and Ftatateeta execute a crisp, choreographed vaudevillian strut and exit, in high show-biz style. Ftatateeta may have retrieved Peggy's spear and handed it to the Pharaoh earlier in the scene, and Ftatateeta and the Pharaoh might use their spears as props in their dance.

Lights down on Egypt as the Pharaoh and Ftatateeta dance off.

STAGE MANAGER. A desperate prayer, go.

Lights up on Mabel's face; she stands downstage center, on a now bare stage. She is plaintive and yearning; she stands high on a mountain top, desperate and unsure of where to turn.

MABEL. Dear God, it's Mabel. Of Canaan. Old Canaan. (*She glances down, collecting her thoughts; she looks up again, to heaven*) I know you've been doing your best. You've given life to—the world. But something's gone terribly wrong. There are tribes everywhere, at war with one another. There is disease, and pestilence, and—the media! People can't seem to live together, to appreciate what they've been given. And Adam and Steve—I don't know what to do! So I've decided that—it's up to you. (*with a new, tough-minded, gritty resolve, making sure God pays attention*) You made it, you fix it! It's time for . . . (*finding the word, for the first time in history*) a miracle!

STAGE MANAGER. Possible miracle, go.

The Stage Manager strikes a bell-tone on her chime. Mabel glances down, touching her stomach. She glances up, with a radiant smile.

MABEL. (*to God, very simply, overwhelmed*) Thank you.

Jane enters, dressed as a shepherd, singing "Ave Maria." She brings Mabel a long blue veil and places it over Mabel's hair.

JANE. (*singing*) AVE MARIA! GRATIA PLENA . . .

The stage is gradually transformed into a life-size Nativity scene. A manger, and perhaps fragments of arches or Gothic windows, appear, designed in a glowing, painterly, Renaissance style. The entire cast appears, entering with a hint of procession, everyone joining in on "Ave Maria," possibly with a re-corded backing, so the song soars and swells majestically. The actors should be dressed in robes and homespun, as shepherds, with head-coverings,

sandals and rope belts. One shepherd leads a life-size, painted camel, an-
other leads a life-size, painted goat. Another shepherd carries a painted
sheep. The animals could be realistic, or have the flat, high-school charm of
awkwardly painted props. Bales of hay appear. The shepherds and animals
arrange themselves in a gorgeously traditional tableau, beneath a single,
radiant star and a midnight-blue Bethlehem sky. The affect should be that
of a Hallmark card, or a painted Nativity beneath a Christmas tree.

ENTIRE CAST. (*singing*) MARIA, GRATIA PLENA
  MARIA, GRATIA PLENA
  AVE!
  AVE, DOMINUS
  DOMINUS TECUM . . .

Adam and Steve have entered from opposite sides of the stage, costumed as
Wise Men in flowing, glittering brocade robes and turbans. They each carry
a gift in a small golden sack or box.

STAGE MANAGER. Wiseguys, go.

Adam and Steve leave the Nativity group, and approach each other down-
stage. "Ave Maria" gradually fades out.

STEVE. Hey.
ADAM. Hey.
STEVE. Long time.
ADAM. How've you been?
STEVE. Sodom was *fantastic*. Of course, it was destroyed.
ADAM. By what?
STEVE. Tourists.
ADAM. Really.

STEVE. And you?

ADAM. Oh, you know. The burning bush, the promised land, the eleven commandments.

STEVE. Eleven?

ADAM. No white after Labor Day.

STEVE. Sure.

ADAM. Well, good to see you.

Adam starts to leave.

STEVE. Hey—remember the flood?

ADAM. (*turning*) Whoa. And Egypt?

STEVE. Right. And the garden?

ADAM. (*passionately*) I missed you so much.

STEVE. I never got to Sodom.

ADAM. So will this be what you need? To finally believe?

STEVE. Mabel's baby?

ADAM. Mabel's miracle!

STEVE. We don't know that.

ADAM. I do! Because ever since Mabel got pregnant, I've been able to read my Bible!

STEVE. You have?

ADAM. (*taking out his Bible and turning to various passages*) And I think it tells a story. So far, I can only make out a few words, but I think they're the most important ones. See? (*the first passage*) "Adam." (*another page*) "God." (*another page*) "Miracle." (*the title page*) "Copyright."

STEVE. Does it say "Steve"?

ADAM. Not yet. It's strange, so far it doesn't say anything about—us.

STEVE. But you want us to believe it. Every line. Without question.

ADAM. It's the word of God!

STEVE. But who wrote it down?

ADAM. (*getting very angry*) Steve . . .

STEVE. (*equally angry*) Adam . . .

ADAM. I don't want to fight!

STEVE. Same here!

ADAM. So—what did you bring?

STEVE. (*holding up his golden sack*) Just—some frankincense. And you?

ADAM. (*holding up his small brass box*) Myrrh.

STEVE. For a baby?

ADAM. (*vehemently*) Babies love myrrh.

STEVE. How would you know?

ADAM. Well, nobody likes frankincense! Why don't you spend some money!

STEVE. I bet somebody just gave that to you and you're just passing it along!

> *Steve knocks Adam's gift out of his hands. Adam knocks Steve's gift out of his hands. Steve knocks Adam's Bible to the ground. Adam smacks Steve in the chest. Steve hits him back. They begin to wrestle, falling to the ground and making loud grunting noises, a real schoolyard brawl. Steve gets Adam in a headlock.*

        Say it!

ADAM. Say what?

STEVE. Say, "I love Steve more than anything," or I'll break your neck!

ADAM. Try it!

> *They wrestle again, just as viciously. Adam gets Steve immobilized.*

        Say it!

STEVE. What?

ADAM. Say, "I love myrrh!"

STEVE. Never!

They wrestle again, until Adam finally begs for mercy.

ADAM. Stop it, stop it, time! Time!

They stop wrestling, lying in a heap on the ground, panting. Adam rises to his knees, and slaps Steve on the butt.

Steve!

STEVE. What?

ADAM. Will we still be like this, will we still be having this fight, in another thousand years? Another two thousand years?

We hear the continual beep of a cell phone. Adam and Steve look around, puzzled as to the source of the sound.

STEVE. Adam, that's you.

STAGE MANAGER. Two thousand years, go.

From within his robes, Adam removes a cell phone. He holds the phone out, unsure of what it is, as it continues to beep. Adam stands. Steve stands and rejoins the Nativity group. Adam moves downstage, gradually figuring out how the phone works. He presses the button to speak.

ADAM. *(into his phone)* Hello? . . . I'm almost done, I'll be right home.

Adam stares at the phone with a mix of wonder and confusion. He presses the button to end the call. As he does so, we hear a bold, very rock and roll, Motown or pop arrangement of a Christmas song begin to blare over the PA system, something wildly propulsive and jubilant, an irresistible, wall-of-sound arrangement of "Jingle Bells" or "Sleighride", with a raucous, soulful vocal.

As Adam listens to the music, he removes his Wise Man robe. Underneath, he is wearing very contemporary clothing, the modern-day outfit he will wear in Act II.

Adam turns upstage to watch the Nativity. As the song soars, it begins to snow on the Nativity.

STAGE MANAGER. Intermission, go.

ACT TWO

Time: Christmas Eve, the present.

STAGE MANAGER. House to half, house out. Sound one eighty-five, go.

We hear the same sprightly Christmas song that ended Act I.

The curtain rises on Adam and Steve's modern-day loft in Manhattan. The loft is large and open but not too luxurious; while clearly designed, it still has a certain industrial rawness. There is a central, open archway, leading to a hallway, with the front door offstage. Additional doors or exits lead to a bathroom, a kitchen, and a bedroom.

The furnishings show more imagination than expense and include low shelves, a central couch, an armchair and ottoman, and several useful stools. A bar has been set out on a table or countertop, with plenty of liquor, soft drinks, ice, and glassware.

At the Moment, the usual decor of the loft is completely obscured by an exuberant excess of Christmas glitz. There is a huge, fully decorated tree, surrounded by piles of gaudily wrapped packages. There are life-size molded plastic Dickensian carolers, huge striped candy canes, an elaborate tabletop Nativity scene, an array of huge plastic Santas and snow-

men, and plenty of plastic snowflakes and gingerbread people. The walls should be smothered in Christmas kitsch, including stockings, wreaths, and at least twelve reindeer pulling a sleigh, along with endless yards of evergreen garland and strand after strand of electric twinkle lights, as yet unlit. All of this has been carefully and lovingly thought out, by a true Yuletide freak, who believes that too much is just a starting point. There might be some Chanukah touches mixed in with the Christmas hurricane, including some Stars of David and a large plastic menorah atop the tree, where an angel usually roosts.

A Christmas Eve open house is being prepared. Colorful platters of food and treats have been set out, along with stacks of plates, utensils, and napkins.

In Act II, the Stage Manager can either stay seated at her desk beside the main playing area throughout the Act, or she can quietly exit after calling the first cues and return to call the end of the first scene, remaining onstage until her final exit.

Steve enters from the offstage kitchen, carrying a punch bowl filled with eggnog. He wears basic, practical clothing, Levis and a sweater. Adam, Steve, Jane, and Mabel will be the same characters from Act I, only with no memory of that Act's events.

Steve sets the punch bowl down on the bar. He turns off the Christmas music, which is emanating from either an audio system or one of those plastic Christmas trees with a singing mouth.

We hear a key in the front door, and Adam enters, wearing a colorful scarf, a striped stocking cap, mittens and a winter coat. He is the ebullient Christmas fan, and he is bursting with holiday fervor.

ADAM. Wait, just wait! One second!

STEVE. Adam . . .

ADAM. I saw it, we need it, you'll love it!

Adam runs back outside. He returns immediately, carrying a nearly lifesize plastic reindeer with a bright red nose.

STEVE. We don't have any more room!

ADAM. But we can't have a party without Rudolph! I was passing by Kmart, and it was the only one left, I had to wrestle it away from this woman with two screaming children, I said, I'm sorry, it's *mine*, you have deductions! Oh, and I also got . . .
Adam runs back outside.

STEVE. No! You may not bring one more piece of holiday shit into this house!

Adam returns, carrying a large, molded plastic statue of the Virgin Mary.

ADAM. But this is so special, this is actually sacred . . .

Adam places the statue on a table or counter.

ADAM. It's the Virgin Mary.
STEVE. Yeah? So?
ADAM. Only—she speaks.

Adam pulls a cord, or presses a button at the base of the statue, and a perky recorded voice is heard, coming from inside the statue.

VIRGIN MARY. Merry Christmas!
ADAM. It's a miracle. A modern miracle.
STEVE. Does she say anything else?

ADAM. I think she got the same microchip as Barbie.

Adam presses the button again, and the statue speaks.

VIRGIN MARY. Math is hard.

STEVE. I like that.

ADAM. (*looking around, taking off his coat*) We have all the food and beverages and ice, and our Yuletide ambiance is almost complete . . .

STEVE. Almost?

ADAM. Shut your eyes.

STEVE. Are you gonna spray me with something?

ADAM. Shut them!

Steve shuts his eyes. Adam turns off the regular lights, so the loft is in darkness.

ADAM. One, two, three . . .

Adam flips a switch, or connects some extension cords, and all of the Christmas lights throughout the loft are illuminated. The effect is kitschy yet dazzling, real Christmas magic.

ADAM. Open!

Steve opens his eyes; he is genuinely impressed with the lighting display.

ADAM. Merry Christmas.

Adam and Steve kiss; they remain deeply in love.

ADAM. You look so great.

STEVE. (*proudly, as in Act I*) I know.

ADAM. (*gesturing to the room*) All of this—is for you.

STEVE. You are very sweet.

ADAM. I just want—to make every day of your life a Christmas party, from now on.

STEVE. Adam, I don't need parties . . .

ADAM. I do. Because I have something to celebrate—your life.

STEVE. Okay, how did it go?

ADAM. No, today isn't about me. No matter how phenomenal my day was.

STEVE. Tell me. I want to hear it. I mean it.

ADAM. (*being noble*) No, I don't have to.

STEVE. Time's up!

ADAM. No! Okay! It was—incredible. It was, if I do say so myself, the most fantastic, deconstructed, trans-holiday pageant in the history of the elite Preston School first grade. Because I am not just a teacher, oh no. I am a post-modern, multi-cultural genius.

STEVE. "Trans-holiday pageant"?

ADAM. Well, I wanted to be inclusive because it's the right thing to do, and because the school is on the Upper West Side and the children's parents are all ultra-liberal, which means that when a kid hits somebody we say he's depressed. So I did the entire Nativity, the Wise Men, the shepherds, even the camels, only everyone in it—was gay.

STEVE. You're kidding.

The intercom buzzes.

ADAM. (*as he moves toward the phone intercom hanging on the wall by the front door*) The kids *loved* it. The parents *loved* it. (*into the intercom receiver*) Hello? Right, three E, come on up. (*He buzzes the visitor in, and hangs up the receiver*) This one little boy, who played Jesus, he ran over to his mother, he was just beaming. And he said, "Mommy, I'm gay!" She was *thrilled*. She hugged him and turned to her husband and said, "Darling, this means *Yale!*"

STEVE. But—the Bible isn't gay.

ADAM. (*triumphantly*) It is now!

STEVE. But—no. I think it sounds terrific.

ADAM. You do?

STEVE. Yes. And I am very proud of you. And so, at least for tonight, I am going to be—a Christmas person.

Steve takes the stocking cap off Adam's head and puts it on.

ADAM. You?

STEVE. Yes. Because of everything you've done. (*as Santa*) Ho, ho, ho!

ADAM. (*amused*) Stay back.

STEVE. Come over here, little boy, and sit on my lap.

ADAM. (*sitting on Steve's lap*) Can I tell you what I want?

STEVE. I can tell you what you'll get.

ADAM. Santa! (*as Adam and Steve embrace, Adam pulls away*) Steve?

STEVE. Yeah?

ADAM. Can I—no, I can't.

STEVE. What? What is it?

ADAM. It's just—there's something I need to ask you, and it's sort of major, beyond major, but—no, it's too weird!

STEVE. What? Ask me!

The doorbell buzzes.

ADAM. Later.

STEVE. Adam!

ADAM. It's fine. (*calling out, to whoever's at the door*) It's open!

Cheryl Mindle enters. Cheryl is a fresh-faced young woman, recently ar-

*rived from Utah; we met her early in Act I, in the audience. She wears a
holly or Santa brooch on her winter coat and carries a potted poinsettia in
foil. She is extremely perky and outgoing, and thrilled to be invited to Adam
and Steve's Christmas party. She is good-hearted and hugely enthusiastic
about everything. She combines all the pep of a cheerleader, missionary, and
fan club president. As she enters, she is dazzled and awestruck by the loft's
Christmas decor.*

CHERYL. Merry merry! *(looking around at the decor, she gasps)* Oh, Adam! Oh my God!

ADAM. Cheryl?

CHERYL. It's *gorgeous!*

ADAM. *(thrilled)* Isn't it?

CHERYL. *(sincerely, as a compliment)* It's . . . it's a *mall!*

ADAM. Steve, this is Cheryl Mindle, my new teaching assistant, from school. She just started.

CHERYL. And I love it! Adam, your pageant! *(Cheryl removes her coat, revealing an extremely Christmasy outfit, including a sweater knitted with blazing red cardinals, a Santa or a Christmas tree, paired with a long, colorfully pleated wool skirt, red stockings, and clunky maryJanes. As Adam takes her coat, she speaks to Steve)* You should have seen it, it was so touching!

ADAM. Cheryl's not going home for Christmas, so I asked her to come and help with the party.

CHERYL. *(to Steve)* And I have heard so much about *you!*

STEVE. Uh-oh.

CHERYL. And I love your loft! Now, you renovated this whole place yourself?

STEVE. I'm a contractor.

CHERYL. And you hate Christmas!

STEVE. Cheryl!

The intercom buzzes.

ADAM. No, it's going to be fine, Steve is being very festive.

STEVE. I am! (*trying very hard to be sincere, ferociously growling his good cheer at Cheryl*) Happy holidays!

CHERYL. That's good!

ADAM. Cheryl, this is the intercom, you just pick it up . . . (*speaking into the receiver*) Hi, come on up. (*to Cheryl*) And buzz. (*He buzzes the visitor in*)

CHERYL. (*impressed*) We don't have one of those, back in Misty Bluffs. That's where I'm from, in Utah.

STEVE. Are you—a Mormon?

CHERYL. Born and bred!

STEVE. (*putting his arm around Adam*) Are you aware that—we're gay?

CHERYL. (*totally sympathetic and chipper*) Of course! And I am not judging you, uh-uh! Adam is a great guy, and I know that you've been together forever, I mean, way longer than most normal couples.

STEVE. Normal?

CHERYL. Uh-huh, and I know that some good Christians, like my Mom, think that gay people are sick and godless, but I said, no, Mom, they are sensitive and artistic! (*She gestures with both arms to all the Christmas decor as sincere proof of gay people's artistic glory*)

STEVE. You go, girl!

Cheryl whoops in agreement and gives a fervently physical, if awkward, two snaps up.

CHERYL. Do you know what you need?

STEVE. Tell me.

CHERYL. *Angels.* They're real, and they're everywhere, watching over us. Back home, I have fifteen different hand-painted ceramic angels, three stuffed angels, an angel poster, an angel T-shirt, oh, and two pairs of angel pajamas!

STEVE. Cheryl, are you—seeing someone?

CHERYL. You mean, like a boyfriend?

STEVE. (*after a beat*) No.

The doorbell buzzes, and Adam goes offstage, into the hall.

CHERYL. Stop it! I bet there are angels in this room, right now! I can feel it! Tonight is gonna be magical!

ADAM. (*stepping in from the hall*) Ladies and gentlemen, a Christmas visitor!

Trey Pomfret strides into the room. He is an acerbic, very gay man dressed as Santa Claus, including the padding, the red suit, the belt, the boots, hat, and a detachable white cotton beard and mustache. He carries a sack over his shoulder.

CHERYL. (*delighted*) It's Santa!

TREY. *Fuck you!*

CHERYL. (*undaunted*) It's New York Santa!

Trey rips off his hat, beard, and mustache, and heads straight for the bar, where he begins violently putting ice cubes into a glass and mixing himself a very stiff drink. He is furious, barely able to contain his rage as he tells his story.

TREY. (*to Adam*) I am so pissed at you!

ADAM. At me? Why?

TREY. Because of all this Bible business!

CHERYL. Bible?

TREY. I am an over-bred, over-educated WASP from Connecticut, so I've always thought of God as, you know—an ancestor. But lately Adam's been going on, about miracles, and his little Bible pageant, so I thought, well, I'll try. (*noticing Cheryl's poinsettia plant*) Oh look, it's a poinsettia—the gift that won't die. So I don this ensemble and I volunteer, on Christmas Eve, at the local homeless shelter. Where I have just allowed countless heartbreakingly innocent, bright-eyed homeless children to sit on my lap. "Ho, ho, ho, and what would you like for Christmas, little Simbali, or Jamal, or Tylenol?" (*going over to shake Cheryl's hand*) I can make these jokes because my name is Trey, and my brothers are named Shreve and Stone, so who am I to talk? And little Advil says, "Santa, whassup? Is you a faggot?"

CHERYL. No!

ADAM. What did you do?

TREY. Well, I took a deep breath, and I said, "Why yes I am, little Midol. And the North Pole is for everyone, gay and straight."

ADAM. That's perfect!

STEVE. And what happened?

TREY. Armageddon. The child's hard-working, down-on-her-luck single parent grabs the child off my lap and screams, "Get away, cock-sucker!" To which I reply, "But darling, look what I've brought for you—Christmas crack." And finally the director of the shelter says that maybe it's best if *I* leave! So I come here, and my question for you, Adam, is this—what the fuck is God thinking?

ADAM. Trey, somewhere in that shelter was a gay kid, who got to see a gay Santa.

CHERYL. (*going to fetch Trey a drink*) You need some eggnog.

TREY. (*as he opens his jacket to remove the pillow padding; he wears a T-shirt under the jacket*) With a chaser.

STEVE. (*to Trey*) This is Cheryl. She's from Utah.

TREY. Oh, I knew that.

CHERYL. How?

TREY. Your smile. Your glow. Your shoes.

CHERYL. Well, I think what you did was just tee-riffic!

ADAM. It's the true Christmas spirit.

STEVE. Oh no, oh no, I'm having a problem, staying Christmasy.

CHERYL. (*flinging open her arms*) Hug alert! Woo-woo-woo!

Cheryl runs across the room toward Steve, to hug him. Adam deflects Cheryl, as Steve flees. Adam goes to Steve.

ADAM. (*to Steve*) You can do it! For the baby Jesus!

STEVE. But Adam—you're Jewish!

CHERYL. You are? Really?

ADAM. (*gesturing to all the Christmas decor*) Duh.

TREY. Of course.

The intercom buzzes.

CHERYL. No, let me! (*into the receiver*) Merry something! Come on up! (*She buzzes the visitor in and speaks to the room*) But you know, I always feel sorry for Jews. I mean, on Christmas Eve.

TREY. I know. When my sleigh lands on a Jewish rooftop, I always look down the chimney and yell, *"Nothing for Goldberg!"*

ADAM. But I want to be clear. I love Christmas, for the decor and the spirit, but I do not want to be Christian. Because my Aunt Sylvia told me, all gentiles are bitter alcoholics who drive German cars and beat their wives.

CHERYL. (*immediately*) Adam! That is a terrible stereotype!

TREY. It's true, but it's a terrible stereotype.

Mabel enters, bursting with giddy Christmas cheer. She wears a winter coat, a knitted Peruvian cap, huge knitted mittens, and mukluks. She carries a cardboard cake box.

MABEL. Merry Christmas!

ADAM. Mabel!

Jane enters. She wears an enormous, distended pair of overalls—she is hugely pregnant. Her belly juts out so far that she cannot close her down-filled coat. She is feverishly, gloriously livid. She has not been physically comfortable for months, and she can barely get around. Her volcanic fury, and her pregnancy, are at peak. Being pregnant has given her absolute authority to majestically blame the entire world for her condition. Her entire first scene is an aria of rage, directed at everyone in the room, at full bellow.

JANE. *There is no God!*

STEVE. Jane.

JANE. (*to Adam*) I blame *you!*

ADAM. Me?

JANE. May you *burn!*

MABEL. (*thrilled, to everyone*) Eight months and counting, raging hormones!

CHERYL. Eight months?

TREY. Jane, should you be here?

JANE. (*to Trey*) Fuck you! (*regarding Mabel*) She tells me we should have a baby . . . (*regarding Adam*) he tells me we should have a baby, everyone's telling me, a baby is a gift, why should gay people be denied!

ADAM. That's right!

JANE. Why? WHY? Because gay people used to be *smart!* But I listened, I said okay, we've been together for fucking ages, why not? A baby, a child, someone to send out for cigarettes!

MABEL. (*to everyone, regarding Jane*) She quit, everything.

JANE. (*regarding Mabel*) And she's looking up at me, with her shining little eyes . . . (*regarding Adam*) and then he chimes in—"Come on, Jane! You're the lucky one!"

CHERYL. You're radiant!

JANE. (*to Cheryl*) FUCK YOU! Whoever you are! I am not radiant! I am not a madonna! I am a WHALE! I am a WAREHOUSE! I've got this bloodsucker sitting in my stomach, and it's trying to punch its way out!

MABEL. It's a brand new life!

JANE. It's the *alien!* I am not supposed to be pregnant—I am a BULL DYKE! It's like if Ralph Kramden got pregnant! I can't stand it!

MABEL. (*sincerely, doting on Jane*) Isn't she adorable?

JANE. Fuck childbirth! Fuck making a family! Fuck the miracle of life! Merry Christmas! I gotta pee!

Jane exits, into the bathroom.

TREY. This is so touching.

ADAM. It's a Hallmark moment.

MABEL. Isn't this *perfect?*

ADAM. Why?

MABEL. (*chattering happily as she skips around the room, pulling many small, brightly wrapped gifts from the shopping bags she and Jane have carried in. Some gifts will go under the tree, and others to party guests. As Mabel speaks, she will not feel sorry for herself, or get at all serious or solemn—she is on a complete Christmas and childbirth high.*) She's been like this for weeks. And at first I felt so helpless. I mean, I wanted this baby so badly, and I tried, I had all those treatments, I had that operation, but it just wasn't going to happen—oh, I love your tree, it's garish! So when Jane volunteered . . .

STEVE. Volunteered?

ADAM. Steve . . .

TREY. As a sublet . . .

MABEL. Yes! And I was so incredibly moved, I thought, oh my God, she would do that for me, for us? And all along, I've been wondering, what can I do to repay her, what gesture can I make that could possibly equal her incredible, selfless act? So I prayed.

STEVE. Good move!

CHERYL. That is so sweet! (*to Mabel*) I'm Cheryl. I work with Adam.

TREY. She's a Mormon.

MABEL. (*thrilled*) Get out! I love Mormons!

CHERYL. You do?

MABEL. (*sincerely*) They'll believe anything!

ADAM. So you prayed . . .

MABEL. Right, and I went to all different churches and temples and ashrams, and then finally I went to the gym.

TREY. The one true God.

MABEL. Amen! And I was doing this spinning class, you know, on the stationary bikes, and, as usual, I offer my fat up to God. And just as we're doing this amazing series of jumps, in and out of the saddle, and the instructor is playing all of these disco Christmas songs, I peak! I have an epiphany!

STEVE. You were dehydrated.

MABEL. And when I get home, I ask Jane—to marry me.

ADAM. Oh my God!

CHERYL. (*whooping*) Whoa!

STEVE. Jesus.

MABEL. And she's sitting there, in her recliner, you know, sort of what she calls, beached? And she's watching her favorite show, *Xena*. And I stand in front of her and I say, "Jane, you are the co-mother of our child and the love of my life. Jane, my beloved, my giver-goddess, my exalted perfect other—will you marry me?"

ADAM. And she said . . . ?

Jane has emerged from the bathroom.

JANE. "You're blocking Xena."

STEVE. Way to go!

As she and Jane reenact the marriage proposal, Mabel will help Jane get settled into an armchair; sitting down, like everything else, is not easy for Jane in her current state.

MABEL. And I grabbed the remote and I turned off the set and I said, "No! I know that I can't really share in the amazing and difficult upheaval you're experiencing—although I bet I can write a poem about it!"

JANE. She threatened me!

MABEL. "And I can make it better—you have to marry me!"

CHERYL. And she said . . . ?

JANE. "Gimme the remote!"

ADAM. And you said . . . ?

MABEL. "Not until you say yes!"

STEVE. That's blackmail!

JANE. And it was the episode where Xena was bathing Gabrielle!

MABEL. *(triumphant)* So we're getting married!

JANE. I had no choice!

MABEL. And we were just wondering if, because you're our very closest friends, and you're all totally a part of us, if we could be married right here. Tonight.

ADAM. Tonight?

STEVE. Here?

MABEL. And we've invited this wonderful woman, Rabbi Sharon, to come to the party and perform the ceremony.

TREY. Rabbi Sharon? In the wheelchair? From cable?

MABEL. Yes! She has that show, it's so motivating, I watch it every morning, at six AM.

ADAM. Of course—what's it called?

MABEL. *Who Believes?*

STEVE. Wait. You invited some handicapped, public-access lesbian rabbi to our Christmas Eve open house to marry you?

MABEL. I just dialed the number on the screen, "one-nine-hundred-She-brew." I told her all about us, she was thrilled!

JANE. Please, you are in no way obligated. Even if the two of you did help get me into this fucking mess.

ADAM. Steve?

STEVE. Adam?

ADAM. I hate to say this, and Steve, you're gonna kill me, but—things are coming together. Steve is feeling so great, he's back at work, he's doing two lofts, I have just presented an all-gay Bible pageant, Jane is about to give birth, and now you're getting married—do you know what this sounds like?

TREY. All the reasons people hate New York?

ADAM. A celebration! We'd love to have the wedding here! We'd be honored!

STEVE. Why not? Merry Christmas!

Adam and Steve kiss, as the intercom buzzes. Cheryl picks up the receiver.

CHERYL. (*into the receiver*) Hello, Rainbow Chapel! Come on up! (*she buzzes the guest in*)

TREY. Will it be a Jewish ceremony? I'm sorry, I'm from Westport, but I did rent *Yentl.* Will there be that wonderful lighting?

CHERYL. Will there be those funny men, with the strange hair, all dressed in black?

TREY. Art dealers?

MABEL. And you know, Adam and Steve, if you want, Sharon could also marry the two of you.

ADAM. No, come on. We can't just decide to get married, on the spur of the moment, as part of a trend. Can we?

JANE. (*needling them*) Can you?

STEVE. Adam, I love you, you know that, I hope everyone knows that, but—why do gay people need to get married?

MABEL. Because we're entitled!

STEVE. But have you noticed how conventional gay people are getting?

TREY. And wholesome?

JANE. We registered.

CHERYL. For a lesbian wedding? Where?

JANE. L. L. Bean.

MABEL. And I have made a savory vegan wedding cake. We could share it.

CHERYL. Vegan?

Mabel has opened the lid of the cake box, to admire the wedding cake. Trey and Cheryl peer into the box.

MABEL. It means that it contains absolutely no animal products. Nothing suffers.

TREY. Except the people who'll eat it.

MABEL. No! It's delicious, it's tofu, and the frosting is made from soy powder and kelp.

TREY. What are the bride and groom?

MABEL. They're two hand-carved wooden seagulls. Because scientists have discovered that there are a great many lesbian seagulls.

CHERYL. How can they tell?

TREY. The ponchos.

JANE. (*feeling a physical tremor*) Whoa!

MABEL. (*running over to Jane*) Sweetie?

JANE. No, I'm fine, I think.

MABEL. (*rubbing Jane's back*) Find your core, like they told us at the birthing center . . .

CHERYL. The birthing center?

JANE. We're in this class, with ten other pregnant lesbians. It's like *The X-Files*. This one woman, she wants to give birth underwater, to reduce trauma to the baby. I said, what are you having, a *trout*?

Kevin Markham enters. Kevin is a hot young go-go boy. He wears a long overcoat, boots and a red elf hat. He is a giddy, muscled Chelsea specimen, with just a hint of Valley Boy syntax.

KEVIN. Like, Merry Christmas! I can only stay a few minutes, I'm working a party down at Twilo.
MABEL. On Christmas Eve?
KEVIN. I'm a go-go elf.

Kevin flings off his coat, revealing just a g-string, or a red wrestling singlet, either garment should have a cluster of mistletoe attached at the crotch.

TREY. Mrs. Claus and I are so proud of him.
KEVIN. How's my baby?

Kevin runs to Jane and kneels, putting his head on her stomach.

JANE. Stop that! I hate it when people do that! I'm not ticking!
KEVIN. But it's so great!
CHERYL. Wait—(*regarding Kevin*) is he the baby's father?
KEVIN. (*proudly*) I'm the godfather.
CHERYL. So—who's the dad?
ADAM. (*shyly, but bursting with pride*) Me.
CHERYL. *You?*
ADAM. I'm the donor.

Cheryl screams and runs to hug Adam; Mabel deftly intercepts the hug, and Adam joins Steve on the couch.

CHERYL. Congratulations!

ADAM. But it's really only technical . . . (*to Jane and Mabel, being respectful*) we signed a contract, I have no legal rights to this child.

MABEL. (*to Adam and Steve*) But you know that we want you, both of you, to be part of the baby's life. And we are so grateful for your sperm.

TREY. I always say that the next morning, over coffee.

MABEL. We need all of you. It takes a village to raise a child.

TREY. Greenwich Village.

JANE. Everyone is pitching in. You promised!

CHERYL. (*starting to circulate, offering guests a bowl of chips or pretzels*) Do you know yet? If it's going to be a boy, or a lesbian?

MABEL. We all went together. We had an ultrasound.

ADAM. You could see her, she was so tiny.

JANE. (*fondly*) She was smoking.

CHERYL. What about a name?

MABEL. Well, we've been thinking about something biblical . . .

CHERYL. I love that!

ADAM. Like Sarah . . .

KEVIN. Or Rebecca . . .

JANE. Oh, or my favorite . . .

CHERYL. (*offering Jane the bowl*) What?

JANE. Satan.

Cheryl stares at Jane, very taken aback. After a beat, she sharply pulls the bowl of snacks away from Jane, and moves across the room, as far from Jane as possible, glancing back at Jane with horror.

CHERYL. But who makes the ultimate decisions? Like, what religion will the baby be?

STEVE. That's interesting. We haven't really talked about that.

MABEL. I'd like to expose the baby to all possible faiths, and let her make any final decision . . .

ADAM. But we can read her Bible stories.

STEVE. Why?

ADAM. Because they're wonderful stories!

JANE. About, oh, guilt and punishment . . .

CHERYL. But what about angels, huh? They're always totally good, and they watch over us, and guide us . . .

TREY. Darling, please. Angels are just Prozac for poor people.

MABEL. Trey!

ADAM. I know. We can take the baby to the Easter Show at Radio City. It's the perfect introduction to the life of Christ.

TREY. Jesus and the Rockettes. I always wish they'd do the Last Supper. "Which of you shall betray me?" (*He looks around, selecting an imaginary showgirl-Judas, and pointing to her*) "Could it be—Lisa?"

STEVE. So Adam, religion is just about glitz.

ADAM. But why not? Isn't that the best part? There's even that one Broadway theater, the Mark Hellinger, that they've rented out as a Baptist church. It makes a strange kind of sense.

TREY. Because it's where gay men once gathered, to worship Carol Channing.

ADAM. Yes! And I've been changing the Bible. I've been making the stories more gay-positive, and upbeat.

STEVE. Then why bother having a Bible at all?

ADAM. So the baby can know, about God.

STEVE. Not in my house.

ADAM. Your house?

KEVIN. Wait, you guys, everybody! Maybe I can help!

ADAM. Please!

KEVIN. Last night, when I was dancing, I had—a vision.

MABEL. A vision?

KEVIN. Okay, this is gonna sound really weird, but—you know what it's like, when the music is fantastic, and the whole crowd is really hot and really into it, and you're on, like, some incredible acid?

A beat, and then everyone in the room looks at everyone else and nods, "Sure, of course."

KEVIN. (*now standing on an ottoman*) And I was up there, on my box, wearing like, my boots and, what was it, oh yeah, a washcloth, and the light hit me! And I looked right into it, and—there she was. Like floating, gazing down at me.

MABEL. The Virgin Mary?

KEVIN. (*with awe*) Olivia Newton-John. Who I always loved from when I was, like, little, and I watched her in *Grease*, where she was like this sort of Australian exchange student, and then in this other flick, *Xanadu*, where she was this goddess who comes to earth and teaches this, oh, this really cute guy how to do roller disco!

TREY. It's her Lear.

KEVIN. And she always seemed like, well, maybe not a great actress, but like a really nice lady, and then I read where she had cancer, but she's doing good, and I'm telling you, she was up there, and she spoke, she said . . .

TREY. "Have you never been mellow?"

MABEL. (*to Trey*) Hush!

KEVIN. She said, "Congratulations! You're going to be part of a baby." And that's the first time it really hit me, like a whole new deal—a baby! I mean, all of us, are we qualified? To have a kid? And I said, Livvy—that's what her friends call her—Livvy, is this right? Is this what God wants?

MABEL. (*eagerly*) And what did she say?

KEVIN. She said—that maybe the baby is going to be *really special*.

JANE. Like what? Like who?

MABEL. You mean, the baby could be what Adam's been talking about, about everything coming together . . .

ADAM. Maybe!

The intercom buzzes.

CHERYL. (*on her way to the intercom*) You mean, Jane's baby could be—the Messiah! The Second Coming! Right here in Chelsea!

KEVIN. It could happen!

TREY. We already have three Starbucks!

STEVE. No, come on, guys! Don't do that to a baby!

JANE. Don't do that to me!

During the previous conversation, Cheryl has privately buzzed the next visitor in.

ADAM. But what if the baby is part of the answer. To my question. The question that's been ruling my life.

STEVE. Which is?

ADAM. Well, it's just that I'm afraid to ask it, out loud . . .

STEVE. Try!

JANE. (*feeling a very sharp labor pain*) Awww!

MABEL. Honey? Should we—should I call an ambulance?

JANE. No! I'm just, oh God—I am so embarrassed!

MABEL. Why, sweetie?

JANE. I mean, you guys know me, don't you? I strip paint. I haul cinder blocks. I'm Jane, right?

MABEL. Of course, honey.

JANE. But it's just, I've been getting so—emotional. Just yesterday I was rebuilding a carburetor, and—I burst into tears.

TREY. (*sympathetically*) You too?

The doorbell buzzes.

CHERYL. I'll get it.

Cheryl runs out into the hall.

JANE. And I've been getting—so scared. I'm turning into such a wuss. I'm not a wuss, am I?

EVERYONE. (*very touched*) Awww . . .

JANE. *Shut up!*

Cheryl wheels in Rabbi Sharon, in her wheelchair. Sharon is an aggressively confident, gung-ho woman, a cable TV diva with a mission. She is stylishly dressed and coiffed, and immediately takes center stage. She relishes an audience, and a challenge; she's a star.

SHARON. Shalom!

MABEL. Sharon!

SHARON. (*to the room*) That's right—I'm a disabled lesbian rabbi. Gimme your money!

MABEL. Sharon!

ADAM. (*going to Sharon, offering his hand*) Hello. Welcome. I'm Adam.

SHARON. (*shaking his hand*) Yes you are!

ADAM. And this is Steve.

SHARON. (*to Steve, totally upbeat*) The guy with AIDS, am I right?

STEVE. You got it. Mabel?

MABEL. And this is Jane.

SHARON. (*very excited*) Who's pregnant!

JANE. No, no. It's beer.

SHARON. So, does everyone watch my show?

MABEL. Only every day!

KEVIN. I tape it! It is so inspirational! Like that time in April, when you wore your hair up?

SHARON. The Power Look for Passover!

MABEL. I loved that!

SHARON. So let's hear it! I'm Rabbi Sharon, and welcome to . . .

EVERYONE. (*copying Sharon's signature arm gesture, in which she points in a wide, sweeping half-circle, and then points to heaven*) "Who Believes"!

SHARON. All right, let's get goin'! I've got two basic weddings—with God and without.

KEVIN. What's the difference?

SHARON. Well, with God is non-sectarian but focused on a higher power, with a pronoun of your choice. God can be He, She, It, Our Mother, Our Father, Our Sister Spirit, Our Lavender Light, The Goddess, The Creator, The King, or Our Lord.

TREY. Excuse me—are those the specials?

JANE. And without?

SHARON. (*eyeballing Trey, sizing him up*) Uh-huh! (*to everyone*) Without is more inner, it's the union of souls, the joining of two perfect beings, let our community bless this day, you get the picture, we hate God—but we want gifts! So?

MABEL. Well, I'd really like to have God, but not if it's going to make anyone uncomfortable.

SHARON. (*to the room*) Kids? Everyone? God? Hands?

There is a beat, as everyone looks at each other, slightly unsure. Then, as everyone raises their hands except for Trey and Steve

ADAM: Sure!

CHERYL: Of course!

KEVIN: Go for it!

JANE: Why not!   (*all at once*)

SHARON. Great! That takes care of the mindless sheep. Santa?

TREY. I'll pass.

SHARON. Mister Kringle?

MABEL. Trey?

TREY. I'm sorry, I'm having a problem, with the entire Judeo-Christian everything.

SHARON. Tell me.

TREY. Well, most of your major-league atrocities are committed in the name of someone's god. And can you tell me any big-time religion that isn't especially vicious to, say, women and gay people?

JANE. Just one.

TREY. Which?

JANE. Oprah.

MABEL. But that's all just interpretation. God doesn't hate anyone.

TREY. I do!

MABEL. Trey . . .

TREY. Oh, all right. Do you know the only thing I really like about God?

SHARON. Spill.

TREY. The art. It's my favorite thing in the world. There's a small private chapel, in the Medici Palace in Florence. And the walls are covered with frescoes by a painter named Gozzoli. It's the *Adoration of the Magi*, but the colors are so delicate, and there's so much gold, that it looks like—Cinderella. I have never seen anything so beautiful.

SHARON. Bravo. And the wedding?

TREY. Fine. God. Maybe.

CHERYL. Sharon? I believe. And I'm a Mormon!

SHARON. (*after a beat*) No, come on, really.

CHERYL. I am! And I think that God is just the best thing ever!

SHARON. Baby, your religion is like—ten minutes old. It was founded by some guy who got caught, cheating on his wife. She said, so where were you, and he said, well, um, um, I met this . . . angel, and she gave me . . . the Book of Mormon! If he'd told the truth, you'd be worshiping a waitress.

CHERYL. Why is everybody picking on Mormons?

TREY. This is New York, dear. You're the Jew.

STEVE. But why are we? Have you ever seen or listened to, a Chasid or a Buddhist monk or the Pope? The only thing that separates their magic tricks from Scientology is a few thousand years. That's the blink of an eye.

CHERYL. Right! So why pick on anyone?

STEVE. No, Cheryl. Pick on *everyone*.

SHARON. And Steve. So handsome.

STEVE. Is that a bribe?

SHARON. Nope. You I respect.

STEVE. Why?

SHARON. Because I've heard you're stubborn. You say show me. You say no.

STEVE. You heard right.

SHARON. Because God did you wrong. AIDS. The homeless. The Holocaust.

TREY. The subway.

STEVE. So?

SHARON. I still believe.

TREY. Why?

SHARON. Because otherwise—I have nothing.

STEVE. You have common sense. You have reality.

SHARON. And self-pity.

STEVE. Excuse me?

SHARON. Come off it. You think about God more than anyone else in this room. Why you? Why now?

STEVE. No, I don't!

SHARON. (*physically pursuing STEVE, in her wheelchair, really going after*

him, picking a fight) And why not? God made you sick! And not your
neighbor, not some fascist dictator, not some creep.

STEVE. It's a virus!

SHARON. Come clean, baby! It's God!

STEVE. Fuck you! And fuck God!

SHARON. Now we're talkin'! Siddown!

Steve hesitates; he doesn't sit.

SHARON. *(gesturing to her wheelchair)* I am.

*Steve, grudgingly, sits. Sharon moves her wheelchair into a position to face
the group.*

SHARON. Five years ago, it's Sunday morning, and I'm walking down
Christopher Street, on my legs. And I've just done a bat mitzvah, for
my gorgeous niece, and I'm carrying my latte, my heavenly date-nut
scone, and the Sunday *Times,* and I'm headed back to see my naked
young girlfriend. And then—a bicycle messenger. Outta nowhere, he
swipes me, my legs go out, the *Times* goes flying, and I'm slammed
smack—into the back of a FedEx truck. Which doesn't see me, so,
as I'm lying in the street with a broken hip and five fractured ribs,
it backs up onto my pelvis. FedEx truck tires! And then—it goes
forward, right in my ribcage—crack! And by this point, people are
screaming and pointing and then, and I swear, I am not making this
up, I am a person of God—a rusty air conditioner falls off a twenty-
story building, onto my face! And, as I finally lose consciousness,
thank you, I see that bicycle messenger *eating my scone!* And I come to,
three weeks later, paralyzed, half-blind, and I think, what the fuck is
going on? Not just why me, but why the fucking air conditioner? And
some nurse gives me this book, called *When Bad Things Happen to Good*

People. And all I'm thinking is, I don't care! What I want to know is, why do *good* things happen to *bad* people! A man can slaughter his wife, and get away with it. A president can start a war, and still get reelected. I'm paralyzed, my girlfriend dumped me, and she got the apartment! And then—it hits me. What doesn't? Why it happened. And what I'm supposed to do, with my useless legs and my messed-up life and my deluxe new nose—do you like it? (*She gestures to her nose*) "The Mindy." So I buy me some airtime and I say, listen up, New York! Take a look! (*She gestures to herself and her wheelchair*) This is your nightmare! This is the ice on the sidewalk, the maniac in the hallway, this is God when she's drunk! So if I can still believe, if I can still thank someone or something for each new day, if I can pee into a bag and still praise heaven for the pleasure, then so the fuck can all of you, mazel tov, praise Allah and amen!

KEVIN. *I love her!*

SHARON. And you know something? Sometimes God delivers. Like these new drugs, these cocktails, am I right?

MABEL. You see?

SHARON. (*to STEVE*) Are you on them?

STEVE. You know it. Twenty-eight pills a day.

SHARON. Twenty-eight prayers. Twenty-eight mitzvahs.

MABEL. Twenty-eight miracles.

STEVE. That is science. And luck.

ADAM. That's God! Steve, do you remember our Christmas party last year?

STEVE. We didn't have one.

TREY. Oh, thank God, I thought I wasn't invited.

ADAM. Mabel had just given birth. To a baby, a boy who lived for two days. In the same hospital where you'd spent the last two weeks, at 125 pounds, hooked up to a torture chamber, coughing up blood. And I sat in that waiting room, and I cursed God. I said, no more desperate prayers, you get down here, you fix this, or—fuck you forever. And tonight—look at Jane. Look at you.

SHARON. Look at all of you. (*regarding Cheryl*) Even the Martian.

CHERYL. Mormon!

ADAM. All right, Sharon, you're a person of God, right?

SHARON. With a Web site and a T-shirt!

ADAM. What does it say?

SHARON. "Oy Gay."

ADAM. So maybe I can ask you—my question. The one I've been trying to get brave enough and strong enough to ask.

SHARON. I can't wait!

ADAM. No, I shouldn't bother you with it, I'll just shut up . . .

EVERYONE. *Adam!*

ADAM. All right! Here goes. All year long, maybe all my life, things have been—building. To this morning. When I woke up and I looked at Steve, who was curled up, snoring, and—smiling. And I looked out the window and it was snowing, just gently, just that perfect MGM snow. And I got my coffee, and I realized that, at exactly that second—I was . . . happy.

SHARON. Mazel tov!

ADAM. No! I ducked, I shivered, I was terrified! I thought, no, don't jinx it, don't call down a flood or a thunderbolt! And ever since then, I've been in this blind panic. So—is it okay? To say it, to feel it? To be in love, to be part of a baby, to have a party, to be—happy?

SHARON. You're Jewish, right?

ADAM. You noticed.

SHARON. (*with genuine compassion, very straightforward*) Sweetheart, I talk to God, all the time. And you know something? God says yes.

ADAM. Yes?

SHARON. Yes.

ADAM. Okay. All right. Since you say so. I am going . . . to be . . . happy.

Adam looks around the room, at everyone, ending on Steve. He shuts his eyes, facing out. A beat. He tilts his head upward. He mouths the words "Thank you." He smiles.

SHARON. (*after a beat, to Steve*) So—how about another miracle? Right now?

STEVE. What?

SHARON. A wedding. With God? You're the holdout.

ADAM. Steve?

STEVE. (*after a beat*) Fine.

SHARON. Damn, I'm good! Mabel? Wedding party?

JANE. Adam and Steve—you're the best men.

ADAM. Our pleasure.

Adam and Steve line up near Jane and Mabel.

CHERYL. (*picking up the poinsettia, for use as a bouquet*) What about a Maid of Honor, huh?

Trey and Kevin both raise their hands. Realizing they are in competition, they face off.

TREY. This is a sacred occasion, and we are both politically ideal gay men.

KEVIN. So there's, like, only one way to settle this.

TREY. Slap fight.

Trey and Kevin start to slap each other viciously, yelping like fiendish, depraved schoolgirls.

MABEL. You guys! You can both be our People of Honor!

KEVIN. (*gesturing, for Trey to take a place with the wedding party*) Father Christmas.

TREY. (*gesturing for Kevin to take a place*) Employee.

Trey and Kevin stand with Adam and Steve and Jane and Mabel, who are gathered in a group near Sharon. Cheryl is about to join the group, when a thought strikes her:

CHERYL. Uh-oh, um, wait—you all seem like wonderful people, but if I participate in a gay wedding, if I don't leave right now, will I go to hell?

TREY. (*rapidly*) Would you rather have a roomful of homosexuals talk about you after you've gone?

The entire wedding party leans toward Cheryl, a bit menacingly.

CHERYL. I'm in!

Cheryl joins the group, or pulls up a stool nearby.

SHARON. (*taking out her Bible*) Tonight our community gathers—female and male, lesbian, gay and bisexual—yeah, right. And is anyone here transgendered?

TREY. Cheryl?

CHERYL. What?

SHARON. (*to Cheryl*) Good for you! (*Cheryl looks very confused*) And now, a lesbian wedding, or as I like to call it, their second date. With the blessing of Our Lord, by Rabbi Sharon. All right. Jane?

JANE. Right here.

SHARON. Do you love Mabel?

JANE. (*gazing into Mabel's eyes*) Yes.

SHARON. And Mabel?

MABEL. Before the eyes of God?

SHARON. Sing it, baby!

MABEL. Yes. No.

JANE. Mabel?

MABEL. (*with great difficulty*) Not always. When my baby, when our baby, died—I hated everyone.

JANE. I know . . .

MABEL. And when you tried to give me everything that had been taken away—I hated you.

JANE. Oh, babe . . .

MABEL. So I bought a gun.

SHARON. (*raising her arm and forming a gun with her forefinger; she makes a clicking noise, as if cocking the trigger*) A piece!

MABEL. A three fifty-seven Magnum. I wanted to do something that was—the opposite of me. And I went to this shooting range, in a warehouse out in Queens, and down at the far end of the alley, where they have the target, I had them put up pictures of Jesus, and Buddha, and Mrs. Wallbauer, my fifth-grade teacher.

ADAM. Mrs. Wallbauer?

MABEL. She knows why!

ADAM. Okay.

MABEL. And then I had them add—a picture of Jane.

JANE. Oh my God . . .

MABEL. A Polaroid, from the day we found out you were pregnant. And I put on my protective plastic goggles, and I raised my Magnum, I held it straight out, and—I fired. (*holding out her arms, as if firing a pistol, really going through it*) I blasted 'em, one after the other, Jesus, BLAM! Buddha, BLAM! Mrs. Wallbauer, BLAM! Because I wasn't being disruptive in class, I was singing my labia song! And Jane—I hesitated, I thought, I can't do this, I can't kill you, but then I thought about my baby, and your belly, and that fucking home pregnancy stick with its little pink plus sign, and—*blam!*

JANE. And—how did you feel?

MABEL. Fantastic. It was this incredible rush, I realized, they're not dead, none of them, but I had killed—my rage, and my envy. And I ran down to the target and I took down your picture and I looked at your face, well, at your chin, and—I kissed it. Because I love you *so much.*

JANE. Oh my God.

SHARON. Jane?

JANE. My water broke!

This revelation sends the room into a frenzy of activity, as Adam and Mabel tend to Jane, while everyone else tries to figure out a course of action.

KEVIN. Her water?

SHARON. Where's the doctor?

MABEL. I'll beep her!

SHARON. Call an ambulance!

JANE. Right now!

CHERYL. Oh my God!

TREY. What should we do?

SHARON. What do you need?

STEVE. *(on the phone)* Hello? I need an ambulance!

JANE. St. Vincent's!

STEVE. *(into phone)* For St. Vincent's. From two nineteen. West Ninteenth Street. Three E. It's an emergency!

CHERYL. *(who has run into the bedroom and returned with JANE's coat)* Tell them it's the Messiah! They'll come faster!

TREY. *(to Cheryl)* You're so young.

MABEL. *(at Jane's side)* Start the breathing, focus on me . . .

ADAM. Should we get her downstairs?

JANE. I'm fine, I'm fine, I can get there . . .

Adam and Mabel start walking Jane toward the front door. Jane collapses; everything is happening very fast.

JANE. No I can't!

SHARON. No she can't!

MABEL. Oh my God!

STEVE. How about the couch?

Adam and Mabel start walking Jane toward the couch.

JANE. The couch is good . . . oh my God . . . NO, NO!

KEVIN. She doesn't like the couch!

TREY. Can you blame her?

ADAM. What about the bedroom?

MABEL. Sweetie?

JANE. Fine! Whatever! AWWW! (*Mabel and Adam get Jane into the bedroom, as Jane moans and screams. Exiting.*) GODDAMNIT!

Jane, Mabel, and Adam are offstage.

STEVE. (*having hung up the phone*) The ambulance is coming, but they said it's Christmas Eve, so it might take some time . . .

CHERYL. I think we should all go in there, and gather around the bed and hold hands, in a birthing circle!

KEVIN. All of us?

CHERYL. We can help the baby be born into a world of hope and trust!

SHARON. It's worth a shot!

STEVE. Let's go!

Everyone runs into the bedroom; Steve pushes Sharon's wheelchair. The stage is now empty; a beat. Then we hear the guys emit a truly blood-curdling group scream, from the bedroom.

ADAM, STEVE, TREY, and KEVIN. (*from offstage*) AHHHH!

Adam, Steve, Kevin, and Trey all hurtle out of the bedroom, gasping with terror; they scatter, clinging to various pieces of furniture. Adam pours himself a stiff drink.

TREY. Oh my Lord . . .

KEVIN. I mean, I know that's how it works, but . . .

ADAM. I am *so* gay!

From the bedroom, we hear Cheryl emit an even more bloodcurdling scream.

CHERYL. (*from offstage*) AHHH!

ADAM. Cheryl?

Cheryl runs out of the bedroom, ricocheting across the room, even more grossed out than the guys.

CHERYL. *I am never having a baby!*

Sharon appears, at the bedroom door.

SHARON. Nice work, all of you! She's in labor, big time! Any word on the ambulance?

ADAM. Not yet.

STEVE. (*already on the phone*) I'm calling the hospital, maybe someone can talk us through it.

SHARON. Good man! I can use another pair of hands!

CHERYL. I can't!

KEVIN. I'm a dancer! I need my hands!

STEVE. (*to the group*) I'm talking to a doctor, and I think he's gay . . . (*into the phone*) Yes, hello, it's an emergency . . . what? (*flirtatiously*) Jeans and a sweater . . .

ADAM. Steve!

SHARON. There's a woman giving birth!

JANE. (*from the bedroom*) FUCK YOU!

SHARON. Trey!

TREY. Oh, all right, I'll pretend I'm a glamorous nurse, on a soap opera!

SHARON. Move it!

TREY. (*on his way toward the bedroom*) I'll need hairspray!

STEVE. (*on the phone*) Trey, he says to keep her on her back, on the bed, with one hand behind each knee . . .

TREY. (*flirtatiously*) Not now, Doctor!

Trey pushes Sharon's wheelchair, and they both exit into the bedroom.

STEVE. (*on the phone*) He says there's going to be a lot of blood, so think about the sheets.

ADAM. What's on there?

STEVE. The Calvin Kleins. The periwinkle.

ADAM. (*panicking*) The new ones?

KEVIN. I love those!

ADAM. JANE!

Adam runs to the bedroom door; Trey meets him, carrying the Calvin Klein sheets in a bundle, which he hands to Adam.

TREY. We stripped the bed.

ADAM. Thank you!

TREY. You should see this, it's sort of extraordinary. But I just can't picture my mother doing it.

ADAM. Maybe she was unconscious.

TREY. No—it was before six.

Jane howls offstage, and Trey runs back into the bedroom.

STEVE. (*on the phone*) He says she shouldn't try to push, or she could tear!

ADAM. (*yelling into the partially open bedroom door*) She shouldn't try to push or she could tear!

STEVE. (*on the phone*) He says, keep your hand on her perineum!

ADAM. (*into the bedroom*) Keep your hand on her—(*turning to Steve*) her what?

STEVE. (*on the phone*) The area between her vagina and her rectum!

ADAM. (*struggling for a beat; he can't bring himself to say it, and then, into the bedroom*) Don't push!

Trey runs in from the bedroom.

TREY. It's happening. It's sort of quasi-neo-semi-miraculous. This creature is demanding to be born. This incredibly messy—Gozzoli.

STAGE MANAGER. Lights two fifty-four, go.

Blackout.

STAGE MANAGER. Lights two fifty-five and the miracle of birth, go.

From the darkness, a pin spot comes up center stage on Jane's face and upper body. She is a mess, drenched with sweat, in the process of giving birth. She is standing, and we see her bare arms and shoulders. She has a dark sheet wrapped around the rest of her body.

JANE. FUCK SHIT PISS! FUCK SHIT PISS COCKSUCKER CUNT! Get it out of me! I'm glad they have white carpeting! (*She starts the rhythmic breathing*) Right, right, don't push, let the baby come out by itself, good baby, natural baby, sweet baby, FUCK YOU DICK-LICKING BITCH CUNT! GET OUT OF MY BODY! (*She resumes the breathing*) Look at Mabel, focus on Mabel, she's covered with sweat, and blood, my blood, her mouth is open, it's like she's watching the sun come up in the Garden of Eden, FUCK MABEL! I WANT A HOSPITAL, I WANT DRUGS! Oh my God, here it comes, the baby's head—CHOP OFF ITS HEAD! WHY DO BABIES NEED HEADS! This just proves one thing, God is a buttfucking, motherfucking MAN! YOU'RE KILLING ME . . . Oh my God, it's out! It's out of me, it's gone, oh my God, this is like the best orgasm I ever had! I love not being pregnant! Just let me lie here, forever . . . wait. Mabel's holding the baby, it's breathing, dear God, let it be healthy, and God, let it go to boarding school. Jesus fucking Christ, I'm a mother! Don't tell anyone! I have a baby . . . she's all ugly and wrinkled. She looks *mean*. (*finally accepting the baby, reaching out her arms*) Come to Mama.

The Stage Manager strikes a crisp, bright note on the chime.

STAGE MANAGER. Lights two fifty-six, go.

The lights fade on Jane, to black.

STAGE MANAGER. Lights two fifty-seven and post-partum, go.

Lights up on the loft. It is a few hours later. Only Adam and Steve remain, cleaning up after the party. Steve carries a small plastic wastebasket. They are both still stunned by the evening's events.

ADAM. We're fathers.
STEVE. Sort of.
ADAM. We've been fathers for almost two . . . (*He checks his watch*) no, three hours.
STEVE. How do you feel?
ADAM. Well, Trey was amazing, but I thought that Kevin was going to faint, when Mabel handed him the placenta.

STEVE. And a fork.

ADAM. And was it my imagination, or once we got to the hospital, was Rabbi Sharon hitting on Cheryl?

STEVE. Really?

ADAM. They were sitting very close, and I heard Rabbi Sharon whisper, "Once you've had a disabled lesbian rabbi, you never go back."

STEVE. It's true!

ADAM. Steve?

STEVE. Yeah?

ADAM. They've—stopped working, haven't they?

STEVE. What?

ADAM. The pills. The new ones. After Jane gave birth, I ran into the bathroom, to see what we had for pain. And I noticed, all of your bottles—they're empty.

STEVE. (*after a beat*) Yup.

ADAM. Were you—were you going to tell me?

STEVE. Look, they don't work for everyone, and no one's been on them that long, and the side effects are worse than the disease, the whole thing was a crapshoot, I mean, come on.

ADAM. Steve?

STEVE. What?

ADAM. How long have you known?

STEVE. I don't know, a week, what difference does it make?

ADAM. It makes a difference.

STEVE. Why?

ADAM. Because I can't believe I said all that bullshit at the party! And you let me!

STEVE. I let you?

ADAM. I said I was happy! I said it was possible! I said that the heavens were smiling down on everyone, while you just sat there!

STEVE. What should I have done? Stood up and said, sorry folks, party's over! Especially for me!

Steve angrily takes the wastebasket out into the hall.

ADAM. (*starting to follow him*) Yes! Because that's the truth! And I can handle that!

STEVE. (*re-entering*) You? And the truth?

ADAM. Why not?

STEVE. Adam—you have spent your entire life lunging for answers and miracles and your little kiddie pageant! You have devoted yourself to everything but the truth!

ADAM. But you're the one who's been lying!

STEVE. Fine! You want some facts? Hard-core? (*very simply, straightforward, without histrionics*) I'm dying. And this could very well be our last Christmas together.

ADAM. (*going to him*) Steve . . .

STEVE. (*backing away*) No! Fuck you! *Handle it!*

ADAM. (*after a beat*) Okay. You're right. You're absolutely right. No more—questions. You are going to die. And I am going to watch you. You win.

Adam sits in the armchair. A long beat of silence. Then Steve goes to the Christmas tree and selects a wrapped gift. He brings the gift to Adam and offers it.

ADAM. Not now.

STEVE. Please?

Adam, still resisting, takes the gift, and removes the wrapping paper. He then meticulously smooths and folds the wrapping paper, to save it. Then, overtaken by anger, he smashes the wrapping paper into a ball and throws it on the floor. Adam opens the box. Inside is a beautiful sweater.

ADAM. Oh my God. You got it. This is just what I wanted. This is cashmere. This is Armani. This cost a fortune.

STEVE. So—do you feel better now? About my dying? And losing your faith?

Adam looks at Steve. He looks down at the sweater. He is overwhelmed by the insanity of the whole situation. He strokes the sweater, almost laughing.

ADAM. Yes.
STEVE. (*smiling*) There you go.

Adam puts the sweater aside and stands up. He faces out, gesturing to God.

ADAM. (*to God*) Fuck you forever.
STEVE. Who are you talking to?
ADAM. I have no idea.
STEVE. Exactly. Believe in that.
ADAM. In nothing?
STEVE. In not knowing. In never knowing.
ADAM. How?
STEVE. Stop looking for comfort, or reasons, or peace. I don't need that. I never have. Take a real risk. Ask nothing. Know nothing.
ADAM. (*after a beat, trying to see things Steve's way, and then*) I can't!
STEVE. Why not?
ADAM. I need . . . a story.
STEVE. A story?
ADAM. I can't believe in the Virgin Mary, not anymore. But I can believe—in Jane, and Mabel. And I can't believe in the baby Jesus. But I can believe in our baby, little Satan. And I won't tell her about the Garden of Eden. But I will tell her—about Central Park.
STEVE. Central Park?
ADAM. And the day we met.
STEVE. May third. Ages ago.

ADAM. Lunch time. The first really fabulous day. And I took off my shirt, to feel the sun.

STAGE MANAGER. Central Park, go.

Scenic elements from the Garden of Eden return, along with the garden's idyllic lighting. If possible, the loft might vanish or recede. As the garden returns, Adam and Steve pull off their shirts, basking in the sunlight.

ADAM. And I thought, I love this park. And I love this city. And I love the air and the breeze and the lake. And I'm alone. And then I turned.

STEVE. (*smiling*) Hey.

ADAM. Hey.

The sultry, sexy saxophone music from the garden is heard. Adam and Steve walk toward each other. As they are about to embrace:

STAGE MANAGER. Curtain, go.

The curtain begins to descend.

ADAM. Wait! Hold on! Hold everything!

The curtain freezes.

ADAM. (*to Steve*) I'm sorry! One second! (*to the Stage Manager*) You! That voice! The Stage Manager. Are you God?

STAGE MANAGER. (*after a beat*) Well, I think I am.

ADAM. (*with overwhelming yearning*) But are you really God? I still need to know! Have you really made everything happen? You have to tell me!

STAGE MANAGER. No I don't. I don't have to tell you anything. What do you want from me? I've been doing my job, and now I'm into overtime . . . (*She checks her watch*) No! I'm done! That's it! I'm outta here!

The Stage Manager pulls off her headset, grabs her script, and strides off the stage and out through the audience.

STAGE MANAGER. (*on her way out*) You people!

The Stage Manager leaves the theater, by a rear or side exit. Adam and Steve watch her go, amazed. After a beat we hear from outside the theater:

TAXI!

Adam and Steve look around. Then they look at each other, mystified but elated—something has been released. Whatever happens next is up to them.

ADAM. What's next?
STEVE. It's your call.
ADAM. (*after a beat*) Sound one ninety-two, go.

An instrumental, bluesy version of "Have Yourself a Merry Little Christmas" is heard; it's very romantic.

STEVE. Merry Christmas.

Adam goes to Steve, and they embrace and begin to kiss. Steve makes Adam aware that an audience is watching them.

STEVE. Adam?

Adam sees the audience. He wants some privacy. With a mixture of sexual anticipation and great good humor, he says:

ADAM. Curtain, go!

CURTAIN

FOUR

The Naked Eye

Cast of Characters

NAN BEMISS

MUMBALI KEEFER

ALEX DELFLAVIO

KATRIN DOWLING

MARCUS DOWLING

PETE BEMISS

SISSY BEMISS DARNLEY

LYNETTE MARSHALL

The Naked Eye

ACT ONE

Scene 1

Time: 3 PM, Friday, 1982

Place: The loft/studio of the notorious photographer Alex DelFlavio. The loft is sweeping and glamorous, with a wide skylight, and floor-to-ceiling windows draped in sheer white linen. The furniture is expensive and eclectic, a carefully edited mix of Mission, Beidermeir and Ruhlmann pieces. Behind these furnishings is a sizeable studio area, a rectangle masked at present by opaque muslin drapes hanging from pipes on the ceiling. Stage left are doors to an industrial elevator. Downstage right is a cluttered desk.

As the curtain rises, the stage is in darkness. We hear a BLAST of highly-charged dance music, which continues at peak volume. Flashes from a photographic strobe are visible from behind the draped area.

The elevator doors open, and Nan Bemiss appears. Nan is a woman of a certain age, the well-bred wife of a conservative senator. She is very attractive, if a bit too meticulously dressed in designer finery. Her hair is ash blonde and carefully coiffed; she carries a quilted Chanel bag and an expensive, slim version of an attache case. Nan is well-meaning and at times aggressively gracious, a born hostess. Beneath her poise and chatter she remains an innocent and a romantic.

NAN. Hi hi! (*there is no reply*) Hello?

Mumbali Keefer appears from behind the drape. Mumbali is a black woman in her thirties. She wears an outfit which is equal parts afrocentric and hardcore lesbian activist. Mumbali is Alex's assistant; she can be impatient and short-tempered with her enemies. She is not shy about expressing her political and social views; she is someone to be reckoned with.

MUMBALI. Can I help you?

NAN. Nan Bemiss. How are you?

Mumbali turns on a tiny desk light, to check an appointment book.

MUMBALI. (*checking the book*) You're from . . . the museum. You called.

NAN. I'm on the board of directors, along with my husband.

MUMBALI. Senator Bemiss.

NAN. Bingo!

MUMBALI. Who wants to be Governor. Jesus.

NAN. Just two weeks till election day.

MUMBALI. You're a Republican.

NAN. It's the Eighties. Aren't you?

There is another flash from behind the drape.

MUMBALI. Alex is shooting right now. I'm his new assistant. We're going insane. And this is in reference to . . . ?

NAN. Oh, just odds and ends, for the opening tonight. Alex DelFlavio's first major retrospective.

MUMBALI. Tell me about it.

ALEX. (*from behind the drape*) Mumbali!

MUMBALI. (*calling out*) What?

ALEX. (*from behind the drape*) Two seconds!

NAN. Mumbali. What a beautiful name. What does it mean?

MUMBALI. "Woman Warrior." In Swahili.

NAN. (*impressed*) Really. Fun.

MUMBALI. And you're here because . . . ?

NAN. Oh, its nothing, less than nothing. It's just, well, you know Alex's work . . .

MUMBALI. Yeah . . .

NAN. And there are just a few pictures, nonessentials, three at most, that . . .

MUMBALI. That what?

NAN. That require, well . . .

MUMBALI. What?

NAN. Editing.

MUMBALI. Editing? Why?

NAN. Why?

Mumbali pulls back the drape, revealing a photo session in progress.

Alex Delflavio is naked and hanging on a large wooden cross; he wears only a crown of thorns. His feet are supported by a small ledge and he has draped his outstretched arms over pegs for a crucifixion effect. Alex is in his thirties; he is lean and handsome. He is a thoroughly self-created personality, and delights in his own wickedness. He can be charming, seductive and viciously direct. He is relentlessly provocative; he is fueled equally by anger and ambition.

Alex's cross stands on a raised platform, backed by a hanging roll of heavy white paper. Alex is beautifully lit by a variety of photographic lights and reflectors. A camera stands on a tripod a few yards from Alex; Alex holds a remote control device in his hand. The camera is equipped with a powerful strobe.

Nan, upon seeing Alex on the cross, steps back, shocked but trying to remain sophisticated.

NAN. Alex.

ALEX. Imagine. Hanging here. Naked. Bleeding. Everyone watching. Forget the God part, the transcendence. Think about the physical reality. Here I am. Your eyes all over me. Spread out. Spread-eagled. I get into it. (*he pushes a button on the remote control. There is a strong FLASH.*) My arms are aching. I'm sticky with sweat. There's a little spot under my balls that just won't stop itching, that's the real torture, I don't want water, I don't want death, all I want is for one of those hunky centurions or Jerusalem peasant women to reach up, lift up my balls and scratch, that would be proof of God's existence. . . . (*another FLASH*) I can barely see but I look down and everyone's vicious and screaming except—that teenage boy with the big eyes, the one who's staring at his first pin-up, the first naked man he's ever really been allowed to study and get away with it, his mother has to remind him to throw his pebble at me, I glance at him, I moan, he comes, don't people realize, they never show a fat Jesus or an ugly Jesus, he's always pretty or handsome and sinewy, he's suffering naked for our dirty sins and we get to watch him and get off,—do you think he knew? How big he was gonna get? Not just the calendars, not just the dashboards, but around people's necks, on mountaintops, cosmic Elvis, Elvis on the cross, die young, die naked, leave a great logo, (*FLASH*) it is all just too fucking hot . . . (*another FLASH, FLASH, FLASH*) Nan—how are you?

NAN. (*like a stern but loving parent*) Alex.

ALEX. What?

NAN. Come down from there. You always do this.

ALEX. What?

NAN. You . . . run around like that. Hang around like that. You try to shock me . . .

ALEX. How?

NAN. Alex.

Alex hops off the cross and picks up a towel, to mop himself.

ALEX. Nan, I'm sorry, I forgot the time, I am sweating like a pig . . .

NAN. Alex, we have to talk.

ALEX. I've been working on this new mutilation series. Some self-portraits, some S&M stuff—you just missed Sharon and Heather, the piercing couple.

NAN. Piercing?

MUMBALI. Heather has a gold ring, right through her vulva.

NAN. *(appalled)* Oh my lord—through her car?

ALEX. Oh, I am just disgusting today. *(he wipes his crotch with his hand and sniffs it; he holds the hand out toward Nan.)* Can you smell?

NAN. Alex, put your clothes on. *(she claps her hands, briskly)* Spit-spot!

Alex begins to pull on a shirt and tight black jeans.

ALEX. What's up? Is this about the gala?

NAN. Partially.

ALEX. Partially? What's wrong?

NAN. Nothing! Nothing, it's going to be sensational. A triumph!

ALEX. It's not the flowers?

NAN. 5,000 trumpet lilies, fresh today from the Philippines.

ALEX. The music?

NAN. Ten pieces, plus a DJ for the dance floor.

ALEX. Press?

NAN. International. Print and video.

ALEX. Acceptances?

NAN. Everyone. Platinum. The calls. The desperation.

ALEX. Angel.

NAN. Madman.

Alex is now dressed; he and Nan embrace.

NAN. And there's only one tiny detail left, it's nothing really, don't give it a thought, but we do need your permission. It's just . . . oh, it's so silly.

ALEX. What?

NAN. Well, its actually Pete's idea, and the rest of the board agreed, we know you won't mind.

ALEX. Won't mind what?

NAN. Well, all right, I'll just say it, just right out, it's less than nothing. They—we—would like three of the photos removed from the show.

ALEX. What?

MUMBALI. You mean before the thing opens?

ALEX. Before tonight?

NAN. They're all gorgeous pictures, I'm sure you can place them elsewhere. It's just . . . the board is worried. About—obscenity.

ALEX. (*very understanding*) Of course.

NAN. I know, it's all so silly, but there's that senator, who went after that performance artist, who received a government arts grant. She stripped naked, drenched herself with chocolate syrup and inserted yams into her—orifices. Yams! It was some sort of statement, about women and—salad.

ALEX. Did you see the piece?

NAN. No, not really . . .

ALEX. Obscenity—it's a real issue.

NAN. And they want the museum to sign a pledge, to receive federal funding. They don't want tax dollars supporting smut.

ALEX. I hear you.

NAN. God bless you.

ALEX. (*very agreeable*) So I'll withdraw the pictures, at least for now, so we can have the party . . .

NAN. The gala!

ALEX. (*very reassuring*) And I am not worried about having to censor my work . . .

NAN. Not censor, remove . . .

ALEX. So I will make a certain, extremely minor sacrifice, for a greater
   good.

NAN. Could you?

ALEX. I could. For you.

NAN. (*thrilled*) Alex!

ALEX. I only have one question.

NAN. (*adorably*) What?

ALEX. One tiny little issue.

NAN. Name it.

ALEX. Are you—that . . . evil?

NAN. What?

MUMBALI. Are you that redneck?

NAN. You're not listening!

ALEX. Are you that incredibly, unbelievably fucked?

NAN. Yes!

ALEX. I'm sorry, I have worked too hard for this show! I have brunched
   with and bullshit and handjobbed half of New York! It's what everyone wants: an uptown event with downtown cachet! If I back off, I
   lose my credibility, I lose my edge. I need *your* party on *my* terms. You
   owe me that!

NAN. So how bad do you want it?

ALEX. Which pictures?

NAN. Well—Number 15.

MUMBALI. By the entrance?

ALEX. The Portrait of Steve?

*Mumbali picks up a remote control. She presses a button, and a slide is
projected on the wall: we see a very large photograph of a sizeable erect
black penis.*

NAN. That's the one.

ALEX. What's wrong?

NAN. Nothing. Could you just—turn that off? Please?

ALEX. Why?

NAN. I know it's just flesh, I know it's beautifully lit and photographed
. . . turn it off! Please!

ALEX. What's it a picture of?

NAN. You know very well.

MUMBALI. Do you?

NAN. Of course.

ALEX. Say it.

NAN. Why?

ALEX. So I'll know. That you can handle it.

NAN. Of course, I can handle it.

ALEX. Then what is it?

NAN. It's . . . it's a composition, in light and dark. It's—a celebration of
the human form, it's a witty essay in erotica, it's a penis, it's a big,
huge, black penis.

ALEX. It's a dick! Say it!

NAN. Say what?

ALEX. Dick! Not "penis." Dick!

NAN. What difference does it make?

ALEX. If it was a picture of a penis, no one would mind. A penis appears
in a medical textbook.

NAN. I've seen those things! They're perfect. They always show everything in cross-section. And everything's all pink, or pale blue, with
branchy red veins, it looks like a map of the tri-state area.

ALEX. Exactly. But I took a picture of a dick—which means it's sexual.
And disturbing. And attached to someone.

NAN. And offensive! (*turning to Mumbali*) To women!

MUMBALI. You know it.

NAN. And black people!

MUMBALI. Now I thought about that. But look at it—it's a symbol of

black strength. It's a proud tower of black supremacy. You have to let
Steve stay for tonight—his parents are coming.

NAN. But how can you work here?

MUMBALI. I'm a black lesbian separatist. Who else would hire me?

NAN. But—all these pictures!

MUMBALI. I like 'em.

NAN. Why?

MUMBALI. 'Cause they're nasty. They get to you. All of you white folks
tiptoe around, going—is that what I think it is? Am I allowed to stare
at it? Should I just yawn and pretend I'm bored? It's what we're not
supposed to look at.

ALEX. But what we think about all the time.

NAN. I don't.

MUMBALI. I don't.

NAN. That's right!

MUMBALI. That's right. I think about vaginas.

NAN. That's right!

MUMBALI. That's right.

NAN. *(catching herself)* No!

MUMBALI. Chickenshit.

NAN. Excuse me?

ALEX. Fascist!

NAN. I am not!

MUMBALI. Bad hostess!

NAN. *(turning on Mumbali, incensed)* Dick! Dick, dick, dick, dick, dick,
dick, dick, dick, dick! *(she grabs the remote control from Alex and decisively
turns off the slide)* There! Are you happy now?

ALEX. Are you?

MUMBALI. Make her say it again.

NAN. No! And you will remove Number 15!

ALEX. But it's just a picture!

NAN. No, it isn't! It isn't just a picture! It's a photograph!

ALEX. Meaning?

NAN. It's so there! It's practically shaking your hand! Now if you look at a Monet you can think, what lovely water lilies. And when you look at a Jackson Pollock it's almost the best, because you can just stand there and make lists for the weekend. But with your pictures you can't make up a little story, it's an assault, it's like—pornography!

ALEX. I hope so!

NAN. You hope so?

ALEX. Nan, you don't understand. I don't think sex should be beautiful and sensual and free. That's so Sixties. I like it filthy. Scary. I don't want "erotica." I want Triple X. A Times Square marquee. Cum-Crazy Cocksuckers. Backdoor Babes. Eat Me In St. Louis. I want my pictures to feel like something you hunt for on your lunch hour, keeping your head down. Something you buy in a hurry from a bored foreigner and slip under your jacket, where it burns through your clothing, something you pray won't fall onto the floor where everyone on the bus will see it, and know what you like, and know who you are.

NAN. That's repulsive!

ALEX. What?

NAN. (*shuddering*) The bus!

ALEX. What happens when you look at porn?

NAN. I do not look at porn.

MUMBALI. Liar.

NAN. Woman are different. Most women.

MUMBALI. *Lady Chatterly's Lover.*

ALEX. What?

NAN. Oh, please—that's D. H. Lawrence.

MUMBALI. It's a boarding school stroke book. The white girl's whoopee. It's about this rich English chick, and she is just as horny as hell.

NAN. That is so vulgar!

ALEX. Keep going . . .

MUMBALI. And there's this one chapter, where she meets this forest ranger . . .

NAN. Gamekeeper!

ALEX. Oh really?

MUMBALI. And they do it outside, like in the rain . . .

NAN. It's very lyrical.

ALEX. I'll bet.

MUMBALI. And she just comes and comes and comes . . .

NAN. It isn't like that!

ALEX. It's not?

MUMBALI. And comes and comes . . .

NAN. You're making it sound so disgusting!

ALEX. (*delighted*) I know!

MUMBALI. And comes and comes and comes . . .

NAN. What is it with all this coming! Stop coming! Human beings make love! The mailman comes! It wasn't the smut I responded to—it was the romance. Between a lonely neglected wife . . .

ALEX. And a man who was off limits. Taboo. A man who could offer her something she sure wasn't getting at home.

NAN. Affection.

ALEX. Excitement. Arousal. The good parts. The private parts.

NAN. No!

ALEX. You were in heat, you were wet and wriggling and so was every pony-loving pre-teen in that dormitory! You passed it around, you read it out loud.

MUMBALI. Under the covers with a flashlight.

ALEX. You were squealing, you were screaming—admit it!

NAN. I was in seventh grade! And *Lady Chatterly* isn't porn! It's literature!

MUMBALI. Only if you finish it.

From outside, a police siren begins to WAIL. Mumbali is immediately on her feet, very alert.

MUMBALI. Fuck.
NAN. What? What's wrong?

The siren grows louder.

MUMBALI. Hit the lights!
ALEX. Mumbali, please . . . Leave it alone!
MUMBALI. Everybody get down!

Mumbali lunges for the light switch, and the stage is plunged into darkness.

NAN. Help! Please! What is happening?
MUMBALI. Shut up! I am not going back there!

The lights come back up. Alex is at the switch. Mumbali has her hand clasped over Nan's mouth, to prevent her from screaming.

ALEX. Mumbali, it's all right. They're not coming to get you. You're on parole.
NAN. Parole?
ALEX. It's nothing. It's fine. She killed someone.
NAN. She . . .
MUMBALI. I did not!
NAN. Thank heavens!
MUMBALI. She didn't die.
ALEX. Mumbali . . .
NAN. What is going on here?
MUMBALI. She was my girlfriend, Allison. She was blonde, and skinny and she had a trust fund, you name it. But that wasn't it. That wasn't what did it.

NAN. Did *what*?

MUMBALI. Gave her a broken collarbone. I got six months. But—it wasn't my fault! That's what the shrink said! It's—a disorder!

NAN. A disorder?

MUMBALI. It's this one thing, when it happens, I just—lose it. It triggers, what did they call it? Justifiable Trans-Social Violence.

ALEX. It's . . . a seizure. It's fabulous.

NAN. But what triggers it? An insult? A threat? A slur?

ALEX. Worse.

MUMBALI. Bad French.

NAN. Bad French?

MUMBALI. From a certain type of person.

NAN. Which type?

MUMBALI. Rich white women.

NAN. (*horrified*) Mon dieu!

MUMBALI. No!

Mumbali lunges at Nan; Alex holds her back. Nan gestures for Alex to release Mumbali.

NAN. (*to Alex*) No! I can do this! (*to Mumbali*) I see you. I feel your rage. I have met with Eartha Kitt. I won't diss you.

After a beat, Mumbali raises her hands, in a grudging truce.

NAN. You must learn some discipline. Some sanity. Both of you. The second picture, Number 17, that couple—in leather—the Barstows. They frighten people. You must remove it.

ALEX. The Barstows? They're married. They love what they do. They're good at it.

NAN. But in that picture, the woman, Mrs. Barstow, she has that . . . that thing hanging from her waist.

ALEX. The dildo?

NAN. Yes. The dildo. Dildo. That's actually a rather sweet word. It's like
. . . some sort of sea chanty. A traditional sailor's dildo.

ALEX. Would you like one?

NAN. No thank you!

MUMBALI. Oh, please. Are you saying you've never been near one?

NAN. Have you?

ALEX. Just her?

NAN. Either of you! I'm sorry, it's so hard to be politically correct every
second! Am I a Mrs. or a Ms.? And what about Columbus? And when
you contribute to the Special Olympics, should you hope that the retarded children from Russia fall down? This is all too confusing, my
mind is about to snap! Should I use a dildo? Would that help?

MUMBALI. They're like dicks perfected. They're always big. . . .

ALEX. They're always hard . . .

NAN. If only they had money.

*The elevator doors open, and Katrin and Marcus Dowling sweep into the
room. They are dressed exclusively and expensively in black; they are the es-
sence of arrogant downtown hauteur. They edit a powerful arts magazine,
and are aware of their status. Everyone hugs and air-kisses.*

MARCUS. Alex.

ALEX. Marcus.

KATRIN. Nan.

NAN. Katrin.

MARCUS. Nan.

NAN. Marcus.

KATRIN. Alex.

ALEX. Katrin.

KATRIN. All our busy bees! We just wanted to drop by and wish you
the best!

MARCUS. The very best! Your big show! The opening of the year!

ALEX. You guys . . .

KATRIN. The Civic Central!

MARCUS. Awfully mainstream!

KATRIN. You know best!

ALEX. Mumbali, this is Katrin and Marcus Dowling. Two of my dearest friends, and the editors of *Artscape*.

MARCUS. And we're married. Don't say it.

KATRIN. We're conceptual.

MARCUS. We have a grant.

KATRIN. We're keeping an intimate video diary of our entire relationship.

MARCUS. So far we have over 1200 hours of tape.

KATRIN. Just the two of us.

MARCUS. Making calls.

KATRIN. *(to Alex, regarding Mumbali)* Oh, Alex, where did you find her? She's perfect.

MARCUS. She's *real*.

KATRIN. She's so deliciously other. We're doing a special issue in June.

MARCUS. "The Black Woman—Why?"

KATRIN. Nan.

MARCUS. Nan Bemiss. I adore you. I worship you.

NAN. Thank you.

MARCUS. Last Halloween, I was you.

NAN. And we have your table. For tonight. Dead center. With Mrs. Astor. And Spielberg.

KATRIN. Sweet.

ALEX. And I'm having a little get-together afterward. Just the inner circle. At that new place.

KATRIN. We'd love to.

NAN. What else do you need?

ALEX. *(handing Katrin an envelope)* The slides. For the interview.

KATRIN. Of course. It's an honor. Alex DelFlavio. Maybe a cover.

MARCUS. You're overdue.

ALEX. Really?

KATRIN. And now Alex, please, there's one more thing, and if it's any inconvenience, we insist you say no.

MARCUS. We won't even ask.

ALEX. What? Name it!

KATRIN. No, you mustn't, your time is too valuable.

MARCUS. It's insulting.

ALEX. Please! Tell me. Anything. What?

KATRIN. It's our little daughter, Guernica. Her birthday. Next week. She'll be six.

NAN. Already!

MARCUS. Can you imagine? It seems like only yesterday, she was still— in her petrie dish.

KATRIN. It's a tiny affair, at Jennifer's loft. Everyone's pitching in.

MARCUS. Eric is deconstructing the cake. It's a return to minimalism— just crumbs.

KATRIN. And we were just wondering, we'd love to have you as a guest, but also—picture it. When Guernica is twenty. And she has memo- ries—by Alex DelFlavio.

MUMBALI. You want him to do birthday pictures?

NAN. Nudes?

KATRIN. Oh no, just candids.

MARCUS. But why not? Children are so innocent, without sin. I think it could be beautiful. (*a pause*) Especially the Stillman boy. (*He shivers*)

ALEX. We'll see.

MARCUS. We'll see?

ALEX. You know I'm crazy about Guernica.

KATRIN. Of course. But don't take too long. Children grow up.

MARCUS. Careers fade.

KATRIN. But we love you!

MARCUS. We adore you!

KATRIN. Of course—we could ask Arliss Tandy. He's been doing some extraordinary work. Bold. Explosive.

ALEX. Arliss Tandy?

MARCUS. He's you, only more—out there.

KATRIN. More right this second.

MARCUS. A young you.

ALEX. How—exciting.

KATRIN. He has done a new series—twelve pictures, platinum printed. Of his rectum. His sphincter.

NAN. Oh my Lord.

MARCUS. They're stunning. Shocking. Yet—strangely lyrical.

KATRIN. Arliss Tandy on our cover. Beyond the future. "The Anus of the Eighties." Quite the coup.

MARCUS. And he is Guernica's favorite.

KATRIN. "Uncle Arliss."

Katrin and Marcus begin to leave.

ALEX. Wait.

KATRIN. Yes?

MARCUS. Arliss? I mean, Alex?

ALEX. I'll do the pictures. I'd love to. For Guernica. Of course.

MARCUS. Of course.

KATRIN. (*regarding Alex*) This man.

ALEX. And the cover?

KATRIN. We'll see.

MARCUS. Que sera!

KATRIN. Till tonight!

Marcus and Katrin stand by the elevator, about to exit.

ALEX. But Katrin, Marcus—I've photographed my asshole. Hundreds of times. Been there, done that. Everyone's seen my asshole. There's a postcard.

MARCUS. Ah, yes. But—you wiped.

Katrin and Marcus blow air-kisses and exit, as the elevator doors shut.

MUMBALI. Arliss Tandy? Birthday pictures?

ALEX. I have to! They're very powerful! They're essential!

NAN. They're vampires!

ALEX. But if the show's a success, we won't need them. Not anymore. But if they hear I backed off, took out pictures, because of Pete—I'm dead. I'm over. Steve and the Barstows—they have to stay!

NAN. But isn't there some alternate route? I try to keep up, to appreciate fresh visions, but—why must everything become so prurient? So overt? So obscene?

ALEX. I have a reputation! Don't you know how hard it is to keep shocking people, day in and day out? Arliss Tandy! Please! That asshole! That—asshole.

NAN. Oh, you don't understand! You're both too young. There was a time, when I was a girl, when no one had sex. Absolutely no one.

ALEX. Do you think that was a good time?

NAN. Yes! Most certainly! There were rules, one knew what to expect. You see, I learned about sex from my mother.

MUMBALI. Uh-oh. Watch out.

NAN. She was marvelous. She had the most beautiful names for everything. I remember, she called our privates "down there."

ALEX. "Down there"?

NAN. Like Australia. Because it's a lovely place, but no one ever goes there.

ALEX. But what about sex? With Senator Petey? Mr. Pig?

NAN. How dare you.

ALEX. Nan—don't you like sex?

MUMBALI. Do you come?

NAN. I am not having this conversation! We are not here to discuss my lovelife! We are talking about pictures!

ALEX. Of people having sex.

NAN. Precisely!

MUMBALI. Which send you into a tizzy.

NAN. I am not in a tizzy! I am attempting to have a mature conversation!

ALEX. About sex.

NAN. About art!

ALEX. So you hate sex.

NAN. Excuse me! Do you think there's some sort of cosmic tradeoff? Do you think that God says to all Republicans, yes, I'll give you wealth and power in exchange for your libido? Do you think that all heterosexual caucasians are frigid and uptight and repressed?

ALEX. Of course not.

MUMBALI. Just you.

NAN. I like sex!

ALEX. Stand back!

MUMBALI. Get the hose!

NAN. I happen to be very good! On our honeymoon, we never left the suite! Fourteen days, fourteen nights! Fourteen midmornings, early evenings and afternoons! I wanted to call my mother and tell her, Mummy—guess where I spent the last two weeks? Australia!

ALEX. (*impressed*) Nan. Still waters.

NAN. I love sex! I just . . . I just . . .

ALEX. What?

MUMBALI. Let it loose.

NAN. I don't have it!

ALEX. Why not?

NAN. I don't know! It's none of your business! Sex is a private matter, that's what you can't seem to understand! These pictures! You have to compromise! That's what Pete said!

ALEX. Pete?

NAN. Yes. He understands negotiation. He's a master.

ALEX. And you agree?

NAN. Of course!

ALEX. Compromise.

MUMBALI. Negotiation.

NAN. A bargain. An informed bargain.

ALEX. Like Lynette? What's her last name?

MUMBALI. Marshall?

ALEX. It was in that paper.

MUMBALI. That tabloid. . . .

ALEX. Thinly veiled, what did it say?

MUMBALI. Um, "Prominent politico . . ."

ALEX. And—

NAN. "Bodacious babe."

Nan is very patient, like a parent with rambunctious offspring.

NAN. (*she is still completely calm*) Yes. Of course. My husband has a mistress. It's common knowledge. And it's off the point.

ALEX. Nan?

MUMBALI. Aren't you something.

ALEX. That is classy.

MUMBALI. Sophisticated.

ALEX. Sensible and sane.

NAN. Thank you. (*she is now examining a matte knife she has found on the desk*) When a man reaches a certain age, when his wife reaches a certain age, these things happen. It's inevitable. Expected. Pete is in the public eye. He's pursued. I have my own life, I can't really expect him to become a monk, he's on the campaign trail, women hurl themselves, it's meaningless, it's nothing, a truly strong marriage can withstand the occasional interlude . . . (*Nan is now drawing the razor-sharp knife across her wrist, drawing blood; she turns to Alex and Mumbali.*) . . . as long as everyone remains discreet.

MUMBALI. (*spotting the blood*) Oh my God. Nan, what are you doing? Give me the knife.

NAN. What?

MUMBALI. The knife!

Mumbali tries to grab the knife from Nan. Alex observes all this; he is interested but dispassionate.

NAN. No, no, I'm sorry, I was just. . . . cutting a thread, it slipped, I'm sorry. . . .

MUMBALI. Give it over. Like right now.

NAN. (*violently keeping Mumbali at bay, using the knife*) No! This is mine! I wish I could run this across his eyes!

ALEX. Nan?

Nan is calm again; she drops the knife, and Mumbali quickly retrieves it. Nan opens her purse and begins wrapping her wrist with a handkerchief.

NAN. I'm sorry, I'm sorry, it's just with the party tonight, there's so much to do, the lilies, the swags, we're draping every table in the palest silver silk taffeta, with matching skirts for the chairs, we're keeping the palette extremely subtle, color can be so jarring . . . (*she erupts again, livid*) she's a centerfold! A *Playboy* centerfold! Lynette Marshall! Miss August! August, can you imagine? When everyone's out of town?

ALEX. Nan.

NAN. What?

ALEX. Let me take your picture.

NAN. What?

ALEX. Mumbali?

MUMBALI. Got it.

Mumbali swings into action; she begins collecting various cameras, loading film, etc.

NAN. What . . . what is she . . .

ALEX. A portrait. Right now.

NAN. Now?

ALEX. It's just what you need. (*to Mumbali*) The Polaroid.

MUMBALI. (*using a light meter*) Five point six.

Mumbali hands Alex a camera. He takes a few quick shots of Nan, who hides her face.

NAN. Stop!

ALEX. Test shots. For lighting. (*to Mumbali, handing her the Polaroid shots*) Thirty seconds.

NAN. A . . . a portrait? Now? I couldn't! I look awful, and now I've been bleeding. . . .

ALEX. You look perfect. Or you will. (*Mumbali hands him the test shots*) The Hasselblad.

NAN. But you should have warned me, what am I wearing, it's last year's Chanel . . . of course, it's still Chanel . . .

ALEX. You won't need it.

NAN. What?

ALEX. I won't photograph you in clothes.

MUMBALI. You know the man's work.

NAN. (*appalled*) You mean . . . a nude?

ALEX. No, no.

NAN. I should hope not!

ALEX. Naked. Raw. Right now. Strip.

Nan, shocked and offended, is about to leave. Taking her belongings, she marches to the elevator. She steps inside. As the door is about to shut, she stops it with her hand.

NAN. *Why?* As revenge?

ALEX. Yes. Against every stitch in your mother's needlepoint. Against every decade of your children's rehab. Revenge against the fact that your hair hasn't moved in over twenty-five years. Revenge against a world that is nothing but greedy and cruel. Bring it down.

NAN. But—you want that world. My world. Uptown. You want it both ways. The bad boy. Outrage and acclaim. Controversy and cover stories. Scandal and sales. You can taste it.

ALEX. *(eagerly)* Every empty calorie.

MUMBALI. I thought you were an outlaw.

ALEX. I am an outlaw!

MUMBALI. With this place? And an accountant and a lawyer and a dealer? And what about your other stuff? Those other pictures, of flowers?

ALEX. They're very dark. They're evil. They're sensual . . .

NAN. They're roses. And tulips. They're pretty. They sell.

MUMBALI. Not everyone wants a dick over the sofa.

NAN. You science the market. Designer decadence. Coffee table filth.

ALEX. I'm an artist!

MUMBALI. You're incorporated.

NAN. So why should I listen to you? Why should I risk everything?

ALEX. Because sometimes, for a micro-second, after meeting with my co-op board, and before I begin wrangling with my contractor, and checking my current prices at auction, I am . . . ashamed.

NAN. You? Of what?

ALEX. Of wanting what I want. Of getting it. Of worshipping sex, and longing for fame. Of hating the people I hustle.

NAN. You mean—me.

ALEX. Until now. Let us laugh our heads off. At Pete. At the museum board. At my tax bracket. At ourselves. A naked picture of Nan? The benefactor stripped bare? As leverage? It might work.

NAN. Your greatest hustle?

ALEX. *Our* greatest hustle. I'll keep my pictures. You'll slaughter Pete.

MUMBALI. For sending you here.

ALEX. For Lynette.

NAN. It wouldn't work.

ALEX. It's your only hope. Maybe I'm an opportunist. A conman. But I want to rub their noses in it. In everything that frightens them. Everything they hate. And I want them to pay me for the privilege.

NAN. Like a pimp. Or a hooker.

ALEX. Even worse.

NAN. What?

MUMBALI. An artist.

ALEX. *(to Nan)* Look at you—all covered up.

MUMBALI. Aren't you a little warm?

ALEX. Aren't you choking?

NAN. Stop it. I won't have it. Both of you. Stop—eyeing me.

ALEX. We're not eyeing. We're ogling.

MUMBALI. Undressing.

ALEX. Unbuttoning.

NAN. Stop it!

ALEX. Your shoe.

MUMBALI. Just that shoe.

ALEX. One shoe.

NAN. No!

ALEX. She's right. We're being mean. We weren't thinking. She probably has—rich white lady feet.

NAN. What?

ALEX. All those years—shoved into slingbacks . . .

MUMBALI. Packed into pumps . . .

ALEX. Four-inch heels . . .

MUMBALI. Two sizes too small . . .

ALEX. Her feet must be gnarled . . .

MUMBALI. Nasty . . .

ALEX. By now they're like—ginseng roots in pantyhose.

NAN. They are not! (*she kicks off one shoe*) There!

Nan immediately tries to pick up the shoe. Alex grabs it, and tosses it to Mumbali.

NAN. Give that back.

ALEX. Give it up.

NAN. Give me my shoe. I cannot leave without my shoe.

ALEX. You've never cheated on Pete, have you?

NAN. Of course not!

MUMBALI. And why the hell not? He's a sleazehole. He dogs out on you. He orders you around. He fucked you over. And now he wants your vote.

Alex is taking off his shirt.

NAN. What are you doing?

ALEX. Getting comfortable. Getting ready. Your turn.

NAN. Stop it!

The elevator doors open. Pete Bemiss steps out. Pete wears a well-tailored navy blue suit, and carries his trenchcoat over his arm. He is a high-flying, born politician; he immediately assesses any situation in terms which turn matters to his advantage. He can be the picture of dignified leadership, a charming, suave snakeoil salesman, or paranoid and vengeful. He will do anything to succeed.

PETE. Nan?

NAN. Pete.

PETE. I've only got a moment. I'm supposed to be at City Hall. No one knows I'm here. (*he looks around, to Alex*) Pete Bemiss.

ALEX. Of course.

PETE. (*regarding Alex's bare chest*) Is it—warm in here? Nan—where's your shoe?

MUMBALI. (*holding up Nan's shoe*) Right here. Senator.

PETE. Nan—I need a certain guarantee. Are we on track here?

NAN. Oh yes. Under control.

PETE. Tonight is going to be massive. Pivotal. Our press coverage has tripled. Does he. . . . (*referring to Alex*) understand our position?

NAN. I've explained it.

PETE. This is not a request. Not any longer. Was that transmitted?

NAN. I believe so.

ALEX. Loud and clear.

PETE. (*satisfied*) Aces! You see? If we all pull together, we can come out ahead. Because we're all Americans. Even if some of us arrived on the *Mayflower* . . . (*he indicates himself and Nan*) Some in chains. . . . (*he indicates Mumbali*) and some . . . (*to Alex*) how did gay people get here?

ALEX. Flight attendants.

PETE. (*to Alex*) Good work! And thank you, for making a very wise decision. It's an ultimate evening, for all of us. You. Me.

ALEX. Nan.

PETE. Nan?

ALEX. It's her party.

NAN. (*after a beat*) Isn't it?

PETE. It certainly is. My cultural ambassador. Involved, yet innocuous.

ALEX. (*helpfully*) Busy yet bland.

PETE. But we all have to cut back. In every sector. The arts. (*to Mumbali*) Welfare. Young lady, let's say you're feeling lonely one evening. And you meet some sweet-talking gangster rapper. And the next morning, you're in trouble. Why should the rest of us pay to support your bastard child?

MUMBALI. Jesus. You know, I cannot believe your crypto-racist, under-class-baiting, patriarchal horseshit. Your little stereotypes ain't gonna play! 'Cause I'm a lesbian!

PETE. Aha. So what if—you're feeling lonely one evening and you meet . . . some gruff older woman in a peasant blouse. Hmm? Why should the rest of us pay to support . . . your small literary magazine?

ALEX. Good point.

PETE. But art is important. Art can inspire us, and give meaning to our days. Art can show us—what boats used to look like.

ALEX. Yes, sir.

PETE. (*to Nan*) So everything's set? For tonight?

ALEX. Everything.

PETE. We're in business. (*to Nan*) Love me?

NAN. You're my husband.

Pete grins and gives Nan a thumbs-up signal, and exits. The elevator doors shut. There is a pause. Alex and Mumbali both face Nan.

NAN. Don't, just don't.

ALEX. Nan.

MUMBALI. Miss Nan.

NAN. I'm sorry! I can't help it! Haven't you ever loved someone?

ALEX. He's a nightmare!

NAN. (*with righteous fury*) But he's my nightmare!

MUMBALI. Yeah!

NAN. Allison!

MUMBALI. Don't! Don't you go there!

NAN. You understand! You loved her even though she did terrible things!

MUMBALI. I didn't love her! No way! It was worse than love, much worse! She was blonde and snooty and she called me Mumby-kins!

She drove a Mercedes, she wore headbands, she was this Upper East Side J. Crew cashmere tennis-Nazi! I hated her! I hated everything about her!

NAN. Then why did you go out with her?

MUMBALI. (*bitterly ashamed*) She was—my *type*!

NAN. Alex?

ALEX. What?

NAN. Who do you love?

ALEX. Who cares? Who've you got?

NAN. Oh, excuse me! You can expose everything, but not that? External organs only?

ALEX. I love lots of people. But that's not what my pictures are about.

NAN. Exactly! That picture of a dick? Yes, that's what it is, that's all it is. Your pictures are nothing. Mud pies. Graffiti. Yes, they are shocking. Shock lasts five seconds. You drop your pants—that's burlesque. I love Pete Bemiss—*that's* shocking! Say it!

ALEX. What?

NAN. What they said. Allison. Pete. When he was nineteen, stammering, looking away, then staring right at me. Maybe he didn't even mean it, maybe I was just—the suitable choice. But it works. And it kills. Say it!

ALEX. What? What did he say?

NAN. Coward.

MUMBALI. Cynic.

NAN. Arliss Tandy.

ALEX. "I love you"?

NAN. Again.

ALEX. "Fuck you" is better.

NAN. "Fuck you" is *Romper Room*. "Fuck you" upsets your mother. "I love you" upsets the world. Come on, Alex—graduate. Really curse someone. Swear with the big kids.

ALEX. No!

NAN. Do you want real filth? Try a Hallmark card. Do you want degenerate art? How about Gershwin? Do you want the three dirtiest little words in the English language? Say it!

ALEX. For your jacket?

Nan removes her jacket. She holds it out to Alex, as a challenge.

ALEX. (*sincerely*) "I love you."

NAN. (*after a beat*) Fuck you.

Alex grabs the jacket, as Nan tries to keep it.

ALEX. Too late!

NAN. It doesn't mean anything! It's just my jacket! It's still a suit! I love this suit. Don't you ever feel like that? Like Chanel is really all you can count on? They say that only cockroaches will survive a nuclear holocaust, but I always see a few quilted bags. And you're asking me to surrender my Chanel, to abandon my faith . . .

MUMBALI. Just dump him! Get real!

NAN. Get fucked! I love Pete! I loathe him! I need him! I'll nuke him! I don't want a divorce! I want an Oscar! I want to slaughter him! No! That isn't enough! I want him to be . . . to be . . .

MUMBALI. Maybe devastated?

ALEX. Or appalled?

MUMBALI. Just plain outraged?

ALEX. Shocked?

NAN. Yes!

ALEX. Nan, I'm not removing the pictures. And your life is not going to change. Not unless you help me.

NAN. Help you? I come here to ask you a tiny favor, and suddenly I'm besieged! You must take those pictures out of the show! I need my party! It's all I have! And I can't have my picture taken! Not even in clothes!

ALEX. Why not?

NAN. Because I'm old! I'm not twenty-three! And I want to have another facelift, except I can barely get my eyes closed since the last one! I look at pictures of myself in the social pages and I look parched. I look like I'm in a wind tunnel. I'm old and I'm saggy and my husband is leaving me! No one wants a picture of that!

ALEX. I do.

NAN. As a vicious joke! Your latest con job! Pickled matron!

ALEX. Why not? There's a demon in you. Something childish and wicked and destructive. Something free. Do something you can never take back. Shock your life.

NAN. *Why?* Why does it all matter to you?

ALEX. One year ago I found a tiny lump, on the side of my neck. Nothing to worry about. I took a test.

NAN. Alex . . .

ALEX. (*cutting her off*) My first response? Blind rage. I will not allow this. Not now. Not me. I am Alex DelFlavio, and I'm about to become very rich and very famous. Let someone else get it, let them all get it, the waiters, the lawyers, the wannabes, the faggots. Not me. I will not become some emaciated bonebag, purple with lesions, the ugliest man at the bar.

NAN. But Alex . . .

ALEX. And after calling in every favor, to get to the very best doctors, for the very latest useless treatments, I decided . . . to kill myself. Rather than become someone I would never fuck. And then, just as I was assembling my barbituates, and my perfect silk pajamas—I got this show. The Civic Central. And I thought—yes. I am saved. I can still win.

NAN. You can win? Win what?

ALEX. Everything. Lights. Cameras. Controversy. Stardom. My cure.

NAN. But I don't understand. Have you told anyone? That you're sick?

ALEX. No! Never! That is not permitted!

NAN. Why not?

ALEX. Sick people don't get museum shows. Sick people don't get cover shots. Sick people don't get laid.

NAN. Alex!

ALEX. (*gesturing to his studio*) This is how I will be remembered! The way I am in my pictures. *All* of my pictures. I will be young and hot and famous. That will be my triumph. And my revenge. Pretty forever! Stars always shine.

NAN. You are Satan.

ALEX. You remember his name.

MUMBALI. Nan, I let Alex take a picture of me.

NAN. When?

MUMBALI. When I got out of jail. I needed it. To feel—right. To feel sexy. To feel like—I still existed. That I wasn't off the map.

ALEX. She looked gorgeous. Pissed off. In just her boots.

NAN. Where is it?

MUMBALI. I mailed it. Allison's folks. Do it, Nan.

ALEX. For women everywhere.

MUMBALI. For first wives.

ALEX. Do it for your mother.

NAN. She would die.

ALEX. You're welcome. Talk dirty.

MUMBALI. Take off those clothes.

ALEX. Wear white *after* Labor Day.

MUMBALI. Blow it all to hell.

ALEX. It's a great five seconds.

NAN. I can't! I can't! You're utterly wrong! I adore my life! I have—position, and security, and French furniture! I'm going to be the Governor's Lady! I have a perfect life! I do!

The elevator doors open and Sissy Bemiss Darnley appears. She is in her thirties; she is the very image of Nan, smartly overdressed, lacquered and poised. She speaks in something of an upbeat, lockjawed, motormouthed drone; no one has ever been able to successfully interrupt her.

SISSY. There you are! Mummy! I can't tell you! My driver! This build-ing! (*to Alex*) Your doorman! This elevator! Soho! (*she air-kisses Nan*) It's me! I'm *downtown*! No, really, it's exciting, it's an adventure, it's another world . . . (*looking around*) it's a *loft*. Alex. It's raw, it's indus-trial, it's a space, it's about freedom, it's about zoning, what was this originally, I see immigrants, child labor, tiny hands stitching, what do you pay, what's the square footage, I hate you, it's divine! (*she air-kisses Alex*) This day, this evening, the occasion, the event, I'm tingling, I'm throbbing, I'm pulsating . . . (*she notices Mumbali*) You're new. You're rugged, you're impressive, you're angry, you're cutting edge, you're . . . African-American, good for me! (*she pats herself on the back and in-troduces herself to Mumbali*) Sissy Bemiss Darnley. A pleasure. I know, three names, I had to, it's a choice, it's a statement, I'm a feminist, I'm a person, I'm empowered, I'm out there, yet still feminine, and so is my husband. He supports me, he nurtures me, we communicate, we share, we're a team, along with the nanny, the au pair and our per-fect Mrs. Ramirez, whom we're very worried about, no green card, no habla Inglese, she cooks, she stays, Olé! You have to have help, otherwise you can't accomplish anything, you can't contribute, you can't make a difference, if it weren't for Mexico and Honduras, there would be no Joffrey Ballet. (*a beat*) Do you ever feel really down? Like your whole life is hollow, just some sort of fraud? Do you ever feel like just grabbing a machete and just hacking your entire existence to bits? (*a beat*) I don't! Mummy, everyone's trying to reach you, Daddy said to try here, I adore Daddy, but he works too hard, he's never at home or at headquarters. Maybe he's having an affair. An affair, Daddy, picture it, Republicans do *not* have affairs. It's like tipping. Mummy, the car is waiting, I'll give you five minutes and then I'm calling 911 and having you listed as a missing person! (*she hugs Nan*) Look at her, isn't she heaven, isn't she bliss, isn't she gorgeous, Dr. Markowitz, Bravo! (*she makes a face-lift gesture*) I can't believe it, I'm here, with my mother, and an artist, and a lesbian, is that the correct word, who knows, Lesbian-American, can-do gal, Martina, rah! Sorry to chat and scoot, but I've got the opening tonight and diabetes tommor-row, then the Red Cross, tuberculosis, hemophilia and the blind. Can you imagine, being blind? How do they shop? What is this world we live in, art, life, money, disease, black, white, beige, cream, egg-shell, bone, wheat, ecru, crime, sex, death, taxes, shelters, *shelters*, the poor—isn't that the perfect word for them, the *poor*? And the home-less, no, worse—the second homeless. Yes! Where's their place at the beach? Reach out, big kiss, ta!

The elevator doors shut. Sissy is gone.

There is a pause. Nan rises.

NAN. Where would you like me?
Nan walks to the posing platform and stands on it, center stage. She glances at Alex, and at Mumbali. She stands straight. She unbuttons the top of her blouse.

CURTAIN

ACT TWO

Scene 1

Time 6:30, that night.

Place: A gallery at the Civic Central Museum. The space is high-ceilinged and well-lit. The main entrance is a pair of doors located atop a wide, curving staircase. Stage left are two doors to the restrooms, marked with the appropriate symbols. Another door, off the staircase, leads to the hallway. At stage right is a bar, set with glassware, a tray of canapes and a vase. At center stage is a display area, currently draped with fabric, covering the large framed photograph beneath. Beside the photo are large black letters reading "ALEX DELFLAVIO: THE NAKED EYE."

As the curtain rises, the stage is deserted. The double doors open, and Nan enters, in a stunning red evening gown. She carries a package wrapped in brown paper. She looks glorious; there is a distinct glint in her eye, and an assurance to her posture. She is ready, and eager for action.

Nan sweeps down the stairs, as lively music plays. She samples a canape. Finally she moves center-stage: she tugs the fabric from the central display, and the "Portrait of Steve," the enormous black erection, is revealed. Nan studies the picture with great satisfaction.

NAN. (*proudly*) Dick. Dick. No. Cock. Cock. Cock and balls! (*frustrated*) Damn. It sounds like an inn. (*calling to offstage*) Pete?

Nan exits, via the door to the hallway.

Pete enters from downstage. He wears a tuxedo.

PETE. *(looking around)* Lynette?

Lynette Marshall steps out from behind the display. She is stunningly, voluptuously beautiful, done up in the somewhat artificial Playboy manner. Her low-cut gown reveals a superb hourglass figure, enhanced by spike heels and diamonds. Her face is both lovely and oddly perfected with make-up; she seems airbrushed. Her hair is an architectural achievement, piled high and cascading over her shoulders. She is wry, self-aware and completely likeable; her downfall is her weakness for powerful men. She speaks with a lively Georgia accent.

LYNETTE. Pete?
PETE. Angel.
LYNETTE. Sugarbear.
PETE. Cinnamon Bun.
LYNETTE. Monkey boy.
PETE. Scooterpie.
LYNETTE. Squirmy.

They kiss. Pete pulls away.

PETE. Did you see? What happened today?
LYNETTE. What?
PETE. The polls! Statewide! It's mine! I'm in! I'm almost Governor!
LYNETTE. Oh Pete!
PETE. People will be arriving—remember, at the party—we're strangers.
LYNETTE. Pete!
PETE. Especially when my wife's around.

LYNETTE. I hate that!

PETE. C'mere.

LYNETTE. No.

PETE. Come on. You know you want to. I know what you find sexually exciting.

LYNETTE. I don't think so.

PETE. A man likes a pretty face, cleavage and curves. But for the female . . .

LYNETTE. It's what?

PETE. *Power.* Not muscles, not some hot young stud. I know what makes a lady twitch.

LYNETTE. No way.

PETE. Come on, baby. I've seen the pinups in your locker.

LYNETTE. I'm warnin' you . . .

PETE. Donald Trump.

LYNETTE. I hate him.

PETE. Benjamin Franklin.

LYNETTE. You're kidding.

PETE. Kissinger . . .

LYNETTE. (*beginning to weaken*) Kissinger . . .

PETE. Think about it. Churchill. Gorbachev. Jabba the Hutt. Me.

LYNETTE. I'm not listening!

PETE. Big bushy eyebrows—can you see 'em, Lynette?

LYNETTE. (*being drawn in, mesmerized*) Growin' every which way . . .

PETE. Gray at the temples, liver spots . . .

LYNETTE. Don't! Don't say it!

PETE. (*innocently*) Say what, Lynette? (*seductively*) Jowls? (*he growls and waggles his jowls*)

LYNETTE. (*trying to resist*) Please! No more!

PETE. It's summer. Bermuda shorts. Pasty white calves, peeking out from behind . . .

LYNETTE. (*moaning*) Black elastic garters . . .

PETE. Ribbed nylon socks, knobby knees . . .

LYNETTE. You're an animal!

PETE. Ear hairs . . .

LYNETTE. Stay away . . .

PETE. Nose hairs . . .

LYNETTE. Shut up!

PETE. A triple bypass!

LYNETTE. (*on fire*) Yes! Yes! Take me! Take me now!

She throws herself into his arms.

SISSY. (*from offstage*) Daddy!

PETE. It's my daughter! Go! Under the bar!

LYNETTE. No, I won't!

PETE. Just until she's gone. (*He takes out his handkerchief, and rubs it on his neck; he holds it out, using it to tantalize Lynette*) Smell it, Lynette. Take a deep whiff.

LYNETTE. (*inhaling, helplessly*) Dentu-creme . . .

PETE. Old Spice . . .

LYNETTE. Dr. Scholl's . . .

PETE. *Ben-gay* . . . (*he tosses the handkerchief behind the bar; Lynette follows it*)

LYNETTE. (*on fire, tormented*) I hate you!

Lynette ducks down behind the bar. Sissy appears at the top of the stairs in an evening gown, something pastel and fluffy, obviously expensive.

SISSY. Daddy!

PETE. Sweetheart!

SISSY. I heard about the polls! It's so exciting! Oh Daddy, when you're Governor, will you still have time for me?

PETE. Will I? Who's Daddy's little girl?

SISSY. I am!

PETE. Who's Daddy's little muffinhead?

SISSY. Sissy!

PETE. Who would Daddy marry if he didn't love Mummy and there weren't all those silly laws?

SISSY. Me! Daddy, there are all these reporters here, and TV crews! They want to set up a press conference!

PETE. (*thrilled*) Of course! The polls!

SISSY. Should I tell them you're coming?

PETE. Whip them into a frenzy!

SISSY. Who do you love the most?

PETE. You, pumpkin!

SISSY. Who do you love more than anyone in the world?

PETE. My little sweetpea!

SISSY. Who's prettier and younger than Mummy?

PETE and SISSY. Sissy!

SISSY. Bye!

Sissy gurgles and exits the double doors. Pete calls out to Lynette.

PETE. Cupcake?

LYNETTE. Stallion.

Lynette appears from behind the bar. At the same time, Nan enters from the hallway.

NAN. Pete?

Lynette runs behind the display area.

PETE. Nan.

NAN. Pete—we need you upstairs. At least to say hello.

PETE. Nannikins.

NAN. (*consulting her clipboard*) We need extra chairs . . .

PETE. Nanny-goat.

NAN. And the lilies are already nodding, it's a nightmare . . .

PETE. Nan! The polls!

NAN. Yes?

PETE. Are you thrilled, are you bursting, are you just ecstatic?

NAN. Pete . . .

PETE. Yeah?

NAN. (*modeling her dress*) Do you like this?

PETE. Sure. Why not?

NAN. I just bought it, this afternoon. Pure silk. It feels wonderful.

PETE. Good for you.

NAN. Without underwear.

PETE. Nan? Was there—a laundry problem? (*examining her*) Well, thank God, you can't tell.

NAN. *I* can.

PETE. Are you—flirting?

NAN. What about my hair? Do you like it?

PETE. Of course. Well, it is a bit—loose. Didn't you get to the hairdresser? Wasn't there time?

NAN. Oh yes. I went. And he was all ready to give me my usual.

PETE. That nice—upsweep.

NAN. The crash dummy.

PETE. Nan?

NAN. I said—let's wash it.

PETE. Yes?

NAN. And brush. I said Carl, today I would like the hair—of a liberal.

PETE. Shut your mouth!

NAN. Shut my mouth? No, I don't think so. I prefer my mouth—open. Wet. Active.

She grabs Pete and kisses him, very aggressively. Pete pulls away.

PETE. Nan! What in God's name do you think you're doing?

NAN. I was kissing you.

PETE. You were not! You were—molesting me.

NAN. What's wrong, Pete? Have I shocked you?

Sissy appears at the top of the stairs.

SISSY. Mummy! Daddy! What are you doing? The press is waiting! We're going mad! Mummy, the caterer has dripped Bernaise sauce all over a DeKooning. It's *so* much better. And Alex DelFlavio called from the car, he says he'll be here any minute! Move it people! (*she claps her hands briskly*) We've got a gala!

Nan exits out through the hallway. Pete opens the double doors; he is greeted by a barrage of flashbulbs and hubbub. He basks in the attention, and exits.

SISSY. (*whispering loudly*) They're gone! Are you here?

Mumbali steps out from the ladies room. She is now wearing a full security guard's uniform, including hat, gun and holster.

SISSY. (*with regard to the uniform*) Mumbali?

MUMBALI. If I do one of these rich white people's $500-a-plate picnics, I work. I do not engage. I will not submit.

SISSY. Oh Mumbali, that's so you!

MUMBALI. Sissy . . .

SISSY. Mumbali . . .

They kiss passionately. Sissy pulls away.

SISSY. Mumby, I just have one question. I know that I called you after I

left Alex's, and we went to your place and made love, and I had sixteen
orgasms in a row, but—I'm not a lesbian, am I?

MUMBALI. What?

SISSY. I mean, I'm married. I have children. Mumbali—(*she holds out her
gown*) Chiffon!

MUMBALI. Excuse me. Were you there? Were we on it? Did you get off?

SISSY. I don't know! It was . . . I felt . . . relaxed. Isn't that strange?
When I was with you, and you were touching me, and looking at me,
and for the first time in my life . . . oh my God . . . I . . . I . . .

MUMBALI. You what?

SISSY. (*with wonder*) I . . . stopped talking.

MUMBALI. That's right.

SISSY. I mean, when I'm with my husband and I, you know, climax, usually I scream, either my father's name or something I forgot to take to
the dry cleaners. But with you, I wasn't pre-occupied, or scattered, or
terrified that if I stopped chattering I'd just—disappear.

MUMBALI. (*romantically*) You didn't. I saw you.

SISSY. Oh Mumbali—*je t'adore!*

MUMBALI. (*lunging at Sissy*) NO!

SISSY. (*wrenching Mumbali's arm behind her back, immobilizing her*) Stop it!
Stop! No! Mumbali—you have to to get over this! This French thing!

MUMBALI. I can't!

SISSY. Count to ten!

MUMBALI. (*trying to control herself*) One, two . . .

SISSY. *Trois, quatre, cinque* . . .

MUMBALI. (*in agony*) I can't! It's bone deep!

SISSY. This is all too bizarre. What's wrong with you?

MUMBALI. I'm losing it! She's back. She's cursed me. Allison.

SISSY. I am not Allison.

MUMBALI. You're rich. You're white. You're father is a fascist.

SISSY. *And?*

MUMBALI. I'm black. I'm a dyke. I'm an ex-con.

SISSY. You're a snob. You're paralyzed. Everything you do, everyone you meet has to be politically perfect, or you detonate. You keep score, you're like some sort of activist maître d'.

MUMBALI. You are evil. You took advantage.

SISSY. You know—I'll bet this can all be traced—to Barbies.

MUMBALI. Barbies?

SISSY. Which ones you played with, what they did. Your childhood. Which Barbie did you have? White Barbie?

MUMBALI. Yeah . . .

SISSY. And what did you do with her? What did you play? Barbie's Dream House?

MUMBALI. No. . . .

SISSY. Barbie beauty salon?

MUMBALI. No . . .

SISSY. Barbie surf shack?

MUMBALI. No.

SISSY. Then what did you play?

MUMBALI. Patty Hearst.

SISSY. You kidnapped Barbie?

MUMBALI. I re-educated her.

SISSY. But now that I think about it, do you know who I played with?

MUMBALI. Who?

SISSY. Velvet, Barbie's black friend.

MUMBALI. Velvet?

SISSY. And I would ask her—where was her dream house? Did she hate Barbie? Did she believe in violent revolution, or working through Mattel?

MUMBALI. This is too sick. Right now, this minute, are you hot for a doll?

SISSY. No. I'm hot—for you.

MUMBALI. Really?

SISSY. And who's getting you all damp and dreamy? Me? Or my pedigree? Barbie? Or Sissy?

MUMBALI. I can't do this.

SISSY. Snot. Priss. Race cadet.

MUMBALI. I'm outta here.

SISSY. Lisa.

MUMBALI. (*shocked*) *What*?

SISSY. You talk in your sleep.

MUMBALI. I am not Lisa! Not anymore! Not since seventh grade!

SISSY. And I snooped around your apartment. You're from Connecticut. Your parents are surgeons. You have a BA from Sarah Lawrence. In French.

MUMBALI. Shut up! I'll kill you! I'll tear you apart!

SISSY. Let's face it, Lisa. You're a rich black woman.

MUMBALI. (*breaking down*) But I'm not! I can't be! It's so—embarassing! It's so pasty and perky and mallomar. It's so—you!

SISSY. And I looked in your Swahili dictionary. "Mumbali" isn't even in there. Who is Mumbali?

MUMBALI. (*in despair*) My horse.

SISSY. (*thrilled*) Really? I had Lucky Star! Were you really in prison?

MUMBALI. Sort of. Minimum Security. White collar crime. In Vermont. It was hell.

SISSY. Really?

MUMBALI. One day, we had a riot. One of the women stood up in the mess hall. She got up on the table and yelled, "You call this *tea*?"

SISSY. My poor baby. But I can help you. I know you don't want to use your honky slave name. Did you know Lisa Wainwright?

MUMBALI. At Miss Porter's? With the knee socks? And the overbite? (*Sissy and Mumbali shriek together. Mumbali catches herself.*) No! I didn't know her!

SISSY. You want to feel proud, of your heritage. But what's wrong with your other heritage? Accept it. Celebrate it. It's a new era. Embrace your inner deb.

MUMBALI. Tell your parents.

SISSY. What?

MUMBALI. Show me you're not Allison. Then I'll be Lisa. I'll—I'll speak French. If you want me, you have to come out.

SISSY. Again?

NAN. (*from offstage*) Sissy! I need your help!

Sissy and Mumbali kiss quickly. Mumbali returns to the ladies room. As Sissy heads toward the display area, Lynette emerges, and they almost collide.

SISSY. Oh, excuse me!

LYNETTE. I'm sorry!

SISSY. Are you here—for the gala?

LYNETTE. Yes. Is that all right?

SISSY. Will you be involved—with a cake?

NAN. (*from offstage*) Sissy!

Lynette ducks down, behind the bar. Sissy pours herself a stiff drink, and downs it, as Nan enters.

NAN. There you are.

SISSY. Mummy?

NAN. We're almost ready. The Great Hall is open, the placecards are under control, but I need you to check the second gallery. Blitzkrieg!

SISSY. (*near tears*) Oh, Mummy!

NAN. What is it, sweetheart? What's wrong?

SISSY. Mummy, do I look—different?

NAN. Different?

SISSY. From the last time you saw me? Do I look—earthy? Outdoorsy? Like at any moment I might found a women's college with my best friend?

NAN. Sissy?

SISSY. Mummy, I . . . I . . . had sex.

NAN. You did?

SISSY. With . . . with a woman.

NAN. Sissy.

SISSY. With—Mumbali.

NAN. *Sacre bleu!*

At Nan's French phrase, there is a loud THUMP from behind the door to the ladies room, where Mumbali hides. The door visibly bulges.

SISSY. Mummy! She's so wonderful and odd and—a woman. I mean, I've never—I just—it was my idea. I just saw her and I couldn't stop thinking about her and—I just did it! And now I can't believe it, I mean Mummy, I'm married.

NAN. Yes, you are.

SISSY. I have children. And a husband.

NAN. You do.

SISSY. Fuck 'em!

NAN. Sissy!

SISSY. I'm awful! What am I doing? I mean, I love my children, and John is so—there, and—where will this lead? A divorce? A custody battle? *Clogs?* Do you hate me?

NAN. *(after a beat)* If you had told me this yesterday, or even this morning, I would never have hated you, but I don't know if I would've quite— understood.

SISSY. And now?

NAN. Now—I think I'm very . . . proud of you!

SISSY. You are?

NAN. Not for being a lesbian, not that there's anything wrong with it, many wonderful women have been lesbians.

SISSY. (*eagerly*) Like who?

NAN. I don't know—Eleanor Roosevelt. Gertrude Stein. Willa Cather.

SISSY. Of course, of course, they're great, but I mean—petites?

NAN. I'm sure. But what I'm proud of is—you've done something outrageous. Something bold!

SISSY. I guess—I have! Oh but Mummy—what will Daddy say?

NAN. Who cares!

SISSY. Mummy?

NAN. I've made some changes too! I'm wicked! I'm depraved! I'm completely different!

SISSY. Are you a lesbian?

NAN. No. Not yet. But—who knows? Why not?

SISSY. Oh Mummy!

NAN. We could be lesbians together! Mother-daughter! We could do talk shows!

SISSY. In matching outfits!

NAN. With crewcuts!

SISSY. With bangs.

NAN. We've been far too well-trained, to hostess, to soothe, to keep things in check. No more! We should live like Alex. Angry! Ambitious! Right on the edge!

SISSY. Mummy, you don't mean . . .

NAN. I do!

SISSY. Take courses?

NAN. I can't just be Mummy, not anymore. I can't even be Nan.

SISSY. But Mummy, you're perfect.

NAN. Don't you ever, ever say that to me again!

SISSY. Mummy?

NAN. You and Mumbali, now there's perfection! Let's make an announcement. At the press conference—tonight!

SISSY. Mummy?

NAN. What an evening! What an opening!

SISSY. Mummy, you're scaring me!

NAN. I hope so! Shock treatment!

SISSY. Mummy, what's happening to us? I'm just so upset and confused! I just feel so all alone! Just like that picture! (*she marches over to the penis picture*) Of that big lonely tree! (*in tears*) I'm sorry!

Sissy runs out, through the hallway.

NAN. Sissy!

Pete backs into the room, speaking to the unseen press corps.

PETE. (*to the press*) Yes! Thank you! We'll begin the conference in just a few moments! Thanks for your support! (*Turning to the room*) Everyone's here. TV crews, newspapers—they know. They can sense it. I'm going to be Governor.

NAN. Really.

PETE. (*he notices the picture*) Nan?

NAN. What?

PETE. That picture. I thought you spoke to DelFlavio.

NAN. You saw me.

PETE. And?

NAN. I think he is—the most remarkable man I've ever known.

PETE. What?

NAN. I think he's a genius.

PETE. He's a menace!

NAN. (*referring to the penis picture*) I think this is one of his very best. It sings. It glows. It speaks to me.

PETE. What does it say?

NAN. "Lunch."

PETE. Nan!

NAN. Tell me, Pete—what's that a picture of?

PETE. You know very well!

NAN. Say it! Don't be afraid.

PETE. I am not afraid!

NAN. What is it?

PETE. That's a picture of what's gone wrong with this country. Permissiveness. Promiscuity. The Sixties. The Seventies.

NAN. But what is it?

PETE. It's an insult to the working man and the farmer and the taxpayer.

NAN. But what is it?

PETE. It's a penis.

NAN. A dick.

PETE. Excuse me?

NAN. Say it. You'll feel better. It's like—a mantra! A battle cry!

PETE. Nan! You're a mature woman. Have some dignity.

NAN. You're right. I am a mature woman. I do have dignity. I am one of the best-dressed, most respected caucasians in this state. How could you do that to me? How could I do that to myself?

PETE. Do what?

NAN. I have campaigned for decades. Until my feet bled and my smile ached and my brain echoed, from telling everyone just how wonderful you are. How caring. How wise. And do you want to know the punchline? The kicker?

PETE. What?

NAN. I believed it. Every word. Every slogan. Every sound bite.

PETE. What is all this? All this—behavior?

NAN. Happy anniversary, Pete.

PETE. Oh my God. Nan, with the campaign, the polls, all of this—I forgot. I'm sorry. I am so sorry.

NAN. Don't worry. It isn't that anniversary. It's only been a year.

PETE. A year?

NAN. Since the last time we touched each other.

Alex enters, from the double doors, in a T-shirt and a tuxedo.

ALEX. Congratulations!

PETE. Thank you, Mr. DelFlavio.

ALEX. You're welcome, darling. (*to Nan*) You look—fantastic.

PETE. I've already told her that.

ALEX. No underwear.

PETE. (*to Nan*) How did he know that?

NAN. What?

PETE. I mean—he's gay. (*he suddenly realizes that Alex might be checking out* his *underwear, and shields himself*) Hey! Hey hey! None of that! No thank you!

ALEX. What?

PETE. I'm a sophisticated man. I know what you are, I know what you do, although frankly I don't know why you do it, or how, really, without screaming. But—there it is. Hands off. Eyes front. Road closed.

ALEX. Excuse me, wait, Pete, do you think—I'm attracted to you?

PETE. You can't help yourself. Homosexuality is like alcoholism. Only unpleasant.

NAN. Alex, you look—superb. In your tuxedo.

PETE. I'm wearing a tuxedo!

ALEX. And it's lovely. Fluid. It—clings.

PETE. What?

ALEX. I'm sorry. You straight guys. You dangle yourselves. A Brooks Brothers tuxedo. A rayon cummerbund. A pre-tied bow-tie. Jesus, Pete, I'm only human!

PETE. Are you mocking me?

NAN. Oh, Pete!

PETE. Is this one of those gay things—anal sex? Whips and chains? Humor?

ALEX. He's been around.

PETE. *(to Alex, gesturing to the exhibit)* Your pictures, all of them—how many of these people are dead?

NAN. Pete!

PETE. We all know what I'm talking about. How many?

ALEX. Several. Not as many as in the Rembrandt show.

PETE. But how can you continue to take these pictures? To display them? Look where they've led!

ALEX. *(in triumph)* To the Civic Central Museum!

PETE. To a plague!

NAN. Pete, stop it!

PETE. Why should I? He's the Pied Piper!

NAN. He's sick!

ALEX. *(furious)* Nan!

NAN. *(to Alex, realizing what she's done)* I'm sorry!

PETE. Oh my God.

ALEX. She's babbling. I'm fine.

NAN. Alex . . .

ALEX. I'm healthy. I'm happening. I swear. Look at me!

PETE. I am.

ALEX. This is my night! This is my shot! This is my coronation!

PETE. *(moving to the penis picture)* And this comes down!

ALEX. Mumbali!

A blast from a police whistle is heard. Mumbali charges in.

MUMBALI. Back off! This is a museum!

Sissy appears, from above.

SISSY. Daddy! Mummy! Everyone is waiting! We have to begin!

NAN. Pete—would you like this picture removed?

SISSY. Oh no! Not the lonely tree.

PETE. Yes! This second!

NAN. Fine—it's gone.

PETE. Bravo!

NAN. Alex—take it down.

ALEX. Not in this lifetime.

NAN. We need the wall space. For—this.

Nan indicates the large wrapped package which Alex has sent over. Alex holds it up.

PETE. What is that?

SISSY. Can we see?

ALEX. It's new.

MUMBALI. It's improved.

NAN. It's . . . me.

PETE. You? It's—you? What do you mean? It's a picture of you?

SISSY. (*thrilled*) Really? A portrait? What are you wearing? The Blass? The Saint Laurent?

NAN. Less.

SISSY. Oh Mummy, not the Donna Karan. Yes, it's simple, yes, it's easy, but it says, "I'm rushing. I'm West Side. I work."

NAN. I am not wearing the Donna Karan.

SISSY. But then what . . . ?

ALEX. Think about it.

PETE. (*the light dawning*) You're kidding.

NAN. Try me.

ALEX. Here we go.

PETE. I don't believe you.

NAN. Well, let's see.

SISSY. (*still not getting it*) Oh yes! I can't wait! Unwrap it!

PETE. No! Don't you dare! Nan—when was this taken?

NAN. This afternoon.

PETE. But, do you mean to say, you . . . you . . . you were coerced into—
    you're nude?

NAN. Naked. Except for the Chanel bag.

PETE. But . . . why?

NAN. It's a classic.

SISSY. (*politely*) Excuse me!

NAN. Yes?

SISSY. Mummy, I don't think I've been following. In this picture, in this
    package, you're, oh, it's too silly, I'm such a dunderhead, Mummy,
    you're not—nude?

NAN. Yes, Sissy.

SISSY. *Nude?*

NAN. Yes.

SISSY. (*trying to be confidential*) Your thighs?

NAN. I have a proposal. Alex removes the offending pictures from the
    show.

PETE. Yes!

ALEX. Wait.

NAN. And replaces them with—me. All of me. Every inch.

ALEX. Your First Lady.

NAN. Full frontal.

PETE. You wouldn't dare!

NAN. Picture it, Pete. Nan Bemiss—bareass blockbuster.

ALEX. Pete Bemiss—Porn Again.

PETE. You mean—if his pictures don't stay . . .

ALEX. (*referring to Nan's portrait*) She will. That's the offer. Bottom line.

PETE. That's blackmail!

ALEX. That's barter. You're the master of negotiation. An eye for an eye.

MUMBALI. Tit for tat.

NAN. So what do we think? Time for the press conference?

MUMBALI. I like it.

ALEX. I love it.

SISSY. Mummy . . .

PETE. (*furious*) You! DelFlavio! What have you done to my wife?

ALEX. I've photographed her. Buck naked. Lots of light.

NAN. Think about it, Pete. He was there.

ALEX. Another man.

MUMBALI. Another woman.

SISSY. Mummy!

ALEX. She was something. You should have seen her.

PETE. I have!

MUMBALI. Not this afternoon.

SISSY. Oh, Mummy—what was it like?

NAN. Degrading. Nasty. Terrifying. I felt more naked, because people were watching. I felt as if—I were on trial. As if my body, my history, every pastry and suntan and stretchmark were being recorded, and judged. Each flashbulb felt like a verdict—guilty, of getting older. Of lying to myself. Of convincing myself that I was a piece of fine china, or Waterford crystal, that if I stayed very still, on a very high shelf, for the rest of my days, I would never shatter. Afterwards, I ran out, convinced I had destroyed everything, ended my life.

SISSY. Mummy . . .

NAN. And then—I ate a Snickers bar.

SISSY. No!

NAN. And then—I bought this dress.

PETE. But I still don't understand—why? Why did you pose for this picture?

NAN. Because I thought that maybe, if I were naked, you would finally—see me.

PETE. You are not the woman I married.

NAN. (*holding the picture*) I hope not! Let's see!

ALEX. This is the hottest picture I've ever taken. And maybe the best. It's a portrait of a woman changing her mind. Let's let everyone see.

PETE. (*exploding*) NO!

Pete grabs the picture.

NAN. Pete!

PETE. I am under attack!

NAN. Excuse me?

PETE. I am under siege!

SISSY. Daddy!

PETE. (*standing before the penis picture*) Look at this, look at it! When I see this thing, do you know how I feel? How any man feels?

SISSY. (*staring at the picture*) Oh my Lord. Oh my Lord.

NAN. Sissy?

SISSY. (*stunned*) Mummy. Daddy. It isn't a lonely tree.

MUMBALI. Oh my God.

SISSY. It's . . . it's . . . it's a doodle! And I'll bet it's not lonely.

PETE. That fellow, in the photo—he's gay, isn't he?

NAN. Pete!

ALEX. Why?

PETE. Because I'm not a bigot! I would never say, of course, all black studs are hung to their knees. But homosexuals—it's true, isn't it? You're all good-looking, rich and hung like mules!

NAN. You see how awful he is?

ALEX. He's not awful. He's right.

MUMBALI. Hold it. You know, there are certain minority stereotypes that I bet were invented by the minority. Well-hung black guys. Smart jews. Gay men with taste.

ALEX. (*challenging her*) Leonardo da Vinci!

MUMBALI. Liberace!

ALEX. Cole Porter!

MUMBALI. Siegfried and Roy!

SISSY. (*incredulous*) Siegfried and Roy?

MUMBALI. Of course!

SISSY. *Roy?*

MUMBALI. Deal with it.

SISSY. (*to Mumbali*) I love you! I do!

PETE. What?

ALEX. Whoa!

SISSY. Daddy—I love her! I need her! I want to have her—pottery!

PETE. *What?*

SISSY. (*terrified*) Oh my God! Oh my God!

PETE. (*to Mumbali*) What have you done to my daughter? To my little girl?

MUMBALI. Your little lesbian.

SISSY. Oh Daddy—I meant to prepare you, to find a time, oh Mummy, please—help!

NAN. You don't need help. You've found someone, someone shocking.

MUMBALI. Nan!

SISSY. Daddy—she makes me so happy! I can't help it! And I'm—I'm going to tell the press conference!

ALEX. Yes!

PETE. I forbid you! You will not tell my constituents about—your little girlfriend!

ALEX. What about yours? (*looking around*) Who said that?

NAN. Pete?

PETE. What?

NAN. Lynette Marshall.

PETE. I don't know whom, or what, you're talking about.

SISSY. Daddy?

NAN. (*to Pete*) Admit it! Expose yourself! (*grabbing the wrapped package*) Or I go out there right now and meet the press. (*she begins to carry the package up the stairs*)

PETE. Stay away from there! I'm warning you!

ALEX. (*to Pete*) You can stop her. Save the election. Make the deal.

SISSY. Daddy—who is Lynette Marshall?

NAN. Pete?

Nan stands by the upper doors. She looks at Pete. She opens the door a few inches. The sounds of the press conference are heard.

PETE. Alright! It's true! I am having an affair.
SISSY. An affair! Daddy!

Nan closes the door. Everyone watches Pete.

PETE. I'm not proud of it.

Pete crosses to the bar. He pours himself a drink.

PETE. Picture it. The campaign trail. A lonely hotel room. There's a knock on the door. Outside stands a nubile young woman, scantily clad. My first response? I think what any other red-blooded American male would think. Muslim terrorists.

Pete looks around. No one is buying his story.

NAN. Pete.
MUMBALI. Senator.
SISSY. Daddy.
ALEX. Darling.
PETE. (*to Nan*) What should I say? That I don't love you? I do! You know I do! You're my wife, you're the woman I want you to be, the woman we created, together. You're flawless, and gracious, and poised—you're terrifying. You scare children.
SISSY. Daddy!
PETE. But love—it's such small change.
NAN. It is?
PETE. Anyone can fall in love. (*to Nan*) You. (*to Sissy*) Or you. (*to Mumbali*) Or even you. But how many people can become Governor?

NAN. Oh my Lord.

PETE. And I want so much more! (*to Nan*) I want you, and Lynette, and the White House and the world!

ALEX. You want everything.

PETE. At least once, before I die! I don't want my picture in an art gallery—that's nothing, who cares? I want my face on the front page, above the fold! I want my profile on a stamp and a coin and a mountaintop! Women fall in love because they can't get elected! I can! So shoot me!

Mumbali unlatches the holster on her belt. She removes her pistol and aims it at Pete.

MUMBALI. One.

PETE. Is that real?

MUMBALI. Find out, baby. You have until three.

PETE. Until three? For what?

MUMBALI. To become someone else. Two . . .

PETE. (*to Alex*) Good God, man! Tell her to put that down before someone gets hurt!

ALEX. Mumbali, think—this could violate your parole.

PETE. Her *parole?*

MUMBALI. Where was I?

ALEX. Two.

MUMBALI. Two.

PETE. Nan, she's causing a scene! Use your influence!

NAN. (*to Mumbali*) Please? He is my husband. For me?

Mumbali reluctantly lowers the gun. Nan holds out her hand, and Mumbali passes her the weapon.

PETE. (*relieved*) Thank God.

Nan aims the gun at Pete.

NAN. Three.
  *We hear a loud BANG. Everyone onstage assumes the gun has gone off, and
  everyone SCREAMS.*

  *Lynette rises from behind the bar, holding an open bottle of champagne, and
  a glass of champagne. The bang was actually the sound of the champagne
  cork popping.*

LYNETTE. Oopsie. (*raising her glass in a toast*) Lynette Marshall. August.

  Nan swings around, now aiming the gun at Lynette.

LYNETTE. No sugar, don't do that.
NAN. Why not?
LYNETTE. You'd only go to prison. You don't want that. Give me the gun.
NAN. No!
LYNETTE. Sugarplum—look at me. I have breasts like twin honeydew
  melons, sweepin' skyward at perfect ninety-degree angles. My legs
  begin somewhere near my armpits, and I have had cameras in places
  most people don't even have husbands. I can't help it. I am the American dreamdate. I'm Barbie with a beaver. Give me the gun.

  Nan hands over the gun.

PETE. Lynette—it's been . . . insane! Nan knows everything! Everyone
  knows everything!
SISSY. (*extending her hand to Lynette*) Sissy Bemiss Darnley.
NAN. Sissy!
SISSY. (*whispering to Nan*) Don't worry. I'm being chilly.
LYNETTE. Pleased to meet you. Formally. You still snorting cocaine?

SISSY. That's my sister.

LYNETTE. Heroin?

SISSY. Pete Junior.

LYNETTE. Bulimia?

SISSY. (*relieved and satisfied*) Thank you!

LYNETTE. Well, you look great.

SISSY. (*sincerely*) Thank you!

NAN. Sissy.

SISSY. (*trying to be chilly*) Merci. (*to Mumbali, very quick and sharp*) No!

LYNETTE. (*to Alex*) And this one . . . (*she points to Alex's name on the wall*) That's you right? Alex DelFlavio. You'd never take my picture, would you?

ALEX. I don't know . . .

LYNETTE. 'Cause you're artistic, and I'm trash.

SISSY. What's the difference?

LYNETTE. Color film.

PETE. Lynette!

LYNETTE. Hold on, hon, just clearin' the air. (*to Nan*) And you, you want me dead. You don't even know what you hate the most—that I'm young, that I'm beautiful, or that I've hogtied your husband.

NAN. Young. I choose young.

LYNETTE. I was raised in a holler. The backwoods. One room. Anyone here know what that's like?

SISSY. Mumbali?

LYNETTE. But, praise Jesus, by the time I was fifteen, I had—blossomed. I was—me. And when I was onstage in the Miss Georgia Peach pageant, they asked me the personality question. Who was my role model? And most of the gals said like Mother Teresa, or Eleanor Roosevelt.

SISSY. Oh my God . . .

MUMBALI. They dated.

NAN. And whom did you select?

LYNETTE. You.

NAN. Me? Why?

LYNETTE. From your pictures. In the social pages. You were ice cold, and elegant, and you looked like you just got everything you ever wanted, without having to put out, or put up, with every sleazeball guy in the world. You looked like you never even heard of the Miss Georgia Peach Pageant.

NAN. True.

LYNETTE. Well baby, now it's my turn.

NAN. Pete?

PETE. Yes?

NAN. Marry her.

PETE. What?

LYNETTE. What?

NAN. You have my blessing.

LYNETTE. *Really?*

NAN. Let her learn. About getting everything she wants. About being your wife.

LYNETTE. Oh my Lord . . .

NAN. On one condition. The pictures stay.

ALEX. Nice work.

NAN. My settlement. My revenge.

ALEX. Grab it, Pete. Plea bargain.

LYNETTE. Pete?

PETE. Lynette . . .

LYNETTE. We have her blessing! Oh my God!

SISSY. A wedding—Daddy and—her?

NAN. Why not?

ALEX. Everyone's happy.

SISSY. We'd better get busy.

PETE. Excuse me?

SISSY. (*to Lynette*) Is this your first marriage? As an adult? Would you like to go classic, antique white satin, or should we do something more—you?

LYNETTE. (*unsure*) Nan?

NAN. Why not Grammy's gown? I wore it.

SISSY. So did I!

ALEX. That's heaven.

SISSY. Perfect!

Sissy, Nan, Lynette and Alex SCREAM with excitement over the gown.

PETE. Excuse me?

SISSY. (*barreling through*) And Alex, you can do the wedding album, can you do that, take normal pictures? I mean it! And Mummy, you and I can be bridesmaids, it's not in perfect taste, but—(*She indicates Pete and Lynette, and then moves on to Mumbali*) And for you, I'm thinking Maid of Honor, in taffeta, maybe peach, maybe pink, why not sunflower. . . .

MUMBALI. *Sunflower?*

SISSY. Fine, khaki!

ALL AT ONCE

NAN. St. Patrick's, or at home?

ALEX. Will you want video?

MUMBALI. Go to City Hall, don't waste the money . . .

SISSY. An announcement in the *Times*, just your picture or the two of you, placecards, linens, appetizers . . .

Everyone except Pete babbles at once, very excitedly, with a rising pitch, planning the wedding.

PETE. Excuse me! Excuse me!

SISSY. Daddy! We're busy!

NAN. Pete?

PETE. I just have one small comment. One minor addition.

LYNETTE. Pete?

PETE. Are you *demented?* Are you all *insane?* Are you on some sort of epic hormonal rampage? There isn't going to be any divorce! And there isn't going to be any wedding!

NAN. Pete, I'm warning you . . .

ALEX. It's a done deal. . . .

PETE. I am running for Governor! And what, two weeks before the election, my wife dumps me and I marry a centerfold? Why don't I just have a sex change? Why don't I just go on a murder spree, through the Vatican? Why don't I just call up Fidel Castro, the Zodiac Killer and Charles Manson, and say, hey guys, let's go dig up the Lindbergh baby! *(to Nan) You* are going home, *(to Lynette) You* are going back to the hotel, *(to Sissy) And you* are going back to your husband, your children and the *Ladies Home Journal!* And I am going to be Governor! Right now!

Pete begins to take down the penis picture.

LYNETTE. I wouldn't.

PETE. What?

LYNETTE. Not if I were you.

Lynette aims the pistol at Pete.

PETE. Lynette.

ALEX. This is amazing. Pete, have you ever noticed, after a woman really gets to know you . . .

Sissy stands in between Pete and Lynette.

SISSY. Don't do it! You'll go to jail! Do you know what kind of women you'll meet in jail?

MUMBALI. What kind?

SISSY. (*thinking fast*) Celebrities!

LYNETTE. Don't worry, sugar—I ain't gonna kill him. I don't want him dead.

PETE. Please—put that down!

LYNETTE. I want him naked. Strip!

The sound of a snare drum begins, as if accompanying a striptease.

PETE. What?

LYNETTE. You heard me. Take it off.

PETE. Are you mad?

LYNETTE. Ain't it your turn?

PETE. My turn?

ALEX. (*to Pete*) It might do you good.

NAN. I highly recommend it.

ALEX. Pete Bemiss—the voice of reason.

LYNETTE. The centerfold.

ALEX. Shock the voters.

NAN. Shock the world.

Pete begins to untie his bowtie.

SISSY. I can't watch this! Daddy, don't!

MUMBALI. Too late!

SISSY. You can't talk! About being naked!

MUMBALI. What?

SISSY. You're black! It's slimming!

LYNETTE. The tux, sweetheart. Lose it. Now.

PETE. Wait.

The music stops.

LYNETTE. Why?

PETE. Alex? You're the linchpin. You want to be famous? Truly, deeply, orgasmically famous? Not well-known, not respected, not esteemed—but hard-core, unauthorized, emblem-of-his-time, T-shirt, *Jeopardy!*-answer and refrigerator-magnet famous?

ALEX. Keep talking.

PETE. Tell everyone.

ALEX. What?

PETE. That you're sick.

NAN. Pete!

SISSY. Daddy!

ALEX. I'd be over!

PETE. You'll be made. (*he gestures to the penis picture*) What's more shocking than life—naked, rude life? (*he gestures to Alex*) An early, black death. That makes a legend. That makes it art.

NAN. Don't listen!

ALEX. (*getting the point, and beginning to get excited*) That makes a fortune.

PETE. Supply and demand,

ALEX. Everyone will want an original Alex DelFlavio . . .

PETE. When there won't be any more.

NAN. That's disgusting!

ALEX. That's inspired.

Katrin and Marcus burst through the double doors, giddily and hiply over-dressed for the gala.

KATRIN. Nan!

MARCUS. Alex!

KATRIN. Senator!

ALEX. (*to Katrin and Marcus*) I have AIDS.

A suspenseful beat. And then:

KATRIN and MARCUS. (*thrilled beyond belief*) *FABULOUS!*

KATRIN. You poor thing!

MARCUS. Our hero!

KATRIN. Our martyr!

Katrin and Marcus look at each other, in total agreement.

KATRIN and MARCUS. *It's a cover!*

KATRIN. I know—announce it at the press conference. With us at your side.

MARCUS. Everyone's here—uptown, downtown.

KATRIN. It's too tragic.

MARCUS. It's too perfect!

KATRIN. Arliss Tandy will die!

ALEX. Not before me!

KATRIN. And Guernica—the birthday pictures. Think what they'll bring.

NAN. You would sell them?

MARCUS. We would share them!

KATRIN. At auction!

MARCUS. With the world!

KATRIN. Senator—this will be so good for you. You'll stand on his other side. You're conservative . . .

MARCUS. But compassionate.

NAN. But that's a contradiction in terms. What in God's name is a compassionate conservative?

LYNETTE. A Republican with a mistress.

KATRIN. We're so excited. After the gala, we're going to have sex.

SISSY. Really?

MARCUS. We've met someone.

Katrin and Marcus scream in gleeful triumph, and exit.

PETE. (*to Alex*) Your pictures can stay. I have only one request.

ALEX. Which is?

PETE. (*gesturing to Nan's wrapped portrait*) That she stay—home. In her plain brown wrapper. And I get the negatives.

ALEX. (*after a beat*) I owe you. Done.

Alex hands Pete the wrapped portrait.

PETE. Done.

NAN. Alex?

ALEX. Nan?

NAN. But, but—what about my picture?

ALEX. It was perfect. It worked.

NAN. But now—no one will see it. No one will know. About what's happened to me. How I've changed.

PETE. Precisely.

ALEX. That's the deal.

SISSY. Mummy, hooray! Now no one will ever have to see you naked!

NAN. But—I want my demon!

PETE. I want to be Governor.

ALEX. I need my show.

Sounds from the press conference are heard.

SISSY. The press conference! We have to get started!

LYNETTE. (*to Nan*) Honey, you're way ahead.

NAN. But how can you say that? You're a centerfold!

LYNETTE. So I know. Horse's mouth.

PETE. Lynette—the hotel.

LYNETTE. (*handing the gun back to Mumbali*) Gotcha. Gone.

NAN. (*apalled*) Are you—going back to him?

LYNETTE. Why not?

NAN. But you're young, you're beautiful—you're in *Playboy*.

PETE. That's not a resume.

NAN. But isn't there anything else you can do? Can you type? Word process?

LYNETTE. Can you?

PETE. (*to Lynette*) I left a stack of videotapes by the bed.

LYNETTE. Oh no . . .

PETE. Cronkite. Khruschev.

LYNETTE. You're evil.

PETE. *Cocoon.*

Lynette moans, and exits.

SISSY. Mummy, it's all worked out for the best. And this can still be your grandest gala ever!

NAN. (*looking for an ally*) Mumbali?

SISSY. (*near the steps*) Come on, Lisa!

NAN. Lisa?

SISSY. Follow me!

Mumbali follows Sissy up the stairs, helplessly. Sissy flings open the double doors. She faces the press.

SISSY. Hello, everyone! It's me, Sissy! And I have an announcement. I hope you won't find this shocking, but—I am leaving my husband. (*flashbulb activity*) For a woman. (*increased flashbulb activity*) A black woman. (*She presents Mumbali to the cameras. A blizzard of flashbulbs.*) But don't worry—she's one of us. And my Daddy is going to make a wonderful governor, because I think he's learned quite a valuable lesson tonight.

PETE. Oh my God.

SISSY. He's learned that this is a perfect, wonderful state, and a perfect, wonderful world, whether you're black or white, gay or straight, rich or upper middle class!

Mumbali turns to Nan.

MUMBALI. (*helplessly*) L'amour!

Sissy grabs Mumbali's hand and drags her into the press conference, into a blizzard of flashbulbs. They exit. A beat.

NAN. (*to Alex*) You've got everything you've ever wanted, don't you? Your pictures, and my party. Every angle.

ALEX. I win.

NAN. So you can die happy.

ALEX. I'll miss the headlines.

NAN. And I was just another rich white lady. Useful. Convenient.

ALEX. You knew the plan. The bargain. Leverage. I never lied to you.

NAN. No. You did something far uglier. You took my picture. And then you took it back. So you owe me. You relentless bastard. One question. One honest answer.

ALEX. Fair enough.

NAN. Was it worth it? Your life? All that shock? All those flashbulbs? All that . . . famous fuck-you?

ALEX. Yes.

NAN. Honestly?

ALEX. But do you know what I am ashamed of? What I truly regret?

NAN. Yes?

ALEX. That for a moment—I got scared. And cowardly. Until Pete. And now—I love being sick. And I'm going to love wasting away. And most of all, I'm going to love the look on peoples' faces, when they tiptoe tearfully into my hospital room, and then shudder at my hollow eyes and rotting flesh. Because I won't be dying. Not me. Not Alex DelFlavio.

NAN. What will you be?

ALEX. Shocking.

NAN. Good God.

ALEX. One question. One honest answer.

NAN. What?

ALEX. Was it worth it? All that love?

Alex exits, into flashbulbs. He pauses, basking in the blinding, warming blast of light. He takes a deep breath. He smiles, and moves into the party.

PETE. Clever fellow.

NAN. Thanks to you.

PETE. You know, I actually—like him. Isn't that odd?

NAN. Not at all.

PETE. (*starting to climb the stairs*) Sweetheart, are you coming? I need you.

NAN. Why?

PETE. The photographers. The press.

NAN. But what about Sissy? And Lynette?

PETE. Kid's stuff. Mid-life whatever. You're a pro.

NAN. Am I?

PETE. We can still pull it off. We can still have everything we've ever dreamed of. This is only the beginning.

NAN. So you—forgive me?

PETE. Of course. The whole day. Everything you've done, every wrong turn—never happened.

NAN. And you don't think that I'm a coward? That I'm terrified of change, of giving offense, of wearing a red dress? Of not wearing a red dress?

PETE. Nan. Come on. You're not shocking. It's not in you. And I think that you're incredibly brave. Brave enough to admit that you were wrong. And foolish.

NAN. And old.

PETE. Mature.

NAN. Wise.

PETE. You said that you believed in me. I'll earn that back. And maybe, just maybe, we can do some good.

NAN. I'll be right up.

PETE. That's my girl! (*He begins climbing the stairs; he turns.*) I love you.

> *Pete exits, into flashbulbs. He beams. Nan is alone. She slowly climbs the stairs, with her back to the audience. She pauses. She reaches up; she undoes her dress, which falls to her ankles. Naked, she steps out of her dress. She heads into the press conference, and a blaze of flashbulbs.*

CURTAIN

FIVE

Valhalla

For Christopher Ashley

VALHALLA was originally produced at New York Theatre Workshop (James C. Nicola, Artistic Director; Lynn Moffat, Managing Director) in New York City, opening on February 5, 2004. It was directed by Christopher Ashley; the set design was by Thomas Lynch; the lighting design was by Kenneth Posner; the sound design was by Mark Bennett; the costume design was by William Ivey Long; the choreography was by Daniel Pelzig; and the production stage manager was Sarah Bittenbender. The cast was as follows:

HENRY LEE STAFFORD / HELMUT / OPERA SINGER	Scott Barrow
MARGARET AVERY / QUEEN MARIE / PRINCESS ENID / NATALIE KIPPELBAUM	Candy Buckley
JAMES AVERY	Sean Dugan
KING LUDWIG OF BAVARIA	Peter Frechette
SALLY MORTIMER / PRINCESS SOPHIE / PRINCESS PATRICIA / MARIE ANTOINETTE / ANNIE AVERY	Samantha Soule
FOOTMAN / OTTO / PFEIFFER / PRINCESS URSULA THE UNUSUAL / REVEREND HOWESBERRY / SERGEANT	Jack Willis

Characters

The play is performed by six actors, with four of the actors playing multiple roles as indicated.

LUDWIG

JAMES AVERY

HENRY LEE STAFFORD / HELMUT / OPERA SINGER

MARGARET AVERY / QUEEN MARIE / PRINCESS ENID /
NATALIE KIPPELBAUM

SALLY MORTIMER / PRINCESS PATRICIA / PRINCESS SOPHIE /
MARIE ANTOINETTE / ANNIE AVERY

PFEIFFER / OTTO / FOOTMAN / PRINCESS URSULA
THE UNUSUAL / REVEREND HOWESBERRY / SERGEANT

A note on *Valhalla*: The play must move rapidly and fluidly, using almost no scenery at all, and the scenes should overlap—we should never have to wait for a scene change. The costumes should indicate the various time periods and the characters' ages. The play also requires a sustained musical score, and Mark Bennett's superb sound design for the play's original production is available from Dramatists Play Service.

Valhalla

ACT ONE

Ludwig of Bavaria runs onstage, dressed in a blue velvet Little Lord Fauntleroy suit and a long curled wig. He will be played by an adult actor, but he's currently ten years old. Ludwig is passionate, highly strung and does not censor his more hallucinatory urges; he's also a true and enduring innocent. The year is 1855.

LUDWIG. I am out of my mind! With excitement! I'm only ten years old, and I've fallen in love! And today—I'm going to tell her! (*James Avery appears. He stares yearningly at a small, beautiful crystal swan located nearby. James will be played by an adult actor, but he's currently ten years old, and he's dressed like a ragged small-town boy from 1930s Texas. James' personality is already fully formed. He's a self-styled aristocrat, and he can be seductive, charming and ruthless. James intends to live a life of enormous possibility, and nothing can stop him.*)

JAMES. (*Staring at the crystal swan.*) It's happenin' again. I'm only ten years old and I shouldn't even be in this department store, 'cause I'm gettin' all itchy. Because I need it!

LUDWIG. I ran all the way down here, to the lake by my family's castle. (*Looking out, toward the audience.*) And here she comes, she's moving like a sunbeam on glass . . .

JAMES. She's one-hundred-percent fine lead crystal, all the way from Europe . . .

LUDWIG. She's so perfect . . .

JAMES. She's so beautiful . . .

LUDWIG. She's so snooty . . .

LUDWIG and JAMES. She's a swan!

LUDWIG. And we'll get married, in a grand royal wedding, Prince Ludwig and his bride . . .

JAMES. And I'll keep you safe in my pocket, and then I'll put you high on my shelf . . .

LUDWIG. And we'll talk about everything, about why everyone thinks I'm so incredibly weird, and about why they're all wrong, maybe . . .

JAMES. And you will fill my whole room, the whole house, you will fill my whole life with light!

LUDWIG. And when you molt, we'll make pillows!

JAMES. So dear Lord, if you want me to have her, if you want me to be happy . . .

LUDWIG. I know you can't speak, I'm not even sure if you have feet, but if your answer is yes . . .

LUDWIG and JAMES. Give me a sign!

LUDWIG. A miracle!

JAMES. I'm begging you!

LUDWIG and JAMES. Please please please please please please please please . . . (*We hear gorgeous Wagnerian music. Both James and Ludwig hear it; they move to the music simultaneously, enraptured.*) Yes! (*As Ludwig leans in to kiss his swan, James grabs the crystal swan and runs offstage.*)

LUDWIG. (*Watching his swan exit.*) But where are you going? Didn't you hear the music? Didn't anyone? Is it just me?

QUEEN. (*From offstage.*) Ludwig!

LUDWIG. (*To the swan.*) Come back! I have breadcrumbs! (*As we hear a police siren wail, Ludwig runs out, pursuing the swan.*)

MARGARET. James. (*Lights up on the Avery parlor, in Texas. James is now lying on the floor, having just been severely beaten. Margaret Avery is standing over James. She is a young Texas matron, in a cheap but clean cotton dress. Margaret is James' mother; while she's concerned for his welfare, she's also short-tempered* *and strict.*) Not so smart now, are you, mister? Now that your daddy's beaten some sense into you.

JAMES. Bitch.

MARGARET. (*Margaret hauls off and smacks James very hard across the face.*) You watch your filthy mouth. This is the third time that I have had to go down to that police station, the third time that I have had to grovel and apologize, and the third time that I have had to live in shame, because my son is a filthy disgrace!

JAMES. I'm not your son.

MARGARET. I wish you weren't!

JAMES. I was switched at birth by gypsies. And they said, let's punish this baby. Let's send him to Dainsville, Texas, let's dump him into a frame house with no books and brown wallpaper and pink chenille bedspreads . . .

MARGARET. You spiteful little jabber-monster . . .

JAMES. Let's give him to a sadistic idiot who runs a hardware store and a vicious, dried-up woman with bad hair and no taste.

MARGARET. (*Raising her hand.*) You are just begging for it . . .

JAMES. Fine. Hit me again. But just look at your dining room.

MARGARET. But why? Why are you like this?

JAMES. Like what?

MARGARET. All I want is to help you. Don't you want to make your daddy proud?

JAMES. But my daddy gets drunk and he hits me. And sometimes he even hits you.

MARGARET. Not as hard.

SALLY. Mrs. Avery? (*Sally Mortimer enters. She is played by an adult actress, but she's currently ten years old. She is very pretty, very cheerful, and she's dressed in a crisp, frilly, almost Shirley Temple-style dress.*)

MARGARET. Come in. James, this is Sally Mortimer, whose family owns the department store.

SALLY. And I'm in the fourth grade, just like you.

MARGARET. And I have asked her to come here, so that you can apologize for your crime, to her face.

SALLY. (*Indicating that she'd like to be alone with James.*) Mrs. Avery?

MARGARET. Oh, of course. This is so sweet! (*Margaret exits.*)

SALLY. Now James, why did you steal that crystal swan?

JAMES. I didn't steal it. I needed it. Because it was beautiful.

SALLY. You mean, like a tree or a sunset?

JAMES. Or you.

SALLY. Well, that's no crime.

JAMES. You see?

SALLY. Now, why don't you kiss me, just right here on my cheek, and then all will be forgiven. (*Sally presents her cheek to be kissed. Just as James is about to kiss it, he kisses her lips instead.*) James! Why did you do that?

JAMES. I've got my eye on a punchbowl.

SALLY. Oh James, I know that deep down inside, you are really a very sweet, very good little boy.

JAMES. I'm a cocksucker.

SALLY. Well, that's fine. I'm a Baptist. (*Lights down on Texas, as Ludwig enters, now thirteen.*)

LUDWIG. I'm sorry! (*Queen Marie, Ludwig's mother, enters; she is played by the same actress who plays Margaret. The Queen loves her son deeply, but she is a fretful, deeply conventional woman. She also has very good reasons for her family concerns.*)

QUEEN. Ludwig! You're thirteen, a young man. Why are you acting like a spiteful, wretched little spoiled infant? Your father is furious.

LUDWIG. I don't care!

QUEEN. He's the king!

LUDWIG. I'm the prince!

QUEEN. I'm the queen!

LUDWIG. Gin!

QUEEN. Ludwig! Why did you fire that footman? He was the third one this month!

LUDWIG. I didn't want to, I didn't mean to. He was kind, he was clever.

QUEEN. Then why?

LUDWIG. (*Tormented.*) He was—ugly! (*Lights down on Bavaria. Lights up on a boy's bedroom in Texas. There is an open window and a bed with someone sleeping in it. The someone is Henry Lee Stafford, played by an adult actor but currently twelve years old. He wears pajamas. Henry Lee is a good-natured, trusting kid, anxious to do well, but he's far less sure of himself than James. Henry Lee has great promise, but he always tries to behave. James climbs into the bedroom through the window. The room is in semi-darkness. James now wears a Cub Scout uniform, including the cap and neckerchief. He carries a wrapped bundle.*)

JAMES. Henry Lee? (*Henry Lee wakes up, still groggy.*)

HENRY LEE. (*Scared.*) Who . . . who is that? Who's there?

JAMES. It's me, James Avery.

HENRY LEE. *What are you doing here?*

JAMES. I've seen you at school, in gym class. You were looking at me.

HENRY LEE. I was not!

JAMES. Do you want to have sex?

HENRY LEE. *What?*

JAMES. Now that I'm twelve, I have it all the time.

HENRY LEE. With who?

JAMES. Me.

HENRY LEE. Get out of my house! I'm gonna yell! (*James jumps onto the bed and yanks Henry Lee's hand behind his back; he covers Henry Lee's mouth with his other hand.*)

JAMES. (*Gleeful.*) Don't make me kiss you. (*Henry Lee bites James' hand and James yells.*) Shit! You bit me! You fight like a girl!

HENRY LEE. I do not!

JAMES. It was a compliment!

HENRY LEE. Get off my bed! Get out of my house!

JAMES. Do you wanna see what I use, for sex?

HENRY LEE. What?

JAMES. (*Holding up the bundle.*) Look.

HENRY LEE. What is that?

JAMES. (*Taking a large art book out of the bundle.*) I got this from the library this afternoon. From the special adult section, behind the front desk.

HENRY LEE. But we're not supposed to go back there.

JAMES. I hid in the bathroom until the librarian went out, and then I grabbed it. It burned my hands.

HENRY LEE. Why?

JAMES. Because when a book is forbidden and sick and evil, when it's in the adult section, it has special, dark powers. Do you know what they call those books?

HENRY LEE. What?

JAMES. Bestsellers.

HENRY LEE. (*Impressed.*) Really?

JAMES. So I dropped it out the window, and then I ran outside and I picked it up.

HENRY LEE. You stole it.

JAMES. I needed it.

HENRY LEE. What's the difference?

JAMES. What do you want, more than anything else in the whole entire world?

HENRY LEE. I want—to make my parents and my teachers and everyone else in Dainsville really proud of me.

JAMES. I love that.

HENRY LEE. You do?

JAMES. So you wanna be an asshole.

HENRY LEE. No!

JAMES. But what do you *need*, in your soul?

HENRY LEE. A Cadillac.

JAMES. Yeah!

HENRY LEE. A midnight-blue convertible, like in that Cary Grant movie, with whitewall tires and real leather seats and all that chrome.

JAMES. Baby!

HENRY LEE. I need it whenever my Little League coach says that the whole team is depending on me. Or when my mom says that "a B-plus is unacceptable." (*Grabbing James around the throat, acting it out.*) I need it when my dad holds a sawed-off shotgun to my head and says, "Boy, if you don't get into Texas A&M, I'm gonna splatter your brains all over the kitchen wall." (*Really going wild.*) But then I grab the gun, and I blast *his* head off, and I blast every window and trophy and piece of fine china in the house! And I set the whole place on fire and I climb out on the roof and I yell, "Come and get me, coppers!"

JAMES. Henry Lee.

HENRY LEE. Yeah?

JAMES. Not the china.

HENRY LEE. Okay.

JAMES. So if we were just walking down the street and we just happened to pass a midnight-blue Cadillac, and the keys were in the ignition and the radio is playing a great song . . .

HENRY LEE. Like Benny Goodman . . .

JAMES. Or Tommy Dorsey . . .

HENRY LEE. Or like, the Andrews Sisters . . .

JAMES. Which one's your favorite?

HENRY LEE. Patti. The pretty one.

JAMES. Me too. (*Very macho.*) Do you know what I'd like to do with her? Do you know what she needs?

HENRY LEE. What?

JAMES. (*Equally macho.*) A solo album.

HENRY LEE. (*Still macho.*) For damn sure!

JAMES. So if you walked past this Cadillac, and it sang to you, so if we took it out for a spin, like to Dallas or Hollywood or Mars, then what would you call that?

HENRY LEE. A dream.

JAMES. Now you're talkin'.

HENRY LEE. A bold escape!

JAMES. Together!

HENRY LEE. A crime.

JAMES. Even better!

HENRY LEE. Get out of my room!

JAMES. Look. (*He points a flashlight at the cover of the art book.*)

HENRY LEE. (*Reading the title.*) *The History of Greco-Roman Art.*

JAMES. But I have to warn you. This book is completely filled with sex.
It's oozing with sex. If you even look at one inch of one page, do you
know what will happen to you?

HENRY LEE. What?

JAMES. Sex.

HENRY LEE. Stop it!

JAMES. Are you ready? Are you man enough?

HENRY LEE. (*After a beat.*) Yes. (*James points the beam of the flashlight at the
book. As he slowly and dramatically opens the cover, we hear:*)

LUDWIG. But I can't! (*The flashlight goes out, as the lights come up instantly
on the palace. Ludwig is standing, facing out. The Queen stands nearby. A uniformed footman, with a powdered wig and a somewhat bloated body, stands
facing Ludwig, with his back to the audience—we will never see the footman's
face. Ludwig, in his reaction to the footman, is not being deliberately mean or
cruel. His aesthetic drive is helpless; he can't control his visceral sense of taste.
He's in torment.*)

QUEEN. But you must. I want you to stare directly at this footman, for a
period of no less than one hour.

LUDWIG. An *hour?* (*Appalled.*)

QUEEN. You can do it. I know you can.

LUDWIG. But—without breaks?

QUEEN. Your father insists.

LUDWIG. But he's grotesque.

QUEEN. He's still your father.

LUDWIG. (*Gesturing to the footman.*) I meant him. He's vile. He's repulsive.

QUEEN. Ludwig!

LUDWIG. (*Sincerely, to the footman.*) No offense.

QUEEN. Darling, one day you're going to be king, of all Bavarians, not just the cute ones. (*Ludwig starts to run.*) Come back here!

LUDWIG. But I have this terrible problem, and I know it's completely my fault, but when I see something—not beautiful, when it's drab and misshapen, when it's—what's the word?

QUEEN. English?

LUDWIG. Yes! I have a physical reaction, a spasm, I can't control it.

QUEEN. You must try.

LUDWIG. I want to, I need to, but I'm frightened.

QUEEN. (*Holding a pocket watch.*) Let's begin. (*Ludwig steels himself; he stares at the footman's face. Blackout on the palace. The flashlight beam appears, illuminating the book, as James and Henry Lee sit on the bed, poring over the pages.*)

HENRY LEE. Oh my God . . .

JAMES. (*Turning a page.*) And this one . . .

HENRY LEE. Look at that.

JAMES. (*Turning the page.*) And two of them!

HENRY LEE. But, but—they're naked. All of the statues. You can see—everything.

JAMES. Of course. This was B.C.

HENRY LEE. B.C.?

JAMES. Before Clothes.

HENRY LEE. Shut up!

JAMES. But why is that guy so big and built, but his dickie is so tiny?

HENRY LEE. You're already bigger than he is.

JAMES. So you looked.

HENRY LEE. I did not!

JAMES. And when I get a boner, it gets even bigger. Do you know why?

HENRY LEE. Why?

JAMES. I'm an American.

HENRY LEE. What are you doing?

JAMES. I'm touching myself.

HENRY LEE. Why?

JAMES. It's like, if I see something, or someone, really beautiful, my hand
     goes right there, like a compass.

HENRY LEE. But my dickie is so hard! It hurts!

JAMES. So touch it. Play with it.

HENRY LEE. But it's wrong. It's dirty.

JAMES. It's beautiful. It says so, right in the Bible.

HENRY LEE. Where?

JAMES. In Ezekiel 12. God says, "Ezekiel, you're twelve. Touch yourself."

HENRY LEE. (*Putting his hand inside his pajamas.*) Thy will be done . . .

JAMES. Look at me.

HENRY LEE. Why?

JAMES. I'm Hercules.

HENRY LEE. I'm Apollo.

JAMES. I'm a gladiator.

HENRY LEE. I'm glad.

JAMES. We're wrestling . . .

HENRY LEE. In the Colosseum . . .

JAMES. In the Olympics . . .

HENRY LEE. In the nude . . .

JAMES. Yes!

QUEEN. (*Consulting her pocket watch.*) Thirty-seven minutes . . .

LUDWIG. (*To the footman, feverishly.*) I'm trying to love you, to be a good
     king, but it's hard. But you're helping me, I can feel it, to appreciate all
     kinds of beauty, it's growing, it's blossoming, a whole new concept, I
     love your ears, I love your eyes, I love your—were you in an accident?

HENRY LEE. The whole Colosseum is on its feet, they're all watching the
     two gladiators . . .

JAMES. The slaves are watching . . .

HENRY LEE. And the citizens . . .

JAMES. And the Emperor . . .

HENRY LEE. Hi, everybody!

JAMES. They're all cheering . . .

HENRY LEE. They're all chanting . . .

JAMES and HENRY LEE. Go, go, go . . .

QUEEN. Forty-eight minutes! You're doing great!

LUDWIG. I can't! I can't! Not one second more!

QUEEN. I have faith! Keep looking! Go, go, go . . .

QUEEN, JAMES and HENRY LEE. Go, go, go, go, go, go, go . . .

LUDWIG. (*Over the go, go, go's:*) But my eyes are on fire! They're going to pop out!

JAMES. It's happening! In front of everyone! We're gonna spurt!

HENRY LEE. We're gonna shoot!

QUEEN. Fifty-eight minutes . . .

JAMES. All over each other and the Emperor and the Acropolis!

HENRY LEE. This is the best book I've ever read!

QUEEN. We're almost there!

JAMES, HENRY LEE and LUDWIG. (*James and Henry Lee are coming, noisily, while Ludwig is crying out:*) AHHH!

QUEEN. One hour! Congratulations!

LUDWIG. But I can't do this! I can't be king!

QUEEN. (*Embracing him.*) Of course you can. And you're going to be the most wonderful king.

LUDWIG. Really, Mummy?

QUEEN. Of course. And next time you'll do even better.

LUDWIG. Next time? What do you mean?

QUEEN. (*To the footman.*) Bring in your wife.

LUDWIG. NO! (*As Ludwig runs out, lights down on the palace.*)

HENRY LEE. James?

JAMES. Yeah?

HENRY LEE. What . . . what just happened? What did we do?

JAMES. I think that, for maybe one hot second, that we both—left Texas.

HENRY LEE. We did?

JAMES. Swear.

HENRY LEE. What?

JAMES. Swear that we will go all the way.

HENRY LEE. What do you mean?

JAMES. Swear that someday, when we get bigger, the minute we can—
that we will get the hell out of here. All the way.

HENRY LEE. To where?

JAMES. To out there. To happiness. To someplace so beautiful it gives
you a boner.

HENRY LEE. But why me?

JAMES. Because I look at everybody in this town. I stare at 'em.

HENRY LEE. Like a hobby?

JAMES. To try and see what's beautiful about them. What they dream
about. Who they love. But most people, they look away. They don't
want me to know. But you looked right back.

HENRY LEE. And it scared me. It was like in *Superman*, when he uses his
X-ray vision, and it starts a fire.

JAMES. Just by lookin' at you, I can make your dickie hard. (*James stares
at Henry Lee, in the eyes.*)

HENRY LEE. Oh my God! And that was so fast!

JAMES. We're twelve.

HENRY LEE. James!

JAMES. You are the best little boy in Dainsville. And I'm the worst. If we
get together, we could explode!

HENRY LEE. Right out of Texas! (*James grabs the art book and holds it out.*)

JAMES. Do you swear? You and me? All the way? Look at me.

HENRY LEE. But if I look at you, I'll say yes.

JAMES. I know.

HENRY LEE. (*Looking right at him.*) Yes. (*Lights out on Henry Lee's bedroom, as
Ludwig sweeps onstage, dressed in a full, billowing nun's habit and wimple. He
faces the audience, kneels and crosses himself in prayer.*)

LUDWIG. Dear Heavenly Father, Today I am fourteen years old, and I am in desperate need. So I have decided to speak to you most humbly, dressed in the habit of your most sainted and elegant creatures. To purify myself completely, for the past two weeks I have fasted. I have taken absolutely no sustenance, except dessert.

OTTO. (*From offstage.*) Ludwig!

LUDWIG. (*To God.*) My little brother, Otto.

OTTO. (*From offstage.*) Luddy!

LUDWIG. (*To God.*) One day, when my father dies, I will become king. So I need to know: When the time comes, how can I make the world as beautiful as You? (*Otto, Ludwig's seven-year-old brother, enters, played by the same adult actor who will later play Pfeiffer. He wears lederhosen and a cap, and carries a rubber ball. He is sweet-natured but far less sophisticated than Ludwig.*)

OTTO. Luddy!

LUDWIG. I'm talking to God!

OTTO. But I want to play! Please, Luddy!

LUDWIG. What did you call me?

OTTO. Luddy! Luddy, Luddy, Luddy!

LUDWIG. (*To God.*) Dear Lord, I seek guidance . . . (*Listening to God's advice.*) Yes . . . yes . . . I'll tell him.

OTTO. What did God say?

LUDWIG. God says that he wants to see you. Right *now*. (*Ludwig chases Otto, who screams.*)

OTTO. No! Stop it! God didn't say that!

LUDWIG. Say it! Say what you're supposed to say!

OTTO. (*As Ludwig grabs Otto and starts to strangle him.*) Stop it! Mama! (*As Ludwig strangles Otto, the Queen rushes in and separates the boys.*)

QUEEN. Ludwig! Stop it! This instant! (*Ludwig reluctantly releases Otto, who lies on the ground, panting.*) You are dressed like a nun!

LUDWIG. I know that!

QUEEN. Then act like one!

OTTO. That's right!

QUEEN. What were you doing?

LUDWIG. I'm trying to learn to be king, but he wouldn't call me by my title!

OTTO. So he killed me!

QUEEN. Do you know what happens to bad little princes?

LUDWIG. What?

QUEEN. You'll end up—like your grandfather.

LUDWIG. How?

QUEEN. When he was king, he became obsessed with Lola Montes, a notorious courtesan. A courtesan—do you know what that is?

LUDWIG. No.

QUEEN. Good. She was an Irish girl, pretending to be an Arabian dancer. She would make a movement with her hips, which would drive men into a filthy, deranged erotic frenzy.

LUDWIG. What was it? (*The Queen, after a Moment's preparation, demonstrates the hip-swivelling movement.*) That's it?

QUEEN. She had lighting.

LUDWIG. And Grandfather?

QUEEN. He ran off with Lola, and the nation was outraged. He refused to give her up, he spent millions, and finally—he was forced to do something horrible. Something unthinkable. Something that no king, of any country, should ever, ever have to do.

LUDWIG. (*Sincerely, shocked.*) His own laundry?

QUEEN. He was forced to leave the throne. To abdicate. In *disgrace*.

LUDWIG and OTTO. No!

QUEEN. Your father has grown very preoccupied, so your future has become entirely my domain. And I'm a normal woman. All I want is for this family to be happy and healthy and to rule Bavaria. Is that too much to ask?

LUDWIG. No, Mummy.

QUEEN. Without any hint of scandal, excess or perversion.

OTTO. Mummy, what's perversion?

QUEEN. It's a Latin term.

OTTO. For what?

QUEEN. Your brother.

LUDWIG. How dare you!

OTTO. You see? Luddy is snooty, because he's going to be king!

QUEEN. (*To Otto.*) But sweetheart, you're just as important, in case Ludwig gets assassinated, commits suicide or goes mad.

OTTO. Really?

QUEEN. You're the spare.

LUDWIG. Mummy!

QUEEN. But that won't happen, not if we all love each other and pull together and wear men's clothing. Do you understand me, Ludwig?

LUDWIG. Yes, Mummy.

QUEEN. So what are you going to do? (*Ludwig, apprehensive but determined, takes off his nun's habit. He stands in his long underwear, which has a royal crest embroidered on the chest. Ludwig is reluctant to remove his wimple.*) And? (*Ludwig removes his wimple.*) Much better.

LUDWIG. But I feel so—naked. And cold. No, worse than that, much worse, I feel—ordinary. Invisible. How will God find me?

QUEEN. He'll find you because He loves you.

LUDWIG. (*Longingly.*) Just the wimple?

QUEEN. No. Now Otto, what's your brother's title?

OTTO. Your Highness.

QUEEN. That's my good boy. And Ludwig, who are you going to be?

LUDWIG. (*Proudly.*) The king.

OTTO. Of my butt.

LUDWIG. Otto! (*Ludwig chases him offstage, as Otto screams.*)

QUEEN. Boys! (*As she pursues the boys.*) I am serious! (*As the Queen exits after her sons, we hear a police siren wail. James appears, standing behind bars, in handcuffs. His clothing and hair are disheveled. Sally Mortimer, now fifteen, runs onstage, very excited. She carries a plate of freshly baked cookies.*)

SALLY. James! Is it true?

JAMES. What?

SALLY. I can scarcely even speak the words. They said, I heard—that you ran off with Henry Lee Stafford.

JAMES. Yes I did!

SALLY. And that before you left Dainsville, you set fire to your family's home.

JAMES. It was so great. It was my fifteenth birthday, and my father beat the hell out of me. So I asked, now, Daddy, what was that for? And he said, "Happy birthday, you little faggot."

SALLY. Oh no!

JAMES. That's right.

SALLY. Was there cake?

JAMES. No. (*Sally gasps.*) But then I thought, maybe he's right. So I asked myself, now just what would a little faggot do?

SALLY. So you burned down your house?

JAMES. I redecorated.

SALLY. And then they caught you and Henry Lee, five miles outside of town, in a stolen pickup truck.

JAMES. You know it!

SALLY. But *why?*

JAMES. We couldn't find a Cadillac.

SALLY. James!

JAMES. We were flyin', we were gone!

SALLY. Where?

JAMES. To some place so beautiful, you can't even imagine it!

SALLY. The state capitol?

JAMES. Picture it, Sally, like if you were with us. We're hittin' eighty miles an hour, the windows wide open, your hair shootin' straight back . . .

SALLY. Oh my Lord . . .

JAMES. I mean, we felt like we could be anybody we wanted!

SALLY. Anybody?

JAMES. Who would you be?

SALLY. I would be . . . I would be . . . I would be me. And I'd stay home.

JAMES. Why?

SALLY. Because I'm popular. Do you realize how many valentines I received, this year alone? So many that I actually gave several of them to Emmeline Atwood, that sweet, brave, wonderful girl, who's blind? I just put them on her desk and I said . . . (*Raising her voice.*) "Emmeline, these are for you!"

JAMES. Did she like them?

SALLY. Especially the embossed ones.

JAMES. What are you doing here? In the police station?

SALLY. I came because I heard that your parents refuse to see you, and that you are being sent away, and that Henry Lee's parents insist that he was a hostage.

JAMES. A hostage?

SALLY. Did you hypnotize him, did you drug him with opium, were you going to sell him to bloodthirsty Chinese pirates as a helpless white slave?

JAMES. Later.

SALLY. I knew it!

JAMES. What are you doing here?

SALLY. I came because no one else would. I came out of goodness and mercy. Ginger snap? (*She begins to feed James cookies, through the bars.*)

JAMES. My favorite. You know why?

SALLY. Because they're tasty yet not all that fattening?

JAMES. Before I bite one, I like to lick it, with my tongue. (*As James licks a cookie, erotically.*)

SALLY. James—that is no way to treat a cookie.

JAMES. You came because you like me.

SALLY. I did not!

JAMES. You came because I once saw your notebook, in geometry class. And you were drawing a picture of me.

SALLY. That was a trapezoid.

JAMES. With my eyes?

SALLY. But I couldn't really get them. Your eyes are so wicked. Like they can see—everything.

JAMES. I can see beneath your clothes right now. You are wearing very clean underwear.

SALLY. That's incredible!

JAMES. And your nipples are hard.

SALLY. It's January!

JAMES. Sally, could you just kind of sneak into the sheriff's office, and kind of grab the keys? (*Indicating the handcuffs.*)

SALLY. Absolutely not! That is illegal!

JAMES. I fucked Henry Lee.

SALLY. James!

JAMES. Well, not yet. He's stubborn.

SALLY. I am leaving!

JAMES. No, please, just stay one more second, just turn around and let me look at you. You are so good and so pretty, you are the prettiest girl in Dainsville. (*Sally pauses and turns, so that James can see her.*)

SALLY. Just for one second. And I am only doing this as an act of charity. Sometimes, when Emmeline gets depressed, I describe myself.

JAMES. While I'm away, will you write to me?

SALLY. I just don't know.

JAMES. Will you pray for me?

SALLY. I will try.

JAMES. And the very first time that you have sex, whenever and wherever, will you call out my name?

SALLY. James Avery! I have tried to help you, to show you some simple human compassion, but everyone is right! You don't deserve cookies!

JAMES. Will you?

SALLY. (*On her way out.*) Yes. (*Sally exits, as James smiles. Lights down on James, as we hear the sound of metal doors clanging shut, followed by a Wagnerian trill. Helmut jogs onstage; he is Ludwig's fitness instructor. He is a handsome, well-built, very energetic fellow, determined to inspire his students. Helmut might have a German, almost Schwarzenegger accent. He is played by the same actor who plays Henry Lee.*)

HELMUT. Five more miles! (*Ludwig, now sixteen, staggers onstage, wearing a long sleeved knit shirt and bloomers, his workout attire.*)

LUDWIG. Are you mad?

HELMUT. Your Highness, I am your fitness instructor. And your parents insist—you need a full program of rigorous exercise.

LUDWIG. But why?

HELMUT. You're sixteen years old, and we must channel your physical urges.

LUDWIG. My urges? For what?

HELMUT. Don't you know?

LUDWIG. I've been kept in the castle since birth. No one tells me anything.

HELMUT. I'll tell you. But first—we shall wrestle.

LUDWIG. But what about my urges?

HELMUT. As we compete! (*Ludwig gets on all fours. Helmuts kneels beside him.*) Wrestle!

LUDWIG. Stop, I'm not ready, I should wrestle someone smaller, someone crippled, someone dead . . .

HELMUT. And down! (*Helmut slams Ludwig onto his stomach and lies on top of him.*)

LUDWIG. I can't breathe . . .

HELMUT. Hormones. When a boy becomes a man, the blood surges through his body, moving directly to his groin. And when he sees a beautiful young lady, alluringly attired . . .

LUDWIG. In say, pale yellow crepe du chine . . .

HELMUT. Her lively eyes sparkle, her luscious bosom heaves . . .

LUDWIG. In her low-cut bodice, in the style of the Empress Josephine . . .

HELMUT. His young heart pounds, his savage mind burns scarlet, when he gazes at her he can think of one thing and one thing only . . .

LUDWIG. Yes!

HELMUT. What?

LUDWIG. The perfect hat!

HELMUT. No! Again! (*Helmut gets on all fours, and Ludwig kneels beside him.*) Put one hand on my forearm, and the other around my waist. (*Ludwig does this.*)

LUDWIG. Helmut, I have been noticing changes. I have gained fifteen pounds, my voice has deepened, and I can now grow a full mustache.

HELMUT. Exactly!

LUDWIG. I am more like my mother every day.

HELMUT. No. Your Highness, have you ever seen a naked woman?

LUDWIG. In my books of mythology.

HELMUT. Good. So let us say that Zeus, he comes upon Aphrodite, lying nude in a secluded forest glade.

LUDWIG. Near Olympus . . .

HELMUT. Her flesh is moist, his desire mounts . . .

LUDWIG. Cupid hovers nearby . . .

HELMUT. Try to pin me! (*Helmut remains stationary, on all fours, while Ludwig climbs all over him, trying vainly to pin him. As they wrestle:*)

LUDWIG. But what happens with Zeus? What do they do?

HELMUT. Pretend I'm Aphrodite! I'm teasing you!

LUDWIG. You little goddess!

HELMUT. Capture me, Your Majesty! Ravish me!

LUDWIG. Here I come!

HELMUT. Oh Your Highness, you overpower me! (*Helmut flips over, allowing himself to be pinned, pulling Ludwig on top of him.*)

LUDWIG. You let me do that!

HELMUT. As will your bride. She'll say yes, Your Highness, plunge your fine silver dagger into my trembling satin pillow.

LUDWIG. Helmut?

HELMUT. Thrust your shining strong rapier into my ripe pomegranate.

LUDWIG. I'm not following . . .

HELMUT. These are metaphors—put your penis into her vagina.

LUDWIG. I like metaphors.

HELMUT. Is it clear, what will be expected?

LUDWIG. I'm more confused than ever. Helmut, are you in love?

HELMUT. Your Highness!

LUDWIG. Are you?

HELMUT. Well, yes. With my Hilda.

LUDWIG. Hilda! Helmut and Hilda!

HELMUT. It sounds pretty.

LUDWIG. Like a puppet show. Is it like in the stories? Like Elsa and Lohengrin?

HELMUT. Lohengrin?

LUDWIG. It's my very favorite legend. Elsa is the innocent maiden, and Lohengrin is a magical knight who appears and saves her. Is it opera?

HELMUT. Why opera?

LUDWIG. That's the test. If your love is truly miraculous, then it rises, it breaks free, it becomes music. So what you've been trying to tell me, about these urges, when you're with your Hilda, do you sing?

HELMUT. Sing? No!

LUDWIG. But this is what terrifies me. That I'll do all that is expected and yet—I'll be alone. Forever. In silence.

HELMUT. But that doesn't have to happen. You can be so happy. I will show you, what men and women do together. (*Helmut grabs Ludwig and kisses him passionately.*) There! Isn't that wonderful? And now let us strip off our clothes and leap into the river! (*Helmut runs offstage, taking off his clothes. Ludwig, still reeling from the kiss, tries to sing, in a small, strangled yet joyously ardent voice.*)

LUDWIG. (*Singing.*) La!

HELMUT. (*From offstage.*) Your Highness! (*Ludwig runs offstage, after Helmut. As Ludwig runs out, we hear the sound of rushing water. Lights up on the Dainsville High School boys' locker room, including at least one locker and a bench. We hear the sounds of guys leaving the locker room, laughing and shouting. Henry Lee, now eighteen, enters, naked except for a towel wrapped around his waist. As he approaches his locker, James steps out from behind the locker. James is now also eighteen, and he wears jeans and a T-shirt. There's a swagger to him; he's grown up a lot faster and rougher than the other teenagers in Dainsville.*)

JAMES. You win?

HENRY LEE. 'Scuse me? Oh my God.

JAMES. Look at you.

HENRY LEE. James? Avery?

JAMES. Henry Lee Stafford, all grown up.

HENRY LEE. I thought—aren't you in reform school?

JAMES. I'm out. A proud graduate. (*Staring at Henry Lee.*) Baby. Three whole years.

HENRY LEE. But what are you doing here?

JAMES. I came back.

HENRY LEE. Why?

JAMES. One reason.

HENRY LEE. What?

JAMES. You. (*We hear offstage voices calling out, "Hank, come on! We're goin'!" Etc.*)

HENRY LEE. (*Calling out.*) Go on ahead, you guys!—I'll catch up! James, I'm getting dressed, could you please go outside?

JAMES. But I have so much to tell you. Reform school was the best. Now I can get into a really good prison.

HENRY LEE. James . . .

JAMES. Man, it is so good to see you . . .

HENRY LEE. James?

JAMES. Yeah?

HENRY LEE. James, a lot has happened since you went away. I've changed. I've shaped up.

JAMES. Nice work. Greco-Roman.

HENRY LEE. Okay, look, I know you've had a bad deal, and I'd like to help you, but I have to get dressed, I have to meet Sally.

JAMES. Sally?

HENRY LEE. Sally Mortimer.

JAMES. Henry Lee—this is James.

HENRY LEE. So what? What's that supposed to mean?

JAMES. I got tattooed, at Laredo.

HENRY LEE. How?

JAMES. With a candle, a razor blade and a ballpoint pen. (*James rolls up his sleeve, revealing a crude tattoo.*)

HENRY LEE. (*Reading the tattoo, stunned.*) "Henry Lee." Oh my God.

JAMES. And it hurt, like a son-of-a-bitch. So I screamed and I spat and I cursed you.

HENRY LEE. Why?

JAMES. Because you have two names.

HENRY LEE. Get out. Right now. Your parents and this town sent you away for a very good reason, but I don't think it helped.

JAMES. But this will. (*James reaches out and grabs Henry Lee's towel.*)

HENRY LEE. Give that back!

JAMES. (*Calling out.*) Help me, someone! Henry Lee Stafford is exposing himself!

HENRY LEE. (*Calling out.*) No I'm not!

JAMES. I can't look! But I will!

HENRY LEE. You don't know what it was like! (*Henry Lee goes to the locker, and starts putting on his clothes.*)

JAMES. When?

HENRY LEE. After you left! Everyone was watching me, every minute, they thought I was—you!

JAMES. Me?

HENRY LEE. But I showed them. I showed everyone.

JAMES. What?

HENRY LEE. (*He takes a football out of his locker; he is now dangerously angry.*) This. (*Henry Lee throws the football very hard and fast, right at James.*)

JAMES. Watch it!

HENRY LEE. Do you know who I am? Do you have any idea?

JAMES. Who?

HENRY LEE. I am the captain and the starting quarterback of the Dainsville Dynamos. I am president of the senior class, the Honor Society, the debate team and the Junior Chamber of Commerce Young Texas Achievers.

JAMES. Why?

HENRY LEE. Because you're not. Because I was voted Most Popular, Smartest, Most Athletic and Most Likely to Succeed.

JAMES. What about Best Looking?

HENRY LEE. I turned it down.

JAMES. Why?

HENRY LEE. Most Modest.

JAMES. But what about your criminal record? Your evil past?

HENRY LEE. Fine, I admit it. Like a million years ago, we . . . we . . .

JAMES. Messed around?

HENRY LEE. But the whole time, I always used to pretend that you were a girl.

JAMES. And I pretended that you were a girl.

HENRY LEE. So it was perfectly normal.

JAMES. If we were lesbians.

HENRY LEE. No!

JAMES. We stole a truck! We tried to run away together!

HENRY LEE. I was a hostage!

JAMES. You—*drove!*

HENRY LEE. So?

JAMES. You are so beautiful.

HENRY LEE. Guys aren't beautiful!

JAMES. You are. Kiss me.

HENRY LEE. No!

JAMES. Fuck me.

HENRY LEE. Get away from me!

JAMES. Hit me.

HENRY LEE. What?

JAMES. If you won't kiss me or, fuck me, then hit me. Because it's the only way you're gonna stop me. Hit me!

HENRY LEE. I won't! I'm a Christian!

JAMES. I'm not. Here I come! (*Henry Lee slugs James, who crumples.*)

HENRY LEE. I'm sorry, but you asked for it, you had it comin'. (*As James remains doubled over. James whimpers.*) Are you okay? (*James pops up, unhurt. He gleefully slugs Henry Lee. Henry Lee crumples.*) Where'd you learn to do that?

JAMES. Recess. (*Henry Lee slugs James, who hits him back. As they fight:*) This is great! This is hot! This is the way Texans have sex!

HENRY LEE. You are disgusting. You are exactly the same.

JAMES. No I'm not. I'm even better at it. I've had lots of time to think about my crimes and my sins and my tendencies. And do you know what I've decided? I love them. They are the very best part of me. And they are gonna save me.

HENRY LEE. They'll destroy you.

JAMES. Henry Lee, I know it's been forever, and I know that your folks and this town and this world have slammed down on you, but that's all over. They can't stop us, not anymore. Look at me.

HENRY LEE. I can't. I can't let my eyes do that. Not anymore.

JAMES. But why not?

HENRY LEE. Because I am getting married. Tomorrow.

JAMES. To who?

HENRY LEE. To Sally.

JAMES. Do you love her?

HENRY LEE. She's so pretty, you should see her . . .

JAMES. Do you love her?

HENRY LEE. Her father owns the department store, I have a future there . . .

JAMES. Do you love her?

HENRY LEE. Yes. (*Ludwig runs onstage. Lights down on the locker room.*)

LUDWIG. I can't do this. It's insane. It's unnatural. (*The Queen enters.*)

QUEEN. It's exciting! You're seventeen, and you get to choose a bride!

LUDWIG. But I need to fall in love!

QUEEN. And you shall. I have hired the most extraordinary man to help with our plans—our new deputy secretary, Johannes Pfeiffer. He's been employed by the royal families of Normandy, Norway, Madrid and Milan. (*Johannes Pfeiffer enters. He is a dignified, perfectly groomed gentleman, wearing an immaculate uniform. He is a superb diplomat; he prides himself on his perfect posture, his ability to instill discipline and his comprehensive knowledge of human affairs.*)

PFEIFFER. *Bonjour. Guten Morgen. Buenos dias.*

QUEEN. (*Delighted.*) Your first task is to find Ludwig a bride.

PFEIFFER. *Arrivederci.* (*Pfeiffer starts to exit.*)

QUEEN. No! He needs to produce an heir to the throne!

LUDWIG. An *heir?*

PFEIFFER. Very well. May I present our first candidate for royal matrimony—Princess Patricia, of Prussia! (*We hear a regal trumpet flourish, and Princess Patricia, a young beauty, enters, in a ballgown and a tiara. She is poised and gracious, and speaks with a demure German accent. She will be played by the same actress who plays Sally. Pfeiffer and the Queen exit.*)

PATRICIA. (*Curtsying.*) Your Highness.

LUDWIG. Good morning.

PATRICIA. I know zis is awkvard, but I'd weally like to get to know you, as a person.

LUDWIG. That's—very nice.

PATRICIA. I only haf vun possible dwawback.

LUDWIG. Yes?

PATRICIA. Vell, to keep our bloodlines pure, most of my ancestors maw-wied zere cousins. Who mawwied zere cousins and so on, for over 2,000 years. So by now, my family has become, well . . .

LUDWIG. Odd? Eccentric?

PATRICIA. Unique. My gweat-aunt, Empwess Cowinthia of Portugal, vas born mute. Shall I do my impwession of her?

LUDWIG. Your impwession? (*Patricia turns away for a Moment, to prepare. Then she faces Ludwig and mouths the word "Hello," silently.*) Bwavo.

PATRICIA. And my uncle, Duke Ferdinand of Finland, he has blue eyes.

LUDWIG. So?

PATRICIA. For lunch.

LUDWIG. Ah.

PATRICIA. And my dearest sister, Pwincess Penelope, is convinced that she is actually a gwand piano.

LUDWIG. But how tragic.

PATRICIA. Not at parties.

LUDWIG. Next!

PATRICIA. Pwincess Enid, of England. (*Patricia exits, and with another trumpet flourish, Princess Enid enters. She will be played by the same actress who plays the Queen. She wears formal riding clothes. She has an English accent and a jolly, chummy, gung-ho quality.*)

ENID. Hallo, Ludwig!

LUDWIG. Hello?

ENID. I've heard so much about you. I think we'd make a marvelous match.

LUDWIG. I can't do this . . .

ENID. But why not?

LUDWIG. You—you remind me of my mother.

ENID. But how lucky!

LUDWIG. Lucky?

ENID. Every fellow secretly yearns to marry his mother.

LUDWIG. Why?

ENID. You can return to childhood, to the womb. Just imagine, getting
chummy with your mummy . . . (*She links arms with Ludwig.*)

LUDWIG. Chummy?

ENID. Feeling plummy with your mummy . . .

LUDWIG. Plummy?

ENID. Let your mummy rub your tummy . . .

LUDWIG. Stop it!

ENID. (*As she caresses him.*) Don't get glummy with your mummy, just
succumb-y to your mummy, put your thumbie in your mummy . . .

LUDWIG. (*Leaping up.*) No!

ENID. (*Threatening.*) Don't play dummy with your mummy!

LUDWIG. Next!

ENID. Princess Ursula the Unusual, of Albania! (*Princess Enid exits, as
Princess Ursula enters, with another trumpet flourish. She is played by the same
actor who plays Pfeiffer. She wears a tiara atop a wig of sausage curls, and a
hoop-skirted ballgown. Ursula is girlishly shy, flirtatious and deeply virginal.
She carries a fan, and speaks in a high, feminine tone.*)

URSULA. Hello, Ludwig.

LUDWIG. Enid, come back!

URSULA. I am not like the other girls.

LUDWIG. Oh no?

URSULA. But the nuns, at my convent school, they tell me I am beautiful.

LUDWIG. They're nuns.

URSULA. In Albania, they have a name for a girl such as I.

LUDWIG. "The big girl"?

URSULA. Oh, no.

LUDWIG. "The tall girl"?

URSULA. No again.

LUDWIG. "The goalie"?

URSULA. It's true! You see, I possess the sexual organs of both genders.
Isn't that marvelous?

LUDWIG. You're a date.

URSULA. (*Very sweet and feminine.*) I'll kiss you and caress you.

LUDWIG. And then?

URSULA. (*Dropping her voice, to a rugged, threatening bass, very macho.*) I'll fuck you raw.

LUDWIG. Next! (*As Ludwig exits, Ursula steps forward.*)

URSULA. And now the greatest princess of them all, in her bedroom, the seventeen-year-old Sally Mortimer, of Dainsville, Texas.

(*Ursula exits. Lights up on Sally, now seventeen, wearing a pretty, frilly bathrobe, seated before her vanity table, facing the audience. A deluxe, full-length wedding gown is worn by a dressmaking mannequin which stands nearby. As Sally speaks to the audience, she might brush her hair and apply makeup. Sally's tone during this speech should never be bitchy or condescending. It's her wedding day, and she's on a sincere spiritual quest.*)

SALLY. Some people think that I had—feelings for James Avery, but that is just not true. But before he—went away, he always used to say something which I will never forget. He would say that he'd been studying the situation since kindergarten, and that he'd made lists and charts and held a personal pageant, and that he had finally determined that I was the prettiest girl in all of Dainsville. And he said that the prettiest girl can give people hope, and brighten their day, and wasn't that just a wonderful thing to say? Especially for a delinquent? And ever since then, whenever I look in the mirror, I see Eleanor Roosevelt. Only, of course, pretty. I mean, Mrs. Roosevelt works so hard, trying to help the poor and the downtrodden, but can you imagine how much more she could do, if she were pretty? And of course, there's also inner beauty, but inner beauty is tricky, because you can't prove it. I've thought a lot about this, you know, about beauty and goodness, and all the different religions? I mean, Buddha is chubby—face it. And Confucius was all old and scraggly and, I imagine, single. And you're not even allowed to have a picture of Mohammed—was it the teeth? I don't know. But Jesus is always really pretty, with perfect skin and shiny hair, it's like God was saying, look to Jesus, for tips. But I know there's that German man, Adolf Hitler, and he thinks that everyone should be perfect and blue-eyed and beautiful, but that's wrong too, because then who would be the best friends? And I don't want to be vain or prideful, so I always remember what James said, in one of his letters. He said that there are only two things which really matter in life: youth and beauty.

(*James enters, dressed as he was in the locker room. He is on the prowl, stalking Sally. She's frightened, nervous and very drawn to James.*)

JAMES. *Truth* and beauty.

SALLY. James? Oh my God!

JAMES. The front door was open.

SALLY. Is that really you? Are you back?

JAMES. For the day.

SALLY. Look at you, you look, well, I'm not even sure what to say, you look—older. Rougher. But what are you doing here?

JAMES. (*Moving toward the wedding gown.*) It's this afternoon, isn't it?

SALLY. Why yes, yes it is. (*As James is about to touch the gown.*) French silk— please don't touch that.

JAMES. You sent me all of those sweet letters, at least once a month, with all of those charming tidbits, about the town and the school . . .

SALLY. Did I tell you about my mother's new car?

JAMES. The Buick.

SALLY. And my Dad's business?

JAMES. Just booming.

SALLY. Although I am so worried about things in Europe . . .

JAMES. I remember—"P.S. It's sad about Poland."

SALLY. Isn't it?

JAMES. But somehow you never mentioned Henry Lee.

SALLY. Well, he wasn't invaded, now was he?

JAMES. Oh really?

SALLY. Now James, I'm sorry, and it's not that it isn't a wonderful surprise to see you, but my parents are at the church, making sure that everything is just perfect, and my Maid of Honor will be here any minute. Do you remember Emmeline Atwood?

JAMES. The blind girl?

SALLY. But I told her—no dog.

JAMES. So we're alone.

SALLY. James?

JAMES. How could you? With Henry Lee?

SALLY. How could I resist? I mean, he is so handsome, and I don't want to brag, but you should have seen us, we were king and queen at the prom. Oh I'm sorry, where you were, did they even have a prom?

JAMES. Of course. And we each picked a younger, smaller boy and pretended he was our date.

SALLY. That is so sweet. Was there a theme?

JAMES. "Just Relax."

SALLY. Now James, I know that I was naughty, not to tell you about our plans. And I'm sorry that I can't invite you to the wedding, but it's a Christian ceremony, and you're, well . . .

JAMES. Satan?

SALLY. (*Sincerely.*) Thank you.

JAMES. Do you love him?

SALLY. He's the president of our class . . .

JAMES. Do you love him?

SALLY. My parents worship the ground he walks on . . .

JAMES. Do you love him?

SALLY. Stop asking that!

JAMES. Look at me.

SALLY. I don't want to. You look crude, and unshaven, and—unreformed.

JAMES. Ever since we were little, I've known all about you. You are so
  good and so pretty and so perfect . . .

SALLY. Because I make an effort. And I stay out of the sun.

JAMES. And today you're getting married, to the perfect boy.

SALLY. Yesireebob.

JAMES. Because you have so much in common.

SALLY. Just about everything.

JAMES. Because in just a few short hours, on your wedding night, you
  will both be thinking about me.

SALLY. You are disgusting! You are just what everyone says you are!

JAMES. A thief?

SALLY. Can you deny it?

JAMES. And a pansy?

SALLY. Well, isn't it true? Isn't that why you want Henry Lee?

JAMES. Not right now.

SALLY. James?

JAMES. I want everything. Everything beautiful.

SALLY. James?

JAMES. I want you.

SALLY. I am getting married! This afternoon!

JAMES. So there's still time.

SALLY. You went away. You left me here. So I started to hate you. So I
  decided to steal something. Something you wanted.

JAMES. What if I came over there, right now, and kissed you? What
  would you do? Would you slap my face?

SALLY. Yes I would. (*James goes to her and kisses her. She slaps him.*)

JAMES. What if I kissed you again? Would you call the police?

SALLY. Watch me. (*James kisses her again. In a tiny voice:*) Police . . .

JAMES. And what if I picked you up and carried you to that bed? What if
  I made love to you? Would you yell stop, oh please, stop?

SALLY. Yes.

JAMES. Then goodbye. I won't make you do anything you don't want to do. (*James starts to leave.*)

SALLY. James?

JAMES. Yeah?

SALLY. Stop. (*Sally drops her robe and stands in just her slip. James picks her up, and carries her offstage, as Ludwig runs on, with a pistol.*)

LUDWIG. I am in crisis. My father is gravely ill, yet my mother is not. I can't find a bride, and I'm not ready to become king. I have been composing a note, to be discovered after my death: (*He takes out the note.*) "To my beloved parents, my brother and the nation, Do not blame yourselves. Although, of course, no one has ever truly understood or appreciated my despair. I'm sure you were all very busy. I have reached a dark crossroads, between aching futility and infinite oblivion." (*Impressed with his own words.*) This should be published. No! I am a ridiculous figure. Bavaria deserves better. Everyone deserves better. I am twenty-one years old, and there is only one solution. (*Ludwig puts the gun to his head, and as he is about to pull the trigger, we hear a gunshot, from offstage, but close by.*) What was that? (*Princess Sophie staggers onstage. She wears a period ballgown, and is played by the same actress who plays Sally. She is holding a pistol and while in great distress, is unharmed. She has a very large and pronounced humpback. Sophie is not your average princess; she's fiercely smart, and blazingly honest. She has an outcast's wit and defensiveness, but she's also just as great a romantic as Ludwig. At the Moment she's tremendously upset, in agony.*)

SOPHIE. Am I bleeding? Am I dead?

LUDWIG. Who are you?

SOPHIE. I'm Princess Sophie, of Austria.

LUDWIG. But what are you doing out here, in the forest?

SOPHIE. I was out—hunting.

LUDWIG. For what?

SOPHIE. For—me!

LUDWIG. But are you all right? Are you hurt?

SOPHIE. My parents dragged me here, to the imperial ball, to be presented to that horrible Prince Ludwig. And I've never even seen a picture of him, have you? Is he so good looking?

LUDWIG. No. He has nice hair.

SOPHIE. What am I doing here? He's turned down hundreds of women. He would hate me. He would humiliate me.

LUDWIG. But why?

SOPHIE. (*Ferociously.*) Why? *Why?* Oh gee, I can't imagine. Let's think about that one. That's a puzzler. Why would Prince Ludwig, the Beast of Bavaria, hate a girl like me? Hmmm . . . (*She uses the pistol to scratch her hump.*) could it be, it's just a wild guess, and I'm really going way out on a limb here . . .

LUDWIG. What?

SOPHIE. I have a HUMPBACK?

LUDWIG. You . . . do?

SOPHIE. (*Turning her back to Ludwig, so he's facing her hump.*) Go ahead, touch it.

LUDWIG. No, thank you.

SOPHIE. You know you want to, everyone secretly does. Some people even think it's lucky.

LUDWIG. They do?

SOPHIE. (*Wiggling her hump, seductively.*) You could get your fondest wish.

LUDWIG. Really?

SOPHIE. I dare you. (*Ludwig touches Sophie's hump, very lightly. She screams in agony, and falls to the ground.*) OWWW!

LUDWIG. Oh my God!

SOPHIE. (*Standing up, amused.*) Kidding.

LUDWIG. What?

SOPHIE. Humpback humor.

LUDWIG. Jesus.

SOPHIE. Who are you?

LUDWIG. I'm a soldier.

SOPHIE. What's your rank?

LUDWIG. I'm—a fancy one.

SOPHIE. What are you doing here?

LUDWIG. I was out guarding the trees.

SOPHIE. Do you work for that Ludwig?

LUDWIG. Sometimes.

SOPHIE. Is it true? Is he a nightmare?

LUDWIG. No, I think he's just—a very solitary man.

SOPHIE. Oh please.

LUDWIG. He's not mean, he's just—well, he's never been allowed to make any real friends.

SOPHIE. He's a snob.

LUDWIG. No, I don't think he means to be. I think that he just spends all of his time—dreaming.

SOPHIE. Is he, you know—feeble?

LUDWIG. That's the mother.

SOPHIE. Well, I hate him. I despise him.

LUDWIG. (*Studying her, trying to be helpful.*) Have you ever thought about . . . a really big corsage?

SOPHIE. No. Wait—do you have a carriage?

LUDWIG. Why?

SOPHIE. Could you take me to the railway station? Maybe I could get back to Vienna, just in time.

LUDWIG. For what?

SOPHIE. You'll think it's insane.

LUDWIG. What?

SOPHIE. But it's all I have left to live for, I've seen it twenty-eight times, but there's only one performance left.

LUDWIG. Of what?

SOPHIE. *Lohengrin.*

LUDWIG. The incredible, perfect opera?

SOPHIE. By the genius, Richard Wagner? Do you know it?

LUDWIG. Only every note!

SOPHIE. Stop it! (*They both scream, with surprise and delight.*)

LUDWIG and SOPHIE. AHHH!

LUDWIG. Elsa, the innocent maiden . . .

SOPHIE. And her brother, who's bewitched into a swan . . .

LUDWIG. And then Elsa's accused of his murder . . .

SOPHIE. Until they're both saved by a handsome young knight! When did you see it?

LUDWIG. Only once.

SOPHIE. Why?

LUDWIG. It was two years ago, in Berlin. I was—on leave. But I'd been dreaming about it for months, I couldn't think about anything else. But then, during the performance, it was all too beautiful, and I was—overcome. I started sobbing uncontrollably, and my body wouldn't stop shaking.

SOPHIE. Sometimes I vomit.

LUDWIG. I foamed at the mouth.

SOPHIE. Sometimes I become completely incontinent.

LUDWIG. (*Impressed.*) You're good.

SOPHIE. But why didn't you go back?

LUDWIG. I was too ashamed.

SOPHIE. I know. Usually I wear a big cape, and I try to sit way in the back, but people still see me.

LUDWIG. My family worries all the time that I'll completely disgrace them.

SOPHIE. And my mother, she keeps saying that I'll never marry anyone. And just before I leave the house, she always tells me the most awful thing.

LUDWIG. What?

SOPHIE. "Stand up straight."

LUDWIG. That's unbearable.

SOPHIE. I hate my life.

LUDWIG. I hate mine.

SOPHIE. Let's kill ourselves.

LUDWIG. Right now. (*They face each other and put the barrels of their guns into each other's mouths. Garbled.*) One . . .

SOPHIE. (*Garbled.*) Two . . .

LUDWIG. (*Garbled.*) Sophie?

SOPHIE. (*Garbled.*) Yes?

LUDWIG. (*They remove the guns from each other's mouths.*) Sophie, I know this is very sudden, but you're the only person I've ever met who doesn't think I'm strange.

SOPHIE. But you are.

LUDWIG. Sophie?

SOPHIE. But that's wonderful. Because I'm even worse.

LUDWIG. How?

SOPHIE. (*Making a bell-ringing Quasimodo gesture.*) Ding-dong.

LUDWIG. But when I look at you, I don't see something strange. I see someone who's—enchanted.

SOPHIE. How?

LUDWIG. You know how in the stories, sometimes there's a magical dwarf or a sly troll?

SOPHIE. Where are you going with this?

LUDWIG. But that doesn't make them ugly. Maybe your hump is a sign of magic. Of true beauty.

SOPHIE. It is?

LUDWIG. You're a princess. You belong in a castle.

SOPHIE. Don't you just love castles?

LUDWIG. More than anything. More than breathing. More than my own life. I love castles more than—chocolate. (*He gasps.*) I can't believe I said that!

SOPHIE. Everyone is happy in a castle.

LUDWIG. But not those modern castles, which are really just big houses, but a storybook castle.

SOPHIE. All the way up on a mountaintop, with banners and turrets . . .

LUDWIG. Floating above the clouds . . .

SOPHIE. The home of the gods . . .

LUDWIG. The most beautiful place on earth . . .

LUDWIG and SOPHIE. Valhalla.

LUDWIG. Marry me?

SOPHIE. Yes.

LUDWIG. Oh my God.

SOPHIE. But wait—I don't even know your name. (*Pfeiffer enters.*)

PFEIFFER. Your Highness?

SOPHIE. (*Taken aback.*) Your Highness?

PFEIFFER. (*To Sophie.*) Prince Ludwig.

SOPHIE. Prince Ludwig? (*Sophie, realizing who Ludwig really is, falls into a curtsy, although she's furious.*)

LUDWIG. The liar.

SOPHIE. Oh no. Oh my God. You are a beast, how could you do this, were you on a scavenger hunt, find one peacock feather and a hump-back?

LUDWIG. No. I would never do anything to hurt you, please Sophie, you have to believe me. Because that was the most perfect conversation I've ever had. And I meant every word.

SOPHIE. You did?

PFEIFFER. I'm sorry, I'm confused. But Your Highness, you must come with me at once. It's your father, I'm afraid he's taken a turn.

LUDWIG. Maybe—I can cheer him.

PFEIFFER. How?

LUDWIG. Pfeiffer, I think, I hope—that I'm engaged.

PFEIFFER. You are?

SOPHIE. (*After a beat.*) Yes, we are.

PFEIFFER. (*Very pleased.*) Well, congratulations.

SOPHIE. Thank you.

PFEIFFER. Have you met?

LUDWIG. Yes. At last.

PFEIFFER. I knew that you could do it. You are becoming such a fine young man.

LUDWIG. I am?

SOPHIE. Yes you are.

LUDWIG. (*To Sophie.*) I'm sorry, I have to go.

PFEIFFER. But first—a kiss?

LUDWIG. (*Taken aback.*) Pfeiffer!

SOPHIE. He means me. We could kiss, like in *Lohengrin.* As if we were in a castle.

PFEIFFER. A castle?

LUDWIG. My Elsa.

SOPHIE. My hero.

PFEIFFER. My prayers. (*Ludwig and Sophie hand their pistols to Pfeiffer, and then they move toward each other, theatrically, like operatic lovers. Ludwig lifts Sophie off the ground. They kiss, as sweepingly romantic music is heard. Ludwig lowers Sophie and they move apart, gracefully.*)

LUDWIG. I have kissed.

SOPHIE. I am saved.

PFEIFFER. Your Highness?

LUDWIG. Adieu! (*Ludwig leaves, on a cloud of joy.*)

SOPHIE. Do I look different? Don't answer that.

PFEIFFER. You look—beautiful.

SOPHIE. He is so special.

PFEIFFER. You have no idea.

SOPHIE. What an incredible day. Just this morning, I was the loneliest humpback in Europe.

PFEIFFER. Was there a contest?

SOPHIE. And then I came out here, to kill myself, and then I meet—my

Prince. And suddenly the moonlight is so warm. Do you know what that sounds like?

PFEIFFER. A fairy tale?

SOPHIE. A happy ending. (*As Sophie exits, elated, the Queen enters, from the opposite side of the stage. She is deeply mournful, and dressed entirely in black.*)

QUEEN. There is tragic news. My husband, the king, is dead.

PFEIFFER. But your son is engaged.

QUEEN. (*Instantly ecstatic, pumping her fists in the air.*) Yes!

PFEIFFER. Your Highness?

QUEEN. Wait—is he engaged to a very beautiful girl? One who will break his heart, and destroy the monarchy? A Lola Montes?

PFEIFFER. She's a humpback.

QUEEN. (*Even more ecstatic, to heaven.*) Thank you! (*As the Queen runs off, Pfeiffer turns to the audience.*)

PFEIFFER. Nobles, citizens, peasants—in the back. We live in extraordinary times. It is with great joy that I introduce your brand new monarch, a regent of only the brightest promise. Please welcome— King Ludwig Freidrich Wilhelm II of Bavaria! (*Grand processional music is heard, along with a roaring crowd. Ludwig enters, as a spotlight hits him. He is now dressed in the full, sumptuous royal regalia of the Order of the Knights of St. George. He is resplendent, in a mountainous cape of heavily gold embroidered blue velvet, trimmed with yards of ermine. He wears a crown, a lace jabot, gauntleted gloves and white satin leggings and shoes. His wardrobe is based on the glorious royal portrait painted by George Schachinger in 1887. Ludwig is radiant, tearful and ecstatic, clutching his golden scepter—he's like someone who's just won an Academy Award. He faces the audience.*)

LUDWIG. I can't believe this! Thank you, thank you all so much . . . um, while I am not accustomed to public speaking . . . (*He takes a scrap of paper from his sleeve and glances at it—his acceptance speech.*) I would just like to say that—I am very proud to be your new king. (*The Queen stands beside Ludwig, hissing directions at him.*)

QUEEN. Shoulders back! And what are you wearing?

LUDWIG. It's a coronation!

QUEEN. (*Regarding Ludwig's outfit.*) That's a couch!

LUDWIG. (*To the crowd.*) First of all, I would like to thank my father, for dying . . .

QUEEN. And who else?

LUDWIG. And I would also like to thank my mother, the grieving royal widow . . .

QUEEN. (*Gesturing, to her all-black outfit.*) It's slimming.

LUDWIG. (*To the crowd.*) And I promise that I will try my very best to be—a good king.

QUEEN. We can't hear you!

LUDWIG. A GOOD KING!

QUEEN. (*To the crowd, grabbing Ludwig's chin, affectionately.*) Is that a face?

LUDWIG. And I'd just like to add that—I adore Bavaria!

QUEEN. Butch it up, Betty!

LUDWIG. (*To the Queen.*) Shut the hell up! (*Another ovation is heard, in response to Ludwig's last remark. The Queen, delighted by Ludwig's newfound strength and command, mimes zipping her lip. Emboldened.*) I would like our nation to become—a beacon of beauty. And so for my very first official act, I am going to the opera, to see *Lohengrin*! (*Ludwig sits on an impressive golden chair or stool, and watches the Dainsville wedding as if he were at the opera, watching* Lohengrin. *He speaks the words of a letter he will write to Sophie. The Queen sits beside him. Enraptured:*) My dearest Sophie, as the curtain rose, I felt a thunderclap of purest happiness.

QUEEN. (*Speaking to heaven.*) My dearest husband, you would be so proud of our son.

LUDWIG. The orchestra, the lights, and then—we approach the close of the act, as the townspeople gather at the glorious cathedral of Brabant. (*Reverend Howesberry enters; he's a fire-and-brimstone Texas preacher. He will be played by the same actor who plays Pfeiffer.*)

REVEREND. Welcome, one and all, to the All Souls First Baptist Church, of Dainsville, Texas! I'm Reverend Howesberry, and we're gonna have us a wedding!

LUDWIG. Lohengrin enters, in gleaming armor!

REVEREND. I like a man in uniform!

QUEEN. (*To Ludwig.*) I like you in that crown. (*Henry Lee, in an army uniform, enters and approaches the altar.*)

HENRY LEE. (*Speaking his thoughts.*) I'm going to get married . . .

LUDWIG. He's going to be married . . .

REVEREND. He's gonna get married!

QUEEN. (*To heaven, regarding Ludwig.*) Our boy is getting married!

HENRY LEE. To Sally . . .

LUDWIG. To Elsa . . .

QUEEN. (*Thrilled.*) To a humpback!

EVERYONE. Here we go! (*We hear the "Wedding March," from* Lohengrin *as Sally enters the church in a wedding gown, with her veil covering her face. She approaches the altar.*)

LUDWIG. As the bride approached the altar, a perfect melody rang forth, stately yet passionate, yearning yet proud. It is called the "Wedding March."

QUEEN. The "Wedding March"!

HENRY LEE. The "Wedding March" . . .

REVEREND. It's a catchy tune!

QUEEN. (*To Ludwig.*) It's our song!

LUDWIG. As the music soared, I entered what I can only call an escalating trance. Note upon note, pleasure upon pleasure . . .

REVEREND. Do you, Henry Lee Stafford, take this woman, Sally Ann Mortimer, to be your lawfully wedded wife? (*As Henry Lee opens his mouth to reply, he begins lip-synching to a glorious tenor aria, from Wagner.*)

LUDWIG. He is strong, he is stalwart . . .

QUEEN. (*To heaven, regarding Ludwig.*) He is strong, he is stalwart . . .

HENRY LEE. (*To himself.*) I am strong, I am stalwart . . .

QUEEN. (*To heaven, regarding Ludwig.*) He is going to be a husband!

HENRY LEE. (*To himself.*) I am going to be a husband . . .

REVEREND. (*To Henry Lee.*) You're gonna be a husband!

LUDWIG. (*Staring at Sally.*) And look at her tiny little shoes! I'm dying!

QUEEN. (*To Ludwig.*) Be a man!

REVEREND. (*To Henry Lee.*) Be a man!

HENRY LEE. (*To himself.*) Be a man!

REVEREND. And do you, Sally Ann Mortimer, take this man, Henry Lee Stafford, to be your lawfully wedded husband? (*As Sally opens her mouth to reply, she lip-synchs to a glorious soprano aria.*) Ain't she purty?

LUDWIG. She's so lovely!

HENRY LEE. She's my wife . . .

QUEEN. (*To Ludwig.*) Girls are good.

LUDWIG. I am there!

QUEEN. We are there!

REVEREND. We're almost there!

HENRY LEE. I need some air . . .

LUDWIG. I am music!

REVEREND. I am ready!

QUEEN. I am complete!

HENRY LEE. I am not beautiful!

LUDWIG. I am in a state of ecstasy . . .

QUEEN. I am in a state of bliss . . .

HENRY LEE. I am in a state of panic . . .

REVEREND. By the authority vested in me, by the glorious state of Texas . . . (*The Reverend begins to lip-synch to something grandly operatic.*)

SALLY. Not so fast! (*Sally has entered, from offstage or the back of the house. She is disheveled, wearing only her slip.*)

HENRY LEE. (*Stunned.*) Sally?

REVEREND. (*Stunned.*) Sally Mortimer?

QUEEN. (*To Ludwig.*) Who is that?

LUDWIG. (*Following the action.*) Ortrud has entered! A jealous pagan princess! She seeks to sabotage the nuptials!

SALLY. He tied me up! Then he stole my gown, and my daddy's Cadillac!

QUEEN. She seems upset.

HENRY LEE. Who did?

SALLY. The bride!

REVEREND. The *bride?* (*A police siren begins to wail.*)

HENRY LEE. The bride?

LUDWIG. (*Thrilled.*) The French horns! (*The bride lifts her veil, so we can see her face—it's James, wearing Sally's wedding gown.*)

SALLY, HENRY LEE and REVEREND. (*Realizing it's James.*) James!

JAMES. I think I'm gonna cry.

QUEEN. I think I'm gonna burst!

HENRY LEE. I think I'm gonna die!

LUDWIG. I think I'm gonna faint!

SALLY. (*To James.*) I think I'm gonna kill you!

REVEREND. (*To Sally.*) I think I'm gonna help you! (*The Reverend takes out a sawed-off shotgun, which he passes to Henry Lee, who hands it to Sally.*)

SALLY. (*To James.*) I think you'd better run.

LUDWIG. It is all too beautiful!

JAMES. Sally . . .

SALLY. (*Aiming the gun at James.*) One . . .

LUDWIG. I am home!

JAMES. Henry Lee . . .

HENRY LEE. Two . . .

QUEEN. You're the king!

JAMES. I think I'm gonna go. (*James, running out, tosses his bouquet to Ludwig, who catches it.*)

REVEREND. God help us all!

SALLY, HENRY LEE and REVEREND. Three! (*Sally fires the shotgun across the stage at James, as he exits. Ludwig faints, dead away, to the floor. The Queen looks at him, then at the audience. She realizes that everyone is staring at her, and her unconscious son. She smiles graciously.*)

QUEEN. Intermission. (*Curtain.*)

ACT TWO

A pinspot appears on Ludwig's face. He is enraptured, transported, perhaps with his eyes shut, and his mouth hanging open in bliss. He is listening to something from Tannhauser *and he is utterly transfixed by the music. He drools.*

PFEIFFER. (*From the darkness.*) Your Highness! (*No response; the music continues.*) Your Highness! (*The lights come up on the throne room, in Munich. This will be suggested mostly by having Ludwig sprawled on the ornate, golden imperial throne. Maps, books and documents are piled nearby. Ludwig wears his crown and a daytime uniform, which is still fairly gaudy. Pfeiffer stands close by, holding a sheaf of documents. The* Tannhauser *music ends abruptly.*)

LUDWIG. (*Gradually returning to reality.*) Yes?

PFEIFFER. You were doing it again. You were gone.

LUDWIG. I was in *Tannhauser.* I was a handsome young knight, lured into an enchanted, sensuous grotto. And I was surrounded by satyrs and satin and orgies.

PFEIFFER. Have you even glanced at the treaty proposal?

LUDWIG. Pfeiffer, what's an orgy?

PFEIFFER. It's when vicious, depraved philistines have sex in a group.

LUDWIG. Is it heavenly?

PFEIFFER. Yes.

LUDWIG. Then let's have one—by royal decree!

PFEIFFER. Your Highness, shall I call in a guard to paddle your buttocks?

LUDWIG. Really?

PFEIFFER. If you focus.

LUDWIG. (*Tossing a pile of documents high into the air.*) But I'm in agony!

PFEIFFER. (*As he begins to pick up the documents, from the floor.*) You're in Munich. And you've only been king for a year. And you've been doing so well.

LUDWIG. I have?

PFEIFFER. But this month alone you've already been to the opera eighteen times. Three *Tannhausers*, five *Tristans*, two *Meistersingers* . . .

LUDWIG. And eight *Lohengrins*!

PFEIFFER. It's like a drug!

LUDWIG. Do you know the true tragedy of *Lohengrin*?

PFEIFFER. What?

LUDWIG. That he could never go to see *Lohengrin*.

PFEIFFER. (*Exasperated.*) Your Highness!

LUDWIG. I know. You're right. And that's why I'm chaining myself to this throne.

PFEIFFER. You're what?

LUDWIG. (*Ludwig begins to handcuff himself to his throne, with cuffs or manacles.*) I want to be a good king. So no more opera, I'm giving it up.

PFEIFFER. Are you sure about this?

LUDWIG. Yes. And here's the key. (*He hands Pfeiffer the key.*) And I forbid you to unlock me, no matter how much I beg, under no circumstances, absolutely no opera.

PFEIFFER. Truly?

LUDWIG. I can beat this.

PFEIFFER. Very good. Because we may very well be going to war.

LUDWIG. With whom?

PFEIFFER. With Prussia.

LUDWIG. Excellent. Now explain the situation. And this time, I promise, I will pay complete attention and follow every word.

PFEIFFER. All right. It's a border dispute. Bismarck, the Prussian Chancellor, has taken control of the Duchy of Schleswig, while Emperor Franz Josef of Austria rules the neighboring Holstein.

LUDWIG. Schleswig-Holstein.

PFEIFFER. Correct. Now, Bismarck wants to build a canal on the Baltic, across Holstein to the North Sea, while Franz Josef demands that Prussia return several provinces annexed a hundred years ago by Freidrich the Great.

LUDWIG. Aha!

PFEIFFER. But Bismarck has been feuding with Denmark, while Franz Josef has engaged in preliminary sessions with the Duke of Augustenburg, a pretender to the Duchies. And here's where it gets really fascinating . . .

LUDWIG. Pfeiffer?

PFEIFFER. Yes?

LUDWIG. Pfeiffer, I need it.

PFEIFFER. What?

LUDWIG. Just a few notes. An aria. A first act.

PFEIFFER. No!

LUDWIG. But the opera house is only a few blocks away, the curtain's in just twenty minutes, I have to go or I'll die, please unlock me.

PFEIFFER. I said no.

LUDWIG. Good. Thank you. I was testing you.

PFEIFFER. I thought so.

LUDWIG. (*Sagely.*) Oo-hoo.

PFEIFFER. (*Agreeing.*) Oo-hoo.

LUDWIG. Instead, I'd like to commission a reliquary. From Faberge, the goldsmith to the tsars.

PFEIFFER. A reliquary?

LUDWIG. I want hammered gold, worked with precious gems. After my death, it will contain my heart.

PFEIFFER. Your heart?

LUDWIG. Shattered! From paperwork!

PFEIFFER. Your Highness!

LUDWIG. Please, Pfeiffer, I'm begging you, I'll give you anything you want, what would you like—a title? An estate? Belgium?

PFEIFFER. No!

LUDWIG. I'm the king, I'm commanding you! You have to unlock me! If I don't see an opera, I don't know what will happen. I'll collapse, I'll explode, I'll start—going to the ballet. Is that what you want?

PFEIFFER. No!

LUDWIG. Or I'll chew off my arm! I'll do it, Pfeiffer, you know I will, I'm starting, I'm gnawing at my flesh, watch me, you'll be held responsible for the cannibal king . . . (*As he chews on his arm savagely.*) It's tasty . . .

PFEIFFER. Why? So you can go see some ridiculous story, like that one about dragons and mermaids?

LUDWIG. *The Ring*!

PFEIFFER. And who was that woman, on horseback?

LUDWIG. Brunhilde?

PFEIFFER. Yes.

LUDWIG. She's a warrior goddess. And yes, I know, you're right, it's ridiculous, that soprano was so—hefty.

PFEIFFER. With those big meaty arms.

LUDWIG. And those legs, like tree trunks.

PFEIFFER. (*Turned on.*) I liked her.

LUDWIG. Pfeiffer?

PFEIFFER. I have always had an affinity for—robust women. My mother was unthinkably beautiful, at nearly 400 pounds. My birth wasn't discovered for three days. And there was my one true love, Calpurnia, at college. She was six-foot-four, all mammoth muscle, but then I lost her forever—even now, how I hate the circus.

LUDWIG. Of course.

PFEIFFER. But then, at the performance the other evening, I was yawning, dozing, wondering will it ever end, and suddenly . . .

LUDWIG and PFEIFFER. Brunhilde!

PFEIFFER. And every midnight since, as I try to sleep, I tell myself, no, Pfeiffer, it was an illusion, no, Pfeiffer, it was the costume—armor can be cruelly deceptive . . .

LUDWIG. Honey . . .

PFEIFFER. I must not allow myself to imagine, to hallucinate, to dream that she is singing only to me, my tiny head wedged like a trembling walnut between the iron cannons of her Himalayan thighs, no, they are not merely thighs . . .

LUDWIG. Oh no!

PFEIFFER. They are twin teutonic armies, pounding, squeezing, drowning me ecstatically in endless amazon acres of pure, pink, powerful woman flesh . . .

LUDWIG. Time for the opera?

PFEIFFER. Let's go! (*Pfeiffer, on fire with lust, runs out.*)

LUDWIG. The key! Pfeiffer, hold the curtain! (*Ludwig, struggling helplessly, still chained, begins to drag the throne offstage with him, pursuing Pfeiffer. Lights down on Munich. We hear the sound of a ship's bell. Lights up on the deck of an army transport ship, somewhere in the middle of the Atlantic. This is indicated by ocean sounds and a fragment of railing. Henry Lee enters, in an army uniform and overcoat. He looks out to sea. He lights a cigarette. James enters, also wearing an army uniform and overcoat.*)

JAMES. Hey there. (*Henry Lee stares at him.*)

HENRY LEE. No. No.

JAMES. Hey there, soldier.

HENRY LEE. *What the fuck are you doing on this ship?*

JAMES. Okay, I know that you're really mad at me and that you hate me and you wish I was dead, so I should just tell you something. Right after I had sex with Sally, and put on her gown, and came to the church, I felt really terrible.

HENRY LEE. Why?

JAMES. The sleeves.

HENRY LEE. Fuck you! (*Just as Henry Lee is about to throw James over the railing, a uniformed sergeant appears. He is very stern and macho, and he's played by the same actor who plays Pfeiffer.*)

SERGEANT. Soldiers! (*James and Henry Lee snap to attention, saluting.*) Ten-hut!

JAMES and HENRY LEE. Sir, yes, sir!

SERGEANT. What are you two doing out here?

HENRY LEE. Keeping watch, sir!

SERGEANT. And is that all?

HENRY LEE. Yes, sir!

JAMES. He was touching me, sir!

SERGEANT. (*To Henry Lee.*) Private, is that true? Are you some kind of butt-toucher? Some kind of pecker-puffer?

HENRY LEE. No, sir!

SERGEANT. But why not?

HENRY LEE. Sir?

SERGEANT. (*To Henry Lee, regarding James.*) He's adorable! Get busy! As you were.

JAMES and HENRY LEE. (*Saluting.*) Sir, yes, sir! (*The sergeant exits.*)

HENRY LEE. What was that?

JAMES. A friend.

HENRY LEE. James, I am warning you. Despite your very best efforts, Sally and I got married, right on schedule. So I do not want to see your psychotic little pinhead, I do not want to hear your perverted little chitchat, I do not want to know that you are within one million miles! Go below!

JAMES. I want to smoke.

HENRY LEE. So do I!

JAMES. Fine.

HENRY LEE. Fine! So you just stay way the hell over there!

JAMES. And you just stay way, way the hell over there.

HENRY LEE. Fine!

JAMES. Fine. (*Henry Lee stands on one side of the stage, James all the way over on the other. They both smoke. Henry Lee is turned away from James, vigorously ignoring him. James watches Henry Lee. He begins whistling a little tune.*)

HENRY LEE. (*Cutting James off, holding out a hand, still not looking at him, still furious.*) Eh!

JAMES. Henry Lee . . .

HENRY LEE. (*Cutting him off, still not looking at him.*) No!

JAMES. Don't you just hate Hitler?

HENRY LEE. Shut up!

JAMES. Henry Lee, I know you. And I know that you are secretly thrilled beyond all measure to see me. Because you need me more than ever.

HENRY LEE. Do you know what terrifies me?

JAMES. Everything?

HENRY LEE. No. What terrifies me is that sometimes, I listen to you. And I realize that you actually believe what you're saying.

JAMES. Because I'm right. Because we have finally done it, just like I promised. We have left Texas! We're on our way!

HENRY LEE. To World War II, you moron! Have you seen the guys on this ship? After lights out, half of 'em start crying.

JAMES. I hear 'em.

HENRY LEE. I'm scared shitless. Why aren't you?

JAMES. If you don't want to die, you just have to be in the right movie.

HENRY LEE. We are not in a movie!

JAMES. Why not? If we're in a war movie, sure, we could get killed, by a tank or a torpedo or a character actor.

HENRY LEE. A character actor?

JAMES. But if we're in, say, a screwball comedy or a musical, everything's deco and beautiful and nobody ever dies.

HENRY LEE. But we're not! We're on a rusty tin crate, like sitting ducks.

JAMES. Like in *Anchors Aweigh* or *Follow the Fleet* or *Soldiers and Seamen*.

HENRY LEE. *Soldiers and Seamen?*

JAMES. That's our movie. And if we sing the title song, we'll be perfectly safe. All of the German U-boats will hear us and say . . . (*In a German accent.*) "Hold your fire! Vait until ze ballad!"

HENRY LEE. Goodbye. (*As Henry Lee is about to exit:*)

JAMES. (*Starting to sing, improvising.*) AHOY THERE, MATEY
    AND SET THOSE SAILS
    WE'RE A TRANSPORT SHIP
    FILLED WITH U.S. MALES
    WE'RE SINGING AND DANCING
    WE'RE A TALENTED BOAT
    BECAUSE SOLDIERS NEED SEAMEN
    TO KEEP THEM AFLOAT

HENRY LEE. What are you?

JAMES. AVAST ME HEARTIES, WE'RE BUILT TO LAST
    MY POOPDECK'S FILLED
    WITH YOUR MIZZENMAST
    YOUR PORTHOLE'S EMPTY
    AND YOU'VE GOT TO LEARN
    THAT SOLDIERS NEED SEAMEN
    FROM STEM TO STERN

HENRY LEE. You should be court-martialed!

JAMES. This is the dancing part. (*As he dances around Henry Lee:*) Work with me.

HENRY LEE. Never.

JAMES. You know you want to.

HENRY LEE. I do not!

JAMES. You're itchin' to. Every cell in your body is cryin' out.

HENRY LEE. I do not sing. I do not dance. I'm married.

JAMES. (*Singing.*) THE ARMY, THE NAVY
    WHO SHOULD BE IN CHARGE?
    WHILE SEAMEN ARE HE-MEN . . .

HENRY LEE. (*Struggling not to say it, resisting every second, angrily.*) OUR PRIVATES ARE LARGE.

JAMES. Henry Lee.

HENRY LEE. What?

JAMES. That was great.

HENRY LEE. I don't care. I shouldn't have said it. I didn't. That wasn't me.

JAMES. SOLDIERS WEAR CUTE COMBAT BOOTS

    SEAMEN SALUTE THOSE RECRUITS

    AN UNORTHODOX HOLE . . .

HENRY LEE. IS FOUND IN A FOXHOLE

JAMES. THE FLEET'S IN, BUT WHO'S IN THE FLEET?

    WE'LL BE ETHEL MERMANS

HENRY LEE. AND CRUSH ALL THOSE GERMANS

JAMES and HENRY LEE. BY SINGING THEM INTO DEFEAT!

(They do a little shave-and-a-haircut dance move together. Henry Lee stares at his feet, shocked at what they've just done.)

JAMES. *(Proudly, to an unseen crowd.)* My husband!

HENRY LEE. *(Furious.)* James! *(Henry Lee strides offstage.)*

JAMES. *(Following him.)* Sweetheart? *(James follows Henry Lee offstage. Lights down on the ship, as Ludwig enters, on horseback. His horse might be a wire and papier-mâché contraption which he wears around his waist. Ludwig wears a parade dress uniform, including a cape and a plumed hat. Both Ludwig and his steed are attired in white and gold. Ludwig's horse is led by Pfeiffer. As Ludwig reviews the troops, he and Pfeiffer look into the audience.)*

PFEIFFER. The Twenty-third Regiment, Your Highness. *(Ludwig nods and salutes.)* The Twenty-fourth Regiment, Your Highness. *(Ludwig nods and salutes.)* The Twenty-fifth Regiment, Your Highness.

LUDWIG. Excuse me, how many regiments in all?

PFEIFFER. Five hundred and twelve, Your Highness.

LUDWIG. *(In despair.)* My *wrist*.

PFEIFFER. These young men are about to go into battle against Prussia.

Most of them have never been away from home. You can give them
hope.

LUDWIG. But how?

PFEIFFER. You're their king, their champion, their—Lohengrin.

LUDWIG. I am?

PFEIFFER. And Prussia resembles—who's the villain, in the opera?

LUDWIG. The brutal Count Telramund, who tries to get rid of Elsa and
steal her land. So she prays for a miracle.

PFEIFFER. And then you appear!

LUDWIG. (*Emboldened, to the troops.*) Gentlemen—you are all so brave
and so noble and some of you are so attractive . . .

PFEIFFER. Your Highness!

LUDWIG. Whenever I seek courage, there is only one source. Many years
ago, on a battlefield much like this, a lovely maiden appeared . . .
(*Sophie runs on, dressed as a medieval maiden, in a flowing velvet gown, with a
long braided blonde wig. Enchanted music is heard.*)

SOPHIE. My knight! My savior!

LUDWIG. Elsa!

SOPHIE. You must save me from the brutal Count Telramund!

LUDWIG. Summon the scoundrel! (*The Queen enters, dressed as the evil
Count, in dashing black and gold; she is hooded, so only her eyes and mouth are
visible. She is also on mechanical horseback—a black stallion. Darker, more
villainous music.*)

QUEEN. Greetings, vagabond!

LUDWIG. Hail, knave!

QUEEN. They say that you dare to challenge my evil.

LUDWIG. I dare!

QUEEN. They say that you champion the pure and the powerless.

LUDWIG. I shall!

QUEEN. And they claim that you possess inhuman, supernatural
powers.

SOPHIE. It's true!

LUDWIG. I'm a tenor!

QUEEN. En garde, knight of goodness!

LUDWIG. Taste my steel, hound of hell! (*Ludwig and the Queen howl war cries and ride at each other, jousting with their swords or lances, to appropriately rousing music. They both miss.*)

PFEIFFER. Miss!

QUEEN. Coward! Stripling!

LUDWIG. Your evil is strong.

QUEEN. Your virtue is pale.

LUDWIG. Your steed is sturdy.

QUEEN. Your stallion is small.

LUDWIG. (*To his horse.*) Don't listen!

PFEIFFER. Ride! (*Ludwig and the Queen repeat their war cries and ride at one another. Just as they are about to joust:*)

SOPHIE. I love you, my hero!

LUDWIG. (*Distracted.*) What?

PFEIFFER. Miss! (*The knights have again missed each other entirely.*)

SOPHIE. I'm sorry! I got carried away!

LUDWIG. (*Regarding Sophie.*) She's a virgin.

SOPHIE. But I don't want to be!

QUEEN. So why haven't you married him? You've been engaged for over two years.

LUDWIG. Hold on—this part isn't in the opera.

SOPHIE. I'm doing my best. I'm here in his fantasy.

QUEEN. I don't care. The real world is waiting. Are you squeamish?

SOPHIE. He's sensitive!

QUEEN. Are you strange?

SOPHIE. He's shy!

QUEEN. Is he a cream puff? A sacher torte? A sissy?

LUDWIG. Who are you, my mother?

QUEEN. (*Ripping off her hood.*) Yes! And I am stronger than your fantasy!

LUDWIG. (*Raising his sword.*) My fantasy will rule!

PFEIFFER. The final joust!

QUEEN. You must behave! You must surrender!

LUDWIG. I must keep dreaming! I must take flight!

QUEEN. But that is madness.

LUDWIG. That is glory!

PFEIFFER. Raise your swords!

LUDWIG. (*Raising his sword.*) For beauty!

QUEEN. For duty!

SOPHIE. (*Regarding Ludwig.*) My cutie!

PFEIFFER. Ride! (*They ride at each other, and Ludwig stabs the Queen, who is mortally wounded.*)

QUEEN. I am vanquished! He has slain me! His own mother! (*The Queen collapses on the ground, dead. The Queen moans, theatrically. She raises her head.*)

PFEIFFER. But lo, she rises!

QUEEN. A prophecy, milord. In fantasy, dreamers flourish. But in life, soldiers bleed. Kingdoms fall.

PFEIFFER. (*Clapping his hands, sharply.*) Your Highness! Your Highness!

LUDWIG. Yes? (*Sophie and the Queen exit, as Ludwig returns to reality.*)

PFEIFFER. You were speaking to the troops, you were sharing an inspirational tale, and you drifted off.

LUDWIG. (*To the troops, sincerely.*) I'm sorry! Be brave!

PFEIFFER. The Twenty-sixth Regiment, Your Highness. (*As Ludwig nods and salutes, lights down on the battlefield, as James and Henry Lee run on from the opposite side of the stage, having just parachuted into Bavaria. Their parachutes billow on the ground behind them, and they try to bunch them up.*)

JAMES. Where are we?

HENRY LEE. We should be about fifty miles from the German border, in Bavaria.

JAMES. (*Looking around, excited.*) Bavaria!

HENRY LEE. Fold your chute!

JAMES. I will, but this is so amazing! We just parachuted out of a plane, behind enemy lines, together!

HENRY LEE. We are not together! We are charting enemy troop positions, and we have to try not to get captured or killed.

JAMES. Right. And we have to stay away from the main roads.

HENRY LEE. Yes.

JAMES. And locate bunkers and ammunition depots.

HENRY LEE. Good.

JAMES. And then we eliminate that Von Trapp family.

HENRY LEE. (*Fed up, leaving.*) See you in France.

JAMES. Come back, I'll behave, I swear.

HENRY LEE. We need to radio the base, and tell them our location.

JAMES. (*Using binoculars.*) Okay, transmit these coordinates.

HENRY LEE. (*Using a walkie-talkie.*) Go.

JAMES. We are standing approximately half a kilometer from the target drop, north by northeast.

HENRY LEE. (*Staring out towards the audience.*) James?

JAMES. (*Still using the binoculars.*) There's open farmland with haystacks and a barn, we seem to have landed in an enormous placemat . . .

HENRY LEE. *James.* (*James lowers the binoculars and sees that Henry Lee now has his hands raised over his head. James immediately takes out his pistol, and points it towards the audience.*)

JAMES. (*Threatening.*) *Achtung! Halten sie! Schnell!*

HENRY LEE. (*To James.*) What are you doing? He's got a gun!

JAMES. So do I. (*To the unseen Nazi.*) Throw it down, or I will kill you. I will shoot you. Bang bang!

HENRY LEE. He threw down his gun! Do it! Shoot him!

JAMES. No.

HENRY LEE. Kill him! Shoot him! He's a Nazi!

JAMES. (*To the soldier, gesturing.*) Run! Go! Now! (*James and Henry Lee watch the soldier run off.*)

HENRY LEE. Oh my God, Jesus Christ . . .

JAMES. Henry Lee!

HENRY LEE. You—you saved my life.

JAMES. Yes I did!

HENRY LEE. But why—why didn't you shoot him?

JAMES. If he had made a move, if he had touched you, I would have took his head clean off, I know it. But I looked at him and—he looked back. It was amazing. I mean, he's our age. And everything about him told me that he didn't want to do it, that's why he hadn't shot both of us, already. He was beautiful. (*A siren begins to sound, and dogs begin to bark, as a searchlight sweeps across the stage, catching James and Henry Lee in its glare.*) Move! (*We hear the sound of machine-gun fire, and James and Henry Lee run offstage. Music rises through the gunfire. Through the music, we hear the voices of Pfeiffer, the Queen, Sophie and others, all calling out, "Ludwig!" Henry Lee's parachute sweeps across the stage, eventually covering Ludwig, who is lying on the stage floor, in his shirt and underwear; the rest of his clothing is heaped nearby. Princess Sophie enters.*)

SOPHIE. Ludwig!

LUDWIG. Sophie?

SOPHIE. They've scheduled our wedding, for this Saturday. But first, I just have to ask—what are you doing out here, at center stage, at the Royal Court Opera House? (*A handsome young opera singer enters, from offstage. He's bare chested, or tucking in his shirt; he's just finished putting on his clothes. He's eager and genuine, if not all that bright. He will be played by the same actor who plays Henry Lee.*)

SINGER. (*To Ludwig.*) Oh, 'scuse me, I thought we were like, alone . . .

SOPHIE. No, it's fine.

SINGER. (*To Ludwig.*) Last night was totally fun, like out here on the floor, but just now, when I was grabbing my stuff, I put it together—you're the king, right?

LUDWIG. Indeed.

SINGER. (*Delighted.*) I knew I recognized you—from the money.

LUDWIG. Yes.

SINGER. And whoa—you're Princess Sophie, of Austria!

SOPHIE. Two for two.

SINGER. (*Thrilled.*) My sister has a humpback—she worships you!

SOPHIE. She does?

SINGER. I mean before, she got like all bummed about it, but now, since you two got engaged, she's super-proud. She collects pictures of you, and the guys are like, all over her. And her best friend, Inga, she's got like a clubfoot, but I'm like, chh!

SOPHIE. Really?

SINGER. (*Gesturing, respectfully, to Sophie's hump.*) Could I?

SOPHIE. Sure. (*The singer delicately touches Sophie's hump.*)

SINGER. (*Beyond thrilled.*) Whoa! (*Holding up the hand that touched the hump.*) I'm gonna keep this! (*To Sophie and Ludwig.*) Later!

LUDWIG. (*The singer exits.*) Do you know who that was? Think about it.

SOPHIE. It can't be.

LUDWIG. Yet it is.

SOPHIE. Don't say it!

LUDWIG. That was Lohengrin, from last night's performance.

SOPHIE. Oh no!

LUDWIG. How can the gods make someone so golden, so beautiful, so Lohengrin—so not?

SOPHIE. My poor Ludwig.

LUDWIG. And in the last six months, I have also been to bed with two Tristans, three Tannhausers, five Parsifals and seven-and-a-half Siegfrieds.

SOPHIE. Seven-and-a-half?

LUDWIG. Understudy.

SOPHIE. Of course.

LUDWIG. Is this what you want to marry? (*Pfeiffer enters, carrying a large, velvet-covered box.*)

PFEIFFER. Your Highness?

LUDWIG. Yes?

PFEIFFER. This has just arrived, from St. Petersburg. (*Pfeiffer hands Ludwig the box, and exits.*)

SOPHIE. What's that?

LUDWIG. (*Opening the box.*) My reliquary.

SOPHIE. A reliquary? Why?

LUDWIG. Because the human heart, the actual organ, it's so hidden and ugly. I was hoping that mine, at least after I died, might become beautiful. And it could be placed in a shrine, where people could pray to it, and lose weight. (*Ludwig takes out the reliquary, which is indeed very beautiful. It's a heart-shaped container in hammered gold, encrusted with precious gems.*)

SOPHIE. But it's all wrong.

LUDWIG. Why?

SOPHIE. Because your heart is so much larger.

LUDWIG. It is?

SOPHIE. Ludwig, I do love you, I will always love you. But I can't marry you.

LUDWIG. You can't?

SOPHIE. You've postponed our wedding for years, and you're not even attracted to women. But none of that matters, because you've given me the most wonderful gift.

LUDWIG. What?

SOPHIE. You're the only person who's ever made me feel beautiful.

LUDWIG. I have?

SOPHIE. Thanks to you, I'm the most beautiful humpback in Europe. I hold my head high. Er. I am envied. Imitated. And men have noticed.

LUDWIG. Which men?

SOPHIE. Among others, a certain French nobleman.

LUDWIG. Not Count D'Amboise, that absolute dreamboat?

SOPHIE. *Mais oui.*

LUDWIG. I hate you!

SOPHIE. I wish I could shrug.

LUDWIG. Sophie? (*He gives her the reliquary.*) Take this away. I don't need it. I don't deserve it.

SOPHIE. But why not?

LUDWIG. (*After a beat.*) I'm a terrible king.

SOPHIE. (*After a beat.*) You're absolutely right.

LUDWIG. I daydreamed my way through the war.

SOPHIE. You vanish for months at a time.

LUDWIG. The newspapers call me "Ludwig the Strange," "Ludwig the Spendthrift" . . .

SOPHIE. "Ludwig the Slut."

LUDWIG. "Ludwig the Slut?"

SOPHIE. *The Daily Bavarian.*

LUDWIG. No!

SOPHIE. And Parliament has formed a committee to investigate your sanity.

LUDWIG. My sanity?

SOPHIE. Imagine.

LUDWIG. Everything I was born to become, every expectation, every test, every opportunity to justify my existence—I haven't even come close. And I have no excuse.

SOPHIE. Ludwig?

LUDWIG. And I have no choice. I'm going to abdicate.

SOPHIE. What?

LUDWIG. I'm going to leave the throne.

SOPHIE. But that isn't the answer. That's insane.

LUDWIG. Like my grandfather? I'll have Pfeiffer draw up the papers. (*Calling out.*) Pfeiffer!

SOPHIE. So you'll never get there.

LUDWIG. Where?

SOPHIE. Valhalla.

LUDWIG. (*Desperately, at the end of his rope.*) Valhalla doesn't exist! (*Calling out, into the darkness of the theater.*) Pfeiffer! Where is he?

SOPHIE. Ludwig, what do kings do?

LUDWIG. They abdicate. *Pfeiffer!*

SOPHIE. I'm talking about true kings, legendary kings, our kings. Ramses. Alexander. Louis XIV.

LUDWIG. (*She's struck a nerve.*) Louis?

SOPHIE. What did they do?

LUDWIG. They soared. They inspired. They dreamed.

SOPHIE. They built.

LUDWIG. What are you babbling about?

SOPHIE. Temples to Apollo. Pyramids to the stars. Gifts to the world.

LUDWIG. The Forbidden City. The Taj Mahal. The Colosseum.

SOPHIE. Versailles.

LUDWIG. (*Moaning, in ecstasy.*) Oooh . . .

SOPHIE. Ludwig?

LUDWIG. I'm sorry, but you know that whenever I hear the word "Versailles," I just get so aroused . . .

SOPHIE. That's your genius.

LUDWIG. It's my curse!

SOPHIE. "Versailles."

LUDWIG. Ooooh . . .

SOPHIE. "Versailles."

LUDWIG. Stop it!

SOPHIE. What do you want, what do you most believe in, with every ounce of your immortal soul?

LUDWIG. I believe—that the world should be beautiful. That God wants the world to be beautiful. But it isn't!

SOPHIE. Then make it so. In many ways, you *are* God.

LUDWIG. How?

SOPHIE. Because you're no good at reality, but you're brilliant at everything else.

LUDWIG. I am?

SOPHIE. Do for the world what you've done for me. And if people,

if parents, if politicians, if they call that madness, well then, my
darling . . .

LUDWIG. What?

SOPHIE. Go mad. (*Sophie tosses the reliquary back to Ludwig, who
catches it.*)

SOPHIE. *Au revoir.* (*Sophie exits.*)

LUDWIG. What is she talking about? I'm supposed to transform the
world? People would think I was crazy. They already do. All right,
what are the signs of madness? Number one—do I talk to myself? No.
Does madness run in my family? Of course not! Well, except for my
grandfather, fifty-eight cousins, three great-aunts, and my brother.
Poor Otto—who for the past fifteen years has been chained in his
room, where he barks like a dog.

OTTO. (*From offstage, barking.*) Ruff, ruff!

LUDWIG. (*To Otto.*) Sit! The third sign—do I hear voices? Sounds that
aren't there? No! I'm not crazy, and I'm leaving the theater, and the
throne! Goodbye! (*Ludwig shuts off all the theater's lights, strides off the stage
and begins to exit, down the aisle and out through the house. Just as he is almost
gone, we hear a single note of music. Ludwig pauses.*) I didn't hear that. No,
I'm fine. (*Another few notes are heard.*) It's just the wind in the rafters.
It's an old building. Please. (*More Wagnerian music is heard, intoxicating
and irresistible. Ludwig clamps his hands over his ears and babbles, trying to
shut out the music.*) Lalalalala . . . shut up! Shut up! (*Ludwig marches back
onstage and speaks to the theater.*) The theater is empty! There's no performance this evening, it's a dark night! I'm not listening! And I'm not
building anything! I don't love you! I'm not mad! (*As the music soars,
a strong, brilliantly vivid shaft of light appears center stage. Ludwig circles the
light, drawn to it, but unsure. With the music urging him onward, he tentatively
puts his hand into the shaft of light. Finally, as the music peaks, Ludwig steps into
the light, so it fully illuminates him. He raises his face to the light, his eyes shut,
completely surrendering to the glorious allure of the music. Silence. Ludwig opens
his eyes. He smiles.*) I'm the king. (*James enters, from the wings.*)

JAMES. Henry Lee? (*Henry Lee enters. He looks out, seeing what James is seeing.*)

HENRY LEE. What is that?

LUDWIG. Pfeiffer? (*Pfeiffer enters.*)

PFEIFFER. Your Highness? (*The two couples will not see each other, but will see the same things.*)

LUDWIG. I want to build something, in the Graswang Valley. Something—rococo.

JAMES. It looks like a huge, demented wedding cake . . .

HENRY LEE. With white marble frosting . . .

PFEIFFER. But you have a perfectly nice estate here in Munich, why do you need another?

LUDWIG. Just wait.

JAMES. Come on.

HENRY LEE. James?

LUDWIG. And underneath the palace, completely hidden, I want—a shocking surprise. I want to excavate, to hollow out at least a full acre . . .

JAMES. There's a secret door, in the side of that hill . . .

HENRY LEE. We shouldn't go in there . . .

PFEIFFER. But what will be in there?

LUDWIG. Think Hansel and Gretel. Think the Arabian Nights.

HENRY LEE. There's a tunnel . . .

JAMES. And a trap door . . .

LUDWIG. Think *Tannhauser*. Think orgies. (*The four men look around them, having entered an underground grotto. The grotto, and all of the subsequent castles, will involve absolutely no scenery. The locations and their beauty will be established entirely through the characters' words, their delighted reactions and lighting effects.*)

JAMES, HENRY LEE and PFEIFFER. It's a grotto!

LUDWIG. Indeed. First we'll fill the entire cavern with an iron armature, and then cover it with plaster and cement . . .

JAMES. It's like a stage set, it's all molded and painted to look like it's carved out of coral . . .

PFEIFFER. This sounds costly . . .

HENRY LEE. This cost a bundle . . .

LUDWIG. Get me the checkbook . . .

JAMES. I feel so rich!

HENRY LEE. And look, there are fake stalagtites dripping from the ceiling . . .

LUDWIG. Draped with endless garlands of lush plaster blooms . . .

PFEIFFER. Perhaps roses and lilies . . .

JAMES. There's honeysuckle and hibiscus . . .

LUDWIG. I want an artificial Eden . . .

HENRY LEE. Don't you think it's kind of spooky?

PFEIFFER. Will your mother be allowed down here?

LUDWIG and JAMES. No!

JAMES. And oh my God, over there, across the whole damn grotto, they built . . .

LUDWIG and HENRY LEE. A lake!

PFEIFFER. You want a full-scale, manmade, underground lake?

LUDWIG. With fifty swans and a story-high waterfall . . .

JAMES. And there's a machine to make waves . . .

HENRY LEE. We could surf!

LUDWIG. I want nature only better . . .

PFEIFFER. It's like nature only more expensive . . .

HENRY LEE. It's like nature . . .

JAMES. If God was gay.

EVERYONE. Yes! (*As the group describes the following lighting effects, they occur, drenching the stage in the most vivid colors.*)

LUDWIG. And I want thousands of hidden lightbulbs to create a continual rainbow, from burning amber . . .

HENRY LEE. To popsicle purple . . .

PFEIFFER. To cockatoo green . . .

JAMES. And Cadillac blue . . .

HENRY LEE. *(To James.)* Stop it.

LUDWIG. I will create architecture . . .

PFEIFFER. As aphrodisiac . . .

JAMES. Just being down here makes me feel sort of secret clubhouse sexy . . .

HENRY LEE. And pirate hideout horny . . .

JAMES. Henry Lee?

PFEIFFER. It's outrageous!

HENRY LEE. Did I say that?

LUDWIG. It's erotic . . .

JAMES. Yes you did!

LUDWIG. Let's see Parisian-whorehouse, pagan-fire-dance, sex-with-the-devil, lusty-lick-me-red! *(The stage bursts into a fiery scarlet as the music soars.)*

EVERYONE. *WHOA!*

HENRY LEE. James?

JAMES. Henry Lee?

PFEIFFER. Your Highness?

LUDWIG. Pfeiffer?

EVERYONE. I think I have a boner . . .

LUDWIG. So it's working . . .

JAMES. This is great!

LUDWIG. But I'm only getting started . . .

PFEIFFER. Your Highness, please don't say that . . .

HENRY LEE. I think I kind of like this . . .

LUDWIG. I think that I'm in love . . .

JAMES. *(To Henry Lee.)* You do?

HENRY LEE. It's true . . .

PFEIFFER. *(To Ludwig.)* With who?

JAMES. *(To Henry Lee.)* You too?

LUDWIG. With me! *(As Ludwig strides offstage, followed by Pfeiffer, James and*

Henry Lee grab each other for a passionate kiss. Natalie Kippelbaum enters. She is a modern-day tour guide, a peppy American woman from Long Island. She wears a gold lamé jogging suit, accessorized with a large button which says "GUIDE," a leopardskin fanny pack, a majorly highlighted hairdo, plenty of jewelry, oversized eyeglasses and hot-pink-and-silver-lamé sneakers. Natalie is a born entertainer and hostess, thrilled to share her enthusiasm for Ludwig and his castles. She is played by the same actress who plays the Queen. James and Henry Lee exit, as Natalie speaks to the audience and her unseen tour group.)

NATALIE. Hi! I'm Natalie Kippelbaum, and welcome to Temple Beth Shalom's Whirlwind European Adventure Castles of Bavaria Plus Wine Tasting and Wienerschnitzel Potpourri Tour. Yes. The bus will be here any second, so let's get started. And I know what you're thinking, you're going, Natalie, from Long Island, what are you doing with Ludwig? Well, three years ago, I hit bottom. First, my husband, he dies, from lung cancer. Fun. And then, my daughter, she loses her job. Then my son, Debbie—enough said. And I'm in my Hyundai, and I'm about to drive off a bridge, like in a Hyundai that's even necessary, and then—I hear music. Gorgeous, operatic music. You know—NPR. And I think, where is that music coming from, I mean, where was it born? So I get on a plane, and I'm here. And the minute I step into that grotto—I'm happy. I'm high. And today we're going to see something even more beautiful, because in 1883, Ludwig decided to build his copy of Versailles. *(She pronounces the word with a thick Long Island accent—"Versoy.")* That's right—Versailles. *(Ludwig enters, now dressed in a glittering waistcoat, pantaloons and a high, curled wig, as Louis XIV, followed by Pfeiffer, who is also dressed in period French style.)*

PFEIFFER. A copy of Versailles?

NATALIE. We're here! Everybody out! Mrs. Kloper, use your walker!

LUDWIG. It's my ecstatic tribute to Louis XIV, le Roi du Soleil.

NATALIE. And why was Louis called the Sun King? Anyone?

PFEIFFER. He was the center of the solar system.

NATALIE. Good answer, Mrs. Weinblatt.

LUDWIG. You're starting to catch on.

NATALIE. And we're moving . . .

LUDWIG. (*As he looks at the palace.*) It's so moving.

PFEIFFER. I'm getting nervous . . .

NATALIE. And we're not touching anything . . .

LUDWIG. It touches me . . .

PFEIFFER. And I'm trembling . . .

NATALIE. Here it comes . . .

PFEIFFER. And what's in here?

LUDWIG. You may wish to shield your eyes . . .

NATALIE. Does anyone have a heart condition?

LUDWIG. May I present, in all its radiant splendor, the heartbeat of the monarchy—the royal bedchamber.

PFEIFFER. (*Seeing it.*) You have outdone yourself.

NATALIE. Look at that bed, I'm palpitating, I'm flushed . . .

LUDWIG. It's entirely gilded in twenty-four-karat gold . . .

NATALIE. It took Parisian artisans over two years to carve . . .

LUDWIG. It's fit for Louis and his queen . . .

PFEIFFER. It's fit for Siegfried and Brunhilde . . .

LUDWIG. It's fit for Venus and Apollo . . .

NATALIE. Donald Trump, eat shit and die! (*The bed has appeared. James and Henry Lee are in the bed; they now wear their T-shirts and army uniform trousers.*)

HENRY LEE. I can't believe this. We just had sex.

NATALIE. (*Gesturing to the bed.*) Can you imagine? For sex?

JAMES. Did you like it?

LUDWIG. Pure silk sheets . . .

HENRY LEE. While we were doing it, I sort of forgot who I was . . .

NATALIE. Forget about it . . .

HENRY LEE. And where I was . . .

PFEIFFER. That bed is evil . . .

JAMES. Is that bad?

LUDWIG. Is it heaven?

HENRY LEE. It's just new . . .

NATALIE. It just kills me . . .

HENRY LEE. It's just crazy . . .

JAMES. So what do you think?

HENRY LEE. It's amazing.

JAMES, LUDWIG and PFEIFFER. It's spectacular!

NATALIE. It's Bed, Bath and Beyond!

PFEIFFER. Your Highness—enough.

LUDWIG. Enough?

NATALIE. So people, let me ask you—do you think we've had enough?

PFEIFFER. They're going to say that you've gone mad . . .

HENRY LEE. They're gonna say that we went AWOL . . .

NATALIE. Someone's gotta say it—are we fatootsed?

JAMES and LUDWIG. Maybe you're right . . .

NATALIE. Mrs. Kloper, am I right?

HENRY LEE. I mean, what about our mission?

PFEIFFER. And Bismarck's coalition?

NATALIE. Are we having a conniption?

JAMES. Should we check our ammunition?

LUDWIG. I shall tell you my position.

HENRY LEE. But there's just one thing I'm wishin' . . .

JAMES. What?

LUDWIG. More.

PFEIFFER. More?

HENRY LEE. More.

JAMES. More?

NATALIE. More? So what do we think?

EVERYONE. *More! (The ghost of Marie Antoinette appears, wearing a high, powdered wig, jewels and a sumptuous gown. Only Ludwig will be able to see her. Marie will be played by the same actress who plays Sally.)*

MARIE. *Bonjour.*

LUDWIG. (*Delighted.*) Your Majesty!

MARIE. Your Highness.

PFEIFFER. (*To Ludwig.*) Who are you talking to?

LUDWIG. For throwing a truly memorable ball, for all the crowned heads of Europe, the queen requires, the planet requires, my soul requires— a Hall of Mirrors. (*The stage is filled with a zillion shards of reflected light, as from a series of mirror balls, so the light dances. James and Henry Lee climb out of bed, and join the group in responding to the light.*)

JAMES and HENRY LEE. Oh my God . . .

PFEIFFER and NATALIE. Oh my God . . .

MARIE. People always say that . . .

LUDWIG. There are over 12,000 separate panes of mirror . . .

NATALIE. Count the fifteen crystal chandeliers . . .

HENRY LEE. It's like getting lost inside a diamond . . .

PFEIFFER. Everywhere I turn, I see myself . . .

MARIE. (*To the group.*) Look, it's you . . .

EVERYONE. (*Seeing themselves in the mirrors.*) Look, it's me . . .

JAMES. (*To Henry Lee.*) Look, it's us . . .

NATALIE. Can't you just see Marie Antoinette?

JAMES. It's like in that movie, *Marie Antoinette* . . .

PFEIFFER. Your Highness, what are you looking at?

LUDWIG. Just the beautiful Marie Antoinette . . .

MARIE. *Merci.*

NATALIE. Although in her portraits, her hips are so huge . . .

MARIE. It's the dress! (*Marie pinches Natalie.*)

NATALIE. (*Reacting to the pinch; she doesn't see Marie.*) Mrs. Kloper?

HENRY LEE. I think I read that she was vain . . .

MARIE. Not vain, French! (*Marie slaps Henry Lee on the back of his head.*)

HENRY LEE. (*Reacting to the slap.*) James?

JAMES. What?

PFEIFFER. They put her head on a spike!

MARIE. Don't remind me! (*Marie kicks Pfeiffer.*)

PFEIFFER. (*Reacting to the kick.*) Your Highness?

LUDWIG. (*To Marie.*) But you still look great!

MARIE. We would always have such dancing . . .

NATALIE and JAMES. This place is made for dancing . . .

LUDWIG. I will create an orchestra, for dancing . . .

HENRY LEE and NATALIE. What did they call it?

JAMES, LUDWIG and PFEIFFER. The gavotte! (*A sparkling gavotte or minuet is heard.*)

LUDWIG and MARIE. *Mais oui!*

NATALIE. This music is available in the gift shop, on CD, along with postcards, slide sets and commemorative plates and keychains . . .

LUDWIG. (*Bowing to Marie.*) Your Highness?

JAMES. (*Bowing to Henry Lee.*) Private Stafford?

PFEIFFER. I'm so alone . . .

NATALIE. The snack bar is to your left . . .

JAMES and LUDWIG. Shall we dance?

MARIE and HENRY LEE. I couldn't.

JAMES and LUDWIG. But why not?

NATALIE. And the restrooms are on your right . . .

HENRY LEE. I'm a soldier . . .

MARIE and PFEIFFER. It's been so long . . .

HENRY LEE. We're at war . . .

MARIE. I have no head . . .

NATALIE. I'm thinking about my husband . . .

PFEIFFER. I'm thinking about my Valkyrie . . .

MARIE. I'm thinking about my Louis . . .

JAMES. That's the reason . . .

LUDWIG. This is your ballroom . . .

NATALIE. He was a fabulous dancer. He'd say to me, "Natalie . . ."

PFEIFFER. (*Turning to Natalie.*) Brunhilde?

NATALIE. (*To Pfeiffer.*) Myron?

JAMES. Henry Lee?

LUDWIG. Marie?

EVERYONE. Let's dance! (*The group begins to dance a gavotte, in couples: James and Henry Lee, Ludwig and Marie, Pfeiffer and Natalie. Then the music grows livelier, turning into a World War II swing anthem, something like "Sing, Sing, Sing." Everyone breaks into an exuberant jitterbug. As Natalie steps forward, everyone else dances offstage.*)

NATALIE. Ludwig couldn't stop building—he was hooked, like on crack. He would race from one construction site to the next, at midnight in a sleigh drawn by six white stallions—goyim! He did a Moorish pavilion, a medieval hunting lodge, and a theater at Bayreuth, with perfect acoustics, where the works of Richard Wagner are still performed to this day. And I know, that Wagner, he was no friend of the Jews. So you know what I call him? (*She uses the soft, American "W".*) Wagner. Dickie Wagner. Ha! He'd die! He did! What's that, Mrs. Slatkin? So what happened to Ludwig? You'll see in just a minute, when we make our final stop. But just remember, if you can't give up everything, even your life itself, for what you truly believe in, well, then why bother? So whenever I'm down, whenever I think about terrorists and starving children and Debbie trying to find shoes—I think of Ludwig. So grab your bottled water and your Instamatics, and look out your window, on the left, because here it comes, all the way up on that mountaintop, it's Ludwig's ultimate dream, his home of the gods, his swan song, I'm kvelling, wait till you see it, if it were a person, I'd have sex with it, and I'm not a young woman. There it is—excuse me, I need a moment. (*She takes a deep breath, composing herself, overcome.*) There it is—Valhalla! (*As Natalie exits, Ludwig enters, dressed as a highly theatrical medieval knight, in armor and velvet. He looks out, and up.*)

LUDWIG. I like to ride out here, at least a mile away, and just gaze up at it. It was finished today. (*Pfeiffer enters, dressed in an outlandish velvet costume, with a tunic, pantaloons and a plumed hat.*)

PFEIFFER. But why are we dressed like this?

LUDWIG. At last, I am Lohengrin. (*James runs on, and stares up at the mountaintop.*)

JAMES. What is that? (*Henry Lee enters.*)

HENRY LEE. I can't see it.

JAMES. The clouds are in the way.

LUDWIG. (*Pointing.*) And next, even higher up the mountain, I'm going to build a temple to Apollo, a parthenon, made entirely of glass. And then I think a pagoda, and something Hindu, and—a Sphinx.

PFEIFFER. Your Highness?

HENRY LEE. I got a letter. I've been carrying it around ever since we got overseas. I've been afraid to open it.

LUDWIG. Yes?

JAMES. Why?

HENRY LEE. It's from Sally.

PFEIFFER. You've been building without pause for over ten years. You've spent every Deustche mark you own, and the royal treasury is over five million in debt.

LUDWIG. What are you saying? (*Lights up on Sally, in a simple dress.*)

JAMES. (*Reading the letter aloud.*) "Dear Henry Lee and James . . ."

SALLY. Somehow I know that you've found each other. And I don't know if I'm jealous, or relieved. But I do know this—James, I wish I didn't love you. And Henry Lee, I wish I could love you more. And please, take care of each other, and stay safe. And don't worry about me, because I'm going to have plenty of company. I'm going to have a baby.

PFEIFFER. You have no more money. (*The Queen enters.*)

QUEEN. Ludwig?

LUDWIG. Mother?

QUEEN. There are soldiers at the gatehouse. With a warrant for your arrest.

LUDWIG. Why?

QUEEN. Parliament has had you declared—insane.

LUDWIG. I don't believe you.

QUEEN. And unfit to rule.

SALLY. One of you is going to be a father.

JAMES. "Love, Sally." (*Sally exits.*)

HENRY LEE. A baby.

JAMES. Go back. Radio the base.

HENRY LEE. I should. I know that.

JAMES. You have a war. And a wife. And a family. And a future.

HENRY LEE. You make all of that sound so impossible. As if no one should ever want those things.

JAMES. I'm not asking you to choose. Not anymore.

HENRY LEE. But what will happen to you?

JAMES. Everything else.

HENRY LEE. You'll be alone.

JAMES. Maybe. But since we got here, to Bavaria, have you noticed something?

HENRY LEE. What?

JAMES. I haven't taken anything. We've been in all of these castles, filled with treasures, and—nothing.

HENRY LEE. But why not?

JAMES. Because from now on, everywhere I go, everything I see, the whole world—it's all mine.

LUDWIG. But there must be money somewhere, to be borrowed or raised. How can anyone see my castles, and not wish for more?

QUEEN. You must prepare yourself.

PFEIFFER. You must defend yourself.

LUDWIG. Why?

QUEEN. The committee claims to have evidence of your dementia. They say that you spend hours speaking to the ghost of Marie Antoinette.

LUDWIG. I adore her.

QUEEN. They say that you hire gilded stableboys to row you about your grotto, in a boat shaped like a duck.

LUDWIG. A swan.

QUEEN. And that you were glimpsed on a hillside, reciting the Song of Solomon, while dressed as a nun.

LUDWIG. It was Sunday!

QUEEN. Ludwig. My sweet boy,

LUDWIG. But who has reported all of this? Who has betrayed me?

QUEEN. A friend.

PFEIFFER. I'm sorry.

LUDWIG. Pfeiffer? (*The Queen exits.*)

HENRY LEE. James?

JAMES. Yeah?

HENRY LEE. I have never hated anyone the way I've hated you.

JAMES. I'm blushing.

HENRY LEE. Since that very first night, when we were kids—you have pushed me.

JAMES. Out of Dainsville.

HENRY LEE. And you have mocked me.

JAMES. Someone had to.

HENRY LEE. And you have tried to make me—like you.

JAMES. You are like me!

HENRY LEE. No I'm not! I don't have half your imagination. Or your courage.

JAMES. Henry Lee?

HENRY LEE. And I'm nowhere near as annoying.

JAMES. Because you don't apply yourself.

LUDWIG. But I'm the king. I have dreamed. I have unleashed my fullest imagination, to create—the purest beauty on this earth. Anyone, everyone can see that. Just look!

JAMES. Look. (*Everyone onstage now faces out, gazing up at Valhalla Castle, as the clouds clear. The view is breathtaking.*)

PFEIFFER. The turrets . . .

HENRY LEE. And the towers . . .

JAMES. The banners . . .

LUDWIG. And the gold . . .

PFEIFFER. It's El Dorado . . .

LUDWIG. It's Nirvana . . .

HENRY LEE. It's Olympus . . .

JAMES. No, it's Oz . . .

PFEIFFER. I love this mountain . . .

JAMES. I love this morning . . .

HENRY LEE. I love this world.

LUDWIG. I love my dreams . . .

PFEIFFER. I can't stop looking . . .

LUDWIG. My soul is bursting . . .

JAMES. That is the opposite of Texas!

PFEIFFER. It soars!

JAMES. It floats!

LUDWIG. It sings!

HENRY LEE. James?

JAMES. Yeah?

HENRY LEE. I'm coming with you. All the way.

JAMES. Why?

HENRY LEE. Because I'm going to say the most dangerous thing I can think of.

JAMES. What?

HENRY LEE. That the world is beautiful.

LUDWIG. Am I mad?

JAMES. So do you love me?

HENRY LEE. What?

JAMES. Do you love me?

HENRY LEE. Why?

JAMES. Do you love me?

HENRY LEE. If I say yes, will it make you just way too happy?

JAMES. Find out.

LUDWIG. (*Gesturing to Valhalla.*) If all this, if all of my dreams, if my entire life is pure insanity; then I have only one response—

HENRY LEE. Yes.

JAMES. Yes!

LUDWIG. Yes. (*We hear a musical phrase from* Lohengrin. *Everyone onstage hears it.*)

HENRY LEE. Listen.

PFEIFFER. Listen.

JAMES. What is that?

LUDWIG. It's the "Prelude," from *Lohengrin.*

HENRY LEE. It sounds like—the beginning of something. (*Henry Lee goes to James. As they are about to embrace, a shot rings out. The bullet hits Henry Lee, who crumples, and then stands and walks offstage. We hear a Wagnerian crescendo. Blackout. Lights up on Margaret, in Texas. She brings a straightback chair onstage and stands behind it. She speaks to an unseen reporter.*)

MARGARET. Yes, I'm James Avery's mother. Excuse me? No, I'm sorry, but this is not a concern of your newspaper. Or of anyone else outside our immediate family. You are misinformed—James did not go AWOL. He was honorably discharged, following a complete and severe emotional breakdown. He had seen Henry Lee Stafford killed before his very eyes. He served his country, he is lucky to be alive, and that is all there is to it. Have I made myself clear? Thank you. Good afternoon. (*Margaret exits. Ludwig enters and sits in the straightback chair. He wears somewhat disheveled, ordinary black clothing, as does Pfeiffer, who stands nearby.*)

PFEIFFER. Do you understand what has happened?

LUDWIG. Thanks to you and your confederates?

PFEIFFER. I'm sorry, I can go, but I've asked the committee if I could stay with you.

LUDWIG. And you shall. You shall witness. That I am imprisoned here, at Valhalla. With holes drilled in every door.

PFEIFFER. Only for observation.

LUDWIG. While my brother Otto has been placed on the throne.

PFEIFFER. Only as a symbol.

LUDWIG. Does he get his own dish? (*Ludwig and Pfeiffer remain onstage. James enters, and sits elsewhere; he's now behind the counter at his family's hardware store in Dainsville. He wears civilian clothes and speaks to an unseen reporter.*)

JAMES. . . . . oh thank you, I'm feeling much better, six months in the VA hospital, good as new. Yes, it was terrible about Henry Lee, I feel so— responsible, somehow. No, no, it's okay, put it in the paper, I want people to know. You see, he was shot by a Nazi soldier, a boy who just a few days before, I had let—live. And after he shot Henry Lee, he just stood there, a few yards away, staring at me. Daring me.

PFEIFFER. Your Highness, Ludwig, I'm sorry, I'm not sure of the proper form of address . . .

LUDWIG. Your Madness.

PFEIFFER. I know this is difficult, but it's only been a day.

LUDWIG. They will never let me out. And they will never let me build.

PFEIFFER. I know.

JAMES. And I shot him. And I kept shooting, until our platoon sergeant found me, three days later, outside this big castle. He said that it was like I was guarding it. And I guess I'd . . . I'd had enough, and I collapsed. And at the hospital I decided that maybe, if I came right back here to Dainsville, I could—well, nobody can take Henry Lee's place, but I can do—what he might've done. So I'm taking over my dad's hardware store, and from now on, I'm a Texas boy. Sally came in, just the other day, with the baby. A little girl. And I held her. She looks just like—her mom. Speaking of which, would you like to see something? Something beautiful?

LUDWIG. Do you think I'm crazy?

PFEIFFER. I think that you're—like opera.

LUDWIG. Why?

PFEIFFER. Because opera is music that's gone mad.

LUDWIG. Could you get permission, for a walk by the lake? Tell them that you will accompany me—as a chaperone. (*Ludwig and Pfeiffer exit; Pfeiffer takes the chair offstage with him. James now holds an object wrapped in burlap.*)

JAMES. Now I can't tell you exactly how I came by this, but . . . (*He takes out Ludwig's reliquary.*) Yes, it's pure gold. It's called a reliquary, yes, I know it's shaped like a heart, but inside—it's the real thing. Well, I guess it is kind of, what did you say, gruesome, but it's almost one hundred years old, and that's how they did it back then, at least for royalty, you know, bigshots. They would bury the body, but the heart, that was precious. (*Ludwig walks onstage, now wearing a homburg and a long black overcoat.*)

LUDWIG. Pfeiffer, come along! (*He gazes out at the lake, towards the audience.*) Look at that. The water. Like glass. How deep is this?

JAMES. (*As the unseen reporter leaves.*) Goodbye.

LUDWIG. (*Still to Pfeiffer, who remains offstage.*) Lohengrin—remember? At the end, after the knight has been betrayed, his ship appears, and he sails off alone. (*Ludwig and James can now see and hear each other.*)

JAMES. Hey.

LUDWIG. Yes?

JAMES. Your Highness.

LUDWIG. James.

JAMES. They found your body the next day.

LUDWIG. When they dragged the lake.

JAMES. Why?

LUDWIG. Because the world is an ugly place, filled with ugly people. And it has nothing to do with physical appearance.

JAMES. There are pretty Nazis.

LUDWIG. And the loveliest humpbacks.

JAMES. So what should we do? Build our own worlds?

LUDWIG. No! My life was utterly selfish. A complete fraud. A waste.

JAMES. Why?

LUDWIG. I was alone. And you stole my heart.

JAMES. I needed it.

LUDWIG. Why?

JAMES. Because you left something out of the story. As Lohengrin sails off, he performs—a final miracle.

LUDWIG. I love miracles.

JAMES. The swan vanishes, and in its place, on the riverbank, there appears . . .

LUDWIG. The maiden's brother. At last! (*Annie Avery, a young woman dressed in the style of the early 1970s, enters. She will be played by the same actress who plays Sally. She moves center stage and speaks to an unseen official. As she speaks, James will hand her the reliquary.*)

ANNIE. Hi, I'm Annie Avery. And I know this is really weird, but, well, last year, my dad passed away, from cancer. But before he died, he made me swear that I would return this. He said that it was the only way that he could be absolutely sure that I would see—the most beautiful place on earth. I'm sorry, are you the right person? Are you in charge, here at the castle?

LUDWIG. (*Turning to her.*) Yes.

ANNIE. (*Looking around, in awe.*) Well, Jesus. I wish my mom could see this, but she hasn't been well. She loved my dad so much, and I promised I'd tell her all about this.

LUDWIG. Then you must. And I believe there are postcards.

JAMES. (*Just to Ludwig.*) And mugs. They say, "I Love Ludwig."

LUDWIG. (*To Annie.*) And mugs.

ANNIE. (*Still looking around.*) Well, my God, for my mom, and my dad, and for everybody—thank you.

LUDWIG. Of course. And, back in . . .

ANNIE. Texas.

LUDWIG. What do you do?

ANNIE. I work in the public schools. I teach.

LUDWIG. Yes?

ANNIE. Music.

LUDWIG. (*Referring to the reliquary.*) Open it.

ANNIE. I'm afraid that I already have. It's empty.

LUDWIG. Try again. (*Annie opens the reliquary. Inside, nestled in velvet, she finds the crystal swan, which James had stolen in the play's opening Moments. She holds the swan up to the light, where it glistens.*)

ANNIE. It's beautiful. (*As music from* Lohengrin *fills the theater, James and Ludwig watch Annie; they are very pleased.*)

CURTAIN

SIX

Regrets Only

REGRETS ONLY was originally produced by Manhattan Theatre Club (Lynne Meadow, Artistic Director; Barry Grove, Executive Producer) in New York City, opening on October 19, 2006. It was directed by Christopher Ashley; the set design was by Michael Yeargan; the costume design was by William Ivey Long; the lighting design was by Natasha Katz; the sound design was by John Gromada; the production stage manager was Martha Donaldson; and the stage manager was Kyle Gates. The cast was as follows:

MYRA KESSELMAN	Jackie Hoffman
HANK HADLEY	George Grizzard
TIBBY McCULLOUGH	Christine Baranski
JACK McCULLOUGH	David Rasche
SPENCER McCULLOUGH	Diane Davis
MARIETTA CLAYPOOLE	Sian Phillips

PLACE
New York City

TIME
The present

Regrets Only

ACT ONE

*Seven PM, Thursday evening. The McCullough penthouse, high above Fifth
Avenue. We're in the drawing room, an expansive, traditional zone with
several entrances, perhaps including a grand staircase at the rear. The room
is decorated in a sumptuous combination of Old Money and high style.
There are various couches, armchairs, tufted ottomans, extravagant floral
arrangements and a fireplace. As the curtain rises, the doorbell rings. Myra
Kesselman, a uniformed maid, enters from a hallway and goes to the front
door. Myra is somewhere in middle age, smart, sane and efficient. Myra's
worked for the McCulloughs for years, and she likes to keep herself amused.
At the Moment, she will speak in a deep, melodious Irish brogue. She opens
the front door.*

MYRA. Why, if it ain't bein' Mister Hank Hadley! (*Hank Hadley enters,
wearing a perfectly hand-tailored tuxedo and carrying his black cashmere overcoat. Hank is a handsome, enormously successful designer, businessman and
an established international icon of perfect taste. Hank is a real gent, a good-
humored, ebullient blend of Cary Grant and a Texas tycoon. He's beautifully
mannered but unpretentious; he's the old school at its best. He's obviously rich
but can put anyone at ease; he's masculine but physically graceful.*)

HANK. (*Very happy to see her.*) Darling.

MYRA. (*As they embrace.*) It's bein' far too long, we ain't been seein' the likes of ye in, begorrah, it's bein' almost bein' a year now, and ain't that a cryin' dirty shame and the work of the devil, may the Good Lord smite him, jumpin' jiminy, Jack and Jehovah!

HANK. Myra, it's great to see you, but why are you talking like that?

MYRA. What are ye sayin', me fine laddie and a blarney blessin' on these old eyes, ye fine figger of a fine fella. Why am I talkin' like what?

HANK. Like a retarded leprechaun.

MYRA. (*Immediately dropping the Irish accent and now speaking in her normal Manhattan honk.*) Because I'm so glad to see you! And because I'm so bored with being the only white, Jewish maid in Manhattan.

HANK. Oh, but that's not how I think of you. I think of you as the most glorious, ravishing, hotly desirable white Jewish maid in Manhattan.

MYRA. (*Passionately.*) I love you.

HANK. (*Even more passionately.*) I want you.

MYRA. (*Even more.*) I need you.

HANK. Take my coat.

TIBBY. (*From offstage.*) Is that really Hank?

HANK. Tibby? (*Myra takes Hank's coat and exits into the apartment. Hank looks around the room; he hasn't been here in some time. He takes a deep breath. Tibby McCullough enters. She's a lifelong Manhattan social heroine, a woman who's wanted nothing more than a fabulously interesting and expensive life. She's wonderfully poised and attractive; her hair is an extravagant ash blonde, not tacky but triumphant. She's wearing an evening gown that's both age appropriate but not at all matronly; she looks sexy and chic and might sport a few snazzy diamonds. Tibby is from a fine WASP background, but fashion is her life.*)

TIBBY. Hank?

HANK. Baby. (*A second before they embrace, they both pause, realizing the potential danger to their outfits and their hair.*) Let's risk it.

TIBBY. We must. (*They embrace, with genuine emotion.*) I have missed you so much.

HANK. You are too sweet.

TIBBY. But it's been forever. I can't believe I haven't seen you in months, not since Mike . . . since Mike . . .

HANK. I know . . .

TIBBY. But I wish he had let me see him, or at least speak on the phone . . .

HANK. He just wasn't up to it . . .

TIBBY. But did he get everything I sent him? I wanted to make sure it was all only things he'd really like, the flowers . . .

HANK. They were perfect . . .

TIBBY. And the treats . . .

HANK. His favorites . . .

TIBBY. And the books and the puzzles and, oh, I wasn't sure about it, that little stuffed giraffe . . .

HANK. It killed him.

TIBBY. Oh no!

HANK. He loved it. And he was so grateful. And tough. I mean, cancer. But do you know, up until the last few days, he refused to take pain-killers?

TIBBY. Really?

HANK. Can you imagine?

TIBBY. I mean, I'm on them *now*.

HANK. Of course.

TIBBY. But how are you? And don't put up a brave front. Because I know that you haven't been going anywhere, or seeing anyone, but this is me, so just tell me—how are you?

HANK. Stop it. Right now.

TIBBY. Hank?

HANK. Here's the deal: Mike and I had thirty-eight terrific years together, which is more than so many people, it's more than most people get. So here's what I don't want, because I know that you're just about to do it. I don't want you leaning forward, with that, "You poor lonely thing, you've just lost a loved one" face . . .

TIBBY. But . . .

HANK. And I don't want you trying to come up with the exact, perfect, desperately compassionate phrase, like, "Is there anything I can do?"

TIBBY. But . . .

HANK. And you are my very best friend, so above all I don't want you acting all moist and sorrowful and taking my hand and murmuring, "Oh my poor darling, he loved you so much."

TIBBY. Oh, my poor darling . . .

HANK. Yes?

TIBBY. (*Very upbeat.*) Death! Yay!

HANK. (*Delighted.*) That's my girl!

TIBBY. (*Smiling.*) Darling.

HANK. Look at you.

TIBBY. Look at you.

HANK. Don't. I'm a wreck.

TIBBY. I'm a mess.

HANK. I'm a liar.

TIBBY. Me too!

HANK. So where are we off to?

TIBBY. (*Calling out.*) Myra! (*Myra enters, carrying a silver tray piled with envelopes and invitations. She now uses a naughty French accent and might wear a beret.*)

MYRA. Bonjour, madame!

TIBBY. Myra?

MYRA. I have all of ze evenink's invitaciones right 'ere, upon zis tray. (*Spotting Hank.*) Ooo-la-la! Eet eez Monsieur Hadlee! Merci, madame, do not let heem peench me ant squeeze me ant make me larch wiz hees childt, so I weel 'ave to be sent away!

TIBBY. Pardon?

MYRA. I am ze good girl! (*Myra runs out.*)

TIBBY. (*Picking up the first invitation from the tray.*) All right, at seven we've got cocktails at Sarah Mortimer's, you have got to see her new face, it's insane, absolutely nothing moves . . .

HANK. We could test it, we could set a fire in her apartment . . .

TIBBY. (*Imitating Sarah Mortimer, her fingertips holding her face immobile.*) "Help! Fire."

HANK. Yes!

TIBBY. And at eight we're expected at the Pierre, there's a fundraiser for multiple amputees . . .

HANK. Will there be dancing?

TIBBY. Hush. And after that we have a choice: the mayor's open house for heart disease, the April in Paris ball for glaucoma, or Muriel Brakeman's midnight supper to fight Attention Deficit Disorder.

HANK. (*After a pause.*) What?

TIBBY. Stop it. (*The front door opens and Jack McCullough, Tibby's husband, enters. Jack is a good-looking success story, one of Manhattan's most powerful white-shoe attorneys. He loves his wife, his family and his own dazzling eminence; he glows with delighted self-esteem. He's come from the office, in a navy suit, with a briefcase and a trench coat.*)

JACK. (*Accusingly.*) I thought so!

TIBBY. Oh no!

HANK. It's not what you're thinking!

JACK. Oh no? I turn my back for only a moment, and I come home to find my wife, and her cheap Manhattan gigolo! (*Myra runs in; she now uses a Cockney accent.*)

MYRA. Oaww, Guv'nor, it's true!

JACK. Yes, lad?

MYRA. I comes in, I does, and I sees 'em together, ruttin' like pigs they was! (*She mimes a sex act by pumping her hips.*) Her ladyship and the games keeper! The sight has singed me eyeballs! I'm blind! I'm blind! (*Myra exits; being blind, she slams into the door frame.*)

JACK. Hank. I was so sorry about Mike.

HANK. Jack. (*They shake hands.*)

JACK. Hey, we're a blue state. (*Jack hugs Hank. As they hug:*)

HANK. (*To Jack.*) Did you see *Brokeback Mountain*?

JACK. (*To Tibby.*) Honey, did we see that?

TIBBY. It was a Western.

JACK. Loved it! (*Jack gives Hank even more of a bear hug. The front door is flung open, and Spencer McCullough enters. Spencer is a gorgeous, fire-breathing, take-no-prisoners corporate attorney. She's dressed in stylish work-into-evening attire, and carries an expensively slim attaché case. At the Moment she's all but levitating, exploding with excitement.*)

SPENCER. Mummy? Daddy? Hank?

TIBBY. Yes, darling?

SPENCER. Alright. Alright, I just have to say something. First of all, I am so proud to have come of age in an era when women, okay, American women, okay, privileged American women, okay, privileged American women with great hair, can be all that they can be. And I am so grateful to all of the pioneering generations of American feminists, yes, I said the "f" word, who have marched and battled and sacrificed, just so that I can have a seven-figure salary, an unlimited expense account and a smokin' hot car. And I take pride in spending two days every month mentoring inner-city teenage girls, who I teach to believe in themselves, to believe in their dreams, and when they go to McDonalds, to at least think about the salads. And I am dedicating my life to making this world a more peaceful, a more equitable and a more compassionate place, but right at this moment I don't really care about any of that bleeding-heart, do-goody, help-the-helpless horseshit, and do you know why?

HANK. Because you're high as a kite?

SPENCER. *And I'm getting married!*

TIBBY. Sweetheart!

HANK. Baby!

JACK. Cupcake!

SPENCER. (*Instantly desperate.*) Where?

HANK. Congratulations!

EVERYONE. YAY!!!

SPENCER. (*Calling out.*) Myra! (*Myra enters; she will now speak with a thick German/Bavarian accent. She also wears a colorful peasant headdress, with trailing ribbons.*)

MYRA. Jais?

SPENCER. Myra, I'm getting married!

MYRA. So I chear! I vill tell all de pipple in de willage!

TIBBY. It's so exciting!

SPENCER. Oh Myra, did you ever think this would happen?

MYRA. No!

TIBBY. (*To Myra.*) Out! (*As Myra exits:*)

HANK. Okay, I've been so out of the loop, so tell me, who's the lucky guy?

SPENCER. His name is Peter Perryman, and I've known him for years, and he's rich and handsome and an investment banker, Mummy, what do you always call him?

TIBBY. (*Happily.*) The Uber-Nazi.

SPENCER. Yes! And tonight we met for drinks and suddenly he gets down on one knee and there's this little velvet box and this ring (*She shows Tibby her ring, and they both scream.*) and this proposal and I was so touched and I just thought—well, why the hell not?

TIBBY. I love it!

JACK. Oh my!

SPENCER. And ever since then I've gone totally bridezilla. Mummy, I want everything you had, I want St. Patrick's and at least twelve bridesmaids and thousands of flowers and the reception at the Pierre . . .

TIBBY and JACK. Of course.

SPENCER. And because I'm a lawyer I can write my own pre-nup!

EVERYONE. YAY!!!

SPENCER. But most of all, what I really want more than anything in the whole world, in the universe, is to be married—in a Hank Hadley gown.

TIBBY. Oh, Hank.

JACK. Wouldn't that be terrific?

HANK. But wait, before you decide, I want to make sure that Spencer has really thought about this. Because there are many other extremely gifted designers.

SPENCER. That's true. I mean, Valentino is amazing.

TIBBY. And you do see his gowns everywhere.

HANK. Especially on prom night.

JACK. Hank?

SPENCER. And of course, Vera Wang makes the most gorgeous wedding dresses.

HANK. And they're always perfect.

JACK. Why?

HANK. Because they're always the same.

TIBBY. Hank . . .

HANK. I know, I should be ashamed of myself. I have a reputation. I'm not just some snitty little fashion designer. I'm considered America's ultimate class act.

TIBBY. And that's just what Donna Karan always says.

JACK. Donna Karan?

HANK. Donna is so brilliant. You should really have her do your gown.

SPENCER. Really?

HANK. Because then you can wear it to work.

SPENCER. No, I insist. It would be beyond good luck, or karma, it would be . . .

TIBBY. A blessing.

JACK. On us all.

HANK. Alright. I'll try. As long as everyone understands the difference between fashion and style.

SPENCER. Which is?

HANK. Fashion is for followers.

JACK. Yes, Yoda?

HANK. But style, real style, in anything, in everything, baby, style is all about you. (*Tibby and Spencer look at each other, thrilled. They clutch each others' hands and squeal.*)

JACK. What an evening. Our daughter engaged. And Hank doing her gown. And do you know the only thing that could make our happiness even more complete? (*Myra runs in.*)

MYRA. (*Pointing to herself.*) Maid of Honor? Get It? Maid? Maid?

TIBBY. Myra.

MYRA. Worth a shot. (*Myra exits.*)

JACK. The thing that will make our happiness even more complete is that I'm having Myra throw some things into a bag because tonight—I would like Spencer to come with me. To Washington.

SPENCER. Why?

JACK. Okay, but before I tell you, I just want all of you to picture something. It's four PM and I'm sitting in my office, in my domain, and I'm gazing at the acres of Brazilian mahogany paneling, and at the silver-framed photos of me and all of the other senior partners, in Aspen, on skis, and at the view from the wraparound windows of a corner office on the seventy-second floor. And all I kept thinking was, I know why those windows are sealed shut.

TIBBY. Darling?

JACK. Because I get this horrible feeling, and it's not just some mid-life thing. Because I mean, I've worked incredibly hard, I've earned my trophies, I'm at the top of my game. This is where all of you agree with me.

SPENCER, TIBBY and HANK. Oh yes, of course, you're doing great, you're the best, etc.

JACK. But I need more. I need excitement. I need something. And then— my assistant buzzes me and she says, get this—it's the president on line four.

TIBBY. The president of . . . ?

JACK. The United States. Or at least some of them.

SPENCER. And?

JACK. And at first I'm thinking, am I in trouble? Is it tax evasion or insider trading or witness tampering, did I do something so terrible that they're actually having the president call me?

HANK. But did you do any of those things?

JACK. Maybe. During a blackout. I take these naps, and when I wake up, there are all these subpoenas. So I'm really flustered, but I say, of course I'll take the call. And I get on the line and I say . . . (*Dropping his voice to sound more macho and impressive.*) "Hello, Mr. President?"

HANK. Please tell me you didn't use that voice.

JACK. I'm a geek, of course I did. And then the President says, he says, "Jack, I need you."

TIBBY. He does?

JACK. It was like phone sex. And so I ask, "Are you alone?"

TIBBY. Jack!

JACK. No I don't. And hey, I'm not gay, but wouldn't it be cool to have phone sex with the President? (*Pretending to masturbate.*) "Iraq . . . Iran . . . clearing brush at the ranch . . ." Boom!

SPENCER. Daddy!

JACK. And okay, he's not my favorite president, and I deal with plenty of important people, but come on—it's the President. Our president. And he's asking for my help. (*To Spencer.*) For our help, because I need you to clerk for me.

SPENCER. On what?

JACK. Well, it's because my doctorate was in constitutional law, and I have a reputation. And so he asked me to help fine-tune a potential constitutional amendment.

SPENCER. Oh my God, oh my God, that's so mind-blasting. It's a once-in-a-lifetime, no, even better, it's a once-in-a-career opportunity. I mean, an amendment.

HANK. But what's it for?

SPENCER. Is it about stem cell research, and cloning? I'm not sure ex-

actly what I think, but could you imagine? Being able to create endless armies of the same person, all with exactly the same face and the
same mind and the same genetic makeup . . .

TIBBY. I know just what you're thinking . . .

HANK. Nantucket.

TIBBY. Yes!

JACK. No, he asked me if I could come up with a more workable and
ironclad definition of legal marriage.

TIBBY. Marriage?

JACK. Between a man and a woman. (*A beat.*)

HANK. Aha. (*The room becomes extremely tense.*)

TIBBY. Alright, as everybody knows, I have only one hard and fast and
absolutely unbreakable rule in this house: no talking about politics,
ever.

JACK. Exactly. And it's nothing to worry about, so you two just have a
wonderful time tonight out at whatever, and Spencer and I will be
back in town by dinner tomorrow.

HANK. Jack?

JACK. Hank, you don't get all hot and bothered over things like this, do
you?

HANK. Hot and bothered?

JACK. I mean, you've always been such a classy guy. And so discreet.

HANK. Thank you. I think.

JACK. And so masculine. Hell, you were a war hero. You've got a bronze
star.

HANK. And that was how I met Mike.

SPENCER. It was?

TIBBY. Oh yes.

HANK. We were kids, we were in North Carolina, basic training. And
we'd seen each other, nothing more. And we're walking back to the
barracks, after evening mess. And it's dark and I'm telling Mike that I
love the army, because it got me out of Illinois. And I ask him, so why

did you join up? And he stops and he stares at me. And there's no one around, and he grabs me, and he kisses me, real slow.

SPENCER. That's so hot.

TIBBY. It's so romantic.

JACK. (*Turned on.*) Whoa.

TIBBY. Jack?

JACK. And then you and Mike were together for all those years. And you didn't need to get married.

HANK. It wasn't an option.

JACK. But it didn't make any difference. And you were both so accomplished. I mean, Mike was a surgeon.

TIBBY. And so handsome . . .

JACK. And look at you, you're one of the world's most incredibly successful designers.

TIBBY. One of?

JACK. Okay, right now, I'm wearing your underwear, your necktie and your aftershave.

HANK. What about your socks?

JACK. Ralph Lauren.

HANK. (*A beat. He stands.*) Goodbye.

TIBBY. Hank!

HANK. No, I'm sorry, I love Ralph Lauren. And I love all of those little embroidered polo players which he puts on everything. Did you know that that polo player is actually a picture of Ralph? And that it's life-size?

JACK. Hank, I love you, you know that. And I consider you a member of our family. And this whole amendment business, it's just a precaution. The president just needs to send a message, to reassure people.

HANK. Which people?

JACK. Well, people on the right. Religious people.

TIBBY. But you know, I've never understood deeply religious people. And I mean, I admire them, and I think their faith is so amazing, but they pray and they pray . . .

SPENCER. And what, Mummy?

TIBBY. And they still look like that.

SPENCER. But wait. I think that I'm like most people, because I'm not sure how I really feel about gay marriage. But if I'm going to help Daddy, then I'd better figure it out.

JACK. Fair enough.

TIBBY. But we have to go out!

JACK. And we have to catch our flight.

SPENCER. But I mean, marriage. For anyone. It's so overwhelming. When Peter asked, "Will you marry me?," it was such an ultimate question.

JACK. It's big.

SPENCER. So what exactly makes a marriage? Is it just the ceremony, and the law? (*Myra enters; she's draped a towel over her head, as a nun's habit. She's now sweet, sincere and pious.*)

MYRA. I can help, because I have a perfect marriage, because I'm a bride of Christ. Jesus is the ideal husband, because he's always there. All through the day, there he is, and all through the night, there he is, he's there every second of my existence, until sometimes I want to scream, excuse me! Get outta here! I'm taking a dump, get a job! (*Very sweet again.*) Bless you all. (*Myra exits.*)

SPENCER. Hank, you and Mike, you were a couple for, what . . .

TIBBY. Thirty-eight years.

SPENCER. So, in your mind, were you married?

HANK. I . . . I don't know.

JACK. You see?

SPENCER. Mummy, why did you marry Daddy?

TIBBY. Why?

JACK. Darling?

TIBBY. I married your father because I was in love with him. And because—he surprised me.

JACK. I did?

SPENCER. How?

TIBBY. Well, when we met, I knew that he was this very traditional, very conservative and very ambitious man.

JACK. Translation: a total catch. Proceed.

TIBBY. I mean, the first time I saw him, he was wearing a LaCoste shirt, and then over that an Oxford cloth button-down, and then over that a crewneck Shetland sweater, and then a navy blazer, with another sweater tossed over the shoulders.

JACK. I was a preppy.

TIBBY. You were an igloo. And I knew that if I married him, it would make both of our families very happy. And that made me nervous.

JACK. She was nuts.

TIBBY. And Jack was just out of law school, and I was about to bolt. Until one night, at a restaurant, he introduced me to Hank.

SPENCER. (*To Jack and Hank.*) But how did you two know each other?

HANK. Well, for years I'd been working for other people, which I hated, but I was finally setting out on my own . . .

JACK. And he needed a lawyer . . .

HANK. And Jack was young·and hungry . . .

JACK. And I didn't even know Hank was gay.

HANK. You didn't?

JACK. Back then, I never thought anyone was gay. It just didn't occur to me. I mean, one time there was this man, in the locker room, and he was staring right at my crotch.

TIBBY. So what did you do?

JACK. I just said . . . (*Proudly.*) "Isn't it neat? And it gets bigger!"

SPENCER. You said that?

HANK. You lied?

TIBBY. And we all got along like mad, and then one Saturday afternoon, the two of them, they forced me to go ice-skating at Rockefeller Center. And they were both horribly mean to me, because I was so hopeless and they were both Olympic caliber. And then the rink played "The Blue Danube" and I just threw up my hands. And then . . . (*Jack stands and bows to Hank. Hank stands, and as Tibby sings the famous tune, the two men waltz together, in a professional-quality routine.*) Da da da da dum, da dum, da dum . . .

JACK, HANK and TIBBY. (*As Jack and Hank waltz, exuberantly.*) DA DA DA DUM, DA DUM, DA DUM . . .

TIBBY. And I just thought to myself, I have to marry that man.

SPENCER. Which one?

TIBBY. Either.

JACK and HANK. DA DUM! (*Jack and Hank end their waltz with an expert flourish.*)

SPENCER. And so why did you move in with Mike?

HANK. Well, we never really lived together, back then.

SPENCER. But why not?

HANK. It was a very different time. And we both had our careers. And so we'd switch off, and go to each other's apartments.

SPENCER. So it was really more of an arrangement.

TIBBY. Spencer!

SPENCER. Which is fine, but it's different from a marriage.

JACK. That's true.

HANK. Excuse me—is this a trial?

SPENCER. Why not? (*Myra enters, waving a gavel.*)

MYRA. Can I be the judge?

HANK. Did you go to law school?

MYRA. No . . .

SPENCER. Have you studied the Constitution?

MYRA. Not really.

JACK. Do you know anything about ethics or civil liberties or basic human behavior?

MYRA. Of course not.

TIBBY. Then you can be the president, but you can't be the judge. (*Myra exits.*)

SPENCER. Mummy, why did you decide to have children?

JACK. *(To Tibby.)* Go.

TIBBY. Well, as I think everyone is aware, my own mother is clinically insane.

SPENCER. Nana?

TIBBY. I love her to pieces, and I know that she did the very best she could, but she was evil.

JACK. Tibby?

TIBBY. She told me that I shouldn't be afraid of lipstick, or a dramatic evening eye.

HANK. That's not so bad . . .

TIBBY. I was four. And when I learned how to read, she said, don't tell anyone. And when I was anorexic, she said, "Good for you! Keep going!"

SPENCER. She did?

TIBBY. And she's been married five times!

JACK. She's a trip.

TIBBY. And so I wanted desperately to have a child of my own, so we could do it right. So we could make you feel loved and safe and special, every day of your life.

SPENCER. And you did! *(Myra enters, dramatically, wearing a shawl.)*

MYRA. I had a child. But I was only a child myself, and so I put my perfect baby up for adoption. And I watched from a distance as my precious bundle grew into a handsome, successful young man. But, until this moment, I have never revealed myself. Because I was terrified, that if my son ever found out that I was a maid, it would ruin his life.

HANK. *(Standing, choking back tears, to Myra.)* Mama?

MYRA. Don't look at me!

HANK. But I've always dreamed of this moment. When at last I could take you in my arms, and ask you the most important question which any child can ever ask . . .

MYRA. Yes, my own sweet baby boy?

HANK. (*Hopefully.*) Does this mean—I'm Jewish?

MYRA. *Shalom,* baby!

TIBBY. (*To Myra.*) Out! (*Myra exits.*)

SPENCER. (*To Hank.*) And did you and Mike ever want a family?

HANK. May I address the court?

SPENCER. Please.

HANK. Your Honors, children are God's gifts. They're sunshine. There is nothing more beautiful than a child's laughter, or a newborn baby's smile.

SPENCER. Hank?

HANK. And the only reason that Mike and I never brought the perfect miracle that is a child into our home is that—*I hate them.*

TIBBY. Hank!

HANK. I'm sorry, and Spencer, you were a delightful child, and Mike adored all of his little nieces and nephews, and I tried to love them, but—eew! It's those squeaky little voices and those sticky little hands, and all of those questions: (*Imitating children's voices:*) "Why don't you have an Xbox?" "Why can't I jump on the sixteen-thousand-dollar antique chair?" "Why is Uncle Hank drinking so much?"

JACK. I hear ya! (*Hank turns away.*)

HANK. No.

TIBBY. Hank?

HANK. I'm sorry, it's just that usually, whenever I'd say things like that, Mike would smack me. Or kick me. And he didn't.

TIBBY. Which is why we should stop all of this, right now.

HANK. No, I'm fine, really. I should be able to talk about Mike, without falling apart.

TIBBY. Are you sure?

HANK. Spencer?

SPENCER. Just one more question, if it pleases the court.

JACK. Counselor?

SPENCER. Mummy, have you ever cheated on Daddy?

TIBBY. Spencer!

SPENCER. It's a critical issue!

JACK. Tibby, you don't have to answer that . . .

SPENCER. But you're asking me to help rewrite the Constitution.

HANK. Yes you are.

SPENCER. (*To Tibby.*) So have you?

TIBBY. (*Distraught.*) Well—could I get a sip of water?

SPENCER. Mrs. McCullough?

TIBBY. This is very hard for me . . .

JACK. Tibby . . .

TIBBY. (*As Hank brings her a glass of water.*) With lime? (*He hands her the water, with lime.*) Thank you, you're very kind. So I'll just say it, just right out loud . . .

HANK. Oh my God . . .

TIBBY. No! I have never cheated on my husband! Dear God in heaven, what is wrong with me?

SPENCER. Never?

TIBBY. I've been so busy!

SPENCER. And Mr. Hadley?

HANK. What?

SPENCER. Did you ever cheat on Mike?

HANK. Hey, we were two men, in New York, it's a very different story . . .

SPENCER. So the president may have a point . . .

JACK. Go team.

TIBBY. Hank, this is none of Spencer's business, it's none of anyone's business . . .

HANK. Do you really want to know? The juicy details? Can you handle it?

TIBBY. Hank?

JACK. Both barrels.

SPENCER. Shoot.

HANK. When we first met, we were wild for each other. Every day, every night, every room, every backseat. Bodies, hands, heat. You know what I mean? Spencer?

SPENCER. Well, yeah!

TIBBY. Spencer?

SPENCER. Freshman year.

HANK. But as the years go by, you look up. You look around. Because there are a lot of very attractive men out there.

TIBBY. Yes there are.

JACK. Tibby?

TIBBY. (*To Jack.*) Oh, darling, not in our building.

JACK. Thank you.

HANK. And so Mike and I, we made a deal. Because haven't you ever loved someone completely, but you wanted someone else too? Haven't you ever said, I want true love and adventure and lust, we're only here once, I want it all?

JACK. Tibby?

TIBBY. Yes, darling?

JACK. Can we be gay?

TIBBY. When you retire.

HANK. And you know where it led us? All of that sex and drama and prowling?

SPENCER. Where?

HANK. Right back to each other. Because at the end of the day, it's all about the two of you . . . and HBO.

TIBBY. You see? Case closed. Taxi!

HANK. Until . . .

SPENCER. Until?

TIBBY. Until what?

JACK. Wait.

HANK. It was almost exactly ten years ago. My birthday. A big one. And so to celebrate, Mike and I, we have a wonderful dinner, and we decide, what the hell, let's go dancing. And so we head downtown, to a club, and it's packed, and everyone has their shirts off, and they're all twelve. But we don't care, because we're together and we're having a blast, and then I'm fighting my way to the john and I brush past this kid, and he says, "Troll."

TIBBY. Oh no!

HANK. And I crashed. And I just think, am I the oldest human being on the planet?

SPENCER. No!

TIBBY. Of course not! (*Myra enters.*)

MYRA. There's a woman in Peru.

HANK. Thank you. (*Myra exits.*) And the very next day, I meet this boy.

TIBBY. You never told me about this . . .

JACK. Watch out.

HANK. And he's blonde and he's cute and he worships me, because guess what he's wearing?

TIBBY. What?

HANK. His Hank Hadley jeans.

SPENCER. I love them!

TIBBY. They're like a drug!

HANK. And so I call him and I say, "I know, let's have lunch at the Plaza."

SPENCER. Lunch at the Plaza?

HANK. And dessert.

TIBBY. Oh my God!

HANK. And we're finishing our lunch and I've got a room reserved upstairs and I'm feeling evil and predatory and unbelievably happy, and suddenly I hear . . .

JACK. "Hank?"

HANK. And it's Jack. And he's seen everything. And as the boy is off getting our coats, Jack says to me . . .

JACK. "Don't."

SPENCER. Daddy?

HANK. And at first I'm outraged, it's my life, how dare he, and then he says . . .

JACK. "Now, I don't know anything about this gay stuff, about this lifestyle, about this sordid underworld, but Mike is just so much way hotter."

TIBBY. You said that?

JACK. I did. And I said, "There will always be boys, what are they called? Ding Dongs?"

HANK. Twinkies.

JACK. "But there's only one Mike. And it's not worth it."

HANK. And I knew that Jack was right, goddamnit, so I put that boy into a cab and I went home.

TIBBY. To Mike. You see?

JACK. Almost. Because Hank, I'm not saying that you guys didn't share something fantastic and special, but the president is talking about traditional marriage.

HANK. Meaning?

SPENCER. Meaning, I guess, did you live together, were there children, were you faithful, including failed attempts . . .

JACK. Did you even want those things?

HANK. Wait . . .

TIBBY. Please, everyone, this is getting very dangerous . . .

JACK. But I'm not saying that I agree with the president, not at all. I'm just saying that I'm willing to hear him out, and if and when it's appropriate, to lend a hand.

HANK. And Spencer?

TIBBY. (*To Spencer.*) Be careful . . .

SPENCER. Here's my closing: I love you and I loved Mike, maybe because you weren't like my parents, because you were something else. Maybe something even more exciting . . .

JACK. Excuse me? We're exciting. We've tried cocaine.

TIBBY. And fondue.

SPENCER. But I think that what I want, for Peter and myself, is—a marriage. Because most of my friends, all of their parents are divorced, or they hate each other. Like, Amanda Fleischmann's mother actually stabbed her father, chopped him up, and put the pieces in a dumpster.

HANK. But why?

SPENCER. He gave her no emotional support.

EVERYONE. (*In complete understanding.*) Oh, of course, duh, can you blame her, etc.

SPENCER. So I've always felt so lucky, and even weird, because my parents had incredible friends, like Hank and Mike, and because you have . . . (*To Jack and Tibby.*) a great marriage.

TIBBY. And so will you!

JACK. In your Hank Hadley gown.

SPENCER. And as for the amendment, it's a very complicated, provocative matter. And it's not a partisan issue—almost every state, red, white and blue, they've all passed a Defense of Marriage Act.

TIBBY. But is that really a good argument . . .

JACK. (*To Tibby.*) Hold that thought.

SPENCER. I'm not sure. And so I need to hear from both sides. And so I need to go to Washington. All in favor? (*Jack and Spencer raise their hands.*) Mummy?

TIBBY. Of what?

JACK. Spencer, stop putting your mother on the spot, you know she doesn't really understand anything legal.

HANK. Tibby?

TIBBY. I . . . I really don't.

JACK. So verdict postponed!

TIBBY. But I do know this: Marriage is a mystery. But we are all friends, and we all love each other, and that trumps everything. And I do know one legal term—court adjourned. (*Myra enters, with two carry-on bags, which she hands to Jack and Spencer.*)

MYRA. All packed!

SPENCER. Oh Myra, do you think that you'll ever get married?

MYRA. To who?

SPENCER. I don't know, maybe a doorman.

MYRA. Get out.

SPENCER. It could happen!

MYRA. No, I mean it—get out.

TIBBY. Is it chilly? Do I need a bracelet?

JACK. And Hank, come on. You and Tibby—you're not political people. You've never marched or signed petitions, have you?

HANK. God no.

JACK. (*To Hank and Tibby.*) And okay, the two of you, tell me, right now— who's our congressman? (*Hank and Tibby look at each other.*)

TIBBY. We know this . . .

HANK. We've met him at parties, a hundred times . . .

SPENCER. (*Trying to help them.*) He's tall and attractive . . .

JACK. He's an outspoken liberal . . .

TIBBY. It's on the tip of my tongue . . .

HANK. I can see him . . .

TIBBY. Richard Sibley!

JACK. No! He's not a congressman! He owns all of those boutique hotels.

TIBBY. But he was indicted.

JACK. You see? So the two of you go to your parties, with the pretty people. And we'll go to ours, with the president.

JACK and SPENCER. (Tingling.) OOOO!!!

SPENCER. And maybe we should ask the president, why did he get married? Or maybe not, I'm sorry, you guys, bridal fever, I'm just hanging on for dear life.

JACK. (*To Tibby.*) I'll call you. And don't you dare worry about any of this amendment business. (*To Hank.*) I miss Mike. (*Jack and Spencer exit.*)

MYRA. (*To Tibby.*) You must be so proud.

TIBBY. Don't start. (*Myra exits, into the apartment.*)

HANK. Tibby?

TIBBY. I'm sorry about all of this, it's just too much to cope with, so I have an idea—let's just not think about any of it right now, let's just go. We're already late for everything—shall we?

HANK. (*Not quite sure.*) Shall we?

TIBBY. Hank? (*Hank is now holding a large, expensive, etched crystal bowl, which had been set in a place of honor.*)

HANK. This was a gift, wasn't it?

TIBBY. My very favorite. From you and Mike. For our twenty-fifth wedding anniversary.

HANK. And it's a symbol of your marriage and our friendship.

TIBBY. Which is why I treasure it.

HANK. Yet at the moment, I have this strange urge to lift it up very high . . . (*He does.*) And then smash it to bits.

TIBBY. Why?

HANK. I think most of all because you just asked me why. (*He lifts the bowl again.*) This might just feel so satisfying . . .

TIBBY. Please, don't! (*Hank lowers the bowl.*)

HANK. I can't. And do you know why?

TIBBY. Hank?

HANK. Because Mike was right.

TIBBY. About what?

HANK. About you and me and all of us. Because when he was angry, he'd say that we deserved each other.

TIBBY. Hank, you're not actually bothered by Jack and Spencer and all of their nonsense, are you?

HANK. But what about my nonsense? And yours? And the fact that we listened to theirs?

TIBBY. Hank, please, I'm begging you. While you were gone, the whole six months, I didn't go anywhere. Or see anyone. I didn't leave the house.

HANK. Why not?

TIBBY. I couldn't. I didn't want to. It seemed—inappropriate. Unfaithful.

HANK. Tibby?

TIBBY. Do you remember what you told me, all of those years ago, at my very first fitting, for *my* wedding dress?

HANK. What?

TIBBY. I still barely knew you, and I was so nervous and so intimidated. And I was wearing a lime green turtleneck with tiny hot pink strawberries . . .

HANK. (*Horrified at the image.*) Don't!

TIBBY. And you were on the phone, and my hands were sweating, and so I picked up what I thought was a paper napkin, only it was . . .

HANK. Three-hundred-dollar-a-yard white China silk . . .

TIBBY. I'm sorry! I'm still sorry!

HANK. And you kept hovering and fidgeting and making these strange little noises . . . (*Tibby makes these noises.*) And finally I just said, sit!

TIBBY. And I did, right on a stack of just-finished sketches for your fall collection . . .

HANK. *Somewhere else!*

TIBBY. And I just burst into tears and I started to run out and you said . . .

HANK. Stop! Wait! Idiot girl!

TIBBY. Yes?

HANK. What do you want?

TIBBY. I want . . . I want . . . I saw this ad, in the *Times*. A full page. And it was a picture of this beautiful girl, in the sunlight, and she's wearing this stunning wedding dress, and she's sitting on a bench in Central Park. And you, you're wearing a great glen plaid suit and a knit tie, and you're sitting right next to her. And the two of you, you're sort of leaning together, and your heads are tilted back, and you're both laughing, not fakey, we-know-we're-having-our-picture-taken laughing, but a real gut-buster. And I was so jealous of that girl, I hated her, because she looked so gorgeous, and so happy, and because she was with you. And because maybe those are all the same thing. And then I saw, down in the lower right-hand corner, these three words. And to this day, that picture and those words, that is all I have ever wanted to be:

HANK. "Very Hank Hadley."

TIBBY. Yes.

HANK. And when you said that, oh my Lord, you wicked, vicious little creature, in your tortoiseshell headband and your debutante pearls . . .

TIBBY. Don't!

HANK. I was yours.

TIBBY. (*Gesturing to the door.*) So shall we? Can we? Please?

HANK. Baby, I would love to, I want to, the thought of seeing you, of being us, it's the only thing that's been keeping me sane. But it's just—Jesus! This thing with Jack. It touched a nerve.

TIBBY. How?

HANK. Over all of our years together, the only fights Mike and I ever had, the only serious ones—they were always over things just like this.

TIBBY. Like what?

HANK. Like the fact that I didn't want to live together, or have kids, and the fact that I would introduce Mike as my friend.

TIBBY. But what's wrong with that?

HANK. He said it made us sound like Quakers.

TIBBY. No!

HANK. And the only time that Mike and I almost broke up was when I made a gown for Nancy Reagan, for one of the inaugural balls . . .

TIBBY. But you're a designer, that's your job. And I thought it was a very great honor. (*Myra pokes her head into the room.*)

MYRA. A ninety-eight-pound, sun-damaged, sixty-four-year-old woman. Strapless. The nation thanks you. (*A beat.*) I'll go. (*Myra exits.*)

HANK. It's just, all of those years, whenever these things would happen, I would tell him, I come from nothing, I have to build my career, or I'd say, look, we don't live in a perfect world, we have to respect other people's feelings, or finally I'd just yell, Jesus Christ, I design ladies dresses, what the hell do you want from me?

TIBBY. Exactly!

HANK. And he would say, very quietly, I want the best. The best possible behavior. The best possible everything. Because I love you. And because I'm not ashamed of that.

TIBBY. Hank—listen to me. I am married to Jack McCullough. And despite everything he says and everything he does, I actually love Jack McCullough, So I am no stranger to shame.

HANK. Tibby?

TIBBY. And over the years, sometimes every morning, I ask myself—has he gone too far? Is today the day, when I leave him, when I shoot him, when I start screaming and can't stop?

HANK. And what about Spencer?

TIBBY. Well, I have a friend. And her daughter turned out to be a thief and a liar and a paranoid schizophrenic.

HANK. Oh no.

TIBBY. I was so jealous. But I love Spencer so much.

HANK. And so do I, and I love Jack, but how do you put up with it? Where do you draw the line?

TIBBY. I don't, I call you.

HANK. But when Mike collapsed, and I rushed him to the hospital, to his own hospital, there was a moment when they wouldn't let me see him. Because I wasn't a member of his immediate family.

TIBBY. But, but—you're famous. Didn't someone recognize you? Wasn't someone wearing you?

HANK. One blouse.

TIBBY. Oh my God!

HANK. And I called my lawyer, but there was a second, more than a second, when I thought, what if he dies? While I'm still in the waiting room, frantically working my cell phone?

TIBBY. But that didn't happen.

HANK. But do you know the worst part? I swear, the real reason I couldn't break that bowl?

TIBBY. What? Why not?

HANK. Because I don't know if I really believe in marriage, for anyone. If you love someone, that's a very private thing, it's the most private thing. So why should you announce it and legalize it and club it to death with a ceremony? I mean, if you want to kill something beautiful, just add crab cakes and God.

TIBBY. Hank!

HANK. And I think that it's really absurd for two men. Because I went to a gay wedding.

TIBBY. You did?

HANK. And there were candles, and wind chimes. And there were the two grooms, right, and they were both wearing tuxedoes and these rainbow-striped bowties. And I thought they were waiters.

TIBBY. Of course.

HANK. And then the lesbian minister, she asks, "Do you, Daniel, take Barry as your life partner, on your journey to coupleness?"

TIBBY. Coupleness?

HANK. I swear. And they wrote their own vows. And I wish I could forget them, but they're burned into my brain. Because Daniel says,

> "I will fly like a man-dove
>
> To Barry, my man-love
>
> I will set out a man-plate
>
> For Barry, my man-mate
>
> And I will build us a man-house
>
> For Barry, my man-spouse."

TIBBY. Please stop!

HANK. I can't! Because the ring bearer was their golden retriever, and their bridesmaids were all bears, these huge, hairy men wearing sleeveless, plaid flannel shirts and carrying bouquets! And I just had to get out of there!

TIBBY. But then why are you so upset?

HANK. Because I always felt that, among the four of us, the two couples, that there was a certain equality. A respect. Only now I'm starting to feel like a servant. (*Myra enters.*)

MYRA. So how do you think I feel?

HANK. Myra, you are a servant.

MYRA. Oh really? How do you know that I'm not actually a top secret agent for a sinister foreign government? How do you know that I'm not infiltrating a powerful American home, for the purpose of eventual terrorism?

TIBBY. Because then you would dust. (*Myra exits.*)

HANK. For the first time I feel like I'm just someone convenient, to take you to parties. That I'm your walker.

TIBBY. You're my life!

HANK. I'm sorry, I'm not like this, you know that, I don't believe in this sort of ranting and raving. But it's just that I, I thought I was starting to get beyond this, to find some distance . . .

TIBBY. From what?

HANK. This whole marriage thing. Mike thought it was important. He thought that we needed, that I needed—to acknowledge that part of my life.

TIBBY. But you're allowed to disagree with him, you disagreed about lots of things, that's what couples do . . .

HANK. But when Mike was lying there, on that last night, when he'd finally agreed to the morphine, and he was sort of floating, thank God, and sometimes he didn't even make that much sense. But then he looked up at me and he squeezed my hand and he smiled. And with his very last words, he said, he asked . . .

TIBBY. What?

HANK. "Will you marry me?"

TIBBY. And what did you say?

HANK. I . . . I sputtered, I was so surprised, I just said, "Mike . . ." and then—he was gone. And I knew, in that split second, why I never wanted to get married. Because sometimes, marriages end. And if we weren't married, we'd never grow old, or get tired of each other, and we'd certainly never die . . . We'd just always be on some sort of eternal first date.

TIBBY. Yes.

HANK. And then, I don't know why, but I got so angry at Mike, I wanted to argue with him, about all of it, and I said, "Wait a minute," because if we could still fight, he was still here. And that's how it's been, ever since. I fight with him, I accuse him of terrible things, I sulk, and then, when I'm at work and something funny or awful happens, I think, Mike will love this, and I reach for the phone. Sometimes I even let it ring, on the demented off-chance that . . . I used to think that one of the reasons I loved designing clothes, doing something so endlessly superficial, was that it was a sort of protection. Against the serious bad stuff. But it's not.

TIBBY. Oh, Hank.

HANK. So what do I do?

TIBBY. What we always do.

HANK. Tibby?

TIBBY. We get up, we get dressed, and we go out.

HANK. How? Why?

TIBBY. Because that's who we are. And that's how we cope. Mike is gone. Jack is impossible. And Spencer, God help her, is getting married.

HANK. I'm sorry, but I need to beg off. Not tonight.

TIBBY. *(Calling out.)* Myra! (*Myra enters, carrying Tibby's fur and Hank's coat.*)

MYRA. But I think that she's absolutely right. I think that you should just ignore all of the terrible things in this apartment and this country and this world, and that you should put on your fancy, gorgeous clothes and get out there and have the very best time you can!

TIBBY. You tell him!

MYRA. And you should dine and dance and get your picture in the paper!

TIBBY. Looking terrific!

MYRA. And when you see a desperate, drug-addicted, alcoholic insane person, what will you say?

TIBBY. "Hello, Muriel, we're so glad we could come!"

HANK. Really?

MYRA. Your boyfriend, he saved lives—big deal. You're a great American designer. Do you know what that means?

HANK. What?

MYRA. It means that you draw pictures of drop-dead beautiful dresses, and then five-year-olds in China sew the sequins onto the sleeves. And then the sleeves are shipped to Mexico, where ten-year-olds attach them to the jackets. And then the final product is shipped to Neiman Marcus, where it's loaned out to a nineteen-year-old soap opera star, who wears it to the Golden Globes. Where it's photographed by the tabloids, and then knocked off for one-tenth of its original price, so that the cheap copy can be worn by an Arizona hooker to a trailer park wedding. And after she spills Tabasco on it, the copy gets torn into rags and shipped back as a T-shirt for that little five-year-old in China. Who can therefore brag to all of his little Cantonese friends . . .

TIBBY. "I'm wearing a Hank Hadley!"

TIBBY and MYRA. YAY!!!

MYRA. So you get out there, because you're not just a label or a brand or a trademark, you're a legendary symbol!

TIBBY. Of taste and style and joy!

MYRA. So fuck unhappiness!

HANK. Fuck unhappiness!

TIBBY. Fuck global warming!

HANK. Fuck global warming!

TIBBY. And fuck everyone in the world who's younger and prettier than we are!

MYRA. I would love to!

TIBBY. And you see this fur? I feel terrible. Because this animal was tor-
tured and mutilated and killed.

MYRA. That's true . . .

TIBBY. So it deserves a night out!

MYRA. With its friends! (*Myra opens the front door and Tibby exits, grandly.
Hank is about to follow her, and just as he's almost through the door, he stops.
He pauses, as Tibby returns, confused.*)

TIBBY. Hank? (*Hank smiles—he's just had an idea.*)

HANK. Let's not. (*Curtain.*)

ACT TWO

Scene 1

Several months later. Spencer, looking disheveled, with her hair yanked back in a ponytail, is pacing back and forth, making phone calls on her cordless headpiece. She's been at it all morning, getting nowhere. The room is littered with fabric swatches, possible place settings, sample slices of wedding cake, bridal magazines, and several vases of grotesquely dead flowers.

SPENCER. *(Into her headset.)* Hello, it's Spencer McCullough, calling about the flowers . . . yes, again . . . still? Really? That's a very long lunch. Yes, just tell him I called. *(She hits speed-dial for another call.)* Hi, Spencer McCullough about the cake . . . the wedding cake . . . my wedding cake . . . well, why don't you know? Fine, just leave word. *(Calling out.)* Myra? Myra! I'm dying! I'm having an anxiety thing, I need decaf! *(To herself.)* I need Xanax. *(She digs a bottle of pills out of her purse. She looks around for a beverage; she dumps some flowers out of a vase, and uses the water in the vase to swallow her pills.)* Myra! *(Another call.)* Spencer Mc-Cullough, for Hank . . . yes, I know I just called five minutes ago and yes, I know that I've been calling every five minutes for the past three hours, so *where is he?* And don't just say you'll leave word, and don't . . . hello? Hello? *(Tibby enters from the front door, wearing a trench coat, oversize sunglasses and a scarf over her hair.)*

TIBBY. Did you get through?

SPENCER. Do I look like I got through? Oh Mummy, I'm sorry, I didn't mean to snap at you . . .

TIBBY. On my way to the hairstylist I even went by Hank's showroom. But there was no one there, only the receptionist. And there were racks and hangers and mannequins, but—no dresses.

SPENCER. No dresses?

TIBBY. It was a wasteland. And then I stopped by the florist, because I was supposed to compare the calla lilies, the French peonies and the freesia, and—it was closed. Locked up tight. And in the window, where Antonio always has some glorious arrangement, well, it was there all right, lilies and lilacs and white tea roses . . .

SPENCER. But that sounds perfect!

TIBBY. All plastic. Dusty, grimy plastic. In a coffee can.

SPENCER. No!

TIBBY. It was like staring into New Jersey. And then I finally got to the salon, but Daniel was out sick, and so were Scott, Jonathan, Eric and Emile Jean-Jacques, you know, the one with all the attitude, what's his real name?

SPENCER. Dwayne.

TIBBY. Yes. But there was only one person working, some sort of temp, a woman named Debbie.

SPENCER. Debbie? Where has she worked? Who does she do?

TIBBY. I asked her, and she said that she used to own her own shop, called Debbie's Curl Up and Dye. In someplace called Bayonne. She said that she was semi-retired, since the accident, but that Daniel had called her, and that her doctor thought it would be good therapy.

SPENCER. For what?

TIBBY. Her Parkinson's.

SPENCER. Okay . . .

TIBBY. So I assumed because of Daniel that she was at least competent, even with, well . . .

SPENCER. What?

TIBBY. The missing fingers.

SPENCER. And? (*Tibby slowly removes her head scarf, revealing that she now*

has very little hair, and that what's left has been greased, spiked and dyed a
screaming mercurochrome red.)

TIBBY. Is it—alright?

SPENCER. Mummy, it's going to be fine.

TIBBY. It is?

SPENCER. I'm a lawyer.

TIBBY. *(Seeing herself in a mirror, she screams.)* Oh my God!

SPENCER. Mummy, something terrible is going on, all over the city. I've
been calling my travel agent and my shrink and my Pilates instructor
and I can't find any of them! And the caterer and the hotel liaison
and the music coordinator have all turned off their phones and none
of my bridesmaids have been able to find Hank or their dresses! And
Mummy, my wedding is tomorrow! *(Hank knocks on the front door and
enters. He's wearing elegant, casual clothes and he's in a terrific mood, jaunty
and gleeful.)*

SPENCER and TIBBY. Hank!

HANK. Kids?

SPENCER. I've been trying to reach you all morning . . .

TIBBY. We've been calling and calling . . .

HANK. And there's no one downstairs. I just walked right in.

SPENCER. Oh my God . . .

TIBBY. Hank, what is going on?

HANK. Well. You know, I've been all out of sorts, over the fact that for the
past two months now, Spencer and Jack have actually been working
on that amendment. And I hate being out of sorts, don't you? And so
I called a few friends, and then they called a few friends, and so forth
and so on, and, well, here's what we were all wondering. What would
this city, what would this world, be like, without gay people? I mean,
what if all of them, what if all of us, what if we all just decided to, oh,
say, take the day off? *(The front door opens and Marietta Claypoole staggers in. She's ordinarily an imposing, impeccably groomed grande dame—she's
Tibby's mother. But at the Moment she's wearing a large black or orange plastic*

garbage bag as a dress, which has been somewhat tailored with duct tape. She's carrying a ratty Kmart shopping bag as a purse, and wears two shoe-boxes on her feet as shoes. She's wearing an orange rubber traffic cone as a hat. When Tibby, Hank and Spencer first glimpse her, they don't recognize her and scream in terror.)

TIBBY and SPENCER. AHHH!!!

TIBBY. Stay back!

SPENCER. We don't have any money!

MARIETTA. Tibby. I'm your mother! *(Marietta removes the traffic cone from her head, although her hair retains the towering beehive shape of the cone.)*

TIBBY. Oh my God . . .

SPENCER. Nana?

HANK. Rough day?

MARIETTA. Hank!

HANK. Darling.

TIBBY. Mother?

MARIETTA. I . . . I . . . I don't now if I can even . . . you have no idea . . .

SPENCER. Nana?

TIBBY. Deep breath.

MARIETTA. I was all prepared for the most marvelous afternoon. I was going to a matinee, of that sensational new musical, I was going with Robert DuMaurier . . .

TIBBY. The shoe designer?

MARIETTA. Of course. Only he called to cancel. He said that there was some sort of unspeakable emergency.

HANK. A fire? A heart attack?

MARIETTA. I don't know, I assumed that it involved shoes. So to fill in, I called Kevin VanDevere . . .

SPENCER. Your stockbroker?

MARIETTA. And then Windham Crowley . . .

TIBBY. Your ophthalmologist?

MARIETTA. And Carstairs Mellon . . .

TIBBY. Isn't he dead?

MARIETTA. I was desperate! Because they were all busy! And I kept howling into the phone, but I have seats for a musical! It won fifteen Tony Awards, including Best Supporting Actress in a Slow Year! And they were still busy! And so I decided, it's the modern age, I don't require an escort, so I arrived at the theater and my *Playbill* was filled with all of these little scraps of paper—announcing that the entire company, and all of their understudies, they were all out of the show!

HANK. But how odd.

MARIETTA. And the curtain rose on an empty stage, and the stage manager walked out and he described what was supposed to be going on.

HANK. Which was?

MARIETTA. He said that usually there was dancing and lip-synching and a standing ovation, and then everyone would rush into the lobby and buy a mug.

HANK. But they didn't?

MARIETTA. No! And I couldn't bear it, so I ran from the theater and I thought, I'll just see something else this evening, something fabulous. And so I called my ticket person and I said, I know, what about that wonderful new one-person show, it's gotten raves in the papers . . .

HANK. Starring?

MARIETTA. Cherry Jones.

TIBBY. I love her.

MARIETTA. Cancelled! And so I asked, well, what about that Shakespeare, from the National, I hear it's miraculous . . .

HANK. The one with Ian McKellan?

MARIETTA. Closed!

SPENCER. Oh no!

MARIETTA. And I said then please, get me a single for that revival, of that marvelous, classic comedy, you know, the one with . . .

TIBBY. (*With apprehension.*) Nathan Lane?

MARIETTA. Dark! And I asked, but what about Matthew Broderick, isn't he going on?

HANK. And?

MARIETTA. And they said he wanted to, but he's afraid of Nathan Lane!

HANK. Really?

MARIETTA. And my ticket person, he said that if I wanted to see anything, that there was only one show performing on all of Broadway.

HANK. And what was it?

MARIETTA. David Mamet.

TIBBY, SPENCER and HANK. (*Aghast.*) NO!

MARIETTA. And there was only one show left off-Broadway.

HANK. Which one?

MARIETTA. Neil LaBute.

TIBBY, SPENCER and HANK. NO!!!

MARIETTA. And then I had a fitting for my dress for tomorrow . . . (*To Hank.*) at your showroom. And the receptionist told me to stand behind a curtain and take off all of my clothes. It reminded me of my favorite childhood game.

SPENCER. Which one?

MARIETTA. (*Fondly.*) It was called "Stand Behind the Curtain and Take Off All Your Clothes." So I did, and then I waited and waited and finally I emerged—and she was gone!

HANK. The receptionist?

MARIETTA. And so were all of my things! And this bag was all I could find to wear, and these shoeboxes. And I stumbled into the street and I ran right into my dearest friend, Evelyn Sheffield. And she stared at me, and she pointed at my outfit and she just said one word.

HANK. Which was?

MARIETTA. "Prada?"

HANK. I see it.

MARIETTA. So I staggered up the steps of St. Patrick's Cathedral and I hurled myself into a confessional. And I pleaded, forgive me, Father, for I have sinned. I am a vain and a foolish woman, but surely I do not deserve this! To have my entire existence usurped, disemboweled, destroyed! No tickets? No clothes? Give me a penance, give me a prayer! (*She holds out her hands, indicating "and there was no response."*) And I peered through the grill and I saw . . . I saw . . .

SPENCER. What, Nana?

TIBBY. What did you see?

MARIETTA. I saw a rabbi! And he said, "I'm sorry, but all of the priests are out today. But I can get you a pair in the orchestra for the Mamet play."

TIBBY, SPENCER and HANK. NO!

MARIETTA. (*In agony.*) What is happening? (*Jack enters, from the front door. He is frazzled and disheveled, but he's trying desperately to appear manly and decisive, a true leader in a time of great crisis.*)

JACK. All right, everyone—just stay calm.

HANK. Why?

JACK. I don't know if any of you have been out there, in the world, but something very strange is happening.

MARIETTA. It's a catastrophe . . .

TIBBY. You have no idea . . .

SPENCER. It's a nightmare . . .

HANK. (*To the women.*) Shhh! Quiet! (*The women shut up. Then, to Jack:*) What's happening?

JACK. I can't quite put my finger on it, but—people are missing.

HANK. Really? Who? Which people?

JACK. Well, when I left here this morning, I went downstairs, and the doorman wasn't on duty. Or the elevator man. And then, when I went to get a coffee, at the place on the corner, only one girl was working, and she was completely overwhelmed. And then, I get to the office, and I try to have a meeting, with three of the junior partners, but they're all out. And I start to think about it, I start to think, what could all of these people have in common. And then, like a light bulb, like a flash of lightning, it hits me. And I know just what's going on.

HANK. What?

JACK. (*Decisively.*) Avian flu. It's happening! It's here!

TIBBY. Sweetheart?

JACK. Don't panic, I think there are pills, or shots, the important thing is
   that we all pull together and don't handle poultry . . .

SPENCER. Daddy . . .

JACK. We can get through this, it won't affect the wedding, we can all
   wear those surgical masks like Michael Jackson.

HANK. Jack?

SPENCER. Daddy?

JACK. What?

TIBBY. It isn't bird flu.

JACK. It's not?

HANK. All of those people, the ones who were missing . . .

JACK. Yes?

HANK. They're all gay.

JACK. What?

TIBBY. It's because of you, and that amendment on gay marriage. All of
   the gay people are taking the day off!

MARIETTA. Wait. Is this all about gay marriage?

HANK. Yes.

MARIETTA. But that's wrong. I'm sorry, but gay people are not ready
   for marriage.

HANK. But why not? How do you know?

MARIETTA. Because I have been married to five gay men, and they were
   not ready.

JACK. Wait. Let me understand this. All of the gay people are taking the
   day off? Or is it just the men? What about the lesbians? (*Myra enters,
   from within the apartment. She wears street clothes, and pulls a small piece
   of luggage on wheels. She struts towards the front door, singing, vaudeville-
   style.*)

MYRA. TOOT TOOT TOOTSIE GOODBYE

  TOOT TOOT TOOTSIE DON'T CRY . . .

JACK. *Myra?*

TIBBY. You're a lesbian?

SPENCER. You're a lesbian?

HANK. You're a lesbian?

MYRA. You got it!

MARIETTA. I just thought she was lazy!

TIBBY. But Myra, why didn't you tell us?

MYRA. You never asked. And so I'm taking the day off!

SPENCER. But you can't! We have so much to do, for my wedding!

MYRA. What wedding?

TIBBY, SPENCER and MARIETTA. *Hank!*

TIBBY. *(To Hank.)* How can you do this?

HANK. You gave me no choice.

JACK. Wait a minute, wait just one minute! Are you telling me, are you actually trying to claim that all of the gay people in New York City know each other?

HANK. Of course not. That's ridiculous.

JACK. That's better.

HANK. In the *world.*

MYRA. I have a Rolodex. Ask me about a lesbian.

TIBBY. Ellen DeGeneres.

MYRA. Funny. Bright.

SPENCER. Rosie O'Donnell.

MYRA. She says what she thinks.

HANK. Jack's mother.

JACK. *(In disbelief.)* My mother?

MYRA. HOT.

JACK. She is not gay!

HANK. Then why did she leave your father?

JACK. They grew apart.

MYRA. And why has she lived with another woman for the past twenty-five years?

JACK. For companionship.

HANK. And why do they have sex?

JACK. It's a one-bedroom apartment!

MYRA. We're everywhere. Think about it, people. For years now, a lesbian has been vacuuming your rugs, washing your china and making your entire home shine. (*She lets loose with a demonic cackle.*) And just think about all of the other legendary gay maids, nannies and housekeepers.

JACK. Like who?

HANK. Tell 'em!

MYRA. Hazel. Rosie, that robot maid on *The Jetsons*. Alice on *The Brady Bunch.*

TIBBY. But Alice had a boyfriend—Sam the butcher.

MYRA. Sam the beard. And the others, they're always called Mrs. Something or Other, only you never see their husbands. Mrs. Danvers. Mrs. Potts. Mrs. Butterworth.

SPENCER. The maple syrup lady?

MYRA. And do you know who she lives with?

TIBBY. Whom?

MYRA. Mrs. Paul.

HANK. It's love!

JACK. Oh my God.

MYRA. And what about Mary Poppins?

MARIETTA. Was Mary Poppins a lesbian?

MYRA. Actually, she was bi. It depends which way the wind blows.

TIBBY. But Hank, and Myra, you're both part of our family.

MYRA. The second cousins. The poor relations.

TIBBY. No! We love you and include you, but now, on the day before a huge family celebration—you sabotage everything?

HANK. We're making a point. And we're not really claiming that all gay people know each other. In fact, we're all very different. But if we can't get married—why should you?

MARIETTA. But I do love gay people. And they've given the world so much. Poetry, and architecture . . .

HANK. And music . . .

MARIETTA. (*Passionately.*) And *drapes.* (*As everyone stares at her.*) What?

HANK. Let's stop it. All of these stereotypes can be extremely harmful. Especially because they're almost always just outright lies. Although, Tibby . . .

TIBBY. Hank?

HANK. I'm sorry, I was just thinking about this room.

JACK. Why?

HANK. Oh, it's lovely now. But in a few years it might require some— freshening. Updating.

MYRA. Something new.

MARIETTA. And if this, this boycott continues . . .

TIBBY. Oh my Lord.

MYRA. No. You'll be fine.

HANK. Because you can just hire a straight decorator. And he will do a terrific job.

JACK. Exactly!

HANK. And everything in this room—will recline.

TIBBY. Never!

HANK. And there'll be a foosball table in the corner, and a giant plasma screen on that wall . . .

JACK. That sounds great!

HANK. And for a bold contemporary touch, I'm going to say it, my mouth is forming the word, this is what you have to look forward to . . .

TIBBY. Hank, no! Mother, don't listen!

MYRA. Here it comes!

HANK. IKEA.

TIBBY, MARIETTA and SPENCER. (*Screaming in horror.*) AHHH!!!

SPENCER. But I don't care about any of that, not right now. Because I'm supposed to be getting married tomorrow, and I don't have lilies or busboys or a gown! They're being held hostage! '

TIBBY. And I'm not sure, but I think, I feel like, if all of this keeps going, that I'm in very real danger—of losing my best friend.

HANK. Tibby?

TIBBY. Hank?

HANK. Are we really friends?

TIBBY. I don't know.

JACK. Friends don't stop the city.

MARIETTA. And friends don't ruin weddings.

MYRA. And friends don't work on amendments.

SPENCER. Well, I'm putting a stop to all of this, right now, and do you know how? I'm calling my fiancé, Peter Perryman. Because he's only the most powerful investment banker in America. The president is going to name him the next Secretary of the Treasury. And he'll take care of all of this, once and for all.

HANK. And where is he?

SPENCER. (*Still very confident.*) I'm not sure, I've been trying to reach him all morning . . . (*As the light dawns.*) Oh my God . . .

MYRA. *Mazel tov!* (*Jack's cell phone rings.*)

JACK. Hold on. (*He answers the phone.*) Yes? Yes? Of course I'll take it. (*To the room.*) It's the President.

TIBBY. Oh my God!

JACK. (*To everyone.*) Shhh!!! (*Into the phone, using his deeper, manly voice.*) Hello? Mr. President?

HANK. Oh my God . . .

SPENCER. Tell him!

MARIETTA. Tell him what's going on!

JACK. (*To the room.*) Shhh!!! He's my friend! (*Into phone.*) I'm sorry, that was my mother-in-law, she's being recycled . . . what? Oh no . . . oh my Lord . . . yes, of course, you too . . . (*He smiles and blushes.*) Stop . . . goodbye. (*He hangs up.*)

TIBBY. Jack?

HANK. What did he say?

JACK. He said that something very strange is happening in Washington. He said that since this morning, no one has been able to find at least five governors, a Supreme Court Justice, or the vice-president's daughter.

MARIETTA. (*Stunned.*) The vice-president's daughter?

MYRA. I'm warning you.

JACK. What?

MYRA. Do not look in my room.

JACK. And almost the entire Navy has gone AWOL.

SPENCER. The Navy? But why?

TIBBY. (*The light dawning.*) It's the only armed force named after a color.

HANK. Ahoy baby!

JACK. And what if this thing keeps growing, and spreading, all across the world? What if there are suddenly no gay people anywhere . . .

SPENCER. In France . . .

MYRA. Latin America . . .

TIBBY. England.

EVERYONE. (*Regarding England.*) WHOA!

JACK. This has gone far enough! This is endangering global security! And the president asked me to deal with it.

TIBBY. He did?

JACK. And I know just how I'm gonna do it. Because this all comes down to one person. Hank?

HANK. You're absolutely right. Because this does all come down to one person. Tibby?

TIBBY. What?

HANK. Tibby, you've heard from Myra, and me . . .

JACK. Way too much!

HANK. And we've heard from your husband and your mother and your daughter, and we've even had a call from the president of the United States.

JACK. (*Proudly.*) Who has my number!

HANK. Yes he does. Because at the moment, the president and his posse, they're all following fashion. Which is easy. And scary. And Tibby, you are my dearest friend, And so I want you to show me what that means. I want you to show me how far that goes. And I want you to stand for something.

TIBBY. But how?

HANK. Show some style.

SPENCER. Oh no. No no no. I love her, but Mummy isn't good in a crisis. She'll just make fun of everything.

JACK. And she's the most wonderful woman in the world, but she doesn't even have a degree.

TIBBY. Excuse me?

JACK. Art History?

MARIETTA. And she's my one, perfect, gorgeous angel, but she's silly and flighty and completely useless.

TIBBY. Mother?

MARIETTA. (*To Tibby, sincerely.*) That was my dream for you.

HANK. How about it, Tibby?

MYRA. Are they right?

HANK. Is that who you are? Is that all you are?

JACK. Tibby, tell him the truth.

TIBBY. (*To Jack, and Hank.*) Are you asking me to choose? Between the two of you? (*Everyone.*) Between all of you?

HANK. Tibby, you can do this. I know you can. Because I know you better than anyone.

JACK. You do not!

HANK. I can put you in satin. I can put you in red. I can make you the most glamorous woman in America.

JACK. But I can give you an orgasm.

MARIETTA. Hank just did!

HANK. I know what you dream about. I know who you want to be.

JACK. Mrs. Jack McCullough!

HANK. Someone very Hank Hadley!

MARIETTA. My darling baby daughter!

SPENCER. The mother of the bride!

TIBBY. But I'm all of those things!

MYRA. In what order?

HANK. And which one comes first?

TIBBY. That's a terrible question!

JACK. (*To Tibby.*) Should I ask Hank to leave?

MYRA. Should I ask Jack to bite me?

TIBBY. No! I don't know! Hank, you've got to do something!

HANK. I already have. Your turn.

TIBBY. But you're not being fair!

JACK. (*To Hank.*) And haven't you caused enough chaos?

HANK. Not yet.

JACK. (*To Hank.*) Hey, you wanna take this outside?

HANK. (*Shoving Jack.*) What's wrong with right here? (*As Jack and Hank begin preparing for a physical fight;*)

TIBBY. What do you two think you're doing?

MYRA. Are they insured?

JACK. Designer!

HANK. Lawyer!

JACK. Pansy!

HANK. Lawyer!

JACK. Pussy!

HANK. Lawyer!

JACK. That's not fair! He keeps winning!

MYRA. Get used to it!

TIBBY. Who are you people? What are you? I thought I had a family, I thought I had a best friend, but—look at you! Look at me!

MYRA. Watch out, she's gonna blow . . .

JACK. Sweetheart, just calm down . . .

TIBBY. Calm down? Calm down? How can I calm down? You are all selfish and self-absorbed and impossible! And you're all thrilled with yourselves!

MARIETTA. (*Grandly, to the others.*) You should all be ashamed.

TIBBY. And I will give you all exactly one second to tell me why I shouldn't walk right out that door!

SPENCER. Because I need my wedding!

MYRA. Because I need a raise!

MARIETTA. Because I'm wearing a garbage bag!

JACK. And because I need my wife!

TIBBY. And Hank?

HANK. I told you what I need. I need the girl I met thirty years ago. I need the beautiful, spirited, hilarious woman whom I take on the town. I need the only woman who ever made Mike jealous. But what I don't need is some spineless, people-pleasing, dithering little society bitch. (*Everyone starts to talk at once, very aggressive, a rising furious hubbub. All of the following should be simultaneous until Tibby's exit:*)

JACK. (*To Hank.*) . . . Are you calling my wife a bitch? . . .

HANK. . . . If that's what she wants to be! . . .

SPENCER. . . . Mummy could never be a bitch! . . .

MYRA. . . . Try scrubbing toilets—that's a bitch! . . .

MARIETTA. . . . My daughter is not a bitch—she takes after me!

JACK. . . . I don't think you really know Tibby, or any of us, at all! I don't think you know what you're talking about, I think you're acting like a self-righteous, overbearing asshole! You have no real idea about the issues on the table . . .

HANK. . . . I'm more married to her than you are, you pompous, reactionary blowhard! All I'm asking for is some acknowledgment, all I'm asking for is for Tibby to wake up and smell the betrayal, your betrayal . . .

MARIETTA. . . . Why are we only focusing on Tibby? Has anyone ever stopped for a moment to consider my day, and my upheaval, and my trauma? I have appeared in public, on the streets of New York, dressed in the contents of a dumpster! There should be an investigation; there should be legal action . . .

SPENCER. . . . Excuse me! I'm the one getting married! I'm the one whose life is being nuked! I'm the one who's facing a church without a single white tea rose and a reception with twenty-five empty chafing dishes! I'm the one whose fiancé has been kidnapped, or brainwashed . . .

MYRA. . . . You people make me sick! You have too much time, too much money, and maybe fifteen brain cells! Do you know what it's like, working for you, do you even consider the emotional toll, do you know what it's like, picking up your underwear, changing your sheets, looking for change in your sofa, you should all trying living my life, for a day, for an hour . . . (*By this point, Tibby has exited. As the front door slams, everyone stops talking, stunned. After a beat:*)

JACK. (*To Hank.*) This is all your fault . . .

HANK. (*Outraged.*) My fault? (*Tibby reenters, livid and determined.*)

SPENCER. Mummy?

TIBBY. Spencer, I love you very much, but first of all, I want you to stop whining and whimpering. Because the world doesn't owe you a wedding.

SPENCER. What?

TIBBY. And Mother, you raised me and I owe you my life, but I want you to stop treating me like a brain-damaged child.

HANK. I'm with ya!

MYRA. Damn right!

TIBBY. And Myra, you are going to start cleaning in the corners!

MARIETTA. (*To Myra.*) It's called a Swiffer!

HANK. Bravo!

TIBBY. And Hank, I think you've got a thing or two to learn about friendship. And respect. And destroying people's lives. So you're going to call up all of your little buddies, up and down the entire Eastern seaboard, because they're all going right back to work, by tomorrow morning.

JACK. (*To Tibby.*) Thank you. Because I know that wasn't easy. And Hank, maybe now you'll finally understand something. Tibby made her choice for the very best reasons. Because I'm her husband. And we're married.

TIBBY. And Jack, you're going to call your new best friend, the president of the United States, and you are going to tell him that you and Spencer are off that amendment.

JACK. (*Shocked.*) Why?

TIBBY. Because you're right. We are married. And if that's what gay people want—let 'em learn! Because you know something? Marriage sucks. Raising a family sucks. And falling in love sucks. And you know why? Because we're all gonna die. But before I do, I wanna look gorgeous. I want hair and makeup and dresses and diamonds, I wanna make the biggest drag queen of all time say, honey, too much. I want a world that doesn't exist, that can't exist, a world where everyone's happy, where everyone's children are perfect, where everyone's mother is perfect, and where everyone's husband has fantastic sex with her, pays for everything, tells her she's beautiful, and leaves. I wanna live inside a Hank Hadley advertisement in the September issue of *Vogue*, the issue that weighs eighteen pounds because it's so packed with lies. That's what I want, and all of you, that's what you're gonna give me. Because I'm a rich white woman, and goddamnit, that's good. We're gonna make it good. And we're gonna have a wedding, because weddings are gorgeous and glorious, and that's how we trick people into getting married. So you just call the president, and you just tell him—I need flowers! I need music! And may God help me, I need cake! (*Myra hands the phone to Tibby, who hands it to Jack. Blackout.*)

Scene 2

Place: The same. The next morning. We hear a joyous, propulsive, wedding-themed song, such as "Going to the Chapel" sung by the Dixie Cups, playing on the apartment's sound system, as the debris of the previous scene is removed, and the wilted floral arrangements are replaced with extravagant displays of all-white flowers. Myra enters, back in her uniform. As she straightens the room, plumping pillows and checking the flowers, she sings along or lip-synchs for a verse, using a feather duster as a prop. As the song ends, the doorbell rings, and Myra opens the front door. Hank enters, very ebullient, wearing formal wedding attire.*

HANK. Have you been out there? Down there on the street? There must be hundreds of reporters, and all of those TV news crews. Since yesterday, this is the wedding of the year! People were cheering: "Hank, we love you! You go, Hank!" Except for this one woman, who ran right up to me and screamed, "Hank Hadley, you're going to burn in hell!"

MYRA. And what did you tell her?

HANK. I said, "Good. We'll have lunch."

MYRA. Very nice.

HANK. But Myra, aren't you excited? It's all done, everyone's gone back to work, and the wedding is going to be flawless.

MYRA. You haven't heard?

---

*See Special Note on Songs and Recordings on copyright page.

HANK. Heard what? I've been at my showroom all morning, wrangling bridesmaids.

MYRA. And no one called you?

HANK. About what?

MYRA. Okay. Last night, after he called the president, Jack went out.

HANK. To get some air. To blow off steam.

MYRA. He still isn't back.

HANK. All night? And he hasn't called?

MYRA. Not a word. Tibby's barely holding it together. But she still told Spencer to get dressed.

HANK. But are they going ahead with the ceremony? And what about all those people downstairs? (*As Myra throws up her hands and exits into the apartment, the front door opens and Marietta enters. She's now completely restored to her customary, elegant self. She wears a dazzling Hank Hadley gown, and her hair and makeup are impeccable.*)

MARIETTA. What a glorious morning.

HANK. Marietta . . .

MARIETTA. I know. You can't decide. Which is more beautiful—the woman? Or her Hank Hadley gown? (*As Hank is about to answer.*) Don't answer. It's a mystery.

HANK. Jack isn't here.

MARIETTA. What?

HANK. No one has seen him. Not since last night.

MARIETTA. Oh no. (*Tibby enters, completely stunning in her own Hank Hadley, her hair and makeup restored to perfection.*)

TIBBY. Everyone?

HANK. Have you heard anything?

TIBBY. Nothing. I've called the police and the hospitals, but he hasn't turned up.

HANK. We will find him, everything will be fine . . .

TIBBY. I'm sure. But it's just—right before Jack left, do you know the last thing he said to me? He was still furious, over everything that had happened. So he asked, "Remind me—why did we get married?"

HANK. Oh no . . .

MARIETTA. My poor baby . . . (*As she goes to Tibby, she catches herself.*) No!

TIBBY. Mother?

MARIETTA. Yesterday, when you accused me of treating you like a child, I was devastated. Because you were absolutely right. And so I went home, and I drank a glass of wine, three fingers of bourbon, and an entire bottle of scotch.

HANK. Marietta?

MARIETTA. I don't believe in drugs.

HANK. Of course not.

MARIETTA. And this morning when I awoke, refreshed, I made a momentous decision. I vowed that I would change. And that from this day forward, I would treat you strictly as an adult, for the rest of our lives.

TIBBY. Oh Mother, do you really mean that?

MARIETTA. I do!

TIBBY. Because you're still drunk?

MARIETTA. (*Proudly.*) I am! (*Spencer enters, in her knockout Hank Hadley wedding gown, very upset.*)

SPENCER. Mummy? Hank? Nana?

TIBBY. Look at you . . .

HANK. Spencer . . .

TIBBY. Hank, you have outdone yourself . . .

MARIETTA. (*To Spencer.*) You are perfection . . .

SPENCER. But—I can't get married.

TIBBY. Darling, I just know your father will be here any second, we just have to have faith . . .

SPENCER. And I'm trying to, but—it's not just that.

TIBBY. Darling?

HANK. Is this because of yesterday, when you couldn't find Peter?

SPENCER. No. Yes.

MARIETTA. Darling, there is no shame in marrying a gay man. As long as he went to a decent school.

TIBBY. Mother—well, actually, that's true . . .

SPENCER. But Peter's not gay. I couldn't find him because—he got scared, about getting married. He said that with the wedding and the gown and the money everyone's been spending, that it's all starting to feel like—a human sacrifice. And so he'd run away, to his family's cabin upstate, to think about everything.

HANK. And what did he decide?

SPENCER. He decided that—he loved me. And that everything else was all up to me.

TIBBY. And do you love him?

SPENCER. Yes. More than anything. Isn't that strange?

TIBBY. Not at all.

MARIETTA. That's how you know when you're in love. When it's strange.

SPENCER. But I can't decide what to do, and I can't get married—not without Daddy. (*The front door opens, and Jack enters. He's wearing his same clothes from the previous scene, from the day before.*)

TIBBY. Jack!

SPENCER. Daddy!

HANK. At last!

MARIETTA. Thank God!

(*As everyone moves towards Jack, he gestures for all of them to stay back.*)

HANK. Where have you been?

TIBBY. All night long? (*Myra enters.*)

HANK. Are you all right?

MYRA. We're supposed to be having a wedding!

TIBBY. (*To Jack.*) And are we?

SPENCER. Daddy?

JACK. Spencer, when all of this started, all of those months ago, when you put marriage on trial, there was one question which you never got to ask.

TIBBY. What?

SPENCER. Oh my God.

HANK. Spencer?

SPENCER. Daddy, have you ever cheated on Mummy?

JACK. Yes.

TIBBY. When?

JACK. Last night.

HANK. Last night?

MARIETTA. Oh my Lord.

MYRA. (*Finding a chair and sitting.*) I really shouldn't be here. No, Myra, stay.

JACK. After I called the president, I was so angry. At everyone and everything, but especially . . . (*To Tibby.*) at you. So I went out.

TIBBY. For a walk.

JACK. For revenge. And I kept walking, spitting bullets, until I got to the Plaza. And so I went inside, to the bar. And sitting there, all by herself, was a stunningly beautiful woman.

MARIETTA. I really don't think we need to hear this . . .

TIBBY. I think we do.

JACK. And so we started talking, and drinking, and she admitted—that she was working.

TIBBY. She was a prostitute?

MYRA. I love this!

HANK. Myra.

JACK. And I thought, why not? Maybe even better. And so I took a room, a suite, on the seventeenth floor. And we went in, and I asked, how much? And she named a figure. And we started to haggle.

TIBBY. Jack?

MARIETTA. (*Regarding haggling.*) You have to.

JACK. Because I said, I want extras. And I said, how much would you charge to tell me that gay marriage is a ridiculous idea. And she said, that's fifty bucks extra. And I asked, and how much would you charge to tell me that all of the gay people going out on strike is not the way to solve anything, and she said, that would be two hundred extra.

MARIETTA. Was there a pimp?

JACK. And I said fine, let's do it, all of it. And she asks me to unzip her dress. And as I start to, I see the label, inside. And I stop.

TIBBY. Because of the label?

HANK. Because it says, "Hank Hadley."

JACK. Yes. And I stop because—it shocks me. Because it made me think about the man who designed that dress. And our friendship. And about how I had insulted him. And so I asked that woman, how much would you charge to tell me that I'm an idiot? And that my wife is so much smarter than me, and that I'm very lucky to be married to her, because otherwise, I would be—nothing. Rich, handsome, wildly successful nothing. (*A pause.*) Incredibly well-educated, polished yet still masculine, driven yet ultimately sensitive nothing. (*A pause.*) Dashing, stalwart, bullheaded yet always somehow adorable nothing.

TIBBY. And the hooker said?

JACK. "Go home."

HANK. She did?

JACK. And so I paid her, and she left.

MARIETTA. Did you tip her?

JACK. Fifteen percent.

MARIETTA. That's plenty.

JACK. And I spent the rest of the night and this morning just working up my courage. To face you. All of you.

SPENCER. And we have to get to the church.

TIBBY. Why?

SPENCER. Because I'm just like Daddy.

JACK. (*Touched, to Spencer.*) Sweetheart.

SPENCER. I'm an idiot. So I'd better get married. Because just like Daddy, I need someone to stop me. To say everything that no one else is allowed to say.

HANK. Are you sure?

SPENCER. (*Becoming very emotional.*) Yes. Because I love all of you. And I love Peter. And most of all, more than any feeling I think I've ever had—I love this dress. (*Spencer exits, out the front door.*)

JACK. Our little girl.

TIBBY. I know.

MARIETTA. (*Very moved, touching her heart.*) Her first marriage.

HANK. Marietta, do you think that you'll ever get married again?

MARIETTA. (*Flirtatious.*) Hank?

HANK. No, not to me.

JACK. But Marietta, why did you marry so many gay men?

MARIETTA. Oh, why does anyone get married? Because you meet someone, and they're kind, and they have house seats.

TIBBY. Mother?

MARIETTA. But you know, since yesterday, I think I'm really beginning to understand, this entire situation. Because, thanks to Hank and his friends, I've realized that all gay people want is the freedom to love. And I'd like to do my part, I would like to appear on television, as a spokesperson, and tell the world, rally round! Because everyone should marry a gay person! (*To Hank.*) You're welcome! (*Marietta exits, out the front door.*)

TIBBY. Myra, would you get our things? (*Myra exits.*)

JACK. Are we okay?

TIBBY. We will be.

JACK. I was talking to Hank.

TIBBY. (*To Jack.*) Get out.

JACK. Hank?

HANK. Save me a waltz.

JACK. Good Lord. (*Noticing what he's wearing.*) I should change. (*Myra enters, carrying a garment bag with Jack's formalwear; she hands it to him.*)

MYRA. At the church.

JACK. But all of you, be careful. Because what would happen if one day, all of the straight, white guys disappeared?

TIBBY. I don't know . . .

HANK. That's a tough one . . .

MYRA. World Peace? Kidding! (*Jack exits, out the front door, as Myra exits, into the apartment.*)

TIBBY. Spill it.

HANK. What?

TIBBY. Are you furious? Are you sorry? Do you hate me?

HANK. Why?

TIBBY. Because it didn't really work. Spencer told me this morning—that after Jack called him, the president just found another lawyer.

HANK. But Jack still made the call. And sooner or later, there will be gay marriage. And gay divorce, and gay pre-nups, and pretty soon gay people will start asking themselves, what were we thinking? And then the president and all of those fierce little evangelicals, they'll be on to something else.

TIBBY. I hate them.

HANK. Don't. That's too easy.

TIBBY. So what should we do?

HANK. Well, Mike always said that he wouldn't waste his time hating conservative idiots or liberal idiots. He said that the only person he'd ever truly hated was—me.

TIBBY. You? But why?

HANK. Because he loved me. And because he said that there was a part of me that was genuinely snobbish, that watched people and made vicious, superficial judgments. I think that we all have that part of us.

TIBBY. The fun part.

HANK. Of course.

TIBBY. And now?

HANK. And now I think that Mike might just be a little bit proud. Of both of us.

TIBBY. Not me. I'm an awful person. A rich white woman. And I'm not a very good friend.

HANK. Me neither.

TIBBY. But would you like to know why I finally stood up to Jack? And why I told him he had to make that call?

HANK. The wedding?

TIBBY. Mike.

HANK. How?

TIBBY. I thought about how much I miss him. And I thought about how, even though you don't like to go on about it, and even though you're a very tough customer, I thought about how much you must miss him.

HANK. Good thinking.

TIBBY. And I thought, what if Jack died?

HANK. Tibby?

TIBBY. Would I be a suspect?

HANK. Get in line.

TIBBY. If Jack died, despite everything, I would be heartbroken. Forever. But if you died, I wouldn't be.

HANK. Good to know.

TIBBY. Because my heart would be gone.

HANK. Please.

TIBBY. You see? You hate it when things get direct and emotional. And sentimental.

HANK. And disgusting.

TIBBY. It makes you a perfect target.

HANK. Don't you dare.

TIBBY. I'm going to say it.

HANK. I'm not listening . . .

TIBBY. Here it comes . . .

HANK. I'm leaving . . .

TIBBY. I love you.

HANK. And I love you.

TIBBY. Really?

HANK. In that dress.

TIBBY. Shut up! (*Myra enters, now dressed in her own knockout Hank Hadley creation, a gown or maybe a cocktail dress. She also carries Tibby's purse and wrap, which she hands to her, or places nearby.*)

MYRA. Can I just say something? I think that this dress, and all of these dresses, they're disgusting. They're almost impossible to wear, they have all sorts of built-in corsets and boning, and they have nothing to do with comfort, durability or a real woman's body. Like all high fashion, they're the deranged product of male homosexual fantasies, which conspire with the male heterosexual power structure to imprison women in outdated iron maidens of silk and chiffon. And as a woman and a lesbian and a human being, I am offended, repulsed and outraged! Oh, and one more thing!

HANK. Yes?

MYRA. I look so hot! (*Myra exits, out the front door.*)

TIBBY. We lead the most ridiculous lives.

HANK. And it gets worse.

TIBBY. How?

HANK. When all of this began, I decided to actually read the Constitution.

TIBBY. (*Impressed.*) You went to the library?

HANK. Please. I Googled it. And I looked at all of the other twenty-seven amendments. And most of them are very big-hearted; they free the slaves, or give women the vote. And the one that tried to stop people from doing something, Prohibition, that one didn't work out so well.

TIBBY. Can you imagine? No liquor anywhere? Not even a cocktail?

HANK. What would we do?

TIBBY. (*Thinking about it.*) We could drive.

HANK. And then I went even further back, to the Declaration of Independence. Remember that line? "We hold these truths to be self-evident, that all men are created equal—" (*To Tibby.*) sorry, ladies—"that they are endowed by their Creator with certain inalienable rights . . ."

TIBBY. Their Creator?

HANK. Don't start. And it says that among those inalienable rights, the ones we're all endowed with, are "life, liberty, and the pursuit of happiness." And when I read that, do you believe I wept, but then I had the most awful thought. And I was so ashamed of myself, because I am just so politically askew, but when I read that wonderful, perfect goal, "life, liberty and the pursuit of happiness," do you know what I thought?

TIBBY. Of course. It's so gay.

HANK. Exactly!

TIBBY. It's like a party invitation.

HANK. We could've written it.

TIBBY. And you know, maybe that's the whole problem with this country, and with this world.

HANK. What?

TIBBY. That no one listens to us.

HANK. It's just wrong. It's just sad.

TIBBY. Remember that "Very Hank Hadley" ad, from all those years ago? That girl in the wedding gown, and you, in the park? I have finally realized what the two of you were laughing at.

HANK. What?

TIBBY. Everything. (*Hank opens the front door.*)

HANK. Shall we? (*As joyous music is heard, Tibby and Hank execute a brief dance step, and Tibby exits. Hank glances at the room, smiles and exits.*)

CURTAIN

E NAKED EYE REGRETS ONLY THE NEW CENTURY JEFFREY I HATE H
LHALLA THE MOST FABULOUS STORY EVER TOLD THE NAKED EYE RE
LY THE NEW CENTURY JEFFREY I HATE HAMLET VALHALLA THE MOST
US STORY EVER TOLD THE NAKED EYE REGRETS ONLY THE NEW CE
FFREY I HATE HAMLET VALHALLA THE MOST FABULOUS STORY EVER
E NAKED EYE REGRETS ONLY THE NEW CENTURY JEFFREY I HATE H
LHALLA THE MOST FABULOUS STORY EVER TOLD EYE RE

SEVEN

The New Century

US STORY EVER TOLD THE NAKED EYE REGRETS ONLY THE NEW CE
FFREY I HATE HAMLET VALHALLA THE MOST FABULOUS STORY EVER
E NAKED EYE REGRETS ONLY THE NEW CENTURY JEFFREY I HATE H
LHALLA THE MOST FABULOUS STORY EVER TOLD THE NAKED EYE RE
LY THE NEW CENTURY JEFFREY I HATE HAMLET VALHALLA THE MOST
US STORY EVER TOLD THE NAKED EYE REGRETS ONLY THE NEW CE
FFREY I HATE HAMLET VALHALLA THE MOST FABULOUS STORY EVER
E NAKED EYE REGRETS ONLY THE NEW CENTURY JEFFREY I HATE H
LHALLA THE MOST FABULOUS STORY EVER TOLD THE NAKED EYE RE
LY THE NEW CENTURY JEFFREY I HATE HAMLET VALHALLA THE MOST
US STORY EVER TOLD THE NAKED EYE REGRETS ONLY THE NEW CE
FFREY I HATE HAMLET VALHALLA THE MOST FABULOUS STORY EVER
E NAKED EYE REGRETS ONLY THE NEW CENTURY JEFFREY I HATE H

THE NEW CENTURY was produced by Lincoln Center Theater at the Mitzi E. Newhouse Theater (Bernard Gersten, Executive Producer; André Bishop, Artistic Director) in New York City, opening on April 14, 2008. It was directed by Nicholas Martin; the set design was by Allen Moyer, the lighting design was by Kenneth Posner; the costume design was by William Ivey Long, the original music and sound design were by Mark Bennett; the general manager was Adam Siegel, the stage manager was Stephen M. Kaus; and the production manager was Jeff Hamlin. The cast was as follows:

HELENE NADLER	Linda Lavin
DAVID NADLER/SHANE	Mike Doyle
ANNOUNCER	Jordan Dean
MR. CHARLES	Peter Bartlett
JOANN MILDERRY	Christy Pusz
BARBARA ELLEN DIGGS	Jayne Houdyshell

Contents

Pride and Joy

PLACE

A high school or community college conference room or small auditorium on Long Island. A sign or banner hangs on a wall or curtain; the banner has the initials: P.L.G.B.T.Q.C.C.C. & O.

TIME

Early evening, a weeknight.

Lights up on Helene Nadler, an attractive Long Island matron, seated on a folding chair. Helene is smartly dressed and accessorized; she's a proud, intelligent, well-spoken woman. She can be gracious, charming and, when necessary, enraged. She speaks to the audience.

HELENE. Good evening. Hi. My name is Helene Nadler, and if I seem a little nervous, it's because this is my very first time here at a meeting of the Massapequa chapter of the Parents of Lesbians, Gays, Bisexuals, the Transgendered, the Questioning, the Curious, the Creatively Concerned and Others. Of Color. With Colds. No, I'm sorry, I'm kidding, maybe we should just call this group, "Why Jimmy Has No Friends." I'm kidding! Because we are all proud, because we are all special. And I am here to tell you, to prove to you, that I am the most accepting, the most tolerant, and the most loving mother *of all time.* Bar none. *You hear me?*

Oh, I know what you're thinking, each and every one of you, you're thinking your child was different, your little *bubbe* went through tough times, your little sweetheart was a total nightmare and you were still warm and nonjudgmental and loving and hugging and giving them self-esteem—well, fuck you. You are nothing. And you will bow down! (*Pulling herself together.*)

I'm sorry. It's just, well, you'll see. What I've been through. It all started ten years ago, with my eldest child, my daughter, Leslie. "Leslie"—what was I thinking? She was twenty-two, she said, "Mother"—so I knew it wasn't happy talk, "Mother, I have something to tell you. I'm a lesbian." And I took a deep breath and I said, Leslie—look at yourself. You're a professional tennis player, you have two cats, named Alice and Mrs. Dalloway, you live with a female social worker and you have the same haircut as a twelve-year-old Amish boy. Of course you're a lesbian. I've been telling you that for years. Helen Keller would know you were a lesbian, from the stubble. And she was so happy, she said, so you don't hate me? And I said, of course I hate you, but not because you're a lesbian.

I hate you because you're so boring. Why can't you be like Melissa Etheridge or Ellen Degeneres, okay, it's always pants, but at least they're Prada. They're cute! They're fun! And we're both thrilled, because it's all out in the open, we're free, we're clean, well, not their apartment. I said, girls, what is that aroma, kitty litter and patchouli? Is that some new Glade spray, Country Fresh Lesbian? Jodie Foster Number Five? But I don't care, I still visit, I sit on their couch, because I am the most loving mother of all time! Wait.

One year later, my middle child, my son, Ronnie, he comes to me. "Ronnie"—do I learn? And he says, Mom, I have something to tell you. And I say, you're gay, it's swell, no problem, *Angels*, Elton John, *Will and Grace*—I loved that show, it was adorable, it was like if Pottery Barn sold people. But Ronnie says, no, it's not that. He says, I was born into the wrong body. And I say, so was I, it's called Atkins, get over it. And he says, no, I was born into the wrong gender. I was meant to be a woman. And I have to sit down. I mean, Ronnie is six three with a beer gut and hairline problems, and all I'm thinking is, Ronnie, which woman? Ed Asner? And he says, Mom, can you imagine what it's like, always feeling so uncomfortable, so totally out of place, he says, Mom, think how you felt when we had to spend Passover with Daddy's family, in New Jersey, and I say, Ronnie, chop it off! If you want a vagina, here's the Visa!

So a year later, I'm riding high, I'm thinking, look at my beautiful family, there's Leslie and Marsha, that's her partner, they announced it in the *Times*, did you see the photo? "Dennis the Menace Marries Opie." And they're having a baby. They wanted to make sure it was multicultural, so at the sperm bank they requested Vietnamese, Jamaican or Nigerian, I said, great, they can just attach the sperm to the menus and slide it under the door. But I'm thrilled for them, and in comes Ronnie, excuse me, Veronica, in her pale yellow ruffles and her pearls, and I just think—she's lovely. And I'm so proud of her. And where do you find a wrap skirt in that size? And then she says, and Mom, I want you to meet someone, my girlfriend, Renee. And in walks this pretty little thing, she's a flight attendant on United, and I say, excuse me, and Veronica says, and I'm also a lesbian. And I pause and I say, Ronnie, didn't you take the long way around? And she, see, I said she, she says, no, when I was a man, I could never enjoy sex with a woman, but now that I'm a woman, I think it's the most beautiful experience ever. And I'm thinking, Jesus Christ, for what we spent on hormones, I could've had a new kitchen. And Marsha starts eyeballing Renee and Veronica's getting all huffy, and Leslie's got morning sickness, and I'm about to jump out the window but I go into the powder room, I splash some water on my temples and I say, Helene—you can do this. You are the most incredible, loving mother on earth, you can go for the gold, for the platinum, and I burst back into the room and I say, you are all so wonderful and so special, and the front door opens, and it's my baby, my David, and he says, Mom, I have something to tell you.

And I'm giddy, I'm flying, I say, so what could it be, you're gay, you're transsexual, you're a pregnant Nigerian lesbian flight attendant—the woman they could never fire. Whatever you are, I love you. And he says, okay, first off, I'm gay. And I say, yawn. Next. And he says, I am also—seriously into leather. And I say, great, I'm into fur. And he says, no, I'm the president of the International Order of Gay Leathermen, which is dedicated to the practice of bondage, sadomasochism, verbal abuse and scatology. And Veronica looks at Leslie, who rolls her eyes and says, "Yale."

And David says, my personal favorite is scatology. (*To the audience.*) This is the clincher. This is my Purple Heart, my Nobel Prize in motherhood! He says that scatology involves enemas. People peeing on each other. And worse. Use your imagination. No, don't. And I look at him, and for a second I lose it, I become so intolerant, I become my mother, and I say, David, in this house we use the toilet, not a friend from Tribeca! And David says, it's all completely safe and careful, it's about the erotic aspects of defecation, he says that children play happily with their own feces until society tells them to be ashamed, and I say, not Jewish children! You never had to play with shit, we gave you Mattel! And he says, Mom, I love you so much, and I just want to share my life openly. And I'm about to say, please don't share anything that leaves a stain. And Leslie touches my hand, and I stop. And I think, so many people's children, they hide everything. They live separate, secret lives. They're like strangers. *I love those children.*

And that night, after everyone leaves, I turned to my husband and I said, Morris, I gave birth to three perfect children—*what did you do to them?* And he said, they're still perfect, and I said, sure, if we're making a documentary. What should we call it—*Guess What's Coming to Dinner? Hide Your Pets?* And he said, don't drive yourself crazy, and I said, but they're our children, doesn't it bother you? And he says, not one bit, and I ask, but why not? And he says, because whenever they come over, I just turn off my hearing aid. And I said, oh my God, and he asks, but who's that big girl, the one who looks like Ronnie?

And he said, come to bed, but I couldn't sleep, and then it's three AM and I fell to my knees and I cry out to God! I say, why me? I go to temple, I pay my taxes, our housekeeper has health insurance, and probably my best diamond earrings! And then I felt ashamed, I felt hopelessly conventional, but goddamnit, I still wanted an answer! And then, just as I was finishing my third all-butter French crumbcake, I had—a vision. Sugar shock, maybe, carb coma, fine—but there she was! An Asian woman, a Chinese, in the little black outfit, standing right near my breakfront. And she said, I am the mother of Chang and Eng, the famous Siamese twins.

And the mother, she says, when my boys were born, I also cried out. I said, why are my children so different, so odd, so—hard to shop for? And I wanted to comfort her, can you imagine, Siamese twins? All I kept thinking about was—long car trips. And the twins are in the backseat and they're fighting, he touched me, he called me a name— and you can't separate them. But the mother, she said, when my babies were born, I looked at them wriggling in their cradle, like paper dolls made of flesh, and through my heartache, a thought arose—at least, they will never be alone. And I thought to myself, I thought, all of my children, with all of their *mishegas*, maybe all they're doing is finding very individual, very new, and very irritating ways—not to be lonely.

And the next morning, not only did I feel so much better, but I realized, not only was I a proud and loving Mom, but—I could compete! That erotic poop thing pushed me right over the top! So here now, I would like you to meet my pride and joy, my Academy Award for Best Mother Ever . . .

(*She points to someone in the audience.*) I'm talking to you, Marilyn Schwartz, with your little bisexual corporate attorney son—big fuckin' deal! May I present *my* son, Dr. David Benjamin Nadler! (*David Nadler enters, dressed head to toe in aggressive black leather, including a motorcycle jacket, a harness and chaps. His head and face are completely obscured by a full leather hood. He waves to the audience.*) Isn't he gorgeous? Well, take my word. Look at him, he's heaven . . . (*She's stroking his leather jacket.*)

He's like a Coach bag. And you know, in many ways, he's the perfect son. He's a doctor, and he's a slave. (*David nods in agreement.*) David— clean your room. (*She unzips the zipper which covers David's mouth.*)

DAVID. Yes, master.

HELENE. Mother.

DAVID. Yes, Mother.

HELENE. (*To the audience.*) Could you die? (*To David.*) Kiss your Aunt Sylvia.

DAVID. (*Whining.*) Do I have to?

HELENE. (*Grabbing his dog collar.*) What was that, slave?

DAVID. (*Obeying instantly.*) Yes, Mother. (*Helene laughs, delighted with her power.*)

HELENE. (*To the audience.*) You can make him do anything except heavy lifting. He has a bad back. I don't know how Jewish men ever built the pyramids.

DAVID. Mother!

HELENE. (*To David, very commanding.*) Come for the weekend, and *stay over.*

DAVID. But I have stuff to do! (*Helene hurls David to the ground, and stands over him.*)

HELENE. What was that, slave?

DAVID. Mother, I'm very busy!

HELENE. Too busy for your own family?

DAVID. I have my own life!

HELENE. What was that, pussy boy?

DAVID. Yes, Mother.

HELENE. I love it! I love all my children! I win!

DAVID. I have to go. (*David exits.*)

HELENE. On the paper! (*To the audience.*) Thank you! Good night! (*The lights dim, as Helene bows and then follows her son offstage.*)

CURTAIN

For Peter Bartlett

Mr. Charles, Currently of Palm Beach

PLACE

A bare-bones public access television studio in Florida.

TIME

Early evening.

A video camera is mounted on a tripod and aimed at a platform which supports the flamboyant, if limited, set for Mr. Charles' cable show. There is a suitably fussy folding screen, a small, ornate French writing desk, holding a silver tea service and an artificial floral arrangement, and a gilded, throne-like French chair set center stage. There is a small table beside the chair.

ANNOUNCER. And now ladies and gentlemen, direct from Palm Beach, cable channel 47 is proud to present, the gayest man in the universe— it's Mr. Charles! (*Buoyant, big band theme music is heard, something very upbeat and welcoming. Mr. Charles enters. He is ageless; he is stylish, haughty and bold. He wears a fairly obvious, fairly blonde hairpiece, a tomato red blazer over a gingham shirt, with an Hermes scarf knotted Apache-style at his throat, colorful espadrilles, white, lemon, or lime green slacks, and a necktie knotted as a belt. His face boasts a not particularly discreet coat of moisturizer, bronzer and a touch of mascara. His image is not transvestite but Palm Beach decorator or antiques dealer. He is glorious. After smiling and posing for the audience, Mr. Charles picks up a letter from the small table.*)

MR. CHARLES. (*Reading from the letter.*) "What causes homosexuality?" (*He puts the letter down.*) I do. I am so deeply homosexual, that with just a glance, I can actually turn someone gay. (*He glances at someone in the audience.*) Well, that was easy. Sometimes, for a lark, I like to stroll through maternity wards, to upset new parents. I am Mr. Charles, and I am currently residing here in Palm Beach, in semi-retirement. In exile. You see, I was asked to leave New York. There was a vote. Today's modern homosexuals find me an embarrassment. This is because, on certain occasions, I take what I call—a nelly break. For example: A few months ago, I attended an NYU conference, on gay role models. And this young man stood up and said . . . (*In an earnest and manly voice.*) "We must show the world that gay people are not just a pack of screaming queens, with eye makeup, effeminate hand gestures and high-pitched voices." And I just said . . . (*He stands and does a nelly break, shrieking and mincing and flapping his wrists; he might burble, "Oh girl! Oh Miss Thing! Oh Mary!" Then he stops and sits, instantly calm again.*) It just happened. I went nelly. I just began babbling, in Gay English. You know, Shebonics. Oh, or another time, I was attending a rally. And a woman approached me and she said, "I would like you to donate five thousand dollars, to support our boycott of Hollywood films which portray homosexuals as socially irresponsible, promiscuous, and campy." (*Another delirious nelly break.*) And so, I was asked to leave the city. As revenge, I have begun to broadcast this program on cable channel 47, a show which I call "Too Gay." It can be found at four A.M. on alternate Thursdays, in between "Adult Interludes" and "Stretching with Sylvia." Poor dear. I would now like to introduce a very popular feature of this program, my devoted companion, Shane. (*Shane, a dim, affable, low-rent hunk enters, wearing a tight tank top, warm-up pants and sneakers, Shane eyes the audience and the camera. Shane and Mr. Charles get along just great; they appreciate each other.*)

SHANE. (*To the audience.*) Hey.

MR. CHARLES. Shane is my ward. I first met him three weeks ago, at a fabulous local night spot, the Back Alley. Shane was appearing atop a plywood cube. He is a gifted performer. (*Mr. Charles motions to an offstage sound booth and hot dance music blares. Shane's head jerks up, and he begins to dance, pinching his own nipples and then exploding into a demented frenzy. Mr. Charles motions for the music to stop, and Shane stops dancing.*) Thank you, Shane.

SHANE. You got it. (*Shane exits.*)

MR. CHARLES. He lives to dance. Since I have begun these broadcasts, I have received many letters and postcards, including this telegram, from the National Gay Task Force in Washington. (*He picks up a telegram from the table.*) It reads . . . (*Reading the telegram.*) "Dear Mr. Charles. Stop." (*He puts down the telegram.*) I would now like to answer several of the many queries I have received regarding homosexuality. Shane? (*Shane enters, now wearing a homemade Robin costume, which includes tight green trunks, a yellow satin cape worn over a tight red tank top, and a black mask. He is not happy about this outfit. He carries a stack of letters, which he dumps on the table. Then he poses, with his hands on his hips, as a superhero.*)

SHANE. Man, I don't know about this outfit.

MR. CHARLES. It doesn't bother Robin.

SHANE. I ain't Robin.

MR. CHARLES. Oh, but you could be.

SHANE. Yeah? Do you think that Batman and Robin, like, do it?

MR. CHARLES. Do you?

SHANE. Yeah, I bet that like, after they nail some robbers and save Gotham City, they're like, all fired up, so they, like, do some X and stay out all night.

MR. CHARLES. Indeed. And we could dress up and go in their place. Only we would fight—bad taste. We would burst into peoples' homes and proclaim, "We have come to save you! From that terrible armoire!"

SHANE. Yeah! (*Shane exits.*)

MR. CHARLES. He hides his pain. (*He picks up a letter.*) "Dear Mr.

Charles, Nowadays, is there any difference between a gay man and a straight man?" None whatsoever. They are identical. In fact, you may be sitting next to a gay man at the theater and not even know it. But here's a clue: He's saving his *Playbill*. And he's awake. (*Another letter.*) "Dear Mr. Charles, Can gay people change?" Of course—for dinner. (*Another letter.*) "Should gays be allowed to serve in the military?" Absolutely! You see, I have this military fantasy. Shane? (*Shane enters, now wearing fatigue shorts, an olive green military tank top, and a military cap. Shane holds a video camera on his shoulder and follows Mr. Charles during the next segment, acting as Mr. Charles' personal cameraman. Mr. Charles stands, and acts out his fantasy.*) I'm serving in Vietnam, with my unit. And one night, I traipse into the shower tent. It's after hours, and I'm just wearing my kimono, mules and a light moisture pack. And I hear the sound of rushing water . . . (*Shane discreetly makes the sound of rushing water.*) And I turn, and there at the end of a row of showers stands a naked marine. John McCain. His flesh glistens as he lathers up, he runs the soap over his firm chest, his washboard stomach, down, down, into his manly areas. My breathing grows heavy as my kimono falls from at least one shoulder, and I stand beneath the showerhead beside him, attaching my plastic shower caddy, which contains my shampoo, conditioner, finishing rinse and scented bath gelee. My eyes are everywhere, feasting on his shining, sudsy, gleaming male flesh. Finally, I speak. "Hello, soldier," I murmur. "Loofah?" We could transform the armed forces. Make remarks, not war. Thank you, Shane. As you were. (*Shane salutes and exits, as military music plays. Picking up another letter.*) "Should gays be allowed to marry?" Of course, wealthy, older women. (*Another letter.*) "Can you always tell if someone is gay?" Well, I can. There's always a giveaway, sometimes it's just a glance on a street corner, or a slight moan during oral sex. But I do have a question. When an English person comes out, is anyone really surprised? Did anyone say, "Oh no, not *Ian McKellan*?" (*Another letter.*) "Dear Mr. Charles, I am a lesbian." Doesn't that sound like some marvelous first line from Dickens? "I am a lesbian. All you do on your show is talk about gay men. What about gay women?" (*He stands and smiles, very graciously.*) Lesbians. I could write a cookbook. But let us not resort to easy stereotypes, picturing all gay women as husky, can-do gals, out hiking in their flannel and sensible shoes. A gay woman is not simply Paul Bunyan with a cat. (*By this point Mr. Charles has poured himself a cup of tea from the silver tea service. He notices that Shane has neglected to provide a lemon wedge on the tray. He calls out, sharply.*) Shane? Shane! (*Shane hurries in, holding out the lemon wedge, which he squeezes into Mr. Charles' cup of tea, and exits, as cheery music plays.*) Danke, Shane. (*He sips his tea.*) Lesbians are charming, endlessly varied people, with all sorts of haircuts, from the flattop to the pixie. I, in fact, have taken a lesbian into my home. (*He holds a finger to his lips—shh!*) She's asleep in the basement until Spring. (*Another letter.*) "How can I raise gay-positive children in today's political climate?" Well, there are many politically aware children's books, including *Daddy's Roommate* and *Heather Has Two Mommies.* I will soon be publishing my additions to this series. My children's books will include *Uncle Patrick Has a Beautiful Apartment* and *Aunt Cathy's Large Friend.* (*Another letter.*) Oh look, here's a letter for Shane. (*He sniffs the letter, which is perfumed.*) Oh, Shane! (*Shane enters.*)

SHANE. Yeah?

MR. CHARLES. (*Pointing to the words as he reads.*) "Dear Shane." (*Shane grins and grunts, very pleased.*) "I think that you are the hottest thing in South Florida. I loved you on last week's show, when you were dressed as Tarzan." (*The Tarzan outfit was Mr. Charles' idea, and Shane grimaces at the memory.*) You see? "But why don't you dump Mr. Charles and get your own show?"

SHANE. (*Pleased.*) It says that?

MR. CHARLES. Well, Shane, do you think you're ready?

SHANE. Well, you know, I've been thinkin' about it. I could help people, I could like go around the country and find poor people and these like amazing families living in shacks with like twenty-eight handicapped kids, and I could teach 'em to dance!

MR. CHARLES. (*Thrilled.*) I can see it!

SHANE. And ya know what I would call it, that show, to like inspire people?

MR. CHARLES. Yes?

SHANE. *The Shane Show.*

MR. CHARLES. By all means!

SHANE. (*Into the camera.*) Watch for it! (*Shane executes a demented martial arts/karate move, with a cry of "Hyah!" and exits.*)

MR. CHARLES. They grow up so fast. (*Another letter.*) "Dear Mr. Charles, Do you enjoy gay theater?" I am gay theater. Alright, I will now give you the entire history of American gay theater, in sixty seconds. Go! (*Mr. Charles stands, and there's a dramatic lighting change, as he free-associates rapidly, using various voices and accents.*) "Jimmy isn't like the other boys—do you know what you are—he's no son of mine! I'm just so lonely and sick of my own evil—he was a boy, just a boy— Skipper was my buddy, and our love was pure and strong, but those things they're saying, they're true about me! I'm so sick and ashamed, Karen! Do you know what you are? I am a thirty-two-year-old pockmarked Jew fairy, and that was when my father saw me backstage, in my wig and my tights, and he said, take care of my son. (*Singing.*) I am what I am! (*In a gravelly, Harvey Fierstein voice.*) I just wanna be loved, is that so wrong? But Doctor, what's wrong with David, with all the Davids? Our people are dying, and the mayor still won't even say the name of the disease—Maria Callas! (*He raises his arms, as graceful wings.*) Let the great work begin! (*He raises his arms again.*) Let the great work begin, part two! When you speak of gay theater, and you will— be kind. Because it's all about love, valour, baseball, and gratuitous frontal male nudity! (*Shane enters, naked, and hands Mr. Charles a bouquet of roses, as triumphant Oscar Night music soars.*) Bravo! (*Mr. Charles bows deeply as Shane exits.*) Which brings us to my favorite part of the program, a forum which I call, "People I *Hate*." This week's person I hate most in the world is someone I've never even met. His name is Theodore DiBenedetto, and he wrote this letter to the editor of our local paper. (*Mr. Charles reads aloud from a copy of the newspaper, using a butch, manly voice.*) "Dear *Palm Beach Sentinal*, I am a gay man who owns the East Bay Hardware Store." (*He looks up with a withering glance and then continues.*) "And I am sick and tired of gay people demanding equal rights when they keep behaving like freaks. As gay people, we must prove that we aren't just stereotypes. We must demonstrate that our lives are normal and wholesome. We must show that we can hold jobs, go to church and raise children, just like anyone else. This is how we will earn our place at the table." (*Mr. Charles puts down the paper. He is now dangerously angry, like steel.*) Darling, I *set* the table. I arranged the flowers. And I would rather have Shane's knife at my throat then share even a brunch with Mr. DiBenedetto and his kind. The nice boys. The good citizens. But please, Mr. DiBenedetto, if you'd like, by all means, be normal and wholesome and responsible, get married, have children, move to the suburbs. I'll wait here. Oh, and Mr. DiBenedetto, by the by . . . (*Mr. Charles stands and launches into a viciously savage nelly break, directly into the camera. He becomes a ferocious nelly whirlwind, making enormous flamboyant gestures to the audience. He might look into the camera and elaborately mime applying lipstick, and licking his forefinger and slicking each eyebrow. Finally he turns, rump to the camera, and minces back to the chair, his heels off the ground, as if he were wearing imaginary spike heels. He turns, sits, and arranges his wrists. With a knife-edge flourish, he crosses his legs. Shane enters, wearing white jeans and an untucked Versace shirt.*)

SHANE. Um, I gotta go out, okay?

MR. CHARLES. Do you have to get your hair cut?

SHANE. Yeah, um, right!

MR. CHARLES. Did you take the car keys?

SHANE. (*Holding up the keys.*) Right here!

MR. CHARLES. (*Like a doting parent.*) And all of the cash on my dresser, my credit cards, and my mother's emerald earrings from my sock drawer?

SHANE. Got 'em!

MR. CHARLES. Do you love me forever?

SHANE. Yeah, of course!

MR. CHARLES. (*Delighted.*) On your way!

SHANE. Later! (*Shane exits.*)

MR. CHARLES. Oh, he's not fooling me. He doesn't need a haircut. Ah, but I am the last of my kind. I shall perish, like the dinosaur. Unless, of course, Steven Spielberg discovers some ancient DNA from Paul Lynde and makes more. But let me ask you something, all of you. Have you ever been in love? Hands? You see, I fell in love quite early. I must have been, oh, twelve? I had just been savagely beaten by . . . (*He tries to remember, quite cheerfully.*) oh, it could have been anyone. But this was at school. I came home bruised, caked with mud. I ran up to my room, and I looked in the mirror. And I thought, all right, whom would I rather be? The boys who beat me up, the boys who played baseball and caught frogs and were already losing their figures? Or would I rather be—Mr. Charles. Who even at twelve knew how to turn his face so the tears would glisten. Who knew enough to immediately put Billie Holiday on the hifi, and lip-synch. Who could transform a schoolyard humiliation into an Academy Award. And that was when I fell passionately in love—with being gay. Oh, there have been men, and boys, and Wedgewood. But being gay—there's a romance. (*Shane enters.*)

SHANE. Hey, Chuck?

MR. CHARLES. You're back.

SHANE. When I was drivin' to the club, I was thinkin' about like, what you said at the beginning of the show, that you can, like, make people gay, just by lookin' at 'em?

MR. CHARLES. In my time.

SHANE. Well, I was kinda wonderin', I mean, nowadays, most gay guys just wanna be, like, regular people. And the world's already got lots of them. So what I was thinkin' was, could you make some more of you?

MR. CHARLES. Oh no, I don't think so, nobody wants to be truly gay anymore. It's passé.

SHANE. So, like, kick their ass! You could do it. Use your superpowers. Your gay ray. Make an army. A planet!

MR. CHARLES. It's tempting . . .

SHANE. Go for it, man!

MR. CHARLES. You're too sweet.

SHANE. Later! (*Shane exits.*)

MR. CHARLES. Well, let me see, how would I do this? Make more? (*He looks at the audience.*) Yes—the receptionist. With the baby. Could you come down here? (*Joann Milderry, the studio receptionist comes on-stage, carrying her seven-month-old baby. Joann is sweet, very young, shy and apologetic.*)

JOANN. (*Timidly, hovering.*) Really?

MR. CHARLES. Yes, it's fine, please, come on down.

JOANN. I'm so sorry, but my boyfriend sort of—disappeared, and my mom usually watches the baby but she was mad at me. She thinks that I shouldn't be working here. She thinks you're too weird.

MR. CHARLES. But why?

JOANN. (*Cautiously pointing to his hairpiece.*) I think it's your hat.

MR. CHARLES. Aha.

JOANN. But I told her that I like it here—I like you.

MR. CHARLES. Stop.

JOANN. (*Joann starting to exit.*) Okay.

MR. CHARLES. Figure of speech. And what a beautiful child. Boy or girl?

JOANN. A boy. Max.

MR. CHARLES. (*To the baby.*) How would you like to grow up like me? How would you like to be—Mr. Max?

JOANN. Could you really make him—like you?

MR. CHARLES. Is there a problem?

JOANN. Well—would he have a difficult life?

MR. CHARLES. Who doesn't?

JOANN. Will people be mean to him?

MR. CHARLES. (*Cheerfully.*) Of course.

JOANN. Will he do those—nelly breaks?

MR. CHARLES. Sometimes—in front of your mother. Think how upset she'll be.

JOANN. (*Firmly holding out the baby.*) Do it.

MR. CHARLES. Are you sure? It's a big step.

JOANN. Well—did you ever see that movie, *The Wizard of Oz*?

MR. CHARLES. Look at me.

JOANN. You know how that main girl, what's her name?

MR. CHARLES. Dorothy?

JOANN. Right, Dorothy, well, at the beginning of the movie, she's back home on the farm in Kansas, and the movie's in black and white. But then, when she gets to Oz, everything's in color. So it's like, my life, and my baby's life, at least right now, we're in Kansas. But someone like you, and I don't know if it's because you're gay or what, but— you're in color.

MR. CHARLES. Then here we go! (*Mr. Charles aims two fingers at the baby and makes a small hissing noise, zapping the baby.*) Ssst! He's on his way!

JOANN. To Oz, or New York or, I don't know, to wherever you buy your clothes?

MR. CHARLES. Who knows?

JOANN. Thank you. (*As she exits, to the baby.*) He's a very nice man.

MR. CHARLES. (*To the departing mother and child.*) Have fun! He will! (*Joann and the baby exit. Mr. Charles speaks to the audience.*) Oh, I know what you're thinking. You're thinking, oh please, he doesn't really have any powers. He's just another shrill, aging Palm Beach queen with too many cocktails and a bad hairpiece. Well, would you like to hear something even more horrible, my pretties? It isn't a hairpiece. (*Mr. Charles cackles gleefully and gestures grandly to his hair.*) It's MINE! (*As the peppy theme music from his show is heard he makes a little pouting face, then he begins blowing kisses and waving goodbye, as the lights fade.*)

CURTAIN

Crafty

Barbara Ellen Diggs stands in a conference room of a municipal building in Decatur, Illinois. Barbara Ellen is a sweet-faced, extremely good-natured, outgoing woman, wearing a sweatshirt with a floral appliqué or a hand-knit sweater. She is surrounded by tables holding many homemade craft items.

BARBARA ELLEN. Hi. I'm Barbara Ellen Diggs, and I'm a craftsperson here in Decatur. And this morning I would like to speak to you, our Junior Chamber of Commerce, on the critical importance of crafts in our culture. Before I discovered crafts, I suffered from clinical depression and had no self-esteem; but today I exhibit my work statewide and I teach workshops at our local women's prison, where a lady who slaughtered her entire family now makes notecards personalized with sequins and dried corn. I have invented over five hundred and twelve different saleables for Christmas bazaars, including doorknob covers, (*She holds up a board holding three doorknobs with crocheted holiday covers.*) microwave bonnets (*She holds up a large quilted microwave bonnet.*) and toilet paper caddies (*She holds up a crocheted cover for a roll of toilet paper.*) And I have recently hand-crocheted a tuxedo for my toaster. (*She holds up a toaster dressed in a hand crocheted black and white cover with a bowtie.*) For wardrobe items I practice appliqué, which is the art of heat-bonding a felt Santa or a three-dimensional chenille snowman onto a garment. (*She holds up a sweatshirt appliquéd with a snowman and a Santa.*) Last Christmas, across a particularly memorable sweatshirt,

I created an entire colonial village, including an ice-skating pond, a blacksmith's shop, and a mischievous Jewish peddler. I also deeply enjoy scrapbooking. (*She picks up a scrapbook and opens it to a page, showing it to the audience as she points to various features.*) For example, on this page, I color-Xeroxed a simple Polaroid of my Aunt Polly, and I placed the image at the center of a piece of oaktag. Then I surrounded the picture with heart-shaped lace doilies, crepe-paper rosettes, and silk ribbon worked to spell out "Aunt Polly." I've also included some ticket stubs from a movie we saw together, *That Darn Cat*, the invitation to her wedding to Uncle Walt, and a tiny burlap bag containing one of her kidney stones. The page now weighs over fifteen pounds, and it can tell you Aunt Polly's entire life story, and I don't even like her.

I am currently applying for a grant for what I consider to be a truly American crafts milestone: I intend to create a series of commemorative plaques, saluting the history of American crafts. Each plaque will be devoted to celebrating a separate medium of expression, including buttons, decals, colored gravel, bottle-caps, poptops, tissue paper, construction paper, mosaic tile, hooked rug, rag rug, needlepoint, needlepoint-in-a-tube, wood-burning, copper tooling, coffee cans, lanyards, embossing, vinyl, leather, leatherette, nauga, look-of-nauga, Dixie cups, styrofoam, balsa wood, spray snow stenciling, corkware, potholder loops, macaroni collage on Michelob beer bottles, popsicle sticks, cheese sculpture, scented soap, scented beeswax, acrylic modeling clay, and human hair. My primary expenses will be for labor, Zoloft, and glue.

Some sophisticated people say that crafts aren't art, but by the same token, some people say that New Yorkers aren't people. Crafts allow me to express myself, to create something worth dusting. When I pick up a crochet hook or a staple gun I'm tingling. I'm transported. This one time I started rubber cementing sea shells onto a keepsake box as a baby gift, and by the time I looked up, that child was in college.

My family has always been very supportive of my hobbies, well, except for my son, whom I loved dearly. Hank was always—very special. He always used to scold me for using words like that, what did he call them—euphemisms. He said, Mom, I'm gay. And I said, no you're not, you're special. And he said no, that makes me sound like I'm re- tarded. And I would say, I wish. And we would laugh. It never really bothered me, even though he did move away and started working for a fancy Broadway costume designer in New York and he didn't come back home all that often. But we would write back and forth, and he would send me trims and braid, all these beautiful expensive things from the costumes and I wouldn't know what to do with them. But to thank him I would send him Hummel figurines, you know, those cute little ceramic children, holding umbrellas or petting kittens, or sit- ting on a swing. And he'd get so angry on the phone, he'd say Mom, don't send me anything you can order from TV. Which upset me, so to express that, I sent him the Hummel sad little clown. And he said that Hummels were originally made by Nazis, and I said they were not, they were made by German nuns who didn't read the newspaper. I just liked the picture of all those Hummels, all lined up in his New York studio apartment, to remind him of where he came from. I'd say Hank, maybe you're still wearing white T-shirts and Levi's, but I remember when you didn't shrink them. I told him, if homosexuality is genetic, then maybe so is home shopping.

And then, well, he got sick. With that terrible disease. And I flew to New York to see him in the hospital, and do you know what I brought? Nothing. I didn't want to embarrass him, in front of his friends. Who were all so sweet, I mean, they all sort of sounded alike and they all kept kissing and hugging me and saying, Henry, we love your mom, she's a hoot. A hoot. That means I wear polyester without irony. But they were all really very nice, and so good to Hank, and when we were finally alone he looked up at me and said, so what did you bring me? A potholder, a picture frame decorated with twine and plastic daisies, two little bunnies on a sled? And I said no, I know all of that just upsets you, makes you feel like a hick. And he leaned back onto the pillow and he said, oh. It's okay. I just wanted to see you.

And I stayed there until, well, let's use one of those euphemisms, until he passed on. Maybe that's why euphemisms get invented, not because people are ashamed, but because—they hate the real word too much. And I hated that word, and I hated that disease, and for the longest time I just went to work and came home and I didn't touch a thing. Not a needle, not a bobbin, not a hole punch or a pair of pinking shears. I would not bring color or beauty or rickrack into this world. I was just too sad.

And then one day I saw on the television, that quilt. All spread out in Washington, right on the ground in front of the Capitol. Over seventy-two thousand squares, each for a different man, woman, or child. And I looked at it and I thought, my Lord, it's like a cemetery created by the *Ladies Home Journal*. And I took all the fancy trims and laces and bugle beads that Hank had sent me, and I went over to Newberry's and I got a rectangle of hot pink felt. And I made his name in embroidered script, and I stitched on one of his report cards and his mittens and one of his T-shirts which said, "No One Knows I'm Gay." Only I changed it so it said, "No One Knows I'm From Decatur." And in the corner I attached one of those labels I always use, that says, "Especially Handmade Just For You By Barbara Ellen Diggs." And I folded up the whole thing and sent it away, so Lord knows where it is now.

But that was ages ago, and now they have all that new medicine, so people, well, at least some people, can keep going. And we've got whole new ways to hurt people, like that 9/11. And I have to tell you something, and you're going to think I'm awful, but when I first heard about it, on TV, and they said Muslim terrorists had attacked those buildings? I swear to God, I thought they said muslin. Muslin terrorists. And I didn't understand and I thought, they're just using cheap cotton? But of course then I found out what it really was, and I saw that all of those people had died and I wondered, will there be a quilt? And I thought, well, probably not in New York, where everyone is so fancy, I thought, maybe they'll make a duvet. I'm sorry.

And about a year or so later, I went back to New York, because I was a finalist, in a cake-decorating competition. It was cutthroat. The woman next to me, from Ohio, she was so sure that she was going to win, because she'd baked a five-layer devil's food supreme, frosted with the entire Battle of Gettysburg. She'd used mocha pudding and shredded coconut for the battlefield, and the Union forces were Necco wafers, and the Confederates were all Gummi Bears. But the judges said it was contrived. No comment.

And I thought that maybe I had a shot, for my special Easter Sunday extravaganza. I had frosted a lemon meringue sheet cake with an exact replica of Leonardo da Vinci's "The Last Supper," only instead of the apostles everyone at the table was either a chocolate bunny or a marshmallow peep. But then that Gettysburg woman made a stink, and said that my work was sacrilegious, because I'd included Mary Magdalene, but I said, I know that it's controversial, but she's a peanut M&M!

So I lost, and the city reminded me of Hank, and people said that you could sometimes still smell the, what was it, the jet fuel from that day. And I just couldn't go downtown because it was so terrible, and because that's where Hank lived and so I walked over, from the Marriot, to Central Park. And they were having this, I didn't really know what to call it, but people said it was an installation. By this French artist named Christo. And it seems that this Christo person goes all around the world, and he wraps up landmarks in fabric. I'm not kidding. That's what he does, he pays for it and he gets all of these helpers and all of these sewing machines and they wrap up buildings and islands and bridges. I'm not kidding! And I wondered if maybe, when he was younger, for Christmas, if Christo once gave someone a particularly bulky item, like a bicycle or an outdoor barbeque, and he had to wrap it. Eureka! And in the park, he'd put up hundreds of these sort of archways, these aluminum gates, and from each one, from the top, there was a bright orange curtain. And I thought, well, now I know what an installation is—it's just a giant French crafts project.

And I stood there and the sun came out and the breeze was blowing all of those orange curtains and it didn't make any sense, but it was very pretty. Like a county fair, at a graduate school. And then I saw this car, this limousine, driving slowly through the park, and this woman next to me, she said that the man in the car was Christo, with his wife, Jean-Claude. And that they drove through all the time, to watch people's reactions. And as the car got closer the window rolled down and inside I could see this little man, Christo, and I waved. And he waved back, and I didn't know what to say, so I just pointed to all of the gates and I said, "Wow! Yardage!" And the car drove past and I asked the woman, I said, does this installation, and all of this orange fabric, does it make people feel better? And I could tell that she was a New Yorker because she said, (*She uses a tougher New York voice.*) "Yes, it does. Because it's free and they're gonna take it down." And I hadn't really talked about him in so long, especially not to a stranger, but I stood under one of those gates and I told her about Hank. And I asked her if she was there, if she was in the city on 9/11. And she said yes. And I asked, did you lose anyone, and she said yes. That her brother was a firefighter.

And it's strange, but when I got back to Decatur, I started to feel a little cheerier, for the first time in years. My friend Susan Deckerman says that maybe I found closure, and I said, Susan, Oprah is just a person. But I've started to make these sock monkeys (*She picks up a pair of sock monkeys from the table.*) and I take them to our local hospital and I hang them on the patient's IV stands. Because maybe when a sick person sees a sock monkey, they'll smile, and I bet they wouldn't do that if they looked up and saw "Guernica."

And that woman I met in New York, in the park, her name is Eileen and we've kept in touch. And after they took those gates down, Eileen got some of the fabric and sent it to me. And so I made this . . . (*She holds up a bright orange, quilted oven mitt.*) It's a quilted oven mitt. And I'm gonna send it to Eileen, with a note that says, "You see? That Christo can make something useful." I don't know if I believe in God anymore. But I do believe in cute. I believe in glue. I believe in hot pink felt. And maybe if I was a New Yorker, I would believe in orange shower curtains hanging in Central Park. Amen.

CURTAIN

The New Century

PLACE

The maternity ward of a Manhattan hospital.
There's some sense of walls, maybe with nursery themed wallpaper.
The newborns are where the audience is.

TIME

Afternoon.

Helene Nadler sits or reclines on a bench, upstage, surrounded by shopping bags.

Mr. Charles enters, cautiously. He's incognito, wearing a drab trenchcoat and a hat. He glances around. Thinking that he's alone, he removes his coat and hat, revealing his customary, flamboyant splendor. He sees the babies, and he's delighted. Facing the audience, he speaks to the babies.

MR. CHARLES. Hello . . . hello there . . . hello . . . hello, you . . . you little sweetheart . . . you tiny darling . . . oh you . . . and you . . . hello!

HELENE. It's you.

MR. CHARLES. Pardon?

HELENE. I know you.

MR. CHARLES. What?

HELENE. When I was down in Florida, I couldn't sleep. It must've been 3 AM and I turned on the TV, and there you were, Mr. Chester . . .

MR. CHARLES. (*Shielding his face.*) No, I'm sorry, you're wrong. That wasn't me.

HELENE. Excuse me?

MR. CHARLES. You're thinking of someone else, happens all the time, it's a mistaken identity . . .

HELENE. Mr. Charles!

MR. CHARLES. Oh no no no no no . . .

HELENE. It is you!

MR. CHARLES. (*Grandly.*) How did you recognize me?

HELENE. You're very distinctive.

MR. CHARLES. And a desperado. You see, I was banned from New York.

HELENE. You were banned? Why?

MR. CHARLES. Do you remember the name of my show?

HELENE. "Too Gay"?

MR. CHARLES. SHHHHH!!!

HELENE. So why did you come back?

MR. CHARLES. It's New York. I couldn't stay away. So I escaped from Palm Beach. It wasn't easy. I traveled by night, sometimes I even wore men's clothing. South Carolina, North Carolina, Virginia—have you seen those people? Until finally, I came here, to this maternity ward, to see the babies. (*Mr. Charles zaps a few babies.*) Ssst . . . Ssst . . .

HELENE. What are you doing?

MR. CHARLES. Nothing. I'm sorry.

HELENE. No, no, I'm sorry, I'm . . . in a terrible state, and I shouldn't be, I have no right. Because last night, my beautiful daughter Leslie and her partner, they gave birth, to that gorgeous baby right over there, in that bassinet . . . (*She reads the nametag.*) "Rebecca Michael Miracle Cilantro Kinkasha O'Malley-Nadler." Isn't that original? It sounds like an appetizer. No no, I think it's wonderful, I think the two mommies, they're wonderful, truly, it's just, oh, I'm sorry, I'm babbling . . .

MR. CHARLES. Tell me.

HELENE. I can't, it's too shameful, it's too selfish, I'm just feeling sorry for myself, and that is disgusting—what, just because I'm a woman and you're a gay man, I'm just supposed to automatically confide in you? Is that how it works? Forget it. Okay. It's just—an hour ago, I was up in that hospital room and all of my kids, they all left, with their friends and their partners, and my husband, he went off to play golf, which believe me I'm fine with, and then Leslie turned to me, and she said "Ma, go home." And I said, No, I can help, I can get you things, and she said, "No, thank you, it's okay, Marsha's here. Go home."

MR. CHARLES. Oh no . . .

HELENE. Go home? To what? To who? Rhetorical. To a photo album filled with ancient history, with pictures of Leslie learning to hold a tennis racquet, and Veronica when she had a penis, and David in diapers—it's from last year. It's just I thought that, maybe if I came up here, and I saw all of this new life, that maybe it would cheer me up. But it's not working. I look at all of this hope, all of this possibility, and I just want—to tell them. I just want to scream, to every last one of these babies, maybe you were only born four hours ago, but think very carefully, don't make any mistakes, don't blow it, (*Reading a name.*)—Tiffany Sierra—because your whole life, it's the blink of an eye, and it's all gonna be over so soon . . . (*We hear all the babies start to wail; it's quite a cacophony.*)

MR. CHARLES. (*To the babies.*) Happy Birthday! (*Barbara Ellen Diggs enters, in a wheelchair upstage.*)

BARBARA ELLEN. Don't mind me.

HELENE. (*Regarding Barbara Ellen, to Mr. Charles.*) Jesus. And look at her. In a wheelchair.

MR. CHARLES. Can you imagine?

HELENE. I would kill myself.

HELENE and MR. CHARLES. (*Both suddenly very cheerful, to Barbara Ellen.*) Hi!

BARBARA ELLEN. Oh, hello!

MR. CHARLES. Can we help you?

HELENE. Can I push you? I always say that to my children.

BARBARA ELLEN. Oh, thank you, that's so sweet, but no, thank you, both of you, I'm fine, I'm just fine.

MR. CHARLES. (*To Barbara Ellen.*) And you're perky.

BARBARA ELLEN. No, I'm not.

MR. CHARLES. Excuse me?

BARBARA ELLEN. I'm sorry, what am I saying, I'm a spunky, good-natured person, I just meant that—if I could just keep busy—excuse me, either of you, do you have any yarn? No, I'm fine, look at all of these babies! Couldn't you just eat them right up?

HELENE. (*To Barbara Ellen.*) Are you all right? Would you like a snack?

MR. CHARLES. Some water? (*Helene and Mr. Charles move to their bags and belongings to find snacks and bottled water.*)

BARBARA ELLEN. Oh, no—sure. It's just I got into town last night, and this morning, I went to Madison Square Garden, for the big annual Cat Show.

HELENE. (*Handing her a bag of nuts.*) Here you go.

BARBARA ELLEN. Thank you. Do you have anything sweet?

HELENE. Sure. (*To Mr. Charles, whispering.*) She's in a wheelchair.

BARBARA ELLEN. I was competing in a kitty couture fashion show, because I've started making little outfits for my cats.

HELENE. (*In disbelief.*) You make outfits for your—no, I'm sorry. Who am I to judge?

BARBARA ELLEN. Are you Jewish?

HELENE. I resent your assumption. Just because someone is critical and articulate and always hungry—fine, I'm Jewish.

MR. CHARLES. And your show?

BARBARA ELLEN. Well, by the final round, it had all come down to me and this one other kitty couturier, this math teacher from Maryland, whose specialty was kitty swimwear. And I'm sorry, but I just said it right out loud, I said a cat does not need a two piece bathing suit. And he said, well, so why does your cat need a pink satin strapless gown, and I said, for evening. And then just as she hit the runway, my cat, my beautiful little Abyssinian, she just got so nervous that she bolted, right out of the exhibition hall, down the escalator and out into the street. And I ran after her, and just as I grabbed her, I got sideswiped by a taxicab.

HELENE. Oh no!

BARBARA ELLEN. But all sorts of people rushed right over to help me, all of those wonderful New Yorkers, you know, it really is a melting pot, because every one of them smelled different. And then an ambulance came and brought me here, and all of the doctors and the nurses have been so helpful.

HELENE. And how's your cat?

BARBARA ELLEN. Oh she's just fine, thank God. She's resting.

MR. CHARLES. And her evening gown?

BARBARA ELLEN. I don't want to talk about it.

MR. CHARLES. Give it time.

BARBARA ELLEN. And nothing's broken, I just have a bruised hip, it's just . . . oh, I'm being such a baby.

HELENE. No you're not, not at all . . .

MR. CHARLES. You've had a dreadful day . . .

BARBARA ELLEN. It's just, well, when you're in a hospital, everything is so upsetting. For the sick people, and the families, except for the maternity ward. It's the only floor where everyone's happy to be there. And it's just, oh, I shouldn't even say this, it was so long ago . . .

MR. CHARLES. What?

BARBARA ELLEN. It's just—this is the hospital where my son died.

HELENE. Oh no. I'm so sorry.

MR. CHARLES. You poor dear . . .

BARBARA ELLEN. He was such a sweet boy. I mean, he was special. Different.

MR. CHARLES. Different?

BARBARA ELLEN. (*To Mr. Charles.*) Are you gay?

MR. CHARLES. Oh no. I'm with Cirque de Soleil.

BARBARA ELLEN. I'm sorry . . .

MR. CHARLES. No, of course I'm gay. Very gay. Too gay.

BARBARA ELLEN. I like your hair.

MR. CHARLES. You do?

BARBARA ELLEN. Did you make it?

MR. CHARLES. (*Touching his hairpiece.*) Yes. It's Abyssinian.

BARBARA ELLEN. (*Charmed by him.*) You're terrible!

MR. CHARLES. Yes I am.

BARBARA ELLEN. You sound just like my son.

HELENE. He does?

BARBARA ELLEN. (*To Helene.*) Do you have children?

HELENE. One lesbian daughter, one transsexual lesbian son, and another gay son who's into bondage and poop.

BARBARA ELLEN. Oh my Lord. So what do they give you for Mother's Day?

HELENE. Cash.

MR. CHARLES. Look at us. All of us.

HELENE. Look at our lives.

BARBARA ELLEN. What do we do with this world? What do we tell all of these babies? You're born . . .

HELENE. You go shopping . . .

MR. CHARLES. You have tea . . .

BARBARA ELLEN. You create a wedding gown for your cat with a catnip bouquet and a three-foot ivory silk train . . .

HELENE. (*After a beat.*) Your cat got married?

BARBARA ELLEN. To our labradoodle. Who wore tails, a bowtie and a top hat.

HELENE. (*Another beat.*) Who married them?

BARBARA ELLEN. Our parakeet. Episcopal.

MR. CHARLES. It won't last.

BARBARA ELLEN. Do you think that, on any level, that these babies can understand us?

HELENE. Well, my mother said that babies have all the knowledge in the world. Except that right before they're born, God smacks them and they forget everything.

BARBARA ELLEN. Did she really believe that?

HELENE. She'd tell me, "Helene, God must've smacked you really hard."

BARBARA ELLEN. Well, if we could get through—what would you tell them? What advice would you give?

HELENE. Don't get old.

BARBARA ELLEN. Don't love anyone.

MR. CHARLES. And if you have no morals but you'd still like to run for public office, move to Florida. (*Shane enters, wearing all sorts of outlandishly gaudy new clothes and carrying shopping bags. He's wildly excited, like a kid.*)

SHANE. Yo, Chuck!

MR. CHARLES. Shane?

HELENE. You're that boy, from his TV show. You were dressed like a gladiator.

SHANE. (*Indicating Mr. Charles.*) He made me do that . . .

HELENE. You looked very handsome . . .

MR. CHARLES. (*To Shane.*) You see?

SHANE. I never been to New York before! Hi, I'm Shane . . .

HELENE. Helene.

BARBARA ELLEN. Barbara Ellen.

SHANE. Whoa. Man, are you like in a wheelchair?

BARBARA ELLEN. Well, at the moment . . .

SHANE. Sweet! So I like come up here with Chuck, and I've been goin' like all over the place! All the like, landmarks! (*He shows everyone his postcards.*) Like Times Square, and the Empire State Building, (*To Barbara Ellen.*) look, it's got a ramp. And then I saw all these trucks, and there was this dead hooker, with her neck all broken, lyin' on the ground in a pool of her own blood.

HELEN. They were shooting *Law and Order.*

SHANE. It was so cool! But then I go, yo, I'm in New York, I gotta do it, I gotta see it, so I go down—to Ground Zero.

HELENE. Oh my.

SHANE. And at first I'm confused, 'cause I get outta the subway and I'm like, where is it? And then I go, right, that's the whole deal, there's nothin' there. It's gone. And it's like I'm tryin' to look at—what used to be there.

BARBARA ELLEN. Yes.

SHANE. And then, I look up. And I swear to God, I see it. Right there.

HELENE. What?

MR. CHARLES. Shane, what do you see?

SHANE. At first I can't believe it, I go, what is that, but it's just shining, just glowing, right over the whole damn thing, over alla that construction shit, there was this bigass neon sign, and it said—"Century 21."

BARBARA ELLEN. Century 21?

SHANE. And I'm goin', what, but I walk over, and I go inside, and it's like the coolest store I've ever seen, in like my whole entire life! They got everything, like Versace and Dolce and Nike and sweats and shades and—alla this! Like everything I'm wearin'! For like, twenty-five bucks! *Total!*

HELENE. And so this discount store, it made you feel better? About— life?

SHANE. I don't know. At first I'm goin', this don't make sense, what happened out there, and what's goin' on in here, and people posin' for pictures in front of the pit, like it's Epcot, and I'm like, I don't know what's goin' on. And I go, maybe we should all just sorta stop. And be respectful. And I try, I swear I did, I'm standin' in that store, with my eyes closed, sorta like prayin'. But then there's all this music, on the sound system, and I open my eyes and it's like—there's this big fat lady, from like I don't know, Czechoslovakia, or the Dominican Republic, and she's got like six kids, and she's tryin' on this dress, and it's got flowers all over, and she's totally packed into it. And you can tell that she's gonna wear it to like, a party or a weddin', and her kids are all goin' like, Mami, lookin' good, and she's laughin', 'cause her kids are right, 'cause she looks so good. And I'm goin', is she bein' disrespectful, or is she—lookin' good!

HELENE. I don't know . . .

SHANE. Okay, like what's your biggest problem? Like right this second?

HELENE. Aside from, say, world peace and disease and hunger? I'm old.

SHANE. Not at Century 21. You could get like a smokin' new outfit, with all like the accessories and the shoes and a bag.

HELENE. Excuse me, are you actually saying that if I just got all decked out, in some designer outfit, that I'd feel better? And that somehow my new shoes would make the world a better place?

SHANE. Yeah!

HELENE. That is ridiculous. And insane. And offensive.

SHANE. It is?

HELENE. Because that is not an answer. That's an evasion. That's denial. And I'm sorry to be such a drag, and maybe I'm just letting my own personal agita color everything, but—I just can't pretend. Not anymore. Buildings fall. People die. Life ends. And a pretty new handbag isn't going to solve my problems or your problems or anyone else's!

SHANE. I'm sorry . . .

MR. CHARLES. Shane, perhaps we should go . . .

BARBARA ELLEN. But it was so nice to meet you . . . (*As Mr. Charles and Shane are almost gone:*)

HELENE. Wait.

SHANE. Yeah?

HELENE. So do they really have bags?

SHANE. They got like this Ralph Lauren bag, from this year, it was like twenty-six hundred bucks, if you could find it, but at Century 21— eighty-nine dollars and fifty cents.

HELENE. It is not.

SHANE. Is!

HELENE. And it's not a knock-off, or one of those bags with the cheap top-stitching which they just make for the outlet stores in Connecti- cut, it's not just some crappy mall bag?

SHANE. Hey, in my like, occupation, I been in some nice houses, and I know real Ralph.

HELENE. I love real Ralph. I worship real Ralph. Ralph Lauren is a Jewish superhero. Ralph Lauren is a Jewish saint.

BARBARA ELLEN. Wait.

HELENE. What?

BARBARA ELLEN. Ralph Lauren is Jewish?

HELENE. Ralph Lauren could make a yarmulke for your cat.

SHANE. And Chuck, you know how you been actin' all like, nobody wants to be gay anymore, not like your kinda gay?

MR. CHARLES. They don't. No one does.

SHANE. Not at Century 21! I saw these guys, they're tryin' on tank tops and cashmere and cologne—it's like, all the nice, normal gay guys and even some of the straight dudes, they sneak down there, to get a fix. You could hear 'em, in the dressin' rooms, they couldn't control them- selves . . .

MR. CHARLES. Did they do nelly breaks?

SHANE. It's like if Patti LuPone was a *store*.

MR. CHARLES. Oh my!

SHANE. (*To Barbara Ellen.*) And you, I bet if you could like, talk to God, or Allah or whoever, I bet you'd be all like, can I have some legs, please, right?

BARBARA ELLEN. But . . .

SHANE. Could I like maybe get up outta this chair? Like probably just the way it happens when you're dreamin'. Man, that's a tough one. I don't know about that. I'm like, really, really, really sorry. (*Shane turns away, upset.*)

BARBARA ELLEN. Your scarf—is that tie-dye? (*Barbara Ellen stands up, and reaches for Shane's colorful scarf.*) That looks handmade. (*Shane is staring at Barbara Ellen, staggered and awestruck by the miracle of her standing up and walking.*)

SHANE. Shit. Shit. Oh my fuckin' *shit!*

MR. CHARLES. Shane?

SHANE. Century 21 is fuckin' *awesome!* (*For the first time, he spots the babies.*) Whoa! Babies!

BARBARA ELLEN. (*Holding Shane's scarf.*) Could I have this? Oh no, I'm sorry, I have no right, you take this right back . . .

SHANE. No, no man, you gotta keep it.

BARBARA ELLEN. Oh, you are just as cute as a bug, and you're almost exactly the same age, as my son. When he—left.

SHANE. You mean like, when he kicked?

BARBARA ELLEN. Yes.

SHANE. Did you love him?

BARBARA ELLEN. Yes.

SHANE. Was he gay?

BARBARA ELLEN. Yes.

SHANE. Was he hot?

BARBARA ELLEN. Yes.

SHANE. Then it's okay.

BARBARA ELLEN. It is?

SHANE. 'Cause see, some people think that heaven is all like white and fluffy, but I think that sounds kinda boring. So I figure maybe it's more like, I don't know, a club, so there's hot music, and God is kinda like Chuck.

BARBARA ELLEN. I like that.

MR. CHARLES. Shane, you're embarrassing me. I'm not God. I mean, look at the world. God obviously has no taste.

HELENE. (*To Shane, pointing to a baby.*) That's my grandchild. Isn't she gorgeous?

SHANE. Yeah. So are you gonna like, babysit for free and tell all your friends where she's gonna go to college and stuff?

HELENE. No! Of course I am. And maybe I can tell her—about my life, and everything I've been through. And everything we've all been through. I'll just bum her right out. Yeah, she's gonna love visiting Grandma. But maybe I should have a little faith. Because my grandchild, and all of these children—they are Century 21.

SHANE. But the Chanel sunglasses? The big round white ones? Buy 'em on the street. Even cheaper.

HELENE. You're a very smart boy. You should have your own show.

MR. CHARLES. I keep telling him.

SHANE. Maybe it's time. And maybe I could have like, special guest stars! 'Cause guess what I got? (*He grabs CD's from one of his shopping bags.*) From this dude who had 'em all spread out on this like blanket? Hot new CD's!

MR. CHARLES. And you can be dressed as the Greek god Apollo!

SHANE. (*Upset.*) Man . . .

HELENE. (*Reassuring Shane.*) That would be very hot . . .

BARBARA ELLEN. Spray glue and body glitter. I have a catalogue.

SHANE. (*Now getting excited about the idea.*) Really? And as one of my Special Guest Stars—Barbara Ellen, the miracle lady of Century 21!

BARBARA ELLEN. Well, I already have my own interactive Web site.

SHANE. What's it called?

BARBARA ELLEN. "Gluetube."

SHANE. And Helene—the smokin' hot Jewish lady!

HELENE. Me? On TV? When I lose five pounds.

SHANE. And you asked for it, the gayest gay guy in the whole entire universe . . .

MR. CHARLES. And the last . . .

SHANE. Mr. Chuck! (*Joann enters, pushing her baby in a stroller. A fabric hood conceals the baby.*)

JOANN. (*Stunned at seeing Mr. Charles and Shane.*) Oh my god . . .

MR. CHARLES. (*Equally shocked.*) Hello?

HELENE. Yes?

SHANE. Hey! You're her! You're that girl! From Florida! You used to work at the TV station.

JOANN. I left. I was living with my mom and trying to work and raise my baby and we were all going crazy. (*To Helene and Barbara Ellen.*) Hi!

BARBARA ELLEN and HELENE. Hi.

JOANN. So you know how, when they're really in trouble, some people ask, what would Jesus do? (*Helene gestures to Barbara Ellen.*)

BARBARA ELLEN. Oh, uh huh . . .

JOANN. Well, I asked myself, what would Mr. Charles do?

MR. CHARLES. You did?

HELENE. Oh my . . .

JOANN. And so—I moved to New York. And it was all so new and scary, and I don't have any money, so I'm really living in New Jersey. But I come into the city every chance I get, just to look at it.

MR. CHARLES. But what are you doing in the maternity ward?

JOANN. I want my baby to be a New Yorker, so I bring him here to the clinic. Because I want him to meet all sorts of different people. (*To Barbara Ellen.*) Like, where are you from?

BARBARA ELLEN. Decatur, Illinois. We're the Soybean Capitol.

JOANN. (*To Helene.*) And what about you?

HELENE. I'm from Massapequa, Long Island.

JOANN. (*Thrilled.*) "Massapequa." That sounds like a wonderful old

Indian name. But what does it mean in English?

HELENE. "Don't touch my hair."

JOANN. You see? That's New York. All of you. And that's what I want for my baby.

MR. CHARLES. And how is your baby?

JOANN. Oh, he's wonderful. Look. (*She pulls the fabric hood off the stroller, revealing the baby, who's now wearing very brightly colored clothes, including huge rhinestone sunglasses, a vivid scarf and a hint of rouge, along with a tiny hairpiece, so he looks just like Mr. Charles. The effect is uncanny.*)

HELENE. Oh my God . . .

BARBARA ELLEN. He looks like a birthday cake. Or a Christmas sweater.

MR. CHARLES. He looks like me.

SHANE. Whoa. *Whoa.* (*To Mr. Charles.*) Chuck. You did it. It *worked.*

JOANN. He's in color!

HELENE. (*To Joann.*) This is your child? You're the mother?

JOANN. Yes.

HELENE. (*Putting her arm around Joann.*) God, we have so much to talk about.

MR. CHARLES. Shane? Ladies? Mr. Max? Maestro? (*The lights go to black. From the darkness, a suspenseful musical vamp begins, and we hear:*)

ANNOUNCER. And now, ladies and gentlemen, it's four in the morning, you can't sleep, so turn to cable channel 47! Because you wanted it, you begged for it, by overwhelming popular demand, it's time for the hottest new public access program in all of South Florida, it's time for *The Shane Show*! Starring everybody's favorite South Florida male superstar, Shane! (*A spotlight come up on Shane, dancing. A sign behind him reads "THE SHANE SHOW!" Hot dance music blasts.*) With Shane's special guest stars, including the former receptionist and the mother of Mr. Max—Joann! (*Joann appears, dancing with Max.*) She's heaven, she's happening—hold on to your handbags, because here's Helene!

(Helene appears and dances. She holds up her gorgeous new Ralph Lauren bag.) She's clever, she's crafty, she can't stop creating—straight from De- catur, she's Barbara Ellen! *(Barbara Ellen appears and dances. She's now wearing a hand-crocheted poncho, or a particularly festive Christmas sweater.)* He's too gay, he's too much, and he's all yours—it's Mr. Charles! *(Mr. Charles appears, dancing.)*

MR. CHARLES. Wait! *(The music pauses.)* We're all so proud to be here, as guests on this Palm Beach premiere. And I would just like to take this opportunity to thank our star and our host . . .

BARBARA ELLEN. The hottest thing in South Florida . . .

HELENE. And a very bright young man, who will soon be attending Palm Beach community college . . .

SHANE. *(This is news to him.)* What?

HELENE. Just a thought.

ALL. *Here's Shane!*

SHANE. *(Very choked up.)* Thank you, thank all of you for bein' here on my very first show, and thank all of you out there, for watchin'. 'Cause we're all in this together, and there's only one way to fix this whole damn planet. And it goes something like this . . . *(The music roars back on, and Shane executes a dance move. His guests all join in, doing the same move. Everyone's dancing joyously.)*

CURTAIN